Best Wishes,

[signature]

The
Title
of
Liberty

Douglas V. Nufer

Distributed by:

PUBLISHING & DISTRIBUTION L.L.C.

Granite Publishing &Distribution, LLC
868 North 1430 West
Orem, Utah 84057
(801) 229-9023 • Toll Free (800) 574-5779
Fax (801) 229-1924

Published by:

**PEEPSOCK
PRESS**

P. O. Box 51082
Provo, UT 84605

Page Layout & Design by Myrna Varga • The Office Connection, Inc.
Cover Design by Steve Gray
Cover Art "Captain Moroni" by Doug Fryer

Library of Congress Control Number: 2003111259
ISBN: 1-932280-25-1

Printed in the United States of America

10 9 8 7 6 5 4 3 2 1

For my best friend and loving wife, Teresa,
and Jonathon, Holly, Merissa,
Hannah, and Joshua who keep
our lives full.

Acknowledgments

Many thanks go to those who have helped and encouraged me in preparing this book. I owe special thanks to Derek Warren, Duane Nufer, Jan and Pat Holman, Ken Nufer, Kevin Tuckett, Michael Rybin, Robin Hansen, and my parents, Harold and Marian Nufer, all of whom have provided insightful feedback and suggestions that have made this a better work.

This work is an adaptation of accounts found in the Book of Mormon. As such, I owe a deep and sincere sense of gratitude to the many brave souls who have written, compiled, translated, preserved and presented that marvelous record.

Table of Contents

Map of Nephite Cities

North Sea

Desolation

Bountiful

Morianton

Land of Ammon
(Jershon)

Mulek

Gid

Zarahemla

Lehi

Sidom

Nephihah

Gideon

Moroni

Judea

Manti

Various
Minor Cities

Cumeni

Antiparah

Zeezrom

West Sea

East Sea

Noah

Ammonihah

Land of Nephi

Prelude to Destiny

74 BC. Deep within the heart of an ancient rainforest.

A large and powerful hand took a firm hold on the edge of the animal skin door-flap. It paused a moment before pulling it open. At first, the contrast between the inner tent and the burning sun left the soldier unable to see within the tent. However, his eyes quickly adjusted and soon he could make out the silhouette of his commander sitting at his writing table on the far end of the opening.

The large, Nephite warrior had to stoop to enter his commander's tent. Once within, he was able to stand erect as he prepared to report his findings. He stood at attention. This was done out of respect, not out of fear of reprimand. The soldier's feet were clad in sandals with their tie-off leather thongs interwoven up his muscular calves. His uniform was a blend of sheepskin about his loins and a leather breastplate covering more sheepskin on his chest. He had removed his helmet before entering and sheathed his long, double-edged sword.

The tent was made of animal skins. The fur had been carefully rubbed off, leaving just the smooth, malleable leather. It was four paces long and half as wide. Three, evenly-space center poles supported the roof, with a pole in each corner and another at the center of each wall. They were tall, sturdy poles, but slender so as to make them more portable. Although the tent could be cleared out and rolled up at a moment's notice, it offered a sense of dignified presence. The poles were straight. The leather walls were clean.

The soldier paused only briefly before calling for his commander's attention, "Captain Moroni!"

Using rigid and calculated military discipline, the soldier, one of Moroni's junior officers, took two more steps within the tent to face his superior officer. At the tender, young age of 25, Captain Moroni had gained the respect of the Nephite nation and had been anointed as its supreme military leader. He was beloved by his army and feared by his enemies. He now sat at a portable, wooden table lashed together with ropes made of indigenous vines to ensure its sturdiness. Parchments with charcoal writing covered the table. Some were unrolled. Others were still curled and lying within their leather and bamboo holders.

Captain Moroni was studying the parchment on the top of the pile. He had placed a leather water flask on one end and a razor-sharp, bone-handled knife on the other, to hold back the edges, which begged to curl back together again. The parchment bore a map of the area etched onto its surface. The commander had heard his officer, but momentarily remained in his thoughts as he completed his study of the map.

He had already begun to look up as the officer repeated his announcement, "Captain Moroni!" Then, he added, "Captain Lehi reports that he and his men are ready."

Moroni now offered the man his full attention and responded, "Excellent. We attack at dawn then. Tell the men to post guards and retire early. I expect heavy fighting tomorrow."

The soldier nodded, turned, and promptly left to fulfill his new orders. Moroni paused. He eyed his map again briefly, then rose and exited the tent. He made his way through his army's campsite, walking between the many tents housing his soldiers. He could catch snatches of conversations as he passed by their tents.

He heard talk of home and family, or of intended loves. He also heard several references to the food, the hike, the living conditions, and of course, what the morning would bring. Word was already spreading that they would engage the enemy in the morning.

He came to the guards he had posted earlier at the camp's perimeter. They straightened up when they saw him, "Captain Moroni, sir, may we help you?" one particularly tall and muscular guard asked as he pulled his vertical spear closer to his chest. His breastplates and armor were polished to a bright and noble shine.

"No, thank you," Moroni replied. "I'm just surveying the area."

"Yes, sir," the guard replied.

He continued a littler farther away, allowing himself to be alone in his thoughts and stood at the edge of a grassy clearing on the hillside. He looked contemplatively down the tree-lined hillside. There were traces of a river in the distance with the dense rainforest beyond. Faint wafts of campfire smoke could be seen rising intermittently throughout the forest on the far side of the river.

In the distance, he could see exotic birds take flight, flutter above the trees and then seek new perches. Just as they settled down, a couple of other birds quickly flew skyward again to make way for some mischievous monkeys who were jumping from tree to tree. If it were not for the smoke, and the enemy that it represented, it would

3

have been a beautifully impressive scene.

In the years that Moroni had led the defense of his people against their mortal enemies, the Lamanites, he had seen more than his fair share of conflict. Words intended for no one other than himself escaped his lips.

"I had really hoped to avoid this," he sighed. "If only they would listen. How can a people be so filled with hate?"

Moroni paused again, deep in thought. The setting sun cast a brilliant orange and reddish hue on his sun-worn face. He sighed again as he thought of the pending conflict. Renegade Nephites had broken off from their society to join the Lamanites and incited them up to war against their former brothers. It was a cycle he had seen far too often and was afraid he was bound to see repeated. He shook his head, dismayed at the apostates' loss of opportunity. Then, with a look of resolve, he turned and headed back up the path to his camp to retire on this eve before the battle. As the last rays of sunlight vanished, he reentered his tent and settled in for the night.

Chapter 1

Mortal Enemies

———◦✦◦———

*D*awn brought a peaceful view of a lush, green field. Colorful flowers were still wet with thick dew that sparkled with the first rays of the day's sun. The morning chattering of exotic birds was gradually overcome by the rhythmic thumping of hundreds upon hundreds of sandal-clad feet. The first soldier crested a rolling hill that lead to the field. The once-tranquil area was quickly filling with Moroni's advancing army. The soldiers were donned in leather and cloth uniforms. Over their uniforms, they bore heavy armor.

Large, brass breastplates protected their chests and stomachs. Similar plates protected their backs, and were firmly attached to the breastplates by leather ties at the shoulders and along their sides. Loose, metal strips were fastened with rings at the base of the plates, to protect their loins. The metal strips separated momentarily as bulging thighs pushed through them then retracted with each step. Lashed to their sandals, protecting their shins, were brass shin-plates.

The soldiers' arms were bare, except where a portion of the sheepskin covered their shoulders and upper arms. Each man wielded a long, unsheathed sword in one hand, and a shield in the other. Their daggers remained at the ready, tied firmly to their sides and resting on their hips.

Protecting their heads, each man had donned a distinctive helmet of brass, which covered their general-issue leather helmets. Those helmets had been fashioned with ornate designs. Some had horns, others feathers, still others bore intricate carvings. Each design represented the symbol of the individual soldiers' family lines.

The march continued forward in wordless, steady earnestness. Each man had cultivated a look of determination in his eye, but not hatred.

The soldiers continued their quick pace. Row after row of them made their way down the tree-lined hillside, with Moroni at their head. The hillside leveled out and the trees gave way to reveal an open field in front of them, bordered by dense, jungle trees and vines. The playful monkeys stopped their games for a moment to turn and see who had entered their field.

Moroni continued to lead his men toward the river, which still lay some two hundred yards ahead, across the field. Moroni's gaze strained forward across the river and into the trees where he had seen the campfire smoke the night before.

Suddenly, a horde of angry men dashed from the trees on either side of the field. They were wild looking and nearly bare all over, revealing the dark redness of their skin, which was a stark contrast to that of the Nephite soldiers. They screamed blood-curdling war cries as they ran forward without any signs of order, waving clubs and swords above their heads. Their faces were painted with wicked designs intended to induce fear and intimidation in their warrior enemies.

Here and there the renegade Nephites could be seen charging side by side with the nearly bare Lamanites. Their lighter skin made them easy to spot, and their fierce expressions made it clear that they were wholly dedicated to this attack. Sweat steamed down their painted faces as their mouths stretched open in shrill cries of pure hatred. Their swords and clubs were raised high over their heads as they charged men whom one would think ought to have been treated as their brothers.

As the two, opposing armies met in a frenzied battle, one of Moroni's soldiers shouted, "For freedom!" and raised his sword high above his head as he energetically charged his foe.

The scene quickly became one of massive, hand-to-hand fighting. Moroni's men were duly protected because of their clothing and shields, but the opposition boasted powerful and determined men. Nephite swords quickly bloodied their bare skin, but Lamanite clubs and swords, swung by powerful arms filled with intense hatred and anger, managed to find their marks in some of the vulnerable areas. Moroni's men remained undeterred and slowly pushed their enemy back across the meadow and toward the river.

One of the Lamanites—a tall, intimidating warrior—looked around and noted the loss of ground. At this moment, three of his men were simultaneously dropped by swords within a few yards of where he stood, as if in testimony that this battle could not be won by shear determination alone. Their bare skin could be no match for the armor with which Moroni had fortified his men. The Lamanite leader's gaze remained toward the river as he motioned with his sword for his men to work their way toward it for crossing and safety.

His men obeyed without question and soon the river was filled with fleeing Lamanites. As escape seemed evident, Captain Lehi and his men emerged from the south, on the far side of the river, cutting off all hope of deliverance. Lehi's men joined the battle fresh and vigorous. The Lamanite enemy was then wholly surrounded, out-numbered and caught literally midstream. Their men panicked and lost all sense of unified attack.

Splashing water obscured much of the view of this routed army as men ran in all directions, not knowing which side of the river provided the most likely means of escape. War cries turned to shouts of frustration and pure anger mingled with fear. In the melee, some of the fleeing soldiers lost their swords or clubs as they fell or tripped over their comrades in the river or by its muddied banks.

The frenzied Lamanites were now in a panic, trampling over each other as they sought in vain for some form of sanctuary. Moroni saw that his enemy had lost all hope of unity. They were now at his mercy to slaughter or spare. As he noted this, he stopped and raised his sword straight and high over his head. All fighting ceased.

"Zerahemnah, come forward!" he shouted with a clear, command-ing voice.

Zerahemnah, a Nephite by birth, but a Lamanite by choice, was the man who had signaled the retreat to the river. He now pushed his way toward Moroni. All eyes were upon him as Nephites and Lamanites alike stepped aside to allow him to pass. Zerahemnah's tall, muscular body was sweaty and his lungs still heaved in and out searching for air, though his expression bore not the least hint of fatigue.

Sweat and water had combined to work away at his red war paint, revealing the true color of his skin and making it clear that this man was not a true Lamanite, but a renegade Nephite who had chosen to bitterly oppose the nation of his birth. His chest and upper arms were covered with battle scars and fresh, minor wounds. He tromped forward, scowling indignantly and with the annoyed expression of a warrior unaccustomed to defeat and unwilling to accept it.

"I'm here, Moroni," he announced and stopped about fifteen feet from Moroni.

"Zerahemnah, you can see that you're defeated. You should also see that God himself has blessed us to prevail. You should now realize that you can't beat us. With this, you should also know that we will crush you into the ground, lest you give up this battle!" Moroni spoke loudly so that as many people as possible could hear him and gain a distinct understanding of the terms of surrender.

Zerahemnah maintained his indignant and defiant attitude. He straightened and retorted with equal volume, "I see no such thing! I don't believe that God is on your side. What I believe is that it's your shields and your armor that lets you prevail!"

Some of the Lamanites nodded in agreement and jeered at their opponents. The Nephites held their ground and returned glaring looks of warning as they poised their swords ready to return to battle.

"Zerahemnah, we don't desire to be men of blood. You know that you're in our hands, yet we don't want to slay you. But, unless you heed my words, I'll loose my men on you and wipe you off the face of this earth!" Moroni warned his nemesis.

Moroni's men leaned forward, swords at the ready, as a show of strength.

"Zerahemnah, I'll let you live only if you and your men lay down your swords and swear an oath that you will never come back to attack my people. If you'll swear that you'll let us live in peace, we will let you live. If you do not swear this, we will destroy you, NOW!" With each word, Moroni's voice grew increasingly threatening and loud.

Zerahemnah looked Moroni in the eye. "I give you my sword, but I'll not swear an oath that I know that I'll break," he declared and threw his sword at Moroni's feet in disgust. "I'll not have my men

9

swear an oath that I know that they'll break. But, take our weapons of war, and let us leave into the wilderness. Otherwise, we'll retain our swords, and we'll either perish or conquer. We're not of your faith. We don't believe that it's God that has delivered us into your hands, but your cunning that has preserved you from our swords."

Zerahemnah stood unflinchingly and defiantly eyeing Moroni. The wind blew his sweaty, dark hair. Two armies now awaited Moroni's reaction. For a moment in time, no one on the battlefield moved. Even the monkeys held their peace. Moroni stared into Zerahemnah's eyes. He saw their firm, unmoving, arrogant hatred and recognized that he was not getting through to his foe.

Seeing no alternative, Moroni dipped his sword and with its tip he flicked Zerahemnah's sword back to its owner. The sword flopped at Zerahemnah's feet with a dull thump. Moroni added with even more firmness, lest anyone that heard him would think that Zerahemnah had gained an edge in the war of words and attitudes, "I can't retract the words which I've spoken. As the Lord lives, you will not leave this field except you swear an oath that you'll not return again against us to war. You *will* swear this oath, or I'll lead my men to your death. . . ."

Moroni was interrupted as Zerahemnah grabbed his sword, and rushed toward him with his weapon drawn, rage in his eyes and murder in his heart. One of Moroni's men, a young soldier named Teancum, quickly stepped forward to intercept the challenge. He swiftly drew his own sword and swung it before the advancing foe. Teancum struck Zerahemnah's sword so hard it broke at the hilt. As Zerahemnah continued his approach, Teancum then struck at him directly. Zerahemnah instinctively attempted to dodge the blow.

Teancum's sword nearly missed its mark entirely, but managed to slice across the top of Zerahemnah's head. Enraged and in pain,

Zerahemnah screamed and collapsed to his knees. His hands sprang toward his head, but he managed to restrain them, fearing to touch his open wound. His severed scalp lay on the ground before him. Teancum picked it up with the tip of his sword and used his sword to hold it high above the armies' heads, so that all could see the grisly object.

"Even as this scalp has fallen to the earth, which is the scalp of your leader, so will you all fall to the earth except you deliver up your weapons of war and leave with an oath of peace!" Teancum loudly proclaimed. "Any of you men who lay down your swords and swear an oath of peace, will be able to leave this field alive. Those of you who don't, won't live to see the sun set!"

Again, there was silence for a moment. A bird rustled, cawed, and flew overhead. One by one, a few dozen Lamanite men pushed their way to Moroni's presence. They were careful to avoid eye contact with Zerahemnah who busied himself attempting to put a makeshift bandage on his head with the aid of two of his soldiers.

The first Lamanite soldier to reach Moroni looked him in the eye and announced without shame, "I am Jeshua. We swear that as the Lord lives and as we live, we will no longer raise the sword against your men. We give you our weapons as proof."

Jeshua tossed his sword at Moroni's feet. The other Lamanites, who had followed him forward, did the same. They stood awaiting Moroni's words—weaponless, vulnerable and at their enemy's utter disposal. Their lives hung by the thread of Moroni's honor.

Moroni faced these former foes and replied, "Jeshua, you have chosen well. We accept your oath." Moroni turned to one of his own men, "Korimur, lead these men through to safe passage."

Korimur stepped forward and led the men away from the scene of battle, through Moroni's army, and toward the rainforest. As they left, Moroni again addressed Zerahemnah's men, "You men see that these brave and wise men have been fairly dealt with. We don't seek your lives. We only seek peace. If you'll swear to let us and our people live in peace, we will let you live. If you do not," he carefully added with an intense sense of warning, "we will not spare you."

Zerahemnah was still in the act of having his head crudely bandaged. But, when he looked up and saw more of his men swearing the oath and leaving, he became further enraged. Pushing away his soldier, disallowing him to complete tying off the bandage, Zerahemnah rose to his feet. Another Lamanite soldier protested and Zerahemnah glared at him with fire in his eyes. The Lamanite backed off. Zerahemnah pushed forward and grabbed a sword from one of his officers.

"Men! We are not dogs that Moroni can beat into submission! We are warriors who have chosen a warrior's path! Forward!"

His shout to his men was intended to incite them to anger. With this, he pointed his sword directly at Moroni. Zerahemnah knew his men well. His remaining men filled the air with the blood curdling screams of frenzied warriors launching a doomed assault. Their response brought a wicked grin to his blood-streaked face.

Moroni could not help shaking his head in disbelief at their stubbornness. He was not caught off guard, however. Even before Zerahemnah was able to make eye contact with him, he had his sword at the ready. He motioned for his men to resist their attack and defend themselves.

Jeshua and his companions were still within earshot of the battlefield. As the muffled sounds of battle edged their way through the jungle growth and surrounded their ears, they stopped. Some of these men tightened, tensely aware of the actions the sounds conveyed. Jeshua was the first to turn and speak to them all.

"Men, this is no longer our battle; no longer our concern. If Zerahemnah is intent on continuing the conflict, he'll have to do it without us."

"But, they're our comrades!" came a concerned reply.

Others nodded agreement, doubting the honor of their retreat.

"We have given our word. We cannot go back or we will deny our souls. You know this to be true," Jeshua stated with forceful conviction.

"Yes, we know. But, that doesn't make it any easier," one of the oath-makers added.

"Jeshua's right. Let's keep going before we do something foolish," another warned.

The repentant warriors bowed their heads. Their heads were not bowed in shame, but pity for their angry brethren. One Lamanite reached up and patted Jeshua on the shoulder in a show of support. The two turned and continued deeper into the forest. The others followed as the group continued wending its way from the field of battle to their homes.

Back among the fury, Moroni's men's shields and armor again offered strong protection. Zerahemnah's men pummeled Moroni's soldiers, but few strokes from the Lamanites' swords or clubs struck the Nephite soldiers' flesh. Those blows were either absorbed by sturdy, gleaming shields, or skillfully parried by swiftly moving swords. To the contrary, Zerahemnah's bare men were quickly wounded and many fell dead.

Those who were first to fall were those wielding clubs. As the threatening but awkward weapons were swung, they were easily deflected and with a small twist of the arm, the Nephite sword could be shifted from a parry to a blow. The Lamanites fell not just one by one, but several at a time across the battlefield, just as Teancum had predicted.

Zerahemnah himself struggled to hold his ground. He could not help but note his own failure to prevail. Now and again, he managed to glance across the field and saw the dead and dying men he led. At times it was necessary to step over dead or wounded Lamanite soldiers as he advanced and retreated during his very mobile hand-to-hand combat. It was not long before he was forced, bitterly, to recognize that the war he waged was a hopeless loss.

Begrudgingly, but desperately, Zerahemnah shouted to Moroni, "Moroni, we will swear! Spare us and we will swear the oath!"

Moroni and Lehi's eyes met from across the battlefield. Lehi nodded approvingly. Moroni again raised his sword straight in the air. His trumpeter sounded the signal. The din of battle slowly faded to a rolling, dying echo across the field. As silence again reigned, Moroni stood on a large rock, so that all could see him.

"Zerahemnah, by all that is holy, if you do not swear this time, you will not live another moment!"

He spoke loudly and forcibly, so that no one could misunderstand him.

All eyes shifted to Zerahemnah. The proud leader ceremoniously lowered his sword. He turned it and held it with its point to the ground. He stood straight with his bandaged head high as he mustered his pride and walked with determination, toward Moroni. When he was within two paces, he quickly kneeled on one knee. He held up his sword horizontally with both hands, one on the hilt and one on the blade. He offered it to Moroni.

Without any tinge of shame or indignity in his voice, he declared, "Captain Moroni, I offer you my sword as a token of my oath that I, my men, and our children will never again come against your people to battle. As the Lord lives and as I live, this I swear. And this my people swear."

The Lamanite people were bold, brash, and fierce, but strictly honored their oaths. Their leader's oath transcended all animosity and anger. To not heed that oath would have been to deny the essence of their society. Zerahemnah knew this. He held off giving the oath until the last possible moment, because he knew too well that the words were more than mere sounds to be uttered. He and his people considered it to be an utterance from their very souls, tying their souls to absolute adherence to the words. Once spoken, they could not be retracted, ignored, or abandoned lest they abandon their very souls.

All across the field, Zerahemnah's men turned ceremoniously solemn. Each one instinctively and immediately obeyed their leader's word of honor and kneeled. Each offered his weapon to whichever of Moroni's men was nearest. These Lamanite and Nephite men, who moments earlier were striking death blows on each other, were now binding themselves together by virtue of the oath which Zerahemnah and his men now swore.

The Lamanite warriors paired up with Moroni's and marched to where Moroni stood. Moroni's officers had also migrated to his vicinity. Each of Moroni's men held a sword or club from Zerahemnah's men. One by one, the Lamanites kneeled with one hand on the weapon held by Moroni's man, in token of their accepting and swearing the oath. With each oath, the men cast their weapons into the pile by Moroni.

The pile of abandoned tools of death grew while Moroni and his officers nodded and allowed each former owner to leave the field of war alive. Neither Moroni nor any of his officers bore the least concern of these former enemies who left the field, unguarded and unescorted. They knew that there could be no more hostilities with these particular men.

As the Lamanites, left one by one, the field revealed the scars of war. In addition to the impressively large pile of weapons at Moroni's feet, other weapons were scattered across the field. They could be seen strewn about like straw from a strong wind. They lay from the top of the hillside down beyond the river Sidon. Their bloodstained blades represented only a fraction of the horrors this field now bore.

Lying near, on, or in some cases, still clasping their weapons, were the bodies of soldiers who would never return from battle this day. Some lay face down in the river. Several of the river-bound bodies had snagged on underwater brush, forming a grisly, human dam. The mighty waters of the river Sidon flowed around them, temporarily widening the river's banks.

Even victories held their bitter tasks. Moroni ordered his men to clear the river. Four large soldiers removed their breastplates and tops. They waded into the stream and tugged at limp limbs. With a mighty pull, one soldier succeeded. He fell backward into the water. The body he freed could no longer hold back the force of the river's water. It rolled forward on a wave bearing with it other bodies that were now loosened by its flow.

The nameless corpses surged quickly down the river several hundred yards until they reached the brim of a towering waterfall. Here they plummeted downward into the mist and foam to be washed out to where the nearby sea waited to receive them into their watery grave.

Moroni would have preferred giving each fallen man a decent, honorable burial. But, he also recognized the efficient mercy the swift river offered. There would be no dishonor in a burial at sea, and his men would not have to linger on the death of their comrades and unrepentant enemies any longer than necessary.

Moroni ordered that the dead be taken from the field of battle and placed into the river to allow nature to finish their task. The sun was setting as Moroni and his men returned to their tents and began to pack for their long march home.

DAYS LATER, MORONI led his men on the final leg of their march home. The ever-ascending path did not slow the feet of his men. They climbed with the eagerness of husbands and fathers returning safely to their loved ones. Finally, the mighty city of Zarahemla stood before them. Its tall wall offered but one gate, wide enough for a large wagon to easily pass through it.

A tower watchman spied Moroni even as his men saw this first tangible sign of home. The men resisted the urge to race to the city. They continued with order and dignity. Each warrior knew that among the quickly-increasing number of little eyes that peered eagerly over the city wall, might be those of his own son. They wanted their sons to see how a true soldier marched, before they returned to their farms and shops.

The city gate opened without Moroni calling out. They marched forward until all the men were safely within the walls. The gate was then closed. Moroni stood in the center of the city square, triumphant. Wives and children rushed from their homes and observation posts to embrace their returning husbands and fathers. Some families were saddened, however, to learn that their husbands and fathers would never be returning.

Moroni's eyes were fixed on the city's central building. The building was tall, large, and shaped like a pyramid, but with a flat top. Its four terraced sides slanted upward and inward forming the pyramid shape. Steep stairs were cut into its face, dissecting the building from its base to its flattened top.

The top bore a single room known as the tower room. Its roof was one, solid piece of stone carved to arch at the top and its four corners rested on firm, thick pillars that rose from the four corners of the pyramid's top. The curved, stone roof was hollowed out in such a way as to become an amphitheater of sorts. A man could stand high up in the tower, yet his voice could be heard with clarity over an impressive distance. This was used on special occasions for making grand pronouncements. It also served as the city's main watchtower.

The central building contained a series of rooms and corridors. Adjacent buildings were made of large, flat stones hewn in such a way that they had been laid together like massive bricks. The largest had a wooden roof, which slanted to one side. From this building Alma, the elderly spiritual leader of the society emerged. He stepped out and paused.

For a moment, his and Moroni's eyes met. Even from a distance, the two were able to communicate Moroni's victory and Alma's satisfaction at their safe return. Alma walked forward and officially met Moroni and his men in the city square.

"Alma, we have secured peace with the Lamanites. Zerahemnah and his men have sworn the oath of peace!" Moroni spoke loudly to allow the people to hear, in addition to his spiritual leader.

"We must give thanks to God for preserving our freedom!" Alma said as he beamed approval and properly directed the thoughts of the city.

Alma kneeled. Moroni and the crowd followed suit. They bowed their heads for a moment of silence. Alma then rose and motioned for the crowd to do the same. He turned to Moroni and summarized with simplicity, "Well done."

"Thank you, sir. Now I can return to my family and my farm. I've spent far too long away from them," Moroni replied.

"I agree. Go and take care of them. They deserve your attention, and your love," Alma bade him well.

Chapter 2

The Passing of the Plates

———⬗———

*A*lma sat at his writing table as he had for year after year. The lashings on the wooden table still held tightly in spite of the weight of the stacks of metal plates it bore. The majority of the plates were bound together with oblong rings that allowed their reader to flip through page after page of historical and doctrinal information. Alma sat hunched over the desk meticulously engraving characters onto a shiny, new, smooth plate. He wrote of Moroni's victory over Zerahemnah and the mercies of God.

His library housed hundreds of such plates, as well as scrolls, on tables, and on shelves that were built into the walls. The shelving was partially covered by cloth curtains. The records gave the history of the Nephite people from the time they set sail from the Old World and arrived in this Promised Land to their present lives.

They included the tales of their prosperity and failures; their wars among themselves and with the Lamanites who shared this land in an all-too-often turbulent existence; their prophecies of the great Messiah who would one day come; and the many miracles and teachings of generation upon generation of prophets and leaders.

The room had a spacious window above Alma's writing table, but it had only one entrance. It was directly behind Alma. Its door was open. Filling its frame was a powerfully built, bearded man. His brown hair was covered by a loose cloth and was held in place with a double band. Both bands entwined within each other. His blue eyes were focused on Alma.

Before the man could announce his presence, Alma instinctively looked up, turned and stated, "Helaman, thank you for coming."

"I came as soon as I got your message. What is it?" Helaman respectfully replied.

Alma's countenance took on an unusually serious demeanor, even for him. He flatly declared, "This is a matter of utmost importance. Do you see these records before you?"

Helaman, whose life had been spent in the shadow of these many plates, responded simply, "Yes."

"You know that these are the sacred records of our people handed down from generation to generation, begun by our father Nephi who left Jerusalem in search of the Promised Land?" Alma continued.

"Yes."

Helaman was unaccustomed to acknowledging the obvious, but still delivered a respectful answer.

"You understand that our very society is founded and governed by the words engraved upon these plates?" Alma persisted.

"Yes, certainly."

Helaman spoke with determination and unflagging agreement. Alma eyed Helaman very closely, as if peering into his very soul.

"You know that these plates also hold the witnesses of many prophets who had been led by the hand of God and have recorded His words so that our people would know His will and of the Great Messiah who shall come and redeem all mankind?"

"Yes, father, I do."

Helaman was growing concerned and confused by the line of questions.

"Do you believe that the things written on these plates are true?" Alma asked bluntly.

Helaman shifted. He was unable to prevent a serious look from growing across his brow. He was both puzzled that his faith was being called into question, and determined to give an answer that would remove all doubt.

He stepped forward and declared, "Father, you know that I believe these things with all my heart and soul. I believed even as a child. As I grew to manhood, I saw many events that witnessed of the truths they hold. I have no doubts, father. You know this."

Alma smiled. He paused, closing his eyes a moment knowingly. He opened them and gestured to Helaman with his hand, "Yes, Helaman, my son, I do know this. That is why I have chosen you."

"Chosen me?" Helaman voiced his confusion.

"I'm no longer a young man," Alma explained. "Soon I will go the way of all the earth. It is time. Time that I pass on all that I have cared for since they were entrusted to me."

Alma paused to allow his words and meaning to sink in. As Helaman realized what Alma was preparing to do, he was visibly moved at the thought of the awesome burden and responsibility he was about to receive. He remained silent.

"Helaman, you have grown to become a good man. A man whom others respect. A strong man, and one who is true to his word. A man who is also true to his God. You make an old father very proud."

Alma smiled warmly with these words. Helaman felt his emotions well up within him, and a sense of satisfaction at the thought of having pleased his father and mentor.

"I have made this a matter of fasting and prayer and the Lord has made it known to me that you are the one who should now be entrusted with these plates, this sacred record of our people. Will you accept them?"

The verbalization of Alma's intent made it all too real for Helaman. He inadvertently stumbled backward and found himself sitting in the chair that was behind him. He sat momentarily with a dazed look, cleared his head, then stood tall and resolutely.

"Father, I accept this tremendous responsibility. I will dedicate my life to preserving this record and adding to it the words and deeds of this great people," he vowed.

"I know you will. Just as I have and my father before me. And king Mosiah before him. And so on back to Nephi. I can now rest well knowing that this record is secure."

Alma spoke with approval. He rose as he said this and put his hand on Helaman's shoulder.

"I wish to leave you with more than just the responsibility. I want to leave you with a blessing to help you fulfill this duty."

Alma gestured to his side. Helaman stood and moved his chair to the designated spot. He sat.

"Before I begin, I've asked two men whom I believe you know well, to witness this."

Alma stepped outside the door and returned with Moroni and Lehi following closely behind. Both men nodded to Helaman as they entered, but remained silent. They stood on either side of Helaman.

As Helaman turned back to his seat, two more men poked their heads into the room.

"Corianton! Shiblon! It's been quite a while! You're looking well." Helaman smiled broadly at the sight of his two brothers. They smiled in return and each gave their brother a warm sibling's embrace.

"Father told us what he has planned for you," Corianton said with his charming smile. "We didn't want to miss it."

"Yes, and we wanted to wish you well," Shiblon added.

"I was beginning to wonder if you'd make it," Alma said to his other sons with a warm chide.

Corianton smiled and shrugged. Shiblon simply added, "It was a long walk."

Alma shook his head warmly, then turned back to Helaman. He patted him on the shoulder and then stepped behind his chosen son. He placed both hands on his head. He then bowed his own head as he reverently closed his eyes. After a momentary pause, and with great reverence and feeling, he pronounced a blessing upon his son and successor.

"Helaman, in the name of God Almighty I entrust you with the power and authority to lead this people and care for their sacred records with the wisdom to say and record only those things that will help lead mankind to believe in the Messiah who shall surely come. Amen."

Alma opened his eyes and removed his hands from Helaman's head. Helaman opened his eyes and stood. Alma looked at his son. Helaman turned and the two respectfully and lovingly embraced as father and son.

Moroni and Lehi took turns shaking his hand and clasping his shoulder with the other hand as they did so. Helaman's brothers stepped forward and did the same.

"May the Lord be with you," Shiblon said.

"We're very proud of you," was all Corianton could add.

After a moment, Alma declared, "Things such as this are not kept secret, my son. We must declare this before the Church."

ALMA STOOD BEFORE his congregation, as he had hundreds of times before. This particular occasion contained one key difference. It would be his last. As he spoke to his beloved people whom he had not only led in righteousness for many, many years, but had also grown to love, Helaman sat in a wooden chair to the side and behind the podium. He kept his silence and looked out at the large congregation that had filled the stone chapel to overflowing.

Not a single additional soul could have fit in any of the hand-carved pews. Corianton and Shiblon sat in the center of the front row. Men, women and children had been summoned to this meeting. Many stood in the aisles listening to their distinguished leader. From the moment the meeting had been announced, rumors and speculation had abounded. Some had come simply to find out which of the many rumors were true.

Alma continued to speak peacefully. His words were calm and pronounced. The congregation's eyes were fixed keenly on him. On a couple of occasions, Alma gestured toward Helaman. At a climatic point, Alma turned to Helaman, who rose. He motioned for Helaman to step forward.

As Helaman approached the podium and passed Alma, Alma whispered into his ear, "All this is now yours, my son. Guard these people's faith and records well and guide them as you know the Lord would want you to." As he turned to leave, he added, "And now I must go."

"Go? Go where?"

Helaman was stunned.

"To my rest," Alma calmly replied. He responded to Helaman's wondering and concerned expression by giving the admonition, "Watch over your people."

Alma gestured to the congregation. Helaman honored his father's final request. After a brief embrace from son to father, he stepped up to the pulpit as Alma quietly walked out of the building. Alma made his way through the fair city of Zarahemla, admiring its sturdy, stone buildings, the pottery sitting at the doorsteps of the many homes, the tapestries hanging in the bazaar, the grandeur of the city square, and the intricate carving in the wooden city gate.

As he made his way toward the jungle that encroached on the city from all directions, he paused. For a moment he looked back. His mind drifted back to his rebellious days of youth. A smile crept across his aged and wrinkled face. He had changed quite a bit since then. Not only had he changed inwardly and outwardly, but he had also effected a massive change on the Nephite people.

Few men could look over their lives without regret. Alma was fortunate enough to be one of those men. He had made his world a much better place for having lived in it. But, it was now time for others to play their parts and continue the quest. For a moment, he wondered what roles those would be, but only for a moment. He turned and headed for the path that led up the mountainside and cut through the jungle.

The mountain was steep and arched. The top of the mountain was enveloped in clouds. He followed the path upward, always upward. They say he was never heard from or seen since that day. The rumor that later circulated among the Nephites was that he had been translated like Moses or Elijah of old. Those who knew Alma best, found it difficult to dismiss that rumor.

Chapter 3

Opposing Objectives

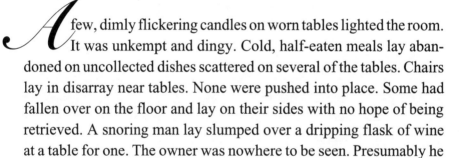

*A*few, dimly flickering candles on worn tables lighted the room. It was unkempt and dingy. Cold, half-eaten meals lay abandoned on uncollected dishes scattered on several of the tables. Chairs lay in disarray near tables. None were pushed into place. Some had fallen over on the floor and lay on their sides with no hope of being retrieved. A snoring man lay slumped over a dripping flask of wine at a table for one. The owner was nowhere to be seen. Presumably he had gone to bed some time past midnight and had chosen to save the cleanup for morning.

Meanwhile, in a corner of the room, seven men sat around a table. The largest was speaking. He slammed his brawny fist hard enough onto the table to make the candles jump. It grabbed the attention of one of his men who had become distracted by fatigue brought on by the discussion having bled into the black hours of the night.

With controlled anger, Amalickiah exclaimed, "I *know* he's the chief priest! And I know that the people follow him. But, that doesn't make him their leader. We're governed by our judges, not our priests!

You five represent the most influential districts for our lower courts. If you support me, I'll see to it that you each become a high judge in whichever court you please!"

The first judge was unintimidated and unimpressed. He viewed the promise as nothing short of preposterous. "How? Even a high judge can't appoint judges on his own. How are you going to do this? You're not even a judge yourself. Are you going to appoint yourself as Chief Judge?"

The formerly-dozing man, Amalickiah's brother, Ammoron, barely looked up. Without attempting to make eye contact with anyone in particular, he interjected, "He's not talking about becoming a judge."

The five judges, who had been leaning forward, with their elbows on the table, were perplexed and sat up straight. They looked at each other trying to see if any of them had a clue as to what Ammoron was referring.

"He's not?" the second judge sought clarification.

"No," Ammoron replied simply, without emotion and with only a faint sign of interest.

"What then?" the third judge demanded with more than a hint of irritation. He had tired of the guessing game.

Amalickiah took advantage of their surprise and edged interest. Ensuring that he had their complete attention, he slowly leaned forward. The five judges followed suit. Amalickiah distinctly spoke one word. "King."

Immediately, four of the judges sat back disputing this as preposterous and futile. They bickered among themselves with their arms and hands gesticulating as wildly as their frustration demanded. One remained leaning forward. He was motionless. His eyes held Amalickiah's stare. A sinister smile crept across his face. Then he nodded his head in knowing approval. Amalickiah nodded in reply and sat back in his seat as this judge slowly raised his hand to silence the bickering judges.

"I see," he announced in a level, unhurried tone, with the arrogance of singular perception.

"See? You see? See what?" the fifth judge demanded. He had managed to hear this observation in spite of his other colleagues' ruckus.

The fourth judge ignored the other judge and responded directly to Amalickiah, "You can count on our complete cooperation and support." Upon saying this, he bowed his head respectfully as he added slowly and with emphasis, "Your Majesty."

Three of the other judges caught on and bowed their heads. The fifth judge remained oblivious to their actions and had still not caught onto the situation. He again demanded to know, "What? What does he see?"

The second judge elbowed the slow judge, who finally looked about him and saw how the others were reverencing Amalickiah by bowing their heads to him. It finally dawned on him that if Amalickiah was appointed king, he would have the power to appoint new high judges, and would be inclined to reward his supporters, as well as punish his dissenters.

With an embarrassed look of recognition, the fifth judge mumbled, "Oh, yes, I see," and awkwardly bowed his head as a token of his support.

Amalickiah was too pleased with the other judges to pay the fifth judge's ignorance any mind. With sinister delight he summarized, "It's agreed then. We need to win over more of the lower judges and convince these people that they need a king to keep them safe from the marauding Lamanites."

HELAMAN HAD TAKEN his new calling to heart. His days were spent traveling and preaching. Zarahemla was only one of many Nephite cities to benefit from his diligence. Within a matter of months, his name and his face had become well known among all the Nephite people. The people flocked to his sermons. Although his topics began with discussions on love, charity, faith, service, or sacrifice, they all concluded by tying them into the concept of the coming Messiah and the great sacrifice He would make for all mankind.

The soles of Helaman's sandals showed extreme wear. His clothing was simple, but his stature was straight, broad, and true. He was a physically powerful man, but humble enough to have an even more powerful ability to draw men's attention to their Lord and God. It was not uncommon for couples to leave his sermons and comment to each other of their surprise at his ability to so clearly articulate and explain gospel doctrine.

On one such occasion Helaman declared the following:

> *I have been privileged to travel among many of you. It does my soul good to see so many faithful men and women yearning to follow the commandments of God. In my journeys, I have also encountered some who are downtrodden and full of woe. They despair because they believe that we are a lost and forgotten people. They say that we are without the blessings of God and unremembered because we are separated from the rest of the House of Israel. I tell you that God our Father knows all of His children. He loves them with an equal love.*
>
> *It is true that we are separated from our brethren*

in the Old World, but we are not forgotten. Our father, Nephi, wisely brought with him the sacred records of the prophets of his day so that we may learn of their teachings, their ways, and their prophecies, that we should not wander in ignorance or disbelief. Many of these prophets saw our day and prophesied that we would be led out of the Old World to this Promised Land.

When father Jacob blessed his 12 sons, he told our father, Joseph, that he and his descendants were as 'a fruitful bough by a well, whose branches run over the wall.' Just as the boughs of a bush run over the edge of a wall, we, the descendants of Joseph, have traveled across the sea to this land. As descendants of Joseph, we still retain the rights to all the blessings of Abraham, Isaac, and Jacob.

The Lord also told the prophet Ezekiel that there should be two records kept of two people. The first record should be of the people of Judah living in the Old World. The second should be of the people of Manasseh, Joseph's son. We are the people of Manasseh, and we keep our record. I have been entrusted with the sacred call to maintain that record.

God knows our doings and He directs your leaders. He loves us and will impart His wisdom to us here in this land of promise the same as in the Old World. The Messiah shall come not only for the benefit of those in the Old World, but for all mankind. This includes us.

I know that some day the record of our people will

be joined with the record of the people of Judah in the Old World and all mankind will be united as one, with one redeemer, one Messiah, one gospel, one truth. Do not despair while we await that great day. Instead, look forward to it with longing, expectation, and joy. For you are a chosen people, a royal priesthood, the elect of God.

AMALICKIAH'S LATE-NIGHT rendezvous was more than mere whispers in the dark. Over the course of many weeks he had actively sought ever-growing audiences. His first meetings were in darkened rooms with limited space. Only those with knowledge of certain key words were permitted to enter. Even then, if their faces were not familiar to those guarding the entrance, they were not permitted to enter until someone else could be found from within the building that could vouch for them.

These closed-room meetings soon gave way as their crowds grew beyond capacity. On one fateful day, Amalickiah dared to hold such a meeting in public. He stood defiantly in the city square speaking of the glories of kingship and the pathetic stalemate of being led by judges. In a bit of irony, the judges were incapable of finding a point of law by that they could detain him, or prohibit such meetings. With the success of the first such meeting, he took a hold of the concept and both continued and expanded the scope of his open-air meetings.

At one such gathering, Amalickiah rose and addressed his crowd in the following manner:

I tell you this plainly. Our government is faulty. It is an offshoot established by deranged and indecisive men who were incapable of making up their own minds. Rather than bare the brunt of actually making and enforcing decisions, they shifted blame and responsibility among themselves as if it were some form of water from a communal well. Just as water spills from a leaky cup, these men's indecisiveness is full of holes and the people's throats dry from thirst. Our fathers surely did not intend this.

Our great father, Nephi, whose name we still proudly bear as a people; whose brilliance led us out of the Old World and to this land of promise; whose keen intellect was the very foundation of the society which we perpetuate; used his uncompromising wisdom to establish a form of government for this people. He himself knowingly and approvingly allowed this people to crown him king, King of the Nephites.

How is it that this people has fallen away from his example, intentions, and established pattern to the point that we have not only lost our king, but we have degraded ourselves to the point that we actually declare the very concept of a king as abominable? Nephi was no abomination! He was a leader! One of the best this people has ever known! Now is the time for another great leader to step forward and shake off the foolish traditions that infest this peoples' minds and acknowledge the responsibilities of proper leadership!

Now is the time for us to return to the true foundations of this society and resurrect the concept of a king! If we ignore this, we will remain a lost and fallen people, doomed to forever wander according to the

whims of noncommittal, uninspired, disagreeable com-
mittees of men who dare call themselves 'judges.'

By what right does this floundering group dare
claim leadership of this mighty people? Leadership
must come from those unafraid to lead. I tell you here
and now, I am unafraid to lead. I am unafraid to make
the hard decisions. I am unafraid to enforce those
decisions. It is your God-given right to be led by him
who is most capable of leading. I am that man, and I
am unafraid of leading you.

The electricity of the speech was inescapable. As one, the crowd
had been mesmerized and wholly drawn into his seductive words.
With one accord they erupted into uncontrollable shouts and applause.
Those with walking staffs pounded the ends into the ground. Those
with bundles in their hands held them high above their heads and
shook them to the rhythm of the pounding staffs. Their clapping also
became rhythmic and a chant escaped a few lips, then was overtaken
by the entire throng. No other sound could be heard over the frenzied
pounding and the chanting of the word, "King! King! King! King!
. . ."

Helaman stood at the back of the city square. He saw the frenzied
looks on the peoples' faces. None of them seemed capable of
individual thought. Their eyes and very thoughts seemed inescapably
affixed on Amalickiah. Amalickiah ate up the attention. He was more
than thoroughly impressed with himself and the effect he had evoked
on his new followers. His expression made it clear that he felt success
was only a few steps away. It was also clear from Helaman's furrowed
brow that he feared the same. He shook his head sadly and with
genuine concern.

Helaman was roused from his despairing musings by a sudden

rush of commotion behind him. He turned in time to see a horde of angry men rushing into the city square from the alleys behind him. Dozens of men leaped over barrels and dodged tables as they charged the square. Helaman could only barely distinguish their war cries. It sounded to him as if some were shouting, "Down with Amalickiah!" others, "No king! No king!"

Before Helaman had a chance to react, the men had raced past him and engaged Amalickiah's newest converts. The initial fistfight quickly turned into an out and out brawl. Men beat upon each other with the ferocity of animals. Walking staffs were turned into clubs and scraps of wood became human-flung projectiles. Blood poured from many wounds before the city's soldiers were called and able to put a stop to the skirmish.

Chapter 4

Re-called to Serve

Aman on horseback rode quickly over a winding trail through valley, field, rainforest, and hills. He arrived at a farm of ancient vintage and dismounted before a large man tilling his field by hand. The young farmer looked up from his tilling and eyed the rider. The rider quickly snapped to attention before the farmer as a distinct show of respect. The farmer, Moroni, recognized his former companion, Lehi, and awaited his message with expectation. He knew his visit represented some form of ill tidings.

"Captain, things have gotten completely out of hand," Lehi declared with earnestness. "Amalickiah's support is growing daily. He has the people in a frenzy clambering over making him king. Helaman is unable to keep the people together. What first began as brawls now bring us onto the verge of a civil war. If the Lamanites were to break their truce and come on us now, we'd have no hope of putting up a unified defense." He paused momentarily, looking his former leader directly in the eye. He removed his helmet and added with sincerity, "We need you again."

Moroni looked to his home and saw his wife carrying their baby while his two boys ran past her, playing. He looked back to Lehi who awaited his reply. Moroni's eyes grew fierce with frustration at Amalickiah. His sense of duty and obligation was not just clear, it was embedded in his very soul. Any pause was not hesitation at making a choice, but a brief last breath of life with his loved ones.

He marched toward the house. As he went, he threw down his hoe and pulled off his cloak. He tore the cloak in a way that allowed him to lay it flat on the ground in front of him. He stooped and picked up a piece of charcoal from the cooling outdoor fire pit.

He wrote with the charcoal on his cloak:

In memory of our God, our religion, our freedom,
our peace, our wives, our children, and our liberty.

Moroni then grabbed a pole that lay nearby and fastened his torn cloak to it like a flag. Lehi held the flag while Moroni entered his home. He knelt in silent prayer, donned his armor, and then came out.

His wife, Sarah, had gathered the children, "You're going again, aren't you?"

"Yes. It seems we have more men grabbing for power by trampling on the freedom of their fellow men," he replied.

"You will take care of yourself, won't you?" she said, bravely holding back tears.

"Certainly, I will. And, may the Lord smile brightly upon you and our children while I'm away," he responded encouragingly.

Turning to his oldest son, a boy of about 17, he added, "Moronihah, you're the man of the family while I'm away. See to it that your mother is cared for and that your brothers and sisters do their part!"

"Yes, sir," Moronihah replied, as he stood a little taller and his

chest swelled. It was evident he was holding back words of importance. He shifted a bit and finally let them out, "But, I should go with
you!" he said at last.

Moroni looked his boy in the eyes carefully. He was hardly a boy
any more. He was fast becoming a man. Moroni could see this, could
sense this. He knew the anguish and angst his eldest son must be
feeling. As respectfully, but clearly, as he could, he replied, "No, son.
You're needed here. Your brothers and sisters need you. Your mother
needs you. And—" Moroni hesitated because of the sincerity of the
moment, "And, *I* need you here!"

"You?!" Moronihah said with surprise, "Why?"

"I need to know that those I care about most are in good hands.
I need to know that when I'm off fighting for our liberty, the ones who
I am liberating are well cared for. I need you to take care of my
family—our family—for me, while I'm away. I need to be able to
leave without fear for my family's well being so I can concentrate on
the task at hand. Can you do this?"

"Yes, father," his son replied with newfound pride and determination. "I will watch over them as well as you would yourself."

"Thank you, son. I can't expect more. Nor could I ask for a better
son. May the Lord smile brightly upon you."

Moroni gave each family member a hug. He tussled the hair of his
youngest child. He paused a moment, taking in the sight of his family.
He held Sarah's hands in his and stared deeply into her eyes. "You'll
be fine. We'll all be fine. Soon, we will be together again."

He hugged her and kissed her again. Tears welled up in her eyes.
Tears that she refused to allow her husband to see. Then her love, her
hero, her husband, aggressively mounted his horse and prepared to go.

Throughout this, Lehi had respectfully held Moroni's makeshift
flag. When he was ready to ride, he handed it to Moroni and then

followed closely behind as Moroni raced toward Zarahemla, Helaman, and his destiny.

MORONI AND HELAMAN clasped hands in an enthusiastic greeting. "Moroni, I appreciate your coming back so soon. I've done what I can, but Amalickiah is too dogmatic. We need your leadership."

"I understand. What's the latest?"

"Amalickiah has been marching from city to city rounding up support. He's very charismatic. I'm overwhelmed by the number of people he has swayed to his way of thinking. His speeches have become more and more direct. He's making his plans very clear. He intends to take leadership of the Nephite nation. I fear that those who are not enticed or deluded by his words will soon feel the point of his sword. He's already amassed a small army that grows with each city he visits."

"He's going from city to city? Well, then so are we," Moroni stated with a matter-of-fact air. "If we can sway these people back to reality, then we can deal with Amalickiah. Apparently, these people need an education on what true freedom is all about. I've brought with me a bit of a tangible reminder."

He held up the banner he had made of his torn cloak. The others read its message and nodded their approval.

MORONI AND HELAMAN RODE from city to city bearing Moroni's flag and gathering ever-increasing numbers of followers. Helaman was extremely vocal in establishing the movement against Amalickiah's seditious ideals. Moroni's visible standard of freedom, coupled with his speeches, had an effective impact on the people. Supporters in many cities duplicated Moroni's flag and posted them high above the city gates.

In a climatic speech, Moroni and Helaman stood side by side on Zarahemla's city wall. They addressed a large crowd gathered below them in the city square. Moroni held his Title of Liberty on a pole as he spoke:

Our fathers brought us to this Promised Land so that we would find freedom and liberty. Not freedom to become enslaved by the whims of an arrogant and power-hungry man, but freedom to raise our children in peaceful communities where they can be taught to love and respect their fellow man. I tell you this plainly, Amalickiah is not seeking after your good, but after your adoration to boost his ego and make his climb to power more attainable.

Once there, he will enslave you as surely as any taskmaster. I call on you to shun his words and seek after true liberty. This banner that I bear, made from my own cloak, represents my commitment to liberty. It bears words that call to remembrance what liberty and freedom truly represent. Whosoever will maintain this title—this Title of Liberty, let him come forward in the strength of the Lord, and enter into a covenant that he will maintain his rights and his religion, that the Lord God may bless him.

Let all those who swear loyalty to God and not this man, Amalickiah, to be gathered together to secure the liberty which God would have us enjoy! We will not allow such a man to enslave our society. Instead, we will preserve our liberty by words if possible, but by

the sword if necessary! Those of you who favor liberty,
gather in this square as a show of might that we will
not blindly lie down and allow this man to usurp
power and authority over this nation!

Moroni's words had a powerful impact on the crowd. Those who
were already opposed to Amalickiah had their opinions confirmed.
Many fence-sitting, indecisive people were swayed to see the light as
Moroni exposed it for them. Each of them determined to take a stand
for what they believed to be right. The people came running together
bearing their armor and swords and gathered before Moroni. They
each tore their own cloaks as a token of their pledge. With this, they
threw their cloaks at the feet of Moroni.

PEOPLE FROM MANY cities had been rounded up as support for both
sides of the strife. This impassioned society had indeed grown to
allow their tensions to increase to a full-scale civil war. Both groups
now met on a large field. Amalickiah's troops chanted, "King! King!"
while Moroni's men chanted, "Freedom!" Both Amalickiah and
Moroni were on horseback and paced before their armies awaiting the
initial attack. Both leaders seemed to be waiting for the other to make
the first move. Amalickiah, however, did not realize that Moroni was
waiting for something more.

Amalickiah's men were proud and swept up in the fury of wanting
a king, pumped up by Amalickiah's vaporous promises. But, as the
time grew nearer for the actual assault of hand-to-hand combat with
men who were their brothers, some, still chanting, began to look at
the swords in their hands and also at Moroni's soldiers, who they
knew were bent on preserving their freedom. They saw Moroni's
banner man proudly bearing the Title of Liberty. Its words called for
the preservation of their rights, freedom and family, as it waved in the

breeze. The sound of Moroni's army's call for "Freedom!" reached their ears and began to hold their attention.

They began to look at each other with more doubt in the justice of their cause, than determination. They saw the vacant expressions on their comrades' faces and now properly guessed that many of them were now questioning the wisdom and validity of their own actions. At this point, both armies were about equal in size. However, within moments, the event Moroni had awaited, arrived. Captain Lehi and his army came rising over the hillside and doubled Moroni's army.

The king-men were clearly disturbed by this and quite abruptly stopped chanting. Some of them simply dropped their weapons and began retreating. Others quickly followed.

Amalickiah's anger grew. "Hold your ground, men! Return to your positions! We can defeat this foe!" He cursed at his men.

None of them listened. Many had now retreated to the outer perimeter of the intended battlefield and had disappeared into the lush jungle that predominated the area. Amalickiah curbed his frustration only enough to keep his wits. Unable to muster his troops, he decided to take charge of their retreat.

"Men! Now is not the day! To the trees! Moroni must not conquer!" he bellowed.

The army fled the field in a uniform, but hurried, manner following Amalickiah's lead. Amalickiah charged his horse to the fringe of the rainforest. The jungle undergrowth was too thick for a man on horseback. He dismounted quickly and ran with his men as they made their escape.

"We can't have them joining the Lamanites!" Moroni shouted to his men. "We'll have to cut them off. Lehi!"

Lehi looked to his leader. Moroni motioned with his sword for Lehi to take his troops around to cut off Amalickiah from the west.

Moroni turned and motioned for Teancum, his youngest and newest commander, to pursue from the eastern side, while Moroni charged with his men straight on. With his army split into three forces, Moroni intended to overtake, surround, and capture Amalickiah and his men.

Although on horseback, Moroni was unable to cross the field and overtake Amalickiah's army before the last of them had successfully retreated into the jungle. Moroni dismounted and joined his men in a foot chase that took place through the jungle. Men leaped over and through the underbrush, slowing, but not by any means stopping. They used their swords to cut their path. It was not difficult to track Amalickiah's men through the shambles they had made of the jungle during their flight.

Farther ahead, Amalickiah kept a keen head during his hasty retreat. Without slowing his pace, he ensured that he met up with a small handful of his best men. He motioned to them to slide his way during the run. The remainder of his army blindly fled at a panicked rate. Amalickiah chose to ignore them and allowed them to run pell-mell as an unled, terrified group. They remained oblivious to Amalickiah's action. None of them noticed Amalickiah and his little group break away from the main troops and secretly run off in a separate direction.

The path they cut was too obscure to be noticed, especially during the heat of the chase. All of Moroni's men passed it by and continued to close in on Amalickiah's main, fleeing army. Neither side was aware that Amalickiah and his small group of loyalists had split off until Moroni overtook and surrounded the main army.

After searching among the prisoners for Amalickiah, Lehi approached Moroni and announced, "Amalickiah is nowhere to be seen. We also can't find his brother, Ammoron, so we have to assume they broke off. They could be anywhere."

"'Anywhere,' yes, but I'm certain they're heading in a straight course for the Lamanites," Moroni responded, with a flare for strategic thinking.

Lehi was shocked at this supposition, "The Lamanites?! He wouldn't stand a chance! They'd cut him down before he'd seen his first sunset in their land."

"I wouldn't count on that," Moroni mused. "He's a slippery one. I don't think we've seen the last of him. Meanwhile, we have to get these prisoners secured before we lose any more. Round them up and let's get back to Zarahemla."

Chapter 5

Infiltration

*A*malickiah and his closest cohorts in crime continued running through the jungle at a desperate pace. Amalickiah stopped and raised his hand for silence. His men all stopped and huddled near him. The only sounds were their heavy breathing and typical jungle noises. Exotic birds squawked and monkeys chided these new invaders of their territory. After a brief pause, it was evident that they were not being pursued. The men smiled, nudged each other in relief, and turned to Amalickiah for guidance. The group included Ammoron and the fourth judge, whose name was Ishmael. He was the judge who had been so quick to swear allegiance to Amalickiah's ploy to become king.

Still breathless and panting, but greatly annoyed, Ammoron managed to nearly stand straight. His shoulders heaved in and out as he tried to catch his breath. He wiped a bit of drool from his mouth and glanced back at the path they had just cut. With the observation of those waking up to a hopeless cause, he muttered, "Well, this is just great! We're 'free,' but we're in the middle of nowhere and we've lost our army!"

"Then we'll have to raise a new army," Amalickiah calmly retorted, without deterrence.

"How?! If we show our faces back at Zarahemla, we're dead men!" Ammoron challenged, more perplexed than annoyed.

"Who said anything about going back—yet?" Amalickiah corrected his less-than-brilliant brother.

There was hidden meaning in his words that only Ishmael caught. He offered the following point to Ammoron and the others, "I believe we won't be returning until we've raised our army." Ishmael turned to Amalickiah for confirmation. "Isn't that right?"

Amalickiah smiled his wicked smile and nodded confirmation.

Ammoron demanded a realistic answer and queried, "But, where will we find an army?! The only other people out here are Lamanites—" His face took on an incredulous expression, mixed with dread, as the dawning of an unfortunate realization emerged. With severe hesitation he began to verbalize it, "Unless—" he looked his brother directly in the eyes hoping to receive a contradiction to his worst fear.

Amalickiah did not oblige him, instead, he confirmed it, "Now you're using your head for something more than carrying around a dumb expression. Follow me men and I'll see you sit in the highest seats of power!"

Ammoron instinctively covered his with his hand and shook his head in disbelief. After a lifetime, he still could not believe his brother's audacity. He would, of course, continue to follow him. The other men rose and followed Amalickiah deeper into Lamanite territory.

MORONI HAD GATHERED the prisoners and marched them back to Zarahemla. Their numbers were such that even crowded together shoulder to shoulder and heel to toe, they still filled Zarahemla's grand city square. They were weaponless and surrounded by Moroni's soldiers. Moroni stood above them, on the catwalk that curled along the city wall wholly encompassing the Nephite capital city. He stood on the section nearest the city gate. The Title of Liberty blew proudly in the breeze behind him. The prisoners mingled in silence, defiantly awaiting word of their fate.

Moroni leaned with both hands on the rail before him and eyed the captives with a mixture of feelings that ranged from disdain to remorse. He had never personally been one to seek for power and had no patience for those others who did. He was a firm believer in pursuing only that which was for the greater good for society. This was the only reason he had accepted commission back into service.

He looked at the imprisoned group of his former Nephite brethren and his heart sickened and ached for those who had turned against their society and attempted to enforce a dictatorial government upon them by the sword. He saw them as lost and deluded souls needing saving, but knew all too well that he could not speak to them in tones of forgiveness and reclamation, as people in this state would not respond appropriately. They would see that tone as a sign of weakness and would remain wholly unrepentant and dangerous.

Moroni knew all too well that this group needed to be dealt with decisively, quickly, and harshly, if he was going to succeed at awakening them and the rest of the Nephites to proper beliefs and behavior. He stood up straight, ensuring that he had the group's full attention.

"You men have been led astray by a wicked and vain man who sought to be king," he boldly declared. "He sought kingship not because he wanted to benefit or protect this people, but because he sought his own, personal glory and riches!"

Moroni began to pace to hold their attention and to give him the ability to see all portions of the crowd. He wanted to see how well received his words were.

"We only seek to protect ourselves, our lands, our families, our religion, and our freedom. We have raised this Title of Liberty as a symbol of our desires and have sworn to uphold this quest." He gestured to the flag above the city gate.

He turned and pointed directly at his captive audience and sternly declared, "Those of you 'king-men' who will swear allegiance to liberty and to no longer fight against our peaceful society can continue to live among us as friends and brethren. Those of you who will not swear this will be put to death. Now!" To highlight the immediacy of the proposition, he commanded, "Those of you swearing this oath, bow down, that we may see."

All but six men bowed down. The six were scattered throughout the captives and stood, defiantly daring Moroni to act. Moroni did not hesitate. He pointed directly to them and gave them the chance to rethink their defiance, "You men, standing there. Do you make the oath of peace?"

"We do not!" the first man declared. A vain grin crept onto his face as he dared defy the man who he had often sarcastically referred to as "the mighty Moroni" in front of his comrades in earlier settings.

"Do you understand my words?" Moroni sought clarification, before exacting justice.

One of the standing men took a few steps toward this fellow prisoner who had spoken. He was unable to walk directly to his comrade, because of the press of the crowd, but the few steps he managed to take made it clear where his allegiance stood.

"We do!" the second man replied, "And we refuse to swear."

Moroni, having given them the opportunity to recant their decision, and being satisfied that they were knowingly choosing to defy liberty, saw no other option than to make an example of the men.

"Then there is only one alternative. Teancum, have these men brought forward," he called out.

Teancum, who stood down in the city square, motioned to his men. The crowd of prisoners quickly parted to enable Teancum's men to grab the six and brusquely march them forward to the feet of Moroni who still stood on the catwalk above the city gate.

Moroni magnanimously gave them one last chance to preserve their rebellious hides, "Do you men now swear?"

"We do not!" the first man again declared.

"So be it," Moroni replied simply.

He motioned to Teancum who had his men toss ropes over the joists in the gate. The six were hanged then and there. As they vainly struggled for breath, the still-bowed prisoners sneaked looks and were more deeply resolved in their decision to swear the oath.

Moroni returned his focus to the captives, "Now, how many of the rest of you want to join your stubborn friends?"

Moroni paced and eyed the prisoners. None of them moved. "Good. You men can now swear allegiance to the Title and must seek no longer to disrupt this people. Do you so swear? Rise and show us."

The men all rose and raised their right hands to the square.

"We so swear," the prisoners stated in unison.

During the course of this incident, Helaman had joined Moroni on the gate.

Moroni concluded the situation with these words, "Lest any man forget what has happened here today, I want the Title of Liberty posted high above each city's gate so that all may remember their oath. You men are now free."

Teancum's men raised their spears and swords so that their tips no longer pointed at the prisoners. Having sworn the oath of peace, the former prisoners were now free to return to their homes. By the rites of their society, breaking their oath now would be a black mark on their very souls. This people, even when rebelling, would not refute their oaths.

MORONI WAS SEATED around a table with Helaman, Teancum, Lehi, and two others. The room was just large enough for them to be able to pace around the table. It was their strategy room. On a far wall was a series of shelves from floor to ceiling. The shelving was covered by a curtain that hung partially open, revealing some of the many maps and documents they contained. The documents were written on scrolls that were loosely rolled.

There were no windows in the strategy room, as it was nested deep within the city's central building. All light came from hanging oil lamps. Only one, wooden door provided access to the room. It led to the main hallway in this building that also housed the council chamber where the judges met, as well as other governmental entities. While many records were kept in that room, the majority were stored in the lower, underground chambers of this complex, secured behind large, stone doors.

These stone doors were somewhat of a marvel. Made from one solid piece of granite-like stone, they were four feet wide, a foot thick, and nearly seven feet tall. While they provided ample security for the records they protected, they were carved in such a way that when the locking stone was removed a man could apply little pressure with one hand and push the one-ton doors open. They pivoted on a beveled corner that acted as a hinge on one side.

In the strategy room, the Nephite leaders discussed ways to prepare for whatever deeds Amalickiah had in store for them. Lehi was particularly concerned about letting Amalickiah remain on the loose. He added the following to the conversation that had been going on for quite some time, "Well, he certainly doesn't dare come back. Should we send a party after them?"

"No, they have too much of a lead and could easily catch our men off guard. I don't want to send my men blindly into some form of ambush," Moroni answered.

"If they do succeed in joining the Lamanites, they won't stay away for long. You can be certain of that," Teancum pointed out.

"I'm afraid you're right. We need to prepare ourselves and our cities for their return," Moroni conceded.

"Our *cities*?" Lehi was a bit perplexed and verbalized his confusion.

Anticipating the question, Moroni added, "Certainly. They know our cities as well as we do ourselves. They know their strengths *and* their weaknesses." He eyed his commanders to see who, if any, would understand what he implied.

The room was silent for only a moment, when Helaman observed, "What we have to do is change our cities in such a way that they can't use their knowledge against us. Correct?"

"Exactly," Moroni smiled.

"But, will we have time?" Teancum saw the point, but questioned their ability.

Moroni presented the following string of logical conclusions, "As we've seen, insurrection doesn't begin in a single day. Infiltration into enemy ranks takes even longer. He has to win friends before he can gain confidences and build up a force. I have no doubt he'll accomplish the climb, but it won't happen in a day. Yes, I'd say we have time. Just not time to waste."

"You have my full support. As always," Helaman dutifully replied.

"And ours as well," Lehi and the others agreed.

"I knew this, but it's good to hear you say it out loud. You are all true men, defenders of the faith and the faithful." Moroni thanked his men for their loyalty. Then he added his own pledge of devotion, "Helaman, in this act of defense I do not in any way mean to usurp the leadership that you represent for this people and myself. Our countrymen and I must still look to you to lead us to trust in the Lord. I wholly realize that swords and spears are powerful weapons, but there is no equal or substitute for having the Lord on our side. I will continue to look to you for spiritual guidance."

"I knew this as well, Moroni," Helaman responded. "And I continue to be impressed with your devotion. For my part, I will step up my efforts to visit each city more regularly; to keep these people in line by making it clear to them who it is that gives them breath and grants them life; to help them gain an appreciation for their role in maintaining the freedom and liberties they now enjoy."

Turning to strategic relations, Moroni added, "Lehi and Teancum, we know that faith is essential, but without works we aren't worthy of His help. We must fortify the cities in such a way that Amalickiah would never expect. Let's begin with our weakest city."

Moroni walked over to the shelves, pulled the curtain aside, and retrieved a scroll. He brought it back to the table and unrolled an old map. He placed some clay drinking flasks at the corners to make it lay flat. The men rose and came around to his side to view the map.

"That would be Ammonihah. Here. It's still not been fully repaired since the last Lamanite attack." Teancum identified the target city, and put his finger on the spot.

Moroni agreed, and began to unfold his plan. "Now, first, we'll dig a trench around the entire city. We won't cart the dirt off. We'll put it to good use. We'll move all of the dirt up against the city walls. We'll have to raise the walls themselves, or rather build higher walls on top of the existing structures. This would make the ditches even deeper. We'll place spears and hurdles in the ditches and along the walls to hinder attempts to scale them. At the top of the dirt walls we'll build a series of reinforced shielding for our archers to peer through. Over the city gate and at each corner we'll build high towers, halfway between each of these towers we'll place weaponry rooms for storing spears, arrows, and boulders for fending off attacks—"

As Moroni described his plans, his officers' eyes grew wide. He sensed their concern, paused and asked, "What is it?"

"Sir, no one has ever built such fortifications before," Teancum stated.

"Yes, I know. That's exactly why we're doing this," Moroni pointed out.

AMALICKIAH AND HIS men were on a tree-filled hilltop. They were crouched down, looking out toward a city of Lamanites. To the far side of the city, farmers could be seen tilling fields. Walking the catwalk along the city wall, two guards performed their routine duties, while additional guards were posted by the city gate. Beyond their line of vision, safely within the city's protective city wall, other Lamanites were going about the duties of a typical day. Merchants plied their wares, couples wandered together, children dashed in and out of hiding spots playing games.

"There it is men. The land of Nephi. Stronghold of the Lamanites," Amalickiah proudly announced.

Centuries earlier, a man named Nephi had led his people out of the Old World to the Promised Land. Lamanite aggression forced them to abandon their first, small settlement. They moved into the wilderness, inland and northward to a find a place where they could be free from Lamanite interference. They had settled in the valley that Amalickiah and his men now surveyed. Here they took the time to build a mighty city. They called it the city of Nephi, out of love and respect for their honored leader.

To further show their respect, the people took on Nephi's name and became known as "Nephites." It was not long, however, before the Lamanites again rose up against the Nephites in a series of wars that seemingly had no end.

The Nephites eventually abandoned their beloved city of Nephi and moved still farther north, hoping to live peaceful lives. They established the even far grander city of Zarahemla. This became the Nephite's new chief city. Although it was much more splendid and offered greater protection than any other city in the land, the Nephites still longed for the day that they would be able to overcome their Lamanite foes and return to their beloved city of Nephi.

Until that time, the Lamanites continued to occupy the envied city and used it as their chief stronghold, out of spite as much as out of any other purpose. This, then, was the city that the Lamanite king considered his home, and which bore his throne room. And, it was here that Amalickiah had dared to lead his men.

Ammoron could not help but cower very low, yet he dared to poke his head up high enough to take in the view. He exclaimed, "I never thought I'd live to see it." He continued to try to make out more of the distant images of life within their enemy's city. Curiously, he noted that there appeared to be no signs of preparations for war.

"You'll see a lot more than its outer gate, I assure you!" Amalickiah prophesied with a self-indulgent smile.

"You're not planning on going *in* there are you?!" Ammoron was again fearful.

"Of course. How else will we gain our army? From the birds and monkeys in the trees?" Amalickiah boisterously slapped his brother on the back of his head while the others laughed.

Undeterred in his apprehension, Ammoron insisted on a plan, "What are you going to do? Walk right into town and ask for enlistments?"

Amalickiah's smile broadened while a plot hatched in his head, only to be hinted at for the moment. "Oh, that's close. But, I'll be a lot more subtle than that. Yes, a lot more subtle. Follow my lead if you value your heads."

Amalickiah began a quick decent toward the city, through the jungle. The others followed. Some half-hour later, Amalickiah stumbled out of the jungle to the clearing nearest the city's main gate. His clothes were disheveled. His men emerged the same. They all stumbled to their knees, panting for breath.

"Guard, guard! Thank goodness, guard!" Amalickiah called out in a desperate, weary voice, maintaining the lead as they crossed the field toward the city, and purposely called attention to himself.

Two guards by the city's gate noticed the commotion and rushed to the Nephite strangers with their spears pointed at their enemies.

"Guards, thank goodness we made it! We must see the king! We must warn the king!" Amalickiah continued.

The first guard was somewhat incredulous, "Warn the king?! You, a Nephite, warn the king? What do you care about our king?"

Amalickiah feigned intense indignation and chided, "Apparently, I care a great deal more than you do! Hurry! I must warn the king!"

The second guard took extreme exception at the gall of this Nephite intruder who dared to chide a Lamanite. He narrowed his eyes, clenched his teeth, moved his weapon into position and firmly declared, "And we must warn you. Stop where you are this instant, or you'll not breathe another breath!"

To the shock and dismay of his brother who slunk toward the back of their group, Amalickiah ignored the threat. "Fine, fine, do with us as you will, but first we must see the king."

The guards were surprised at the audacity of this man who should have been pleading for his life. They recognized that there must be something unique about this warning he claimed to have for their king. They stepped back and spoke to each other in hushed, hurried tones, while keeping a watchful eye on their captives.

They discussed the likelihood of Amalickiah actually bearing news for which, should they prevent it from reaching their king, they could be held accountable. During this discussion, three more guards rushed out of the city gate and moved in to surround Amalickiah and his men.

"What's all this about?! Where did these Nephites come from?!" the largest of the three additional guards demanded.

"I haven't a clue," the second guard replied. "They've just appeared from the jungle, claiming to need to warn the king. They seem in earnest."

"A warning for the king? What sort of warning?" the tall guard queried.

"We don't know yet. We've been trying to find that out," the first guard pointed out. "I say we bring them to the captain and let him decide what to do."

"Agreed," the third guard stated. Then, turning to Amalickiah's men, he sternly ordered, "Up, you men! Step in line!"

They bound Amalickiah and his men's hands behind their backs and took them through the gate into the city. The group was marched to a prison while curious and concerned Lamanites watched them pass. Amalickiah observed the guards speak to their captain, but was unable to overhear the conversation.

The captain disappeared through a doorway. Amalickiah and his men awaited word on their fate while continuing to be well guarded. The captain finally returned and motioned for them to be led to the throne room. The throne room door opened widely, bringing the room into their full view, as they cautiously entered.

The throne room had obviously seen better days. The tapestries on the walls were fading. While the humid air had taken its toll on them, it was evident that the years, and perhaps centuries that had passed since they were first hung there, had taken an even greater toll on their once-brilliant colors. An ancient chandelier of jewels and gold, lit by candles hung from the central rafter. Torches filled each walls interspersed between the tapestries.

The stone floor had a long, hand-woven carpet that led directly from the throne room door to the throne itself. Its reddish-purple color was fading, and the edges of the carpet were frayed in many areas. The throne itself was made of both stone and wood.

Its dais had a stone foundation that had once been carved with images of serpents and vines. Over the years, these images had all but worn off. Two wooden steps built to cover the original, stone steps. These were made of dark wood and also carved to depict the original vines and serpents.

Much of the same treatment had been given to the throne itself. The king's seat, chair back and armrests were covered with a dark wood with ornamental carvings imitating those found in the original stone. Simple, dark red cloths had been placed on the wood, for the king to sit upon. The king himself now sat in his throne, governing all things pertaining to the Lamanites. At this time, that included conversing with these unlikely visitors from the north.

"Who are you and what is this news you wish me to hear?" the Lamanite king demanded. He had on a loose vest made of monkey skins. His bulging belly protruded uncomely from within the confines of the vest. The jewels in his golden crown were interspersed with brightly-colored feathers. His mood looked ill and suspicious.

As Amalickiah attempted to step forward, a guard blocked him with his spear. The king waved the guard aside. Amalickiah was able to step forward. Behind him, his men remained encircled by several guards pointing spears at them. Amalickiah bowed and knelt before the king, showing all the deference he inwardly wanted others to show to him.

"Oh, great king, I thank you that I might speak to you this day. I am Amalickiah, a Nephite by birth, as you can plainly see by my pale, uncomely skin. But, I am your humble servant from this day onward."

The king was pleased with the prospect of a Nephite who knew his manners and his place. He maintained his gruff exterior, however and repeated, "What is your news?"

"Oh, great king, I wish to save you. You and your beautiful people."

"Save me? From what? From whom?"

"Oh, great king, from the Nephites." With the dropping of this bit of news, Amalickiah bowed himself low to the ground and lowered his eyes to the floor, implying submission to the unfortunate "truth" he had been compelled to reveal to the king.

The king sat upright, wholly surprised by this news. "The

Nephites? The Nephites! They've sworn to leave us in peace. Why should I need to fear them?"

Amalickiah turned and spoke to his men, but with the obvious intent that the king overhear him. "You see. You see that this king is a man of his word and he does not take oaths as trifles. He would not refute his word."

The king was irritated that Amalickiah would dare to speak to others in his presence, but was even more impatient to learn to what Amalickiah was referring. "Of what do you speak?" he demanded in a deep voice that echoed through the hall.

Amalickiah turned back to the king and again feigned humility and deference as he perpetuated his lie, "Even as we speak, great king, the Nephites prepare for war, in spite of their supposed oath. I am a man of honor. I cannot live among a people who don't honor their oaths. I have come to warn you of their treachery, lest they take you and your peaceful people unawares."

"The Nephites prepare for war?!" the king stood at this news.

Amalickiah nodded. The king flumped back down onto his throne, sat back and pondered the implications of the Nephites breaking the oath that they themselves forced upon the Lamanites.

"Unheard of!" the Lamanite ruler muttered to himself. Then, with a resolute look he declared to his court, "Very well. We will not be taken off our guard."

Already the king had begun to ignore Amalickiah and his men as he began to give orders of preparation for another war. Amalickiah would not be so easily forgotten, however, and dared to interrupt the king's intentions by calling out, "Oh, great king, I have come to aid you."

The king turned his gaze and attention back to Amalickiah, who continued to kneel before him. He incredulously asked, with more than a subtle hint of indignation at the thought, "Aid me? I need no aid! My armies are mighty enough."

"Yes, great king, they are," Amalickiah continued. "They are the mightiest of armies with brave, bold warriors, but I can make the battle quick and spare your men from trouble."

"How? How can you do this?"

"I am a Nephite by birth. I have lived my days among them. I have dwelled in their cities." Amalickiah rose to his feet as he continued. "I have seen their fortifications. I know their strengths—and their weaknesses." Amalickiah paused to allow this to sink in. "And I wish to share all of this knowledge with you, great king. For I wish that you will be *my* king, and I will be your servant."

The king smiled as Amalickiah bowed with exaggerated subservience. He had completely fallen for Amalickiah's ploy. Ammoron and the others, still guarded, looked at each other and nodded approvingly in admiration of a master schemer.

WITHIN A FEW short days, a proclamation from the king had been written, copied, and was in the process of being posted throughout the Lamanite city. The proclamation declared the Nephite's intention to attack them. It further stated that all men were to arm themselves and report for duty. Husbands and wives read the proclamation on various city walls. Wives cried and men shook and scratched their heads in disbelief. It was beyond their capacity to believe that the Nephites could possibly go against their word of honor.

Other men, who boldly longed for war and the splendors of battle, read and nodded with enthusiasm. The people became split in whether or not they believed there was a real threat. Rumor had it that the supposed war was a hoax, generated to take their minds off of this year's poor crops. The king's men called for representatives from each of the Lamanite homes. Some men risked public censor and potential execution by refusing to take the weapons offered to them.

The king required weekly updates on the preparations. Guards bore the unnerving task of reporting protests to their superiors. As word got back to the general populace that many were refusing to take up arms against the Nephites, others took courage and joined in the protest. An increasing number of men spoke out about not breaking their oath by taking up arms.

Chapter 6

In Pursuit of Power

The Lamanite king paced furiously. He had become accustomed to having his orders meticulously obeyed. Reluctance he could handle, but out and out refusal was wholly unthinkable. Amalickiah was by his side, dressed in the fineries of an advisor.

"How can they disobey me?! I won't tolerate this!" the king ranted.

"They claim they don't want to break their oath. The oath they swore to the Nephites, that the Nephites themselves have broken," Amalickiah slyly egged on the king.

The king caught the meaning behind Amalickiah's dig, "Their oath to the *Nephites*! What about their loyalty to *me*?! I can't allow this! This is insurrection!"

"They need to be taught to honor their king and obey his will."

"Yes, and follow his orders! Amalickiah, in this short while, you have served me well. You have proven your loyalty by risking your life to bring me your news. I want you to take charge of those who are loyal to me and round up those who are not. In this way we can put an end to this disloyalty. Will you do this?" The king looked searchingly at his new advisor's face.

Amalickiah straightened and attempted to display pure and total loyalty, "Yes, your majesty. It would be an honor. What do you wish me to do?"

"What I wish is that you will take my army and round up these rebels, these—these 'oath-keepers' and teach them to obey their true and rightful king."

"As you wish it, so shall it be done." Upon this, Amalickiah bowed respectfully to the king. The king nodded approvingly. Amalickiah left to carry out his orders.

Neither of them paid any heed to the king's guards who stood silently protecting the entrance to the throne room. One in particular had overheard the orders. As soon as his shift replacement arrived, he slipped out of the building and made his way through the city streets. He entered a small building where a large group of people had huddled together for a clandestine meeting.

The oath-keepers turned for word from the king's guard. He spoke with an air of disappointment and concern, "It's just as we feared. The king has given orders to round us up and 'teach' us to obey. He's put this Nephite, Amalickiah, in charge of finding us."

A charismatic leader named Lehonti spoke up, "It's good that we had anticipated this. Give the order to have everyone move out. Go from house to house to those who have sworn to uphold their oaths. We should be long gone by morning. With any luck we can reach the hill Antipas within a week's march. We should be able to hold up there for quite some time."

THE BLACKNESS OF the moonless night was disrupted by a splattering of campfires at the base of the hill Antipas. Amalickiah's soldiers restlessly waited for the dawn and their attack. They knew full well that with Lehonti and his men, encamped at the top of this steep, natural fortress, success would be much more awkward than had they overtaken them on the plain.

Some peered up the hillside trying in vain to get a feel for the size and strength of Lehonti's force. They wondered if it were dozens, hundreds, or more. All they could manage to discern was the reflective glow of many campfires now and then lighting the trees and brush that surrounded the upper end of this craggy hill.

Amalickiah sat hunched over a makeshift, portable wooden table in his tent. His concentration was poised on his writing. A soldier stood at the ready patiently awaiting his orders. With a final stroke of his charcoal pen, Amalickiah sat upright. He held his latest masterpiece in his hand and silently reread it to himself. A wicked smirk crept across his face, and his eyes lit up with delight as he read. Upon conclusion, he nodded approvingly. It would do.

He rolled the note up as a scroll and stuffed it gingerly into a standard message tube, made of bamboo with leather caps on either end, held in place by leather ties. He finished tying on the top cap and handed the tube to his soldier. The soldier was already pulling the longer strap that was attached to either end of the message tube around his shoulder for safe keeping as Amalickiah gave his final instruction, "Take this up to Lehonti. Don't fail me!"

"Yes, sir," the messenger responded with only moderate interest, only wanting to fulfill the order quickly and then retire for the night.

The messenger stepped out of the tent and looked up the black hillside. It qualified as a "hill" in only the most academic of terms, being simply too short to be considered a "mountain." This one fact did not make the ascent any simpler. Even with the switchback hairpin turns, the climb was tedious and taxing, not the kind of jaunt one looked forward to in broad daylight, let alone by torchlight.

The noble warrior reached the crest of the climb only to be met by Lehonti's guards.

"I bear a message for Lehonti from Amalickiah. I seek admittance," he stated.

Lehonti's guards admitted him. They led him quickly to Lehonti's tent. He delivered his message and awaited the reply.

As Lehonti, the fugitive leader, read Amalickiah's message, he could not help but allow a few words of surprise escape his thoughts and become verbalized, "'Come down and meet him?' I will do no such thing! It's obviously a trap."

Upon completing his reading, Lehonti turned to Amalickiah's messenger, "Tell your esteemed leader I will do no such thing."

"Did you wish to write a message?" the messenger braved the question.

"No, I do *not* wish to write a message. I wish you to tell him he need not bother waiting for me. I won't be coming," Lehonti replied with a tinge of sarcasm and derision.

The descent was physically no better than the climb. In some ways it was more awkward to maintain balance. The soldier's thoughts, however, were not on his balance. He was more concerned about sharing Lehonti's refusal with Amalickiah, especially since it was to be done devoid of any tangible evidence that the message came from Lehonti.

Upon return to base-camp, the messenger allowed Amalickiah's guard to announce him. Amalickiah called for him to enter without delay. To the messenger's relief and surprise, Amalickiah was not deterred by Lehonti's refusal. For a moment, he sensed that Amalic-kiah had actually expected it.

"Ask him once more," Amalickiah announced, taking the messenger further off his guard.

"But, he's already refused—" the messenger made the potentially fatal error of questioning the order.

Amalickiah held his tone, but with more than just a hint of threat stated, "Humor me. Or, do I need a new courier?"

"No, sir. That will not be necessary," the messenger replied while observing Amalickiah finger his sword.

"I didn't think so. Be quick!" Amalickiah added as he gave an ominous grin and nodded approvingly.

The foreboding ascent was again undertaken. Rocks, potholes, twists, turns, and brambles that were once unknown emerging obstacles, brought into consciousness by the flicker of torchlight, now appeared as familiar milestones on the thrice-taken path.

Again the guards admitted the messenger into Lehonti's tent. Again Lehonti shook his head. This time, he shouted his refusal to the hapless courier and ushered him back to the arduous path. This time, the messenger's thoughts were even more grim as he contemplated, step by step during the descent, the reconfirmation of the traitorous leader's refusal to satisfy Amalickiah's request.

With heavy feet and prolonged steps the soldier shamefully noted his hesitation to return to Amalickiah's tent. He was, after all, a warrior not a whimpering boy. "Who is this Nephite who should order me about in the night?" In answer to his own question, the thought formed, "The ambassador of your king, with the power to take life with more ease than you trod this path."

Regardless, when the time came, the soldier announced his return and was led into Amalickiah's tent. He found his leader pacing impatiently. Amalickiah turned and demanded to know Lehonti's reply, "Well?!"

The soldier nearly shook, but again mustered his warrior's pride and courage to give his report, "He refuses to come, sir."

Amalickiah maintained his unpredictability and calmly responded, "I anticipated that. Give him this reply."

Amalickiah handed him a new scroll he had already prepared, much to the surprise of the courier. The soldier was at first perplexed, but glancing at Amalickiah's sword, he did not question the order and headed back up the hillside.

For the third time, the sleepless messenger found himself standing in Lehonti's tent watching the man read a note. In this case, Lehonti was nodding approvingly and even managed a smile. Again Lehonti mumbled to himself while reading. "Bring as many men as I wish? . . . He'll be alone halfway down? . . . Well, I'd certainly see if he tried to bring his men. . . ."

Lehonti paused only momentarily, and then looked up at the courier, "Tell Amalickiah I'll be there by the time he arrives. *With* my men."

The soldier dutifully replied, "Yes, sir," and turned to leave.

LEHONTI AND HIS guards stood awaiting Amalickiah on a landing on the hillside. They had both torches and swords. Amalickiah emerged from the darkness. He was clearly alone. Even his tireless messenger had been left behind for this trek up the hillside. The scheming emissary of the king began to speak even as he walked into view of the torchlight.

"Lehonti, thank goodness you have agreed to this meeting! You are a wise and prudent man. This fighting is clearly wrong. I don't know what more we can do to help the king see this. He seems bent on destroying the Nephites. Our men need to be united in our efforts to stop this conflict."

"I thought *you* were the cause of the king's proclamation," Lehonti stated with suspicion.

"Me?!" Amalickiah feigned surprise. "I seek only peace! That's what I told the king upon our first meeting! You and I must join forces to secure peace."

"Join forces? How? Your men are on a quest to destroy mine," Lehonti was taken off guard.

"I know this," Amalickiah agreed. "That's why it was imperative that we meet tonight. I know how we can join forces and unify the loyalty of both our men."

"And what do you propose?" Lehonti was intrigued.

"Under the cover of night, bring your men down and surround my army. When they awake, they'll see that they're at your mercy. You'll be viewed as a wise and powerful adversary. My men will appeal for mercy. I'll step forward and negotiate with you. When you agree to allow my men to join yours, rather than destroy them, you'll win their hearts. And, I'll save face for having negotiated this great truce with you."

Lehonti considered the proposal and surmised, "This sounds reasonable, but then what? What more will you want of me once this is done?"

"All I ask is that you allow me to retain a portion of my position. I will deliver up my army to you, if you will let me be your second in command," Amalickiah offered.

"My second? Nothing more?"

"That is all. I seek only peace."

"Do you swear that this is your intent?"

"I swear that as the Lord lives and as I live, if you do as I have said, I will do the same. These armies will be yours and you shall be their unquestioned leader."

"So be it," Lehonti nodded. "We meet at dawn. I go to muster my men."

"So be it."

Amalickiah and Lehonti shook hands then both turned to go. As Amalickiah faced away from Lehonti, he paused only long enough to allow a wicked grimace creep across his face. Its sinister intent was heightened by the shifting shadows from the torches. He headed back down the mountainside.

DAWN ARRIVED. As Amalickiah's army awakened. They saw that Lehonti's men had entirely surrounded their camp and stood ready to attack. The main officers rushed to Amalickiah's tent. Amalickiah dashed out feigning surprise. The men watched with intense interest as the officers negotiated with him. They anxiously encouraged Amalickiah to follow his officer's recommendations. Although the other soldiers were unable to overhear the officers' negotiations with Amalickiah, it seemed to them that they were recommending that he surrender. This seemed the most prudent course to them. They were greatly relieved when it became clear that Amalickiah had finally nodded in agreement.

He approached the place where Lehonti stood. The king's army again watched as their newest leader negotiated with Lehonti. The two leaders shook hands. Amalickiah faced his troops. It was made evident to all that he had agreed to fall in with Lehonti when he ceremoniously handed Lehonti his sword, who returned it with equal ceremony. Amalickiah's men cheered. The army was one.

STILL ENCAMPED, LEHONTI and Amalickiah and their chief officers dined in the officers' tent. Amalickiah's chief officers consisted mainly of Ammoron, Ishmael, and two of the Lamanite king's key officers. Amalickiah nodded to Ishmael across the table. Ishmael acknowledged the nod. As the servant with the wine began to fill Ishmael's glass, Ishmael purposely knocked his spoon to the ground.

As the servant bent to retrieve the utensil, Ishmael reached for his half-filled glass. He leaned forward as he slipped a small bag containing powder out of his pocket. Ensuring that no one noticed, he poured a portion of the powder into the glass. The servant stood and placed the spoon back on the table and finished filling the glass.

"Please, give my drink to our leader," Ishmael instructed the servant. "He is more deserving of its refreshing qualities than I."

The servant was confused, but decided it was better to not question. He gave the glass to Lehonti, filled with both wine and the powder. Lehonti acknowledged receipt and raised the glass to drink a toast, "To the wisdom of Amalickiah for knowing how to bring peace to two warring armies!" All toasted him and drank.

Later that night, Lehonti lay on his bed, he rolled back and forth in severe pain, unable to sleep for sickness. He was sweaty and fitful. He called to a servant, "Bring me a drink! Something to tame my burning tongue! Anything!"

Ishmael had lingered nearby. He filled a glass with more powder and wine and handed it to Lehonti's servant when he hurried out in search of a drink for his master. He thanked Ishmael and entered

Lehonti's tent. Lehonti drank. His pains did not subside throughout the long night.

By morning, he was unconscious from the pain, not from sleep. Amalickiah approached Lehonti's tent. Lehonti's servant paced fretfully in front of the tent door's flap.

"I'm here to see Lehonti," Amalickiah announced.

"Yes, but, Lehonti is not well," the servant replied, wringing his hands with concern.

Amalickiah, the master of feigning surprise, concern, and a host of other emotions, wrinkled his brow and cried out, "Not well? What's the matter?"

"I don't know. He hasn't slept well in the night. He tossed and groaned continuously. He's burning with a fever as well," the servant responded, appreciating Amalickiah's apparent concern.

"It must be the jungle fever. It's not uncommon in this area. We should move him out of this place. This is an evil place. The land smells of death and woe," Amalickiah concluded.

"Yes, we should do whatever it takes."

"I'll give the command and order stretcher bearers to care for Lehonti on the journey."

"That would be very thoughtful. I'll see to it that Lehonti's things are packed."

"Do so quickly. I'll have the camp moved immediately."

Within the hour, the army marched onward. Row upon row of men with spears, swords, and clubs led the march. Toward the center area, protected by the army both before and behind, was the stretcher bearing Lehonti. Lehonti laid on it with an ashen, deathlike expression on his face, making the stretcher resemble a bier, more than a means of rest and rescue.

Suddenly, Lehonti curled up in obvious pain at a cramp in his stomach. He twisted and groaned. The stretcher-bearers could not help but notice his agony and shook their heads with pity and concern.

Later that evening, the army sat in groups around their various campfires. Amalickiah sat with his officers discussing the day's events. Lehonti's servant approached Amalickiah.

"Is our leader any better?" Amalickiah asked, looking up quickly.

The servant shook his head somberly.

"It's a genuine pity. Why should such a great man be forced to suffer so? You must take good care of the man," Amalickiah offered.

The servant nodded and left. Amalickiah watched to ensure he was out of earshot. Then he pulled a little bag out of his clothing and handed it to Ishmael.

"You make sure he gets the right amount two times a day. No more. No less. I don't want to raise suspicions by having it take full effect too soon," Amalickiah instructed him.

"Understood," Ishmael acknowledged, and tucked the bag away as he sauntered off.

He headed directly to Lehonti's tent area, where the servant sat fretfully. Ensuring he was not seen, Ishmael poured an amount of powder into a cup. He then poured some water into the cup and swirled it to mix the powder in with the liquid. With a turn of his head, the servant now noticed Ishmael's presence.

"He must be thirsty," Ishmael stated. "Give him another drink to tame his bitter thirst."

"Yes, you're right. Thank you," the servant gratefully responded.

The servant took the cup into Lehonti's tent. Ishmael smiled as the tent flap closed.

This scene was played out countless times over the succeeding days. Lehonti groaned and twisted on his bed. Amalickiah led the army on a continuing march. Lehonti struggled on the stretcher during the march. And, Ishmael made regular visits to the servant, always carrying his sachet of powder.

On one particular night, Ishmael asked, "Is he any better?"

"No, I fear he grows worse." The servant restated the oft-repeated response. He added, "I don't know how much more of this he can take."

"Death would seem to be an escape to rest," Ishmael surmised.

Without looking up, the servant woefully nodded, "Yes, I must agree."

For a final time, Ishmael offered, "Please, give him more to drink, to give him strength."

The servant nodded and took the cup Ishmael offered and entered the tent.

It was still early morning as Amalickiah quickly approached the tent. His gait had an eager spring to it, in spite of his efforts to conceal his anticipation. When he was nearly at Lehonti's tent, he paused for a moment, ensuring to remove any trace of hopefulness from his face and replaced it with a look of grim foreboding. He wakened the servant who had fallen asleep by the door.

"How is our leader?" Amalickiah reverently inquired.

The servant, startled from his uneasy sleep, stretched and acknowledged, "I don't know. I've never heard anyone have a worse night."

Amalickiah did not really wait for the answer as he entered the tent. Lehonti lay with one leg off the bed. His arms were twisted unnaturally. Blankets were strewn all over the bed and floor and wrapped around him from his tossing and turning. It was evident that he had suffered a painful and complete death. Amalickiah knelt in feigned mourning and despair. He let out an enormous, loud cry that startled the camp.

Lehonti's guards rushed forward and entered the tent. They saw Lehonti's corpse and offered to help Amalickiah to his feet. He refused their aid. They watched him mourn for a few moments, then Amalickiah gave the air of one gathering his wits. He lifted his head, while still kneeling, and held out his hand to one of the guards for help to his feet. Both guards helped him up.

"The world has lost a truly great man," Amalickiah said with resolution. "He would want us to carry on and so carry on we must. As his second I will now endeavor to fill the gap that his passing has created. Can I count on your support?"

Lehonti's men were impressed with his supposed compassion for the man that they did not realize he had murdered. They gathered to encourage him to go forward in spite of what they perceived to be his loss, by showing an increase of support.

"Amalickiah, you can count on us for total support," Lehonti's men replied.

"I appreciate that. Unquestioned unity and support is what the Lamanite nation needs at this critical time. We must now return to the king," Amalickiah responded with a veiled hint of warning.

Chapter 7

A Royal Greeting

The officers' tent now consisted strictly of Amalickiah's closest confidants. Lehonti's leading officers were conspicuously and permanently absent from further discussions of strategy and intentions. Even more telling, the Lamanite king's officers were also indefinitely uninvited to all future such meetings. Amalickiah sat at the head of the table.

Ammoron raised a glass in toast of his mentor, "Well, brother, you've done it. You've gotten your army. I can't believe it. But, somehow you've done it."

Amalickiah smiled at the acknowledgment and added, "Yes, I'm almost ready to take on Moroni."

"*Almost*, what more do you lack?" Ammoron was a bit surprised and sought clarification.

"Position."

"*Position*? You're the commander of the entire Lamanite army!"

Ammoron opened his arms widely to emphasize the immensity of the forces Amalickiah now held within his grasp.

Ishmael, always one step ahead of his leader's brother, pointed out, "I don't believe your brother had his sights set on being a mere general."

Ishmael said this while reaching for his glass of wine. As he began to sip it, he turned his eyes to Amalickiah who returned his gaze approvingly. Ishmael gave a slight nod to Amalickiah, signifying he recognized there was more scheming afoot. Amalickiah returned a slight smile.

He paused then leaned forward to unfold the next step in his plan. He looked each of his men in the eye one by one to ensure he had their full attention. No one spoke. Only the crackle of the campfires and muffled speaking of soldiers in surrounding tents could be heard. The conspiring leader then stated in a hushed and serious tone, "Ishmael is correct. We have one more key step before we return our revenge on Moroni. First, we must return to the land of Nephi with this army and meet the king. . . ."

ON A CLEAR, crisp morning when the winds bore the lush smells of the surrounding rainforest, a guard posted in the city of Nephi's main watchtower saw Amalickiah's army approach.

The guard had maintained strict allegiance to his king and was pleased to see the king's army return from putting an end to the sedition of the "oath-keepers" who had dared to defy the king's direct orders. He had hoped to join in on the march to catch and capture his rebellious brethren. Duty called him to sit in the tower, however.

He had taken pride in fulfilling that duty and now hollered down to a soldier below, passing on the news of what appeared to be a successful return. The foot soldier passed the news onto another soldier, who rushed to the city's main building, and told a guard. The guard rushed to tell a throne room guard, who respectfully approached the king.

"Your supreme majesty, Amalickiah returns. He appears victorious."

The king was visibly pleased, stood and quickly hurried out of the throne room.

Outside the city walls, Amalickiah's army continued marching toward the city. Amalickiah's main officers were about 100 yards forward from the rest of the army, signifying a successful return. The guard in the watchtower saw Amalickiah's officers disappear from his view as they neared the city gate far below him.

He turned and saw the king and his personal guard approach the gate from the city square. They too disappeared from his view as they exited the gate to greet the officers. He had wanted to at least view the greeting, but was frustrated in this desire because his vantage point denied him a view of the platitudes that would be exchanged.

As the king and his guards had exited the gate, they left it ajar, and allowed it to follow its natural course, slowly closing behind them as they approached Amalickiah's men. This left none but those directly involved, the opportunity to watch the customary greeting of the victorious Lamanite army.

"Wonderful! Wonderful! Welcome back my mighty warriors! I'm so pleased to see you back with so few casualties!" The king was nearly bubbling with enthusiasm.

Amalickiah's officers reverently knelt before their king, with heads bowed. The king approached the first, Ishmael, to ceremoniously touch his head and raise him to his feet.

"Rise, my faithful servant," the king declared.

"Oh, great king, we are glad that our return brings pleasure to you," Ishmael spoke as he rose.

Suddenly, Ishmael plunged a dagger deeply into the king's heart. The king collapsed forward onto Ishmael with a look of surprise on his face. He slumped forward, and Ishmael allowed him to fall to the ground. Ishmael straightened and ran to be within view of the tower guard. He pointed and shouted as Amalickiah's other officers rose to their feet, feigning anguish over the king's demise.

"Hurry, the king's guards have killed the king! Open the gate! Open the gate! The king's guards have killed the king! Amalickiah, hurry! The king is in peril!" Ishmael shouted loudly enough for the guard in the watchtower to hear that something unfortunate had transpired.

Amalickiah rushed up just as more of the king's guards came out of the city gate and saw the king lying dead on the ground. His original guards had seen what had happened and were just realizing that the blame was being placed on them.

"What?! No, it was—" the king's guards were interrupted in their attempt to declare their innocence.

Ishmael verbally burst in and increased the volume of his accusation, "The king's guards have killed the king! They must be taken!"

Seeing that the likelihood of maintaining their innocence was doubtful, they saw no other recourse than to flee. With Amalickiah bringing his massive army up the main road from the east, the quickest escape route they could see was to make a frantic dash for the jungle to the north.

"Whoever loved the king, let him capture those who did this! After them!" Amalickiah boldly appealed to the remaining guards' loyalty.

The additional guards pursued the original guards into the jungle. The four framed guards were well into the jungle by the time their pursuers entered. The terrain was difficult as the rainforest grew quickly leaving only well-traveled paths any form of easy access. The path they chose was not a path at all. The thick vines draped from tree to tree and dense undergrowth beneath the towering trees gave this area the look and feel of a place never before disturbed by man. Monkeys and birds chided the intruders who nimbly made their way along the ground far below them.

The men hurdled the lowest hanging vines as well as small bushes. The thicker vines were pushed aside, or ducked under. They forced their bodies through the thickest brush. Their only advantage was leaping into the jungle a matter of seconds before their pursuers. They realized all too well that they could stay alive only so long as they could stay ahead of their pursuers. They also knew from experience that tracking anything, or anyone, through the dense jungle could be difficult. They carefully chose to use that to their advantage, being careful not to break many branches or vines.

They had also wisely chosen to not run in a straight path lest they be overtaken simply by chance. Shortly after entering the forest they zigged northeast. A few hundred yards later they zagged northwest. They continued their course alterations, marking a continuous path northeast, but avoiding a straight line. Within a few miles it became clear that they would either need to be heard, or leave a distinct trail, in order to be successfully overtaken. They carefully ensured that neither of these options occurred.

Their pursuers were equally clever and determined. They loved their king. The thought of his betrayal burned in their souls. They were determined to avenge him. The fire burning in their eyes sped their feet. To their dismay they lost the trail too quickly. Moments later, it was discovered again quite a way from the original trajectory.

Again in hot pursuit they lunged forward, ignoring both snakes and vines as they angrily cut their way forward. The trail was lost and rediscovered three more times before it was lost again for good. It was near nightfall before they had to concede failure and return to the city of Nephi without their prey. It was a bitter return.

THE NEXT MORNING found Amalickiah and his army camped outside the city wall. Amalickiah stood, waiting just outside the city gate for his emissary to return from delivering his message within the city. The emissary came outside the gate and approached Amalickiah.

Amalickiah spoke loudly enough to be overheard. He was determined to both perpetuate the ruse that he was concerned about the king's betrayal, and to reinforce the lie that the king's servants were to blame.

He asked, "Did you inform her majesty of the king's servants' treachery and the tragic death of our beloved king?"

"Yes, sir. She at first feared that you would attack the city, but I assured her that you were not the ones who killed the king, that you sent guards to apprehend the murderers. She then asked that you come to her and bring witnesses of this terrible deed. Will you come with your witnesses?" the emissary requested.

"Witnesses? Certainly! Let her majesty know that we will be there straightaway!" Amalickiah responded.

The emissary left to inform the queen. Amalickiah turned to his men and beckoned his conspiring officers. Ishmael, Ammoron, and the others stepped forward. Amalickiah signaled with his hand that they should keep silent.

The gate was opened. Other Lamanite guards greeted them as they entered the city square. These guards acted as their escorts through the city streets and to the chief building. The king's own guards replaced them and ushered the group through the halls and to the throne room.

Once there, the throne room guards took charge of these witnesses of their beloved king's demise. All of them were somber and silent. The disturbed, but regal queen sat upon her throne. Amalickiah and his men entered a short distance into the elaborate throne room and knelt in a semicircle arching toward her. Amalickiah was closest to the queen.

"Your majesty," he spoke as he respectfully and gracefully waved and extended his right arm before him in token deference to his leader.

"Arise, Amalickiah. You had become my husband's confidant and one of his most trusted servants. What can you tell me of this terrible act?" the queen requested.

"Oh, queen, my sorrow is greater than words. I wish that I had returned sooner and rooted out this terrible plot. I was not there when the deed was done, but I have brought my advance party who were first upon the scene. Please allow this humble man to relate what he saw and heard," Amalickiah gestured, indicating Ishmael.

"He may speak." The queen shifted her glance to Ishmael, who rose only long enough to step forward. He knelt again before speaking.

"Thank you, oh great queen. I thank you that I may speak to you. I have seen terrible things. My men and I were nearly to the city gate when the king and his guards came out to greet us. My men and I were just kneeling to honor our great king when one of his servants rushed the king and stabbed him to the heart. I was horrified and jumped to the king's aid. I was the first one to him. Sadly, I was too late. The wound was too deep. I could not stop the bleeding, as you can see on my hands and clothes. He was dead before he could even speak."

Ishmael's voice cracked with emotion. He looked downward feigning humility and sorrow. He had learned his actions well from his master.

She shook her head at the outright betrayal. "What became of the servants who did this?" the queen demanded.

"Alas, we were so concerned about the king that before we had a chance to react, they had fled. Amalickiah sent men after them." Ishmael gestured to Amalickiah again, returning the queen's focus and investigation back to him.

"I sent my swiftest men, but they have now returned with word that the fiends have run to the Nephites to join their armies." Amalickiah added, "Isn't this a witness of their guilt?"

"Such a tragic thing! How can such a thing happen? We trusted them with our lives."

The queen shuddered at the thought of her most trusted servants betraying her. Without consciously intending to send an accusing glare, she looked over to the guard who stood beside her throne. The guard caught her gaze, perceived her question and straightened up attempting to display unrelenting obeisance to his queen.

This silent exchange was interrupted by Amalickiah's persistent words, "Great and beautiful queen, it is clear that this is a plot by the Nephites to overthrow your peaceful kingdom."

The queen looked up with sudden concern, "The *Nephites*?!"

"This is a thing to mourn, but we must not be caught unawares." Amalickiah unfolded the final stage in his plan to avenge himself on Moroni, "We must prepare ourselves for their attack. Better still, we should prepare to strike them before they have the chance of attack."

"Yes, yes, I suppose you're right," the queen conceded.

"Great queen," Amalickiah added, "I know that this is burdensome for you. As leader of this great army, I pledge my all to lead these people in the absence of the king." He bowed again.

"Amalickiah, you are truly a man with a noble heart and a clear head. You are, of course, right. We must prepare ourselves."

The queen had kept her feelings silent on this matter, but the thought of the Nephites breaking their oath had always been a source of puzzlement for her. While she agreed that the oath-keepers were wrong to rebel, she understood their point.

With this turn of events, she sadly had to admit that there seemed to be a reason, even internal treason, to acknowledge that there appeared to be some conspiring taking place in favor of the Nephites. This fact pointed to justification of Nephite involvement, and hence the likelihood of their breaking their oaths. Preparation for war now seemed not just inevitable, but inescapably necessary.

Chapter 8

Regal Requests

*T*he royal dining chamber was a place of elegance. Tapestries covered the hewn stone walls. An intricate, hand-woven rug covered the floor nearly wall to wall. The tabletop was one solid piece of dark wood, nearly black and buffed to an impressive shine. The table's legs were broad and sturdy. They curved inward then outward to where they joined the four corners of the table. Their feet were carved as giant eagle's claws grasping nearly perfect spheres.

Each wall bore torches evenly spaced. They burned brightly, but did little to add to the light of the room, for hanging from the center of the ceiling, positioned exactly over the table, was a large, elaborate chandelier. The glass of this piece of handiwork consisted of crystal on the outer edges, but also rubies and gems of green, yellow, and purple. They were all held together by a polished gold framework that wound like a web throughout the outer rim of the light and then inward and upward to the ceiling above.

The chairs were as black as the table. Their seats and legs were of one solid piece of wood that had been carved, steamed, and bent to arch in a most unique fashion. The arms and backs of the chairs worked their way upward with the resemblance of jungle vines intertwined and arching upward and outward to form a most comfortable resting place for the arms and back.

The table bore a spread of food that soldiers on a lengthy march could not even hope to witness in their dreams. Flasks of multicolored wines were interspersed between place settings. Three large trays of meats formed the centerpiece. Fruits and breads were positioned for ready access and were in considerable abundance.

Those at this table had feasted well. Their gluttonous appetites had barely managed to make a noticeable subtraction from the bounteous spread. Ishmael clumsily raised a golden bejeweled goblet filled to overflowing with wine.

"A toast to the masterful mind of our leader. May his strategies always lead true!"

"To our leader!" all of Amalickiah's officers cheered, banging the table. They clinked glasses together slopping the wine on both table and rug alike, and drank.

"Brother, you are nothing short of amazing! Each time I believe I've figured you out, you surprise me again. I don't know how you do it!" Ammoron offered with an incredulous smile, in addition to the toast.

"That, dear brother, is why you are about to only become the *brother* of the king, and not the king himself." Amalickiah returned the compliment.

Ammoron nearly dropped his goblet, "*Brother* of the *king*?" He looked about himself, particularly at Ishmael who continued to smile at his leader. Then he added, "I see your plotting is not yet done."

"I've only just begun. If you think you've seen plotting, just watch me woo a queen." Amalickiah took a large gulp from his goblet. The

men looked surprised at first, then laughed and slapped each other on their backs.

OVER THE NEXT several days and weeks, Amalickiah became a common visitor to the throne room. His first visits were very formal and full of the pomp and circumstance any person should be expected to give to a nation's queen. Amalickiah initiated several conversations speaking of his respect for the late king and his dismay at his tragic, untimely end. He vowed several times to bring the traitors to justice and punish the Nephites for infiltrating the Lamanite people and stirring them up to plot against their own.

As the visits continued, his speeches turned to be of himself and how he managed to track down Lehonti and the oath-keepers. He alluded quite directly to his cleverness in merging the two armies without shedding blood. He did not miss opportunities to share impressive details about his past accomplishments. Nor did he withhold expressions of deep remorse for those that had been lost, such as Lehonti's supposed unfortunate bout with jungle fever.

"We did all we could to make him comfortable. We moved him from that wicked place. We carried him on our very backs. He wanted for no attention. I ensured that his servant kept a constant vigil. I also sent my top officers to check on him each evening and throughout the day. It was a cursed experience for a noble warrior," Amalickiah said with pity.

"Perhaps it was the gods punishing him for leading those who dared break their word to their king. If so, nothing you could have done could have prevented his end," the queen offered.

"Perhaps, my queen. I had not thought of it in those terms. I merely saw him suffering and wished I could end it, and soon," Amalickiah said with his notorious double meaning.

As the visits became daily, the queen grew to expect and anticipate them. One day, when Amalickiah entered and knelt, the queen bade him to rise, "Amalickiah, you have become a true and trusted servant of this court. Please, take this seat I have had prepared for you."

The queen pointed to a finely adorned chair that sat to the side of her throne and the empty one of her slain husband. It was turned on an angle to face her throne, but was on ground level, leaving it about two feet lower than the throne she occupied, as the thrones themselves resided on a small platform with two steps leading up to them. Amalickiah gave a shocked expression.

"My queen, I could not but kneel in your presence!" he said.

"Good Amalickiah, please take hold of my generosity. I wish you to sit in comfort so that we may converse with more ease," the queen explained.

"I thank you, my queen. This is a rare and heartwarming offer." Amalickiah bowed his head and glided his right hand to his chest and then outward to his side in a show of full deference.

He rose and crossed to the chair, walking, if not strutting, with a noble gait. He eyed the lavish chair as being satisfactory, but only for the time being. As he sat, he again nodded to the queen, but his eyes fell upon the empty king's throne. He knew that in time, that seat would be occupied. He fully intended to become that occupant.

On a later occasion, the queen asked Amalickiah how his plans for defeating the Nephites were progressing. Amalickiah sat upright with genuine interest in elaborating on the topic. A rare scene unfolded as Amalickiah's enthusiasm exceeded his normally carefully calculated communications.

Words raced from his mouth. His arms gesticulated wildly. The queen became overwhelmed by the unusual vibrancy of his descriptions. Her eyes grew wide, then a small laugh escaped her lips. It was a sound not heard in this throne room, or this kingdom, for many, many months.

Amalickiah was in mid-sentence when he heard the laugh. He had been so caught up in his description that he had actually lost consciousness of the fact that he was speaking to someone other than himself. The sound of the laughter disrupted his train of thought. His initial thought was to smite whoever it was that dared intrude upon and mock his thoughts. It was only for a moment, however, as he caught himself and regained awareness of both his position and who his audience was.

He simply stopped talking, and let his formerly flailing arms fall limp to his sides. He found the queen with his eyes and asked, "What?"

"Don't look so hurt, dear Amalickiah, I was merely overwhelmed by your enthusiasm. This is a side of you I am not accustomed to. You seem to be quite taken by your plans," the queen responded.

"Yes, my queen, I guess I am. I am pleased that my words have entertained you, although that was not their intent," Amalickiah added.

"Oh, yes, Amalickiah, they have entertained me. To be honest, I have grown to look forward to your words." She paused then added, "and your presence."

"Again, I am glad that I can please you, my queen." Amalickiah bowed his head respectfully, and saw this as a prime time to add some flattering words, "And, I must confess, my queen, that I find myself longing for these brief visits and conversations. I find them to be the highlight of my otherwise drab days."

"I am truly pleased to hear that." The queen was surprised to feel

95

her cheeks flush and hoped that no others could see the effect this man seemed to have on her.

Not too many days after this exchange, Amalickiah found himself the invited guest to dine privately with the queen. The dinner was by far the most impressive Amalickiah had ever had the privilege of attending. He wore his most impressive robes and remained in his best of manners. Servants kept their distance, but surrounded the table ready to serve the tiniest whim of their queen and her guest.

Both queen and commander were oblivious to the servants. The two dinner guests lingered at the table long after both had finished eating. They were enwrapped in conversation. The queen was intrigued by Amalickiah's every word.

Amalickiah, meanwhile, was choosing his words carefully to ensure they continued to maintain that effect upon his prey. Even in matters of the heart, his every word was coldly calculated to elicit the effects he desired. He saw that the queen would soon be his, and thus the kingdom. Soon, Moroni would learn to tremble at the very mention of his name.

THE WEDDING WAS inevitable. Only the Lamanites of the highest birth were permitted within the throne room. All others were ordered to spend the day in celebration and commemoration of the queen's new mate and their new king. Amalickiah's officers and henchmen were given seats of honor, toward the front. The Lamanite minister wore a stately robe of monkey skins and toucan feathers. His words were a confusing mixture of religion and paganism, but their intent was clear. Once spoken, the queen had a husband, and Amalickiah had a kingdom. Upon their conclusion, the queen's face beamed a beautiful smile of love rekindled. Amalickiah's face beamed as well, but for a much darker reason.

AMALICKIAH SAT UPON his new throne, without the queen present. His key men who had witnessed and aided him in his climb to power knelt before him. Amalickiah wore a large, red, regal robe.

"My brother, you have finally done it!" Ammoron said out of continued respect for his ever awe-inspiring brother's ability to achieve his highest goals.

"That's 'king'," Amalickiah sternly corrected his insolent subject.

Ammoron was at first taken aback, not sure if this was a sarcastic correction, but the tone of Amalickiah's voice, and his glare made it clear that it was a sincere correction.

"Pardon me, my king. I meant no disrespect," Ammoron forced himself to bow his head respectfully.

"You are pardoned," Amalickiah magnanimously declared.

Ammoron appeared to be withholding a bristling at the pardon, but Ishmael interrupted, and removed attention from the king's small-minded brother, "Great king, I compliment you once again for your foresight and ingenuity. Might I ask if you are ready for your final conquest?"

Ishmael's platitudes were not missed by Amalickiah's ego. He had longed to hear such words and fully appreciated hearing them delivered with such ease and respect.

"Yes. Now I am ready," Amalickiah responded.

"Wonderful! I am eager to expand the power of your mighty kingdom. When do we attack?" Ishmael queried.

"Within a fortnight, just as soon as we have assembled the troops once more."

"And where do we attack first, great king?" Ishmael asked.

"Zarahemla?" Ammoron guessed, still ignorant to the verbal formalities of addressing his new king.

"Oh, no, no. Not yet. I want to play with them first. Sting them in some vulnerable spots to let them know we're still around. Once we've made our point, then we'll hit their capital city, their blessed Zarahemla," Amalickiah disclosed.

"Interesting. Where do you propose to 'sting' them first, my king?" Ishmael persisted.

"Where else, but their most vulnerable spot?" Amalickiah offered.

"Ammonihah? The city's still practically a ruin from the last Lamanite invasion—" Ishmael spoke with more than a twinge of surprise mingled with satisfaction.

"Precisely. What better place to test out my new army than by giving them some easy target practice?" Amalickiah smiled, and paused allowing the men to enjoy the comment. The king then added, "Ishmael, you have served me well. You have shown the greatest understanding of what must happen and when. I'd like you to lead this first assault."

Ishmael was visibly surprised, nearly losing his balance from his kneeling position, "Me? I'm keenly honored. But, aren't you coming?"

"No, not this time. I want to plan our little party in Zarahemla. Our new armor coupled with Ammonihah's weaknesses should make this an easy quest. Besides, you deserve this. Go and enjoy." Amalickiah said the words with the attitude of a boy tossing his playful puppy a meaty bone.

"Thank you, thank you, my Lord. I am honored. I will endeavor to make you proud." Ishmael bowed respectfully. He was keenly delighted and flattered with this unexpected assignment.

"I'm sure you will. Just don't weary my men more than necessary. I've got a busy schedule planned for them." The king's smile increased as he pleased himself with words he had longed to utter for many, many months. On this day, his dreaming and scheming were coming to fruition. Ishmael and the others bowed respectfully before leaving his regal presence.

Chapter 9

First Assault

*I*shmael led his troops down the path to Ammonihah. He was atop one of the rare, but stately horses the Lamanite army had at their disposal. He sat erect and proudly displayed the airs of the king's favorite. The Lamanite soldiers marched in an unusually unified gait, for Lamanites at least. They were more accustomed to storming their foe with reckless abandon. The drills and tactics their new, pale officers had ingrained in them by the king's command in recent months had been grudgingly accepted, but followed nonetheless.

In spite of their march into battle, or perhaps because of it, they progressed with a degree of levity. They obviously saw this as an easy conquest. It was well known by all that Ammonihah was a pitifully weak city. "Give it a good kick and let the rest of it fall down!" one of the men joked.

As they marched, they continued to admire their new armor. Occasionally, they jostled each other to demonstrate its strength and protective qualities. Too often they had seen their Nephite foes benefit from such metal strength. Now, it was their turn to save their tender skin from the direct impact of sword, spear, or arrow. It was enough of an intrigue that the men longed to try it out in a real battle, especially when the odds were so much in their favor.

As the army rounded the final curve, the city showed itself like none they had ever seen before. Moroni's preparations took them completely off guard. They saw a massive trench surrounding the city with a towering wall of dirt protecting the once-broken wall.

The top of the wall was spiked with spears as well as the trench itself. Spaced along the top of the wall were several small towers for archers, and a few taller, larger ones for lookouts. The tower guards had already noted the Lamanites' approach and several Nephite archers could be made out readying themselves along the wall.

Ishmael and his army were abruptly taken aback by these preparations. The once-boastful, brash warriors dashed behind trees that lined, and ever encroached upon, the road. In their hurry, Ishmael's horse was startled, nearly causing its rider to lose his mount. Ammoron, the only other soldier on horseback, hustled over to Ishmael's side.

"My word! Have you ever seen such!?" Ammoron declared with utter astonishment.

"Never in all my life!" Ishmael found himself saying.

"What are we going to do? Amalickiah said this would be an easy quest!" Ammoron was concerned not only of their attack, but also of the wrath of their king should they come back anything less than victorious.

"Well, I'm certainly not going back without a victory! We'll need to attack," Ishmael declared.

"Attack?! How?! Where?! There's not a clear area to be seen.

We'd be picked off like flies from a horse's back!" Ammoron felt compelled to point out.

"We're not turning back without a fight!" Ishmael vowed resolutely.

Ammoron turned his horse and faced his men. He waved them onward. The previously fearless Lamanite soldiers shrank back out of sight around the bend. Ammoron waved them forward again. Again, they refused. Ammoron rode over to them and shouted at them. Finally giving up, he returned to Ishmael.

"The men won't attack, sir," Ammoron announced.

"They'd attack if Amalickiah was here!" Ishmael said with disgust.

"Yes, that's true. But, he's not here—you are," Ammoron dug into his leader.

Ishmael was outraged by this attack on his leadership. "Curse their tanned hides and cowardly hearts! All right! We'll leave this place, but I swear to you by all that is holy, and by all that is unholy, we'll attack the next city or I'll lay into the men myself!"

"Where do you propose attacking?" Ammoron asked. He then added with more than just a hint of irony, "Are we just going to march around until some helpless city presents itself?"

"Watch your tongue, or you'll feel my wrath." Ishmael fingered his sword, but Ammoron did not flinch. "There's a city not far from here that is as equally unprotected as Ammonihah is—or was."

"You mean the city of Noah?" Ammoron demonstrated his memory of geography.

"None other," Ishmael stated flatly.

"I've been there. You're right. That should be a worthy target." Ammoron could not help being at least slightly impressed that

Ishmael had managed to pull a potential victory from an otherwise disastrous first assault.

"Of course I'm right! Send out the order! We leave immediately!" Ishmael added with irritation and defensive impatience.

As the Lamanite army turned to leave, one particular pair of eyes took note. Teancum stood on the center of the city wall, above the city gate. His scouts had brought back warnings of Ishmael's march, long before their arrival. Teancum had a clear view of their arrival and was thus able to fully enjoy the shock their new fortifications provided against the Lamanites. Although he could only guess at the conversation between Ammoron and Ishmael, it was not difficult to extrapolate its content.

Upon the retreat of their enemy, Teancum smiled at the victory and raised his sword high over his head in triumph. His fellow Nephites, posted strategically on the wall, did the same and cheered. They had witnessed their first victory without raising a hand in combat. Moroni's strategy was so far proving quite wise. The Lamanites withdrew too quickly to be able to hear their forfeited prey's cheers.

They embarked on a fairly long march. By midday, Ishmael and his army finally rounded a bend and saw the city of Noah. To their utter dismay, it was protected in a similar fashion as Ammonihah was, only even more so. The men were visibly distressed. A man walked the city wall purposely exposing his presence. Although he was high above, the Lamanites and their leaders recognized him immediately from their earlier encounter by the river Sidon.

"It's Lehi!" one marching Lamanite soldier perceived.

"Not the same Lehi who fought by Moroni's side!" another exclaimed.

"There's no hope!" a third declared with palpable dejection and dismay.

The soldiers stopped their march with their eyes fixed with fear on the city, its wall, and its commander. Ammoron's eyes were no exception.

"What are you men looking at?! This is our target!" Ishmael sternly declared. "Ammoron, send your men left, I'll take mine right."

Ammoron was shaken out of his fearful trance enough to stammer a meager reply, "But?—"

"Do it now, or die this instant!" Ishmael threatened, swinging his horse around directly between Ammoron and the city. He faced Ammoron, brandishing his sword as evidence that this was not an idle threat.

Ammoron nodded attempting to conceal his reluctant submission, and beckoned to his men. "Forward men! In the name of your mighty nation, attack!"

Ammoron kicked his horse into action charging forward with his sword raised. His men, trained to do battle, ignored their fears and their instincts and charged the spiked wall. The Lamanite archers vainly attempted to send their arrows up against the foe behind the wall. The top of the wall had many layered, wooden hatches with gaps between them.

The Nephites could easily peer between them and even hurl objects down below. But, the Lamanites on the plain far below had a slim chance at best of targeting people between the narrow openings. Of the many arrows sent skyward, none hit their mark.

While the flurry of arrows soared overhead, the foot soldiers attempted to charge the city intent on scaling the massive wall. Their first obstacle was a series of sharp sticks the length of spears, set at alternating 45-degree angles all along the lip of the deep trench that surrounded the city. Not only did these block clear passage into the trench, but also another series of these sticks were placed within the heart of the trench itself. The first few men who managed to make it passed the sharp sticks lost their footing on the loose earth and tumbled into the freshly dug trench. These hapless souls were easy targets for the Nephites' stones and arrows from directly above.

In their frantic haste to charge, the second wave failed to notice that men were entering the trench, but not managing to scale the wall on its far side. They pushed their way past the blockade, only to also tumble into the trench. They tangled themselves with their dead and dying comrades who preceded them into the deathly pit while being pummeled from above by a seemingly endless barrage of stones and arrows from the Nephites. Few made it more than a matter of yards up the wall's face before becoming extinct targets.

A very few soldiers managed to push their way back out of the trench, between the wooden spears that barred passage across the ditch. Others, who had been charging forward, finally saw their bloody comrades' retreat and stopped in their tracks unsure of what to do or which direction to run. Ishmael saw the men floundering. He became insanely enraged at the men's lack of success.

His hatred toward Moroni increased in equal proportion to his growing fear that the campaign was doomed to failure. He was determined to not let his first campaign be turned into a total fiasco. He rode forward on his horse to encourage his men, shouting blind orders.

"Onward men! Forward! You lousy, cowardly heathen! Attack now or by God I'll—" Ishmael's curse was cut off in mid-word as an archer's arrow pierced him through the neck.

He staggered on horseback, still clinging onto his sword. As his body tensed up at the impact, he inadvertently pulled on the reigns, causing the horse to slowly circle and stutter step in place. He attempted to raise his sword triumphantly, but failed as his life ebbed from his now-slumping body. As he slowly fell forward onto his horse's mane, he turned his head upward toward the city he had hoped to defeat.

His eyes caught those of Lehi's who stood boldly and dignified atop the wall that Moroni had instructed him to build to protect a god-faring people which he, Ishmael, had abandoned and tried to enslave for his own, personal honor and glory. The irony escaped him as his last breath of life dissipated and he fell from his horse into an undignified heap upon the unrelenting ground.

With the loss of their leader, even a poor one at that, the Lamanites' defeat was complete. Some looked to Ammoron for guidance. He sat on his horse looking at Ishmael. His mouth slowly opened and closed repeatedly, but no words were uttered. The Lamanites began to flee. One bumped into his horse and shook Ammoron from his stupor. He looked at the city, the dead, the failing archers, and the fleeing men. He shook his head as if to clear it and sat up tall on his steed. He attempted to take command of the retreat. He saw the trumpeter fleeing.

"Trumpeter, sound the alarm and head for those trees!" he commanded.

Ammoron motioned to the nearest trees. The trumpeter sounded the call on a brass, curved horn of ancient design. Those Lamanites still capable of movement retreated quickly to safety. Some limped, badly wounded and fearful of being pummeled by Nephite arrows during their retreat. At the first sign of retreat, however, all Nephite arrows ceased, allowing their foe to abandon the battle without further injury. Ammoron urged his horse on and was among the first to

disappear into the jungles. The Nephites cheered boisterously and congratulated each other.

IN A QUIET part of the kingdom, a guard entered the Lamanite throne room and approached Amalickiah, who sat arrogantly on his throne. Amalickiah had military scrolls laid out on a table nearby. They contained maps identifying the locations of Nephite cities. One map was unrolled on his lap. He had been reviewing this particular map as he schemed the next phase of his attack on the Nephites. He ignored the guard's entrance until the guard knelt before him on one knee with head bowed.

"Your majesty, I bear news," the guard reported, awaiting his majesty's reply.

Amalickiah did not look up from his maps and replied flippantly, "And what news do you bear?"

"The tower watch guard has seen that your army is returning," the guard announced.

Amalickiah looked up quickly and nearly stood with excitement. He cleared his lap in one swift swipe of his hand and threw the map aside.

"They return?! So soon?! Splendid! Wonderful! This is going to be even easier than I thought. Tell General Ishmael to report to me as soon as they're within the city walls," Amalickiah replied.

"Yes, your majesty!" the Guard stood, bowed, then turned and left.

Amalickiah rubbed his hands together in excitement and gloated. "Ah, Moroni, where is your mighty army now? You thought you could stop me so easily. We'll see who cuts down whom very soon now."

Amalickiah was still pacing before his throne, impatient to hear the news of his victory and move on to phase two, as another guard entered with Ammoron close behind.

"Your majesty—" the guard began.

Amalickiah turned and saw the two. He cut off the guard and impatiently demanded, "Where's Ishmael?! I ordered Ishmael to come here directly!"

"Your majesty—" the guard attempted to continue.

Ammoron, whose fear of his brother had turned to disgust on the long, lonely trek home from defeat, interrupted. "He's dead!"

"Dead? Dead?! What do you mean he's dead? He can't be dead!" Amalickiah denied.

"Yes, dear brother, he's dead!" Ammoron's anger was now so thick that it was almost a satisfaction for him to contradict his brother's arrogance.

"How can this be? You had the finest armor and shields this army has ever seen!" Amalickiah questioned.

"Shields and helmets are small protection from rocks and arrows when you're stuck in a trench filled with the dead and dying," Ammoron added flatly.

"What?! What nonsense is this?" Amalickiah demanded.

"This 'nonsense' is the reality of warfare. You thought you could walk in and take Moroni by surprise. Well, Moroni had a few surprises for you, dear king," Ammoron announced.

"What has he done? Where's Ishmael?" Amalickiah repeated.

"I told you. He's dead. Fallen by an archer's arrow while leading a hopeless cause. Moroni has fortified his cities in ways you've never even dreamed!"

"'Cities' what do you mean 'cities?' Didn't you attack Ammonihah?" Amalickiah questioned, suffering his anger to merge into confusion.

"We tried to, but when we got to it, we saw that Moroni had dug a trench around the whole city and built a massive wall with sticks and staves guarding it. It's impregnable. When the men saw it, they refused to fight," Ammoron explained.

"The cowardly fools! If I had been there, they would have fought!" Amalickiah said, rekindling the anger in his eyes.

"And they would have died! And you along with them!" Ammoron countered.

"Watch your tongue, brother, I'm in an ill mood!" Amalickiah warned, "So, if the men didn't fight what became of Ishmael?"

"We left Ammonihah and marched to the city of Noah."

"Yes, that's a good, weak spot. I would have gone there, too."

"When we got there, we found it was even stronger than Ammonihah, and Captain Lehi himself was on the city wall guarding as if he expected us."

"Lehi?!" Amalickiah was clearly surprised.

"Yes. The men again refused to fight, but Ishmael told them to fight or die by his hand."

"I knew he'd make a brave and cunning leader," Amalickiah lamented.

"And a dead one. He died futilely leading his men to their deaths."

"Bravery is never futile. At least he took a great deal of Nephites with him," attempting to find a noble point of victory in this account.

"I beg to differ," Ammoron again contradicted.

"What?!"

"I didn't see a single Nephite wounded, let alone killed. While at least half of our men were lost." Ammoron attempted to dispel any hint of victory.

"What?! Not one?!"

"They were safe atop their high wall. None of our archers could take a true aim. None of our men could climb more than a few paces before being dropped by arrows or rocks. Moroni's wisdom has outdone us!" Ammoron could not see even a hint of a moral victory in the slaughter he helped lead his men into and intended to drive that point home to his blindly arrogant superior.

Amalickiah, whose rage had grown throughout this entire discourse, was now furious beyond words and screamed so loudly it was heard throughout the long halls of the entire stone building. Children playing in the street outside looked up upon hearing the noise, horses reared up, and guards looked clearly disturbed.

"I swear to you, dear brother, that I will drink Moroni's *blood*! He and his men will feel my wrath, and then we'll see whose wisdom prevails!" Amalickiah vowed.

Chapter 10

The Point of Liberty

*A*lone figure jogged quickly over trails, through the jungle and to the city of Zarahemla. The city gate was opened and the man was allowed in without slowing. He hurried to the city's central building. He took a quick drink from the wooden ladle that sat, beckoning to visitors, in the fresh water supply that was stored just inside the main entrance, in a cement basin built into the wall. The water cooled his hot thirst after the long run and gave him just a moment to catch his breath. He then hurried down the stone passageway into the room where Moroni, Helaman, and Teancum sat in discussion. They looked up to see Lehi entering enthusiastically.

"Captain Moroni! Helaman! It worked! I never thought I'd call warfare beautiful, but this was the most beautiful battle I've even seen. Not a man was killed on our side. A few of their arrows made it over the wall and found a mark on a leg or two, but not a soul was lost!" Lehi's enthusiasm was contagious. He then added with sincerity, "I'm sorry to say, the Lamanites weren't so lucky. I take no pride in saying we sent a goodly number of them to their final reward."

"They never even drew their swords at Ammonihah!" Teancum told his fellow patriot. "My men and I were at the ready, but they took one look at the city and tucked their tails between their legs."

"Captain, it was just as you predicted!" Lehi exclaimed with admiration.

"Yes, unfortunately, it was. Teancum reported he saw Ammoron and Ishmael among them. Amalickiah is definitely behind all this," Moroni responded.

"I never saw Amalickiah. It looked to me that the former judge, Ishmael, was leading them." Lehi paused then added in a somber tone, "But, we won't have to worry about him again."

"How so?" asked Helaman.

"One of my archers has a very keen hand. He fell quickly. I believe without too much pain," Lehi explained. His meaning was easily understood by all in the room.

"He was one of the finest judges in his day," Moroni lamented. "It saddens me to see how once a person so enlightened can be turned so deeply into evil. I believe a person who turns from truth becomes more fierce and godless than those who never knew it."

Moroni paused, allowing a silence to fill the room. He was moved by the thought of those Nephites who had gone astray.

"Amalickiah must be stopped, and for good," he finally uttered.

"But, we did stop him," Teancum said with youthful determination.

"No, we've only hurt his pride," Moroni corrected. "I'm afraid he's going to be more angry than ever. And an angry man with an army at his disposal is never a healthy combination. We'll need to fortify our cities, and our people, even more than ever before. He's seen our cities and will doubtless come up with clever ways to pick away at any perceived weaknesses. Teancum and Lehi, I want you to oversee the increased fortifications."

"Yes, sir," Lehi committed.

"With pleasure!" Teancum declared with unflagging enthusiasm.

"We'll want to especially watch our border towns. If we can pull enough people from our inner cities perhaps we can build some new ones to fill in some of the larger gaps that would be difficult to watch otherwise," Moroni perceived.

He paused again and sighed. He stood with both hands on the table, bracing himself as he leaned forward looking over the maps. Something significant was weighing on his mind. The others waited to hear his words.

He looked up slowly and finally spoke, "A nation is only as strong as its people's hearts. When people's hearts turn to evil, they become ripe for destruction. We need to fortify our people as much, and perhaps more so, than our city walls. Helaman, it's time to double our efforts at making sure this people know who their God truly is and what He expects of them."

"I will be honored to do whatever you feel is needed. What do you have in mind?" Helaman queried.

"I'm concerned." Moroni paused again. As he began to speak, his voice was filled with emotion. "This is a good people. God is on their side. You are all good men. God will prosper your efforts. But, I worry. I worry because we are about to make this people strong and safe in the ways of warfare. Teancum and Lehi, if you succeed—and I believe you will—we will make this people the strongest and most secure generation to ever set foot in this land."

"And that bothers me," Moroni added to the surprise of his men.

"Bothers you? Why in name of liberty would that bother you?" Lehi asked.

"Because, Lehi, when a people feel secure, especially if they feel it is because of their own doing—because of their walls, and forts, and arrows—because of their own might—they begin to feel that they have brought this security on by themselves. They begin to forget where the wisdom and inspiration came from that made them great. They begin to forget God. And when a nation forgets God, they damage themselves more than any outside foe ever could. I fear this people's own prosperity much more than I'll ever fear Amalickiah and his men," Moroni explained.

The men stood for a moment as they were, looking at Moroni and allowing his words to sink in. Helaman was the first to stir after the momentary pause. "Understood. We'll get right on this," he stated.

"Yes," Lehi committed. Turning to the others he added, "We know our duties, now let's get to them."

The men all turned and left. Helaman lingered last of all and momentarily put his hand on Moroni's shoulder as a show of support and respect. Moroni continued to stand looking at the maps, still leaning on the table before him.

LEHI AND TEANCUM took their mission to heart. They divided the land of the Nephites between them and marched from city to city beefing up their defenses. In each case, they educated local leaders in the new arts of fortifications. Word of the successes at the cities of Ammonihah and Noah preceded both Lehi and Teancum. The Nephites were eager to learn from them.

Dozens of families accustomed to living in rural areas or farms flocked together. Moroni's trusted duo joined forces to direct them in creating new cities. They ensured that these new cities were fully fortified, particularly the ones closest to the Nephite-Lamanite border.

HELAMAN DID HIS part as well. He doubled his efforts to meet with his congregations. He sought out the honest and true in each city and from among their most valiant, he ordained leaders to the priesthood to lead and teach the congregations in his absence. He carried with him the sacred records of their people.

He read from them the account of Nephi, their revered forefather. The recounting of his faith and devotion to God and his untiring dedication to his people, inspired them to remember their God. Moroni frequently joined in the prayer services. The people farmed and worked in a prosperous, contented manner. They began to experience a level of peace and prosperity that they had not known for many, many years.

HELAMAN, AS THE spiritual leader of this grand society, presided in the war room. He deferred strategic planning to Moroni, however, offering opinions and insights as needed. Moroni's current discussion with Teancum, Lehi, and Helaman had been progressing for quite some time. Teancum rose and pointed to an animal skin map on the table.

". . .And as soon as my men finish the city wall here the entire southern defense will be completed. We won't have a vulnerable city at any point along the Lamanite's border," Teancum said with pride.

"I don't think the Lamanites could smuggle a troop of army ants across our southern border without us first seeing and stopping it," Lehi added with an uncharacteristic touch of humor.

"Excellent progress, gentlemen. We have too many insects up here as it is." Moroni nodded allowing an appreciation for a little dip in the seriousness of their discussion.

"The new city by the sea is almost complete, too," Teancum eagerly pointed out.

"Yes, we believe you'll especially like it," Lehi added. He looked Moroni in the eye for only a moment, before he turned away, hiding a smirk.

"Oh, how so?" Moroni innocently requested.

Teancum and Lehi tried in vain to keep from smiling.

"The people of this new city asked if they could name it after someone great," Teancum managed to state.

"That's our tradition," Moroni responded. He looked at his two officers and saw their odd behavior. "What's so unusual?" he asked.

"They asked if they could call it the City of Moroni," Lehi finally revealed.

For a brief moment in time, two highly unusual and infrequent conditions occurred at the same time. This assault on Moroni's modesty caused him to blush, and it left him momentarily speechless. Grasping out for a strain of dignity, he only managed to stumble out a few awkward words and sounds in response, "Oh. I see. Well, um, yes."

Seizing the moment, Teancum could not resist adding, "We knew you'd approve—"

"So we gave them our blessing," Lehi offered the crowning touch.

"Wonderful. You've done just . . . wonderfully. I don't know how to thank you," Moroni responded with embarrassed sarcasm masking an inevitable bit of gratitude at the honor.

Wanting to change the topic, Moroni turned to Helaman. Teancum and Lehi continued to grin. Moroni managed to ignore them.

"What do you have to report?" he asked the only other somber face in the room.

"I wish I could give an equally glowing report for our internal defenses," Helaman stated.

"Meaning?"

"I'm hearing rumors of power-hungry—"

Helaman was interrupted when a young woman in her early twenties burst into the room followed by an apologetic, indignant soldier who had just failed his duty to keep their meeting private. The guard caught and held her by her wrists as she struggled to free herself. She was dirty and her clothes were ragged. There were traces of dried blood under her nose. One eye and her upper lip were swollen.

"Captain Moroni! I have to—" the girl demanded.

"Captain! My apologies, sir, I'll remove her—" the guard interrupted. He began to pull her toward the exit.

"No, Captain, sir! I must—" she struggled to free herself and stay in the room.

"Quiet girl! Captain, I'll—" he continued to pull at her. He was on the verge of simply picking her up with the intention of bodily removing her.

"No, stop," Moroni interrupted. "Let her speak. She appears in earnest. I want to see what's so urgent that has possessed this girl to get the better of my best guards."

The girl manifested a heartfelt smirk at the guard who still held her tightly. The powerful guard looked over to Moroni quickly with embarrassment in his eyes. Moroni ignored his guard and looked at the young woman.

"What is it?" he calmly asked the girl.

Moroni motioned and nodded to the guard to release her. She broke away defiantly, gave the guard another glaring look, and then stepped toward Moroni.

"I have news from the land of Morianton," she declared.

"Morianton?! That's where the unrest is that I was just beginning to tell you about, Moroni!" Helaman interjected.

"Yes, I know a little about this. Apparently, they aren't content with their own city and are interested in 'inheriting' the land of their neighbors. What can you tell me?" Moroni pursued.

"I am Sephara, the maid servant of Morianton. Morianton wanted more than he could have. First, it was his own city. Next, it was the neighboring cities. Then he wanted me. When I refused, he beat me. I was able to escape and have been on the run for three days, trying to bring you news," Sephara explained.

"Yes, I can gather that from your appearance. What news do you bear?" Moroni asked.

"Morianton assembled an army of men to attack their neighbors, who have fled and left their city empty. Morianton feared they would join your army and that you would come down and attack him. Rather than that, he has fled northward. He plans to gather support and attack you from the north while you blindly look southward, watching for the Lamanites," she continued.

"They'd catch us wholly unaware!" Lehi exclaimed.

"Exactly," Sephara confirmed, gaining a degree of satisfaction that her words were laying credence to her having forced her way into their presence.

"If the Lamanites weren't bad enough, we're killing ourselves from within," Teancum observed.

"Teancum, can you gather your men and cut Morianton off?" Moroni asked.

"It will be a dubious honor, captain. Consider them captured," Teancum said.

Teancum stepped toward the map table and motioned for the young woman to join him there. He pointed generally at the map.

"Do you know where Morianton planned to go?" he asked.

"Yes, unfortunately for him, I know more than he would want. Let's see—" she looked at the map, trying to decipher its locations.

Teancum pointed out some general reference points. "We're here in Zarahemla. The city of Morianton is here. Gid is there, and Manti is there."

"He was heading to the land of Desolation, because he knew few people ever travel through there." She continued to look for it as she talked.

Teancum pointed to it dragging his finger from the city of Morianton to the land of Desolation as he spoke. "The land of Desolation? Then the terrain is on our side. He's got a series of densely overgrown hills and small mountains between him and his goal. We're a straight shot through nearly level ground. We can easily catch him and head him off—probably here—"

Teancum confidently pointed to a spot on the map. He straightened up and turned to Moroni.

"We'll leave in the morning. I should catch up with him in about two days' time," he said with resolve.

"Good. Let's take care of this quickly, before the Lamanites get word of it and try to take us while we're distracted," Moroni cautioned.

"Yes, sir," Teancum stated.

As Teancum left, he motioned for the young woman to go with him. As they retreated into the hall, he spoke to her with partial sarcasm. "Come with me, I'll take you to meet our 'committee for wayward waifs.' They'll help you get cleaned up and find a new place to stay. Meanwhile, you can tell me more about Morianton, to help me beat him at his own game. You've become quite a valuable little asset—"

"Very funny. I just want Morianton to get what's coming to him," she said bitterly.

"That's what I'm here for," Teancum declared.

Teancum missed the final stage of planning, back in the war room.

"This is exactly what I feared," Moroni lamented once the door had again been secured.

"You can't reach everyone, Moroni. We're doing our best," Helaman pointed out.

"Yes, but that's small comfort when former friends turn to foes," Moroni countered.

"I'll pass on the word to all of the cities' watch guards to be on the alert until Morianton is taken care of," Lehi offered.

"Meanwhile, Helaman, we need to again increase the efforts to clear these peoples' heads so they can see straight. Liberty isn't about power and conquest. It's about the right to raise a decent family without fearing one day your child will return home on a stretcher with an arrow in his heart. Freedom from fear. That's liberty," Moroni proclaimed.

Chapter 11

Close Encounters

$\mathcal{T}$eancum led his men through the jungle. The Nephites were a strong, physically powerful race. But, Teancum and his men were unusually large and muscular, even for Nephites. They looked and acted as formidable warriors, but with hearts set on the needs of others and their quest for liberty. They progressed at a steady pace. The front soldiers hacked at vines and small trees with their swords literally cutting a path in a straight direction toward the land of Desolation. Monkeys chided overhead as the army passed through, but kept a safe distance. Teancum and his men ignored their chatter as they continued onward.

The path they cut became broad and distinct with logs and branches flung to the sides in the wake of the army's fast-paced advance. Teancum and his men ignored the humidity and heat. They bore stern, determined expressions. None of them had any degree of tolerance for either power mongering or treason. Morianton had chosen to commit both. They were determined to stop him before his aligning with others of his ilk could do more damage.

MORIANTON LED HIS men over hills and across rivers that snaked along the base of the hills. The men began to dread the rivers. Too often a crossing of the deceptively peaceful looking, murky-green, lazy-flowing waters were interrupted by the agonizing screams of men encountering the jagged, unrelenting teeth of the piranha who thrived in the area. Morianton insisted on speed, but finally relented to his men's demand that they fell trees to be used as bridges over the upcoming rivers. Swords used as axes made for slow work, but Morianton put several men into motion.

The first three trees felled were stripped of branches and hastily lashed together parallel to the river on the near bank. A long rope was tied to the far end of the makeshift bridge. Two additional, shorter ones were tied to the center area. Stakes were pounded into the ground at the base of the free end. The long rope was stretched across the length of the three-tree bridge, the stakes, and beyond. A dozen men heaved on the rope and slowly dragged it taut. Half as many others stood at the base of the bridge ensuring that it stayed within the bounds of the stakes.

As the far end of the forty-foot bridge began to be pulled upward, more men grabbed hold of the rope and added their muscle to the struggle. Soon the bridge was wholly vertical. The men on the long rope worked carefully to keep their structure slightly off-balance, letting it lean to the far side just enough to allow their ropes to pull back and fight the gravity pulling on the opposite side.

Two other groups of men now jumped into action. They grabbed the two loose ropes dangling from the center of the now-vertical bridge. They spread outward in opposite directions. They pulled their ropes taut and began to circle the lashed trees in a manner reminiscent of some ancient May Pole, using the ropes to help turn the bridge. The men at the base awkwardly stepped over the stakes as they fought to help turn the beast. They struggled successfully to turn it, keeping it between the stakes and the river. More stakes were added to be parallel with the river.

Finally, the proposed safe passage was ready for its drawbridge descent across the lethal, meandering waters. The men on the short ropes attempted to help keep it steady, but as the bridge lowered, the shorter ropes lost any form of strategic benefit and the men's tugs became meaningless. They let go of their ropes and allowed them to droop into the river. The loose ropes then began to be gently tugged by the casual flow of the river. The men on the long rope sweated and strained, to keep the bridge's descent slow and controlled.

They dug their feet into the earth, fighting to keep from losing their footing, and their grip, while also attempting to stay out of each other's way. One misstep by any individual would pose a chain reaction stumbling block for the others. The men at the stakes continued to push the base downward, forcing it to stay in line with the stakes. The descent quickened unexpectedly. The men on the long rope let out a fierce groan and pulled back.

The rate was slowed momentarily. But, just as it was believed to be controlled, the front rope man lost his footing and fell forward. His feet tangled with those of the men behind him. They fell and inadvertently released their grips. The far end of the bridge tumbled the last dozen feet and collided with the far bank with a loud, but muffled thud.

Some of the rope men had not managed to let go in time and were dragged forward at a tremendous rate. They slammed into those who had tripped. The front man was forced forward and bodily pressed into the vertical stakes that had temporarily held the bridge at bay. His shoulder was dislocated, but they were able to pop it back into place. He survived in spite of the pain.

Morianton, who had stood by simply supervising, gave the order to cross. The men were relieved to finally cross a river without wading into it. They were admittedly a little excited to try out their new bridge, as well. They shouldered their gear and stepped onto the bridge in single file groups of three. The slender logs could not handle much more weight than this.

Even still, the bridge bowed under the weight. The men noted how it seemed to bounce with each step and took it a little more slowly than they had at first planned. After the fifth of six groups had crossed, Morianton's patience was taxed to its limit as he saw his men gingerly crossing at too slow a pace for his liking. He urged them to step up the pace.

As they did so, the sagging bridge bounced even more abundantly. The middle man in this group was the same man who had dislocated his shoulder during the lowering of the bridge. He had shouldered his allotment of equipment, but was trying to keep its weight on his good shoulder. On one particularly large shudder of the bridge, his bundle shifted onto his tender shoulder.

He stiffened suddenly with the unexpected, searing pain and instinctively heaved his bundle away from the shoulder and off of his back. It swung backward and took the man to his rear off guard. The man first tried to catch the bundle, trying to steady it, but lost his own balance in the process. He teetered momentarily, then, dropping his own bundle and swinging both arms in large circles as he fought to regain his balance, he tipped off of the safety bridge and fell face first into the warm, brownish waters.

He probably would have been all right, but as he fell, one of his struggling feet became entangled in the strap of his pack. The weight of the equipment pulled his foot to the bottom. Entirely submerged, he reached for his ankle and frantically worked to free himself of this unanticipated anchor. He had only been in the water for a matter of seconds when an angry school of sharp-toothed fish moved in on their prey. The man's efforts quickly gave way to panic. Gurgling shrieks of pain escaped his lips in large blasts of bubbles.

Up above, his two companions on the bridge called in vain for their fallen comrade. The one nearest, with the dislocated shoulder, hesitated diving in, out of concern of being able to lend much assistance. His guilt for having been the cause of the fall had added to his hesitancy. The man who had been in the lead was only now figuring out what had happened. His offer to help was stopped short as he saw the once-calm water begin to churn voraciously at the spot of the plummet. Soon the telltale sign of red liquid rose to the surface and began to slowly drift away with the lazy current. Their friend was now beyond their help.

All of those who had witnessed this sad event were left with somber thoughts. The remainder of them took even greater care as they finished porting their equipment across the river. Morianton was much more patient. Within a handful of minutes the place was again vacated. The makeshift bridge lay across the river, abandoned. Its center ropes continued to skim across the top of the water like snakes forever winding left and right.

Deep footprints and scrape marks on the bank where they had successfully struggled to lower the bridge, were all that remained. The entire ordeal of cutting, lashing and lowering the bridge was repeated again and again as they continued to ford rivers. The men silently agreed that the strain was preferable to the hidden terrors of the devil fish.

The rivers, however, posed only one obstacle for the advancing army. The mountainous terrain also taxed their strength and resolve as they hefted their gear up steep hillsides, hacking their way through the distressingly dense growth as they climbed. The summits provided little reprieve, as many simply descended again after only a few dozen yards. The base of most of these hills more often than not were bathed by yet another river forcing the need for what had become an all-too-common felling and lashing of trees.

Finally, the descent from one hill, and the crossing of the river led to a welcome sight. The jungle and the terrain gave way to an appealing clearing. It appeared the men would receive a respite from their laborious and ill-intentioned march. Their mood brightened as they emerged from the jungle and into the clearing. Their relief was quickly quelled, however, when they saw Teancum's army standing on the far end of the clearing. Morianton shouted hastily-contrived orders to his men. They lunged forward against their former brothers.

Teancum and his men were unaware of the near proximity of their foes until the very moment that Morianton ordered the attack. Morianton's army obeyed and charged Teancum's men. Teancum attempted to prevent the pending battle. He shouted several times for Morianton, attempting to establish a peaceful negotiation, but neither Morianton nor his men would respond or acknowledge their country-man. They simply charged forward with fire in their eyes and swords held high.

Within a moment, both armies were engaged in mortal combat. The sap stains on their swords from trees and vines were quickly concealed by blood and sweat. The tranquil area was filled with the clinging and clanging of swords and the shouts of the aggressors, the defenders, and the dying.

Morianton's men were weary, but determined. They had endured too much to have their quest end in some forgotten clearing. They fought with aggression bordering on frenzy. To his wicked delight, Morianton noted that his army was not just holding their ground, but pushing forward. Teancum's army was now decidedly losing ground. Morianton flashed an evil smile and urged his men forward.

With the suddenness of a cloud burst, the second half of Teancum's army charged into the battlefield from the north and joined the fray. Morianton and his army were dismayed to learn that there was still a great number who had not yet reached the clearing when their attack began. Morianton's army became wholly surrounded and quickly lost confidence. Teancum and Morianton fought hand-to-hand.

Teancum turned to deflect a blow being laid on an already-wounded fellow soldier. With Teancum's back to him, Morianton took full advantage and raised his sword high above his head intent on bringing it down and snuffing the life out of Teancum. As he brought it down, Teancum turned swiftly and stuck his knife into Morianton's belly. Morianton had not counted on Teancum using his other hand. Morianton froze, then slumped and tumbled to the ground clumsily.

With the felling of their leader, his treasonous, overwhelmed and weary army dropped to their knees begging for mercy. Teancum raised his sword high above his head, signaling the cessation of fighting. His men obeyed. Teancum looked about him. He saw the dead and the dying Nephites and those who were now holding back from further carnage. He was incensed at the disruption of peace, society, and lives, which their quest for unearned power had generated.

"You men disgust me! You're worse than fleas on a dog's back! How can you turn so quickly from the standard of truth to follow the lies of an arrogant and greedy man? Throw down your swords and step in line! You're going back to Zarahemla where I'm certain Moroni will have you swear allegiance to the Title of Liberty, or die. Either way suits me just fine," he shouted.

The kneeling men stood, leaving their swords at their feet, and slowly backed up. Teancum's men picked up these weapons and marshaled the captives into a line five men wide. They headed back into the jungle toward Zarahemla. They followed the path Teancum's army had recently cut. The going was considerably easier than that which Morianton's men had undergone previously.

TEANCUM HAD GIVEN his accounting of the death of Morianton to Moroni, Lehi, and Helaman. Before he left the strategy room, Moroni offered his gratitude for a grizzly job done well and swiftly, "Thank you, Teancum, I knew we could count on you to settle this quickly."

"I only wish he'd have given us the chance to reason with him. To not even talk before attacking . . . How can a man become so filled with hate?" Teancum bemoaned.

"Some men put pride and passion for power ahead of their senses, their people's welfare, and their God. This is what this whole conflict is all about. You did the right thing, Teancum. It's unfortunate, but it was right," Moroni reassured him.

"I guess you're right. No, I know you're right. It's just not an easy task," Teancum said.

"If you thought it was, I'd be concerned about you. Why don't you take a day or two to clear your head?" Moroni counseled.

"Yes, sir. Thank you, sir," Teancum nodded appreciatively.

Teancum turned and left the room. He made his way through the stone hallways that led to the outer area of the central building. As he worked his way through the building, his thoughts were on the senseless struggle with Morianton. His frustration unintentionally caused him to quicken his pace as he went.

He reached the outer door and opened it quickly as he made his exit. His timing was impeccable, for he bumped a passerby with the sudden opening of the door. The passerby was taken off guard and lost her balance. Teancum peered around the door and found her sitting on the ground in the alley that passed by the building. Her hair was draped over her face from the fall. He stooped to help her to her feet.

"I'm terribly sorry. I didn't see you," he offered.

The young woman sat on the ground and pulled her long, brown hair from her eyes as she looked up. It was a face Teancum had seen before, but much changed from the ragged, swollen appearance she had had the last time they were together. It was Morianton's maidservant, Sephara, who had come and warned Moroni of her master's treachery. Then, she was a ragged mess after a three-day flight through the jungle. Now, she was clean and freshly dressed. He was stunned by Sephara's natural beauty.

"Well—why—it's you!" Teancum stammered, inadvertently retracting his hand in surprise and standing upright again.

"Well, of course it's me! I am who I am. Who would you expect?" she said sarcastically.

Teancum regained his composure and slipped into stride with her sarcastic lines.

"I don't normally expect wayward waifs to be wandering the streets. But, I see you've graduated from that school," he said still staring down at her with admiration.

"Thanks. Are you all talk, or are you going to give me a hand up?" she quipped.

Teancum was so taken by her appearance he had forgotten that she was still sitting on the ground. He reached out his hand and helped her to her feet.

"There you go. Back on your feet again. Anything broken?" he asked, attempting to bring about some manners.

"No, thank you. Don't overestimate your own strength," she responded dryly.

"Morianton certainly did," he pointed out under his breath.

The two began to walk down the alleyway together.

"Yes, so I heard," she acknowledged.

"He didn't even give me the chance to negotiate. The moment he saw my men, he instinctively attacked," he said somberly.

"He wasn't exactly a gentleman," she added, referencing her own experience with the man.

Her inference was not lost on Teancum, "Yes, I know. I remember what he did to you. You looked so, so—so horrible." He looked at her with renewed pity for the pathetic state she had been in when they first met.

"Thanks a lot," she repeated with renewed sarcasm.

"No, that's not what I meant," Teancum added attempting to present a better impression. "I just can't imagine a man treating a woman that way."

Teancum paused, and then added in a more subdued tone, "Especially one so beautiful."

Sephara was caught off guard by the compliment and blushed. She responded with intrigued surprise, "Why—thank you."

In an attempt to change the topic somewhat, but not totally, Teancum added, "So, where were you off to, when I so rudely interrupted you?"

"To be honest, I was on my way to the market to get some food. Eating has become a habit I've grown somewhat fond of." Sephara had managed to regain her composure and returned to her sarcastic emotional defense.

"That's a habit I tend to enjoy myself, although there are times out in the field when it can be somewhat difficult to fully indulge in it. And, we rarely have good company. Do you mind if I join you?" Teancum had a fondness for her use of language and was finding that he was gaining a fondness for her as a person as well.

"Oh, I suppose a little companionship might be tolerable," she conceded. She found this Nephite somewhat intriguing herself.

"Thanks. I'll take that as a compliment. I get the feeling that might be as close as I'm going to get," Teancum surmised with a wink.

"You never know, now do you?" she responded as an irrepressible grin brightened her face.

Teancum laughed and offered her his arm. She linked her hand inside his elbow and the two continued down the alley together looking at peace in each other's presence. This was a feeling neither had experienced in quite some time.

TEANCUM AND SEPHARA sat together at a small, round wooden table near the city's center square. Fruit vendors and vendors of other types of foods and goods milled about in the background hawking their wares. This new couple was oblivious to the many people walking back and forth or haggling boisterously with the vendors. Teancum and Sephara barely touched their meals. They were deep in discussion.

Teancum gesticulated with his hands and arms to illustrate the words of his current story. Both smiled in a way that those who knew them best had not seen in many a year, if ever. Both had lived adventurous, but lonely lives. They found this to be a strong, yet unspoken bond between them. As unlikely as it may have seemed to them both as they awoke that morning, a new relationship was being solidified.

TEANCUM'S CUP WAS once filled with a bright, purple liquid. Now, it sat empty, having been drained sip by sip during only infrequent pauses between stories and topics, or during the time he eagerly listened to his new friend's tales. The two remained wholly engaged in conversation, not noticing how dark it had grown. Nor did they notice that the once-bustling city square was now nearly empty. Carts and baskets were gone. Torches had been lit.

Teancum, still in mid-story reached for another sip, picked up the cup and found it empty. He reached for the pitcher to pour more drink, and found it was empty too. He looked from the pitcher to Sephara.

"Well, we seem to have run dry," he said.

He took his eyes off of Sephara for the first time in hours, looked around and only now noticed the lateness of the hour and the lack of other people.

"And the people all seem to have run off. I'm sorry. I hadn't noticed the time. I must have held you captive here for hours!" he apologized.

"I've been a very willing prisoner. I haven't enjoyed a day like this in—I don't think I've *ever* enjoyed a day this much," she stated with sincerity.

"Nor have I. It's a pity the sun has called it to an end. I'd better see you safely home," Teancum replied.

"Yes, thank you," she accepted.

Teancum rose and helped Sephara up. They continued to walk arm in arm.

"Now, which of these paths leads to your noble abode?" he asked with mock dignity.

Sephara laughed and pointed.

"'Modest' is a much better word. It's down this way," she offered.

They began their walk again arm in arm. They passed by many homes with torches in their windows. Here and there they could over-hear parents tucking their children into bed, or saying their nightly prayers. It was a peaceful, clear evening. The stars provided a surpris-ingly bright light as they walked through the streets of Zarahemla. For the most part, they remained oblivious to the world around them and were still engaged in conversation when they arrived at her door.

"This is the place," Sephara declared.

"And a wonderful place it is. May I see you again tomorrow?" Teancum asked.

"I'd be terribly disappointed if you didn't," she admitted.

"Good, because I'm afraid you'd be seeing me nonetheless. Good night, sweet fair one!" he vowed.

He smiled, bowed with exaggerated politeness, and gave her a wink as he stood up again. Sephara laughed as she went inside and shut the door. Elated, Teancum whirled around with a big smile. As he sauntered off, he passed a large, clay pot and slapped its lid with his hand. The lid fell off and shattered. A dog barked. A voice from within the house with the pot called out.

"What's that? What's happened?" the voice queried.

"Nothing of any concern. Go back to sleep, dear world," Teancum reassured everyone and no one in particular.

He continued to head home. The most splendid day—and evening—of his life had come to a close. Fortunately, there was a strong prospect that even better days were near at hand. For the first time, he was beginning to fully understand just what it was Moroni had been saying about fighting for the liberty of their loved ones.

Chapter 12

Union

*S*ephara's door was made of several, wide, thick pieces of wood lashed together. The frame was of stone bricks offset from the stone walls. There were decorative metal hinges holding the door fast against the frame. The door opened and her face peered out smiling warmly. Teancum stood in the doorway. He pulled a single flower from behind his back and offered it to her.

She smirked and looked at his token offer. It was clear she was surprised and amused, but had also politely hoped for something a bit more grand. Teancum then pulled his other hand forward and revealed an abundantly large bouquet of wild flowers. Sephara blushed and laughed. She took the flowers. Teancum offered his arm. She set the flowers down in a vase by the door and followed him out.

The two spent the day doing many things together. They strolled through the city square teasing vendors, went for a walk through the rainforest that surrounded the city on three sides, and stepped on rocks to cross a gentle river. They sat on the bank together and passed the time, just enjoying being in each other's presence. The breeze was gentle and warm. The ground was soft and inviting as they sat leaning back on a 100-foot tall, ancient rubber tree. Time seemed to stand still.

MORONI, LEHI, AND Helaman were again in the war room. They were pouring over maps and in the middle of a discussion when the door opened quietly. Teancum entered, obviously trying to hide the fact that he had rushed to get there. He attempted to join them without drawing attention to himself. He failed, however, as Moroni and Lehi could not help looking at each other. Moroni did a better job of hiding his smirk.

Lehi could not resist a comment, "I understand you've taken Captain Moroni's council to take some time to relax, to heart," he jabbed.

Teancum walked fully into the room shifting uncomfortably, but trying to fend off any hint of his new romance.

"Yes, well, it was good advice," he acknowledged.

Even Helaman added, "And, it's nice you've seen fit to make our visitor from the city of Morianton feel more at home."

Helaman and Lehi were having a terrible time holding back their smiles. Teancum looked up quickly at Helaman. Before he could comment, Moroni interrupted.

"I think this is a fine thing. If anything it makes me realize how long it's been since I've seen my own, sweet wife."

Teancum took heart at Moroni's encouragement and tacit approval. This meant much to Teancum who looked up to Moroni as a mentor.

"Thank you, sir," Teancum stated.

"Now, if we're done with this inquiry, I'd like to get back to

Lehi's report," Moroni changed the subject, much to Teancum's relief.

Teancum stepped up to the map table. Lehi gave him a hearty slap on the shoulder. Teancum smiled then focused on the map. Lehi shifted and also turned his attention back to the map.

"As I was saying before our relaxed friend entered, the latest fortification efforts have focused on these three cities—" Lehi began.

SEPHARA STOOD OUTSIDE the building where Moroni's strategy meetings were held. She waited for Teancum. Teancum walked into her view. She smiled and held out her hand. Teancum took it eagerly and they walked together. Teancum walked quickly, but not overly rushed. It was evident from his gait that he was simply trying to get out of sight of Lehi, before taking more ribbing about their fledgling romance. As they walked, Teancum led them around a couple of corners to ensure there were no accidental meetings with his comrades in arms.

"Well, how'd it go, was it as bad as you feared?" Sephara asked.

"You make it sound like I went in there to resign my commission," Teancum commented.

"You're the one who acted so paranoid about what they were going to say about us," she countered.

"I know, I know. I admit that it was a bit embarrassing at first," he said.

"An embarrassed warrior? I'd like to have seen that!" Sephara smiled.

Teancum stopped and smirked at her sarcasm, but then looked deeply into her eyes and added. "Yes, well, it's all worth it to ensure that we can be together."

"Nice come back!" Sephara added with more than just a slight bit of teasing.

"I mean that, Sephara," Teancum stated with bold seriousness. "You're the best thing that's happened to me in many years—in my whole life. I feel like my life has been a waiting period, waiting for when I would meet you and find completeness. I want you to know that in a very short time, you've become very important to me."

Sephara was moved by his words and unable to continue her shield of sarcastic and teasing words. "I know. I feel the same way about you. I've never experienced anything like this. I've never had anyone actually care about me before."

"I find that hard to believe," he said with earnestness.

"That's because you've never been a maid servant. That's all they'd see, the little servant girl. 'Maid, come here! Do this! Do that! Fetch me this! Fetch me that!' No one ever saw me for anything beyond that, just a servant. Just an object that could make their life so much easier. But, you—you don't ask for my service. You give to me. Your time. Your undivided attention. Your presence—" she paused, fearfully stumbling on words that crept from her heart in an unaccustomed manner.

"My love," Teancum completed her words for her and confirmed her innermost desire.

Sephara blushed and looked downward.

"It's true, Sephara, I love you. You've completely stolen the heart of this 'embarrassed warrior'."

Sephara continued to look down. Teancum became concerned. He reached out and gently held her chin with his index finger and pulled it upward. Sephara looked down and then to the right, avoiding eye contact. Teancum determined to find out the cause of this reaction.

"Sephara, what is it?"

"Oh, Teancum, it's just that no one's ever said such things to me before. I—I don't know what to say. I don't know what to feel."

"Just feel what's in your heart, Sephara. And know this, I love you. I don't understand it, but I have a feeling of love for you that is stronger than any force I've ever felt in my life. The time I spend away from you feels like an agony of wasted years, leaving me longing for your gaze, your voice, your sweet perfume, the touch of your soft hands, your very presence calls to my heart. I live to be with you," he declared.

Sephara was overwhelmed and suddenly wrapped her arms around Teancum, with tears streaming down her face. Teancum quickly returned the embrace.

"Oh, Teancum! I love you so!" she cried.

After a long embrace, Teancum backed up and looked into Sephara's questioning eyes.

"I hadn't really planned on doing this now, but—" he began.

"But, what? What?" she asked searchingly.

Teancum held her hands in his and knelt.

"Sephara, would you be my wife?" he nobly requested.

"What?!" Sephara was both shocked and elated.

"Will you marry me?" he restated.

Sephara fell on him hugging and kissing him.

"Yes! Yes! Yes!" she repeated.

The warm jungle breeze eased its way over the city wall, down the city streets and enveloped the two. Its external warmth was insignificant compared to the burning love that both held within their hearts, for each other. For a long moment, they stood embracing. They both appreciated the new found love and devotion the one had committed to the other. Both of them realized they now stood on the brink of a different and wonderful new phase of their lives. In many ways, they felt as if this was not a change, but a beginning of life.

THE BREEZE CONTINUED to lend life to the peaceful city of Zarahemla. The jungle foliage lent a beautiful backdrop to this city of stone and wood. Near the center of the city, an archway was covered with exotic flowers and greenery marking the entry into a square that had been decorated for an important celebration. The archway led into a Nephite church. The church was full of well-wishing parishioners filling the congregational pews.

Toward the front of the church was a sacred altar covered with soft, colored cloth. Helaman stood behind it, facing the congregation. Teancum stood before the altar, appearing both anxious and excited. He was dressed in his finest apparel. His wavy brown hair was neatly combed. His large, brown eyes looked off to the side with expectation.

Moroni entered the room. He stood tall and dignified. All eyes turned in his direction, but none landed on him. Instead, they fell upon the woman he escorted. Sephara had her hand in his arm. She was dressed in beautifully woven wedding attire. Moroni and Sephara paused momentarily as they entered the room.

Teancum and Sephara's eyes met. The electricity of the moment caused Sephara to blush and smile. Teancum swallowed, smiled, and stood taller hoping to be worthy of what he considered to be an approaching goddess.

Moroni continued forward, with Sephara keeping in step. He brought her to the front of the altar and put her hand into Teancum's. He smiled, nodded his approval to Teancum and then turned to sit in a chair beside Helaman. Lehi was already sitting in the witness chair on the other side of Helaman. Helaman nodded to the couple and extended his arms to them indicating that they should kneel.

"Please kneel and join hands," Helaman said as he began the ceremony.

Teancum and Sephara knelt on the padding on either side of the altar. There was an intricately woven, white cloth about six inches wide and 16 inches long, lying lengthwise across the top of the altar. The couple held hands while resting them over the cloth.

"My brothers and sisters in the Lord, we meet this day to witness the joining in marriage of two noble and sweet spirits who are willing to pledge eternal devotion to each other. They have met and shared their thoughts and dreams and now wish to publicly proclaim their love as they begin to share their lives together," Helaman declared.

Helaman leaned forward, toward Teancum. As he spoke, he took hold of the near end of the strip of white cloth. He pulled it upward and over Teancum and Sephara's hands. He held it there in place, not allowing it to fall as he spoke the words of the ceremony.

"Teancum, do you vow to take this lovely daughter of God into your life with a devotion that will outlast the eternities and a love that will span the heavens?"

He looked Teancum directly in the eyes. Teancum turned his gaze from Helaman and looked Sephara directly in the eyes. In keeping with the solemnity of the moment, he attempted to suppress an irresistible smile.

"Yes, I do. Now and forever. Beyond the time when the moon grows pale and the sun grows cold, my heart, mind, and soul will belong to my darling Sephara," Teancum vowed.

Helaman placed the end of the cloth away from him, so that it lay across the top of the couple's clasped hands. He bent forward and grasped the other end of the cloth. As he pulled it upward and toward him, he turned to Sephara.

"Sephara, do you vow to take this noble son of God into your life with a devotion that will outlast the eternities and a love that will span the heavens?" he asked.

Sephara, who had turned to Helaman as he spoke, now turned to meet Teancum's gaze. She made little attempt to hold back a smile that arched across her beaming face.

"Yes, I pledge my life and love to Teancum from now and for always, my love will grow for him beyond the time that birds sing songs and the flowers bloom. Teancum will always be my main concern and my love," she vowed.

Helaman took the two loose ends of the white cloth and symbolically tied them together.

"As I tie this cloth, so I tie your hearts and souls together as one. May the God of Heaven smile brightly upon your lives and futures together and pour blessing upon you beyond your ability to need or want. In the name of our promised Messiah. Amen." Helaman nodded his head in conclusion of the ceremony.

Teancum and Sephara repeated the "amen" then leaned over the altar and kissed each other warmly.

A LAVISH CELEBRATION feast followed the wedding. Teancum and Sephara sat together at the center of the main table. An archway of exotic flowers towered over their heads. Moroni, Helaman, and Lehi sat at their table, along with many others. Little children danced in the foreground. Sephara pointed at their cute attempts to imitate the adults. Teancum laughed with her. Moroni stood to give a toast.

"Teancum, I didn't think there would ever be a woman so strong, yet so tender as to tame your bold heart!" he stated.

Teancum leaned to Sephara and commented with a smile, "Neither did I!"

"But, it does my heart good to see that it has happened nonetheless," Moroni continued. "Sephara, welcome to your new life. May it bring the fulfillment of your many hopes and wishes. Teancum, take good care of your sweet wife. She deserves nothing but the best from you."

Teancum nodded and added, "She deserves better than my best, but I will try to make her happy!"

"You already have!" Sephara stated.

Teancum and Sephara kissed again, while the guests applauded.

Chapter 13

The Voice of the People

*M*oroni's war room held three familiar officers discussing strategies with each other, but with an air of distraction. They awaited word of potentially distressing news. The door opened. Helaman entered. Moroni, Lehi, and Teancum immediately stopped their conversation and listened for the news he bore.

"Moroni, it's just as we feared, chief judge Nephihah has lived a long and fruitful life and has now been called home to the Lord who gave him breath. His son, Pahoran, will succeed him. May he judge in righteousness as his father did before him."

Helaman had confirmed their fears. The men bowed their heads respectfully.

THE NEPHITE COUNCIL chamber was the most tangible representation of the Nephite's civil government. Its stone walls were decorated with colorful tapestries, but with modest designs so as not to distract. Pahoran sat at the head of two tables joined together in a wide "V"

arrangement. A series of lower judges sat behind the tables, to Pahoran's left and right. Various men sat and others stood facing the judges from the audience chamber.

One of the men stood in the center facing the judges. He spoke passionately. The others in the room were emotionally attached to the points he was contending. Pahoran raised his hand to command attention and silence the man. To add emphasis, he broke tradition and actually rose part way, with his other hand supporting him on the table.

This support was merely for balance, not brought on by age or other need. Pahoran was a powerful-looking man in his mid-thirties, dignified and well-bred, but also with an air of keen understanding of the ways of the common people. Pahoran spoke loudly and with authority, but avoided yelling, though it was clear that he was on the verge of losing his temper. He was a man accustomed to controlling his passions.

"No, Elam, no. It's that simple. We are NOT changing the law. The law stands clear and will stay clear. We are ruled by judges by choice, not by accident. Haven't you learned anything from the trouble Amalickiah has caused this people?" Pahoran restated.

"Yes, I've learned that our leaders are so cowardly that they have to hide behind walls of dirt and sticks rather than offer true leadership and rid our land of our enemies!" Elam chided.

"We fight and we kill, but we only do so out of the necessity to protect our rights. When there's an alternative, we follow it," Pahoran clarified.

"That's because you're cowardly fools," Elam scoffed.

"No, that's because we value life, even those of our enemies," Pahoran corrected.

"You are fools who bring disgrace to yourselves, your families, and this people. The law must change to allow this proud people to be led by a man capable of leading," Elam added.

"We're not changing the law in any way that will allow you—or anyone else with high aspirations—to crown themselves king. Your words are bordering on insurrection and treason. I highly recommend you cease this prattle, now!" Pahoran warned.

Pahoran looked to the guards who stood in the wings by either end of the tables. They straightened and turned their gaze on Elam, indicating their preparation to engage in their unique duties to quell disturbances caused by either crowds or individuals.

"I will not be silenced, and your peasant army isn't going to stop me. Oh, you can silence me here for the moment, but this isn't the end." Elam defiantly whipped around and left without allowing Pahoran to respond, and in direct contradiction to chamber room protocol.

Pahoran began to respond, but stopped himself as he saw that Elam was intent on leaving, and he recognized that any more words would be just so much more contention. He continued to stand as Elam and his cronies left. Once the judges had the room to themselves, Pahoran sat and spoke.

"We had a king and that nearly led to our total downfall. The system of judges is still the best way to lead this people."

"And how do the people receive these judges? By common consent," one of the judges pointed out. "Elam is only one, representing dozens of angry king-men. We'll not put an end to this strife until we put this to a vote."

"A vote?" Pahoran's eyes brightened, "Now there's the best words I've heard spoken in this chamber since I took on this seat. Most certainly. We'll put this to a vote of the people. When the king-men lose by a public lack of support, they'll have no grounds to contend,"

Pahoran paused, pondering his own words. "Yes, very well. It's time to send out word for a public vote." Pahoran slapped the table with his hand to add enthusiastic emphasis.

"What if they vote for a king? And what if that turns out to be Elam?" another of the judges asked with a worried look.

Pahoran turned and looked the judge directly in the eye. He intended no malice. He simply wanted to drive his point home. He stated with emphasis, "Then the people will deserve exactly what they get."

ZARAHEMLA, THE CAPITAL city of the Nephite civilization, stood nobly surrounded by the dense rainforest and hills. Today, it was filled with citizens anxious to determine the future of their way of life and the means of directing their society. By sunset they would know if they would continue to be ruled by judges, or if they would revert back to a system of kings. Too few generations had passed for the memories to have faded of a time when they had suffered under the hands of a power-hungry and arrogant king who corrupted their government, weakened their military, and allowed them to become enslaved by the Lamanites.

The square was crowded with people waiting to voice their feelings on the matter through a public vote. Many stood in a long line that led to the voting apparatus. Those who had already voted milled about. Pahoran and two judges sat in chairs above the apparatus, overseeing the judging.

Moroni, Helaman, and Lehi were present down below in the city square observing and informally helping to ensure that this was a peaceful event. Teancum and Sephara also stood there hand in hand. Sephara was quite noticeably pregnant. There were scattered arguments between the king-men and the freemen throughout the square, but no serious confrontations.

The line of voters moved slowly, but continuously. The next man in line stepped forward. He was a simple man dressed in modest means bearing the demeanor of one unaccustomed to having his opinion heard. Yet, today, he had the opportunity to choose his society's destiny. A guard allowed him to step forward and he walked up a ramp to the top of the city wall's catwalk.

Once there, he approached a table at the feet of the judges, who sat in chairs on a platform above the voting apparatus. The voter picked up a token and walked over to the voting apparatus. He showed the judges his token before turning his back to them and facing the voting apparatus. The apparatus had a small platform on the top, with a hole on either side of it. By the hole on the one half was a symbol of a crown. An etching of the Title of Liberty was carved by the other opening. Placing his token in the hole adjacent to one of the two symbols would determine his vote.

The man on the voting platform was in full view of the city square, so that all could see him. Because he was on a raised platform, the people would not be able to see how he voted. The judges' presence behind him ensured that no one was swaying his vote. The holes were close together so that with his back to the judges, they too could not see how the man voted. In this way, public voting was kept secure and democratic, while also preserving the confidentiality of individual preference.

As the man dropped his token into the slot, he paused for a moment to listen to it drop. The voting apparatus consisted of a wooden funnel that went down and split into two separate tunnels. It spread out in two directions at forty-five degree angles, forming an upside down letter "Y."

A large holding area at the base of each funnel held the voting tokens. These funnels were tilted outward at a forty-five degree angle, evidently for allowing them to transfer their contents into some sort of external container. The bottom of each funnel was closed by a trap door.

The anxious crowd pressed toward the voting apparatus, hoping to discern which way the vote was going. The guards kept the area clear, however. With each dropping of a token, the crowd would fall silent, hoping to tell by the sound which side the tokens fell. But, the dull thudding of the tokens cascading downward through the apparatus and coming to a rest on previously-deposited tokens was too muffled and the funnels too close together for anyone to be certain.

Hours passed. Finally, the line of voters had completely dissipated. Pahoran stood and faced the city square.

"Is there anyone who has not voted?" he called out in a booming voice that echoed throughout the square.

The people looked about them. No one stepped forward. All eyes returned to Pahoran as a hush fell upon the crowd. A sense of deep anticipation hung in the air. The moment of decision was nigh.

"Bring in the Vote Scale!" he loudly declared.

With this, the crowd's eyes turned toward a large door that opened with a sudden push from within. A series of itchy, rolling squeaks could be heard coming from the recesses of the building. They continued to crescendo until at last the Vote Scale began to come into view.

Two, large wooden wheels were the first portions of the apparatus to catch the rays of the sun. Two more sets of wheels also emerged from the building, bound together by a wooden platform four feet square. Each wheel had a man leaning into it, forcing the wheel to turn and pushing the apparatus forward.

An eight-foot tall beam rose directly up from the center of the platform. It was topped by another beam of equal length that rested horizontally on the support beam. The top beam was balanced with equal portions extending to either side of the support beam. It was held in place by a crude hinge that allowed either end of the top beam to dip and climb as the men continued to push the Vote Scale forward.

Hanging from either end of the top beam were long ropes that descended to within a yard of the ground. Both sets of ropes held within them a metal tray the length and width of a man's shield. The trays lied horizontally, ready to bear whatever would be poured into them.

Two guards preceded the Vote Scale on its brief journey. Two more guards followed it. These guards were followed by a single, dignified man in official garb, similar to what was worn by Pahoran and the judges on the voting platform. He was the Vote Judge. The crowd parted and allowed the cart to be wheeled to the center of the square. It stopped just below the voting apparatus.

The Vote Judge turned and motioned for two men to step forward. Each carried a large basket. They each dumped a large weight out of their baskets and onto the ground. They then placed the baskets on each side of the scale. The weight man on the left placed his weight into his basket. The crossbeam tipped quickly, its metal tray plummeting to the earth accepting his weight. The second Weight Man then placed his weight on the other end of the balance. The crossbeam tipped back into equilibrium.

The Weight Men looked at the Vote Judge. He looked up at Pahoran who nodded. The Vote Judge looked down and nodded to the Weight Men. They pulled their baskets off of the Vote Scale and switched them. They replaced the baskets on the opposite sides and validated that the scale balanced either way. They looked to the Vote

Judge who again received visual confirmation from Pahoran and turned to the crowd.

"I declare this a valid measurement! Let the vote judgment commence!" the Vote Judge decreed.

The Weight Men removed their weights from the baskets and ensured the scales were directly beneath each trap door of the voting apparatus with the empty baskets positioned directly beneath each funnel ready to receive the voting tokens. The Weight Man that was on the king-men's side of the balance pulled the lever on that trap door.

The voting tokens spilled into the basket and the crossbeam tipped at an increasing rate, indicating a healthy number of votes for a king. Elam, who had been pacing the square all day, nodded and smiled approvingly. His supporters patted him on the back.

Sephara maintained her strong character in spite of her pregnancy. However, she could not help but let out a gasp of dread at the distressingly high number of king-men votes. She looked to Teancum who patted her hand that was now wrapped firmly around his arm. He nodded for her to keep watching.

The other Weight Man pulled the trap door from under the Freeman bin. It spilled its contents into the basket in a continuous rain. The scale tipped quickly beyond equilibrium and then the Free-man scale was plastered onto the ground as more voting tokens poured onto it to overflowing. Tokens continued to tumble for several moments. The crowd cheered enthusiastically. Elam and a handful of his cohorts gained bitter faces and turned and left in disgust. Pahoran observed their exit, as did Moroni.

Amidst the cheers, Teancum shouted to Moroni, "We did it! We've won!" and he gave his wife an excited hug.

"Yes, it appears we've won the vote," Moroni confirmed. "I

believe it's safe to assume that the results from the other cities will bear that out. But, I'm afraid we haven't won the heart of every man. I fear this is not yet over."

Pahoran nodded to Moroni from above, giving him an indication of the complete results. Moroni acknowledged and returned the nod.

The celebration within the city square continued. Meanwhile, on the other side of the great city wall, nested far away among the thick trees of the jungle that surrounded the area, westward toward a brilliant red sunset, something else was transpiring. Faint wisps of smoke were beginning to rise up through the tall trees and wend its way through their tops and up into the open air.

This was the first indication that an unrelenting enemy was on the move. Amalickiah himself stood speaking angrily to Ammoron and a handful of other officers. They bore armor and their faces were painted with war paint.

In Zarahemla, a watchtower guard turned to admire the splendid sunset. But, he paid more attention to something else that caught his eye. What was it he saw? Was it smoke? Mist? Clouds? No, it must be smoke. Once he felt certain that his eyes did not deceive him, concern filled his soul. He knew that this could only mean one thing: campfires.

His mouth opened in a shout of alarm, "Lamanites! Lamanites!"

He turned and shouted directly down into the square. "Lamanites! I see Lamanite campfires! Captain Moroni! The Lamanites are coming!"

There was a bustle of activity below as word got out. Moroni dashed up to the watchtower.

"Where?!" he demanded.

The Tower Guard pointed, "There, directly west!"

155

"I see it," Moroni confirmed.

Moroni shouted to the guard on the opposite wall, "Sound the alarm! We must have every man prepared!"

The man blew an ancient-looking horn that gave an immense reverberating low pitch that was heard throughout the city. He gave two long, slow blasts followed by three short ones. He repeated the signal three times. Birds in the jungle shrieked and took flight. Frightened monkeys and other jungle animals jumped and chided. Far off where the campfires burned, Amalickiah looked up at the sound of birds shrieking and flying. He also made out the distant echoes of the warning horn tapering off.

"Good, our presence has been noticed," Amalickiah smiled. "I want Moroni to know what I'm up to. His little kingdom is about to be disturbed."

In Zarahemla, Elam and his men, who had stormed angrily beyond the square, stopped in their tracks. Elam turned at the sound of the horn. His countenance again opposed that of his fellow, worried Nephites. His showed a sense of actual glee and enthusiasm.

"Well, isn't that wonderful timing?! It sounds like our old friend Amalickiah is making a come back. Let's go see the party," he said to his men.

He and his men returned to the city square that was quickly filling again with people. Moroni was busily shouting orders from where he stood on a platform, a few paces from where Pahoran and the two judges still sat. Elam and his men worked their way forward until they were directly below Moroni, in the square.

". . . All men grab your weapons! Each man is to take his position just as we've gone over in past drills!" Moroni ordered.

The men scurried about obeying orders. Moroni noticed Elam

standing with his legs spread and arms folded, defiantly looking back at him.

"Elam, get your men to the east wall!" Moroni ordered.

Elam remained stoic.

"Elam, get your men to the east wall! Now!" Moroni repeated.

Elam still refused to move, and stood stubbornly defiant, digging his heels into the sandy dirt that covered the city square.

"Elam, now is not the time! Get your men to the east wall!" Moroni shouted with as much of a threatening edge as he could muster.

When Elam still refused to move, Moroni turned to Pahoran. "Pahoran, chief judge, our enemy is nearly upon us and these king-men, who have lost their grievance through a true and proper vote of the people still refuse to support the cause of liberty. Their refusal to take their places weakens our defense and poses a threat to the safety of our society. As such, it is tantamount to treason. In accordance with our laws, I ask for your permission to compel these men to fight. Or, if they refuse to fight, I ask that the law be honored and the treasonous men be put to death, lest their rebellious insurrection spread further."

"As my father, the chief judge before me, had great trust in your judgment and advice, I do the same. I know the law, and you are correct. As you are our nation's military leader, I grant you your request. Do what you must to compel these men to protect the cause of liberty among this people, but ensure that what you do stays within the bounds of the law which has been established by the voice of this people," Pahoran decreed.

"I understand, and will obey," Moroni responded. Then, he turned again to Elam. "Elam, the chief judge himself has granted me the right to compel you to fight in our defense. You and your men will go to the east wall and protect this people or you will forfeit your lives!"

Elam responded by drawing his sword and pointing it at Moroni. Moroni did not allow Elam to perceive the dismay he felt. He knew there was only one way to deal with such defiance and that was to carry out his threats. He knew all too well that if he let Elam get away with his actions, there would be others who would later try the same defiance. He had to stem off this insurrection here and now if he was going to ensure lasting unity among his Nephite brethren.

Moroni motioned for his men to march forward toward Elam and his men. Rather than submit, Elam and his men began a desperate sword battle. Elam's men fought vigorously, with Elam giving the lead. They were defiant, bold and daring, but no match for Moroni's men. Three quarters of Elam's men fell by the sword.

Elam himself scrambled to the top of a well and fought while standing on the edge. A sword cut into his side and he fell into the well. His body came to rest far below inside the well's large bucket. Elam did not move. His life and his insurrection both came to an abrupt halt. The remainder of Elam's king-men quickly gave up. They knelt and surrendered their swords to Moroni's men.

It was not long before these begrudgingly repentant men found themselves guarding the east wall. They were far from happy about it, but they were guarding it nonetheless.

Chapter 14

Conquest

It was still pre-dawn. A jungle mist surrounded Amalickiah's camp. Most of the men still slept. Amalickiah and Ammoron sat at a campfire.

"So," Ammoron asked his now-royal brother, "when do we hit Zarahemla?"

"We don't," Amalickiah replied, "Not today, anyway."

"We don't?!" Ammoron said with a start, "But, I thought you wanted to take on Moroni? Make him hurt. Drink his blood. That sort of thing."

"Don't mock me brother!" Amalickiah warned.

"I'm not," Ammoron countered, "I'm just confused."

"I want Moroni to believe we're after him first, yes," Amalickiah explained. "But I'm no fool. His best men guard that city. Moroni knows we're near and with his 'walls of terror' as your men so glibly put it, we wouldn't stand a chance. No, we won't be going there today, but soon. Although I'd love to get a peak of the scrambling

Moroni's people must be going through now that we've been seen," Amalickiah laughed.

"If not Zarahemla," Ammoron asked, "then where?" He wondered inwardly if he would ever understand his brother's scheming mind.

"We hit them first where they least expect it," Amalickiah said, "at the cities along the sea."

"But, they hold no strategic benefit! It would be pointless," Ammoron pointed out.

"Exactly! So, then, which cities do you believe are least guarded and the easiest targets?"

"Yes, but, what's the point?"

"To make him squirm!" Amalickiah retorted sharply, "To catch him off guard! To hurt his little kingdom one step at a time! A man like that feels for and bleeds for every insignificant man in his outfit, including those doomed to wile away their time in pointless little cities watching the surf hit the shore. We'll pick off a few of these cities first, gain a foothold in his lair, and let him see that his muddied walls are no match for our physical might and cunning! He'll learn to quiver at the mere mention of my name and I will not only defeat him, I'll see him squirm under my knife! And, *yes*, dear brother, I *will* drink his blood!"

During this tirade, Amalickiah had become wholly impassioned. His fists were clenched. His voice rose. His men stirred from their sleep. He stood by the time he completed his description. Ammoron was staggered by his brother's soul-consuming obsession. He managed only a blundering comment. "My word—"

"Call the men to order!" Amalickiah snapped, "It's time to march!"

Amalickiah turned with a flurry, the tails of his red cloak flew up

and outward then swung inward toward him as he stormed off.

THE MORNING SURF lightly, but regularly, pounded the sandy shore. Each wave retreated leaving behind a foamy trace of its brief existence only to be covered by another wave that left its own, temporary mark on the shoreline. It was difficult to say which wave owned the foam. It both lingered and was renewed by the constant succession of waves. At once it was generated by them, but it also owed its existence to no wave in particular. The foam just was. It was temporary, yet permanent. Visible, yet transitory. Constantly waning yet always renewed. It remained a perpetual feature of the pristine shoreline.

The shoreline led to a city wall similar to those Moroni had ordered to be built for all of the Nephite cities, only this one was not quite as high and insurmountable as others were. A singular watch guard kept vigilance at this early morning hour. The sun was only now beginning to bring to light the city that he had guarded throughout the blackness of the night.

The city square was silent. No vendors had yet ventured out to hawk their wares. The shops and homes remained still. It appeared that no one stirred in this sleepy community. All was as it should be. As it always had been. As it seemed it always would be. For one more night, the guard had fulfilled his duty. The city remained safe.

Not far from the city wall, but beyond earshot of the guard, there was a stirring in the forest. The lush jungle foliage continued to within a few yards of the shore, leaving only a very narrow beachfront. Morning mist still rolled off the waves and onto the shore. Less than one hundred yards from the city wall, Amalickiah's army broke forth from the jungle and onto the beach.

They dashed at a wild pace toward the city wall. They bore

swords, hatchets, armor, ladders, and crude, little spades for digging footholds in the dirt-covered city wall. They were within 60 yards of their target before the watch guard, who had only momentarily looked out toward the sea, spotted them. In spite of his remote and quiet post, his training did not allow him to be shocked or surprised.

He instinctively and immediately reacted by sounding the alarm. He faced the sleepy city and blew furiously into his horn and continued to do so up until one of Amalickiah's archers struck him through the back of the neck. He slumped forward, still pressing the horn to his dying lips.

The warning was not absolutely in vain, Nephite soldiers emerged from buildings near the city square. Unfortunately, as they prepared to scale the inner wall and reach the catwalk from which their archers intended to defend their city, Amalickiah's men were already halfway up the outside of the wall. They hacked away at the spears that had been secured in the ditches, and dug footholds with their climbing spades. They climbed over each other in waves like ants devouring a leafy tree. One wave stopped to hack away or dig a foothold while others used these footholds to aid their progression.

Amalickiah's first wave of men won the race between competitors who could not yet see each other; as they reached the top of the wall before the Nephites made the catwalk. They quickly drew quivers on the newly awakened soldiers and picked them off as they scurried into battle. Those that did make it to the wall's ladders and ramps were cut down by Amalickiah's soldier's swords. Amalickiah, in his distinctive red cloak, climbed the wall and stood atop the center of the city wall just as the battle was clearly won and his soldiers were rounding up the surviving Nephite soldiers.

Amalickiah stood with arms raised high above his head, his hands clenched the Title of Liberty flag by the fabric. As he tore it in half, his face contorted in a hideously vile shout of triumphal glee at his first and indisputable victory. Below his victorious perch, the once-tranquil city square was now a scene of desolation of bodies and damage that his victory had imposed on the Nephite city.

After completing his gloating, Amalickiah addressed his officers, who stood in the city square, "I want two dozen of our most brutal soldiers to remain behind and take control of this city."

"Remain behind?" the ever-questioning Ammoron asked, "Where are we going?"

"This is just the first of three little parties I've planned," Amalickiah said. "We've got places to go, things to do, and people to conquer. It's time to head inland."

As Amalickiah led his conquering army toward the main gate, he passed by the solider he had left in command. The soldier stood at attention. As Amalickiah passed, he irreverently tossed the torn Title of Liberty at the soldier's feet. He commanded the man, "Burn this!"

Amalickiah and his soldiers left the city and joined his other men who waited outside the city wall and had no need of making the climb. The twenty-four remaining men were spread out with three archers on the city wall, pointing their attention inward at their new captives, and the remaining spread out in the square ushering groups of war prisoners to areas of containment. Amalickiah and his army headed inland following the road between this city and the next, which was about an hour's march.

IT WAS STILL early morning, but this city had awoken, and its guards were more alert than at the previous city. There was a bend in the road about a half mile before the city. Amalickiah had halted his men prior to this final bend and ushered them into the jungle. He conferred again with his officers.

"I want five dozen men, to swing wide and approach the city from the far side. They are to stay hidden and silent until they're in position. Then I want them to rush the city with as much noise and speed as possible, leaving the trees in groups of three. I want them staggering their attack so their guards won't know how many are rushing them."

An officer inadvertently vocalized his concern, "They'll be wholly exposed and picked off like monkeys during target practice!"

"They'll be serving their commander!" Amalickiah corrected his officer sternly. His tone quickly mellowed and he added with a sinister lilt, "Besides, I've decided to send you along with them to ensure their safety."

He returned his focus to the other officers. "And they won't be exposed for long." He continued, "This is where our point man earns his keep. Once we hear their shouts, I want that man to keep his eye on the nearest tower guard. Unless I miss my guess, he'll be irresistibly drawn to the clamor. These distant cities are too lonely and boring for him to not want a glimpse of the only action he's bound to see all summer. When he moves over, we move in. And, I want our men to move in silence. I want to scale that wall as noiselessly and quickly as a python going for the kill. By the time they detect us, they'll be at our mercy. Is this clear to everyone?"

Ammoron and the other officers were clearly impressed and nodded approval.

"Then spread the word and be quick about it!" he concluded.

FIVE DOZEN MEN, in waves of three, charged the city shouting boisterously. The concerned officer was in the center of the first wave. City guards and archers rushed to the wall's top and began raining arrows on their attackers. The officer was the first of Amalickiah's soldiers to drop. New ones continued to pour out of the jungle. Finally, the key tower guard left his post and rushed to witness the excitement.

Amalickiah's point man waved his makeshift flag and Amalickiah's full army quickly and silently rushed the city wall from the far side. Without being under fire from above, it was a small matter for them to push aside the spears and sticks that blocked the way to and inside the ditch that circled the city like a dry moat. The men began to scale the wall with vigor.

As predicted, Amalickiah's forces were near the top before they were noticed by the distracted guard. He was felled quickly by an arrow and tumbled from the wall into the city square. His collapse alerted other soldiers to the invaders' presence. They turned to counter, but were quickly overpowered by the rush of Amalickiah's men who poured over the wall and filled the city square. Victory was without question.

Amalickiah's soldiers opened the main gate. He arrogantly strode through the gate.

"Where's their petty leader?" he demanded.

A soldier rudely whisked the city's judge forward before Amalickiah and forced him to his knees. He pushed his head down.

"I found him cowering in a hall," the soldier mocked.

"So," Amalickiah mused, "you're one of Moroni's little men."

"I serve under Pahoran," the judge corrected, "not Moroni."

"Silence!" Amalickiah demanded, holding back the urge to strike the insolent captive across the face.

The soldier used no such restraint and slapped the judge's head. The judge ducked his head, but the soldier grabbed him by his hair and forced him to look up at Amalickiah. Amalickiah spoke sarcastically and demeaningly.

"Well, my little chief judge," he mocked, "This is your lucky day."

The sarcasm was not lost on the judge, as shown by his expression of detest for Amalickiah and in anticipation of what he was about to propose.

"I can use a man like you," Amalickiah added, "Where are your assistants?"

The judge remained silent.

"Refuse to answer if you will," Amalickiah said, "but bear in mind, I can easily learn where your family is housed. If you'd like to see your wee ones again in this life, I suggest you start being a bit more vocal."

The judge's expression betrayed his mental debate. He finally uttered with shame, "They're in the council room." He bowed his head with a sense of betrayal.

"See, now," Amalickiah taunted, "That wasn't so bad was it? Doesn't it feel good to cooperate?"

MOMENTS LATER, AMALICKIAH addressed his officers in the city square. The judge and his two assistants stood nearby, guarded, with their hands tied. A soldier approached Amalickiah carrying clothes similar to the robes the judicial trio was wearing. He handed the garb to Amalickiah, Ammoron, and a big, burly soldier. Amalickiah addressed his captive judge.

"Well, gentlemen, this is a fine day for you. Not only am I going to spare your lives—for now anyway—but you have the blessed opportunity of accompanying me as we pay a visit to your neighbors."

"We'll never help you!" the judge swore.

"Suit yourself," Amalickiah replied. "You can make this easy on us both, or you can die. It makes no difference to me. I'll still win either way. Only you'll be dead. What good would your bold heroics do for you then beyond earning you a flowery epitaph? 'Here lies so-and-so, he was brave and bold, now he's dead. What a shame.'"

A couple of Amalickiah's men laughed.

Amalickiah stared the judge deep into the eyes. His cold, unblinking gaze seemed to pierce the judge and send a shiver through his spine. Amalickiah added with a factual air that chilled the man, "Besides, we know where you live. We have your wives already in hand, and your children... ."

"What? You don't!"

"Oh? No?" Amalickiah smiled and while keeping his face turned toward the judge, never letting his eyes leave the man's, he reached his arm back and with a flick of his fingers waved two of his soldiers forward from a concealed corner.

The hapless judge nearly fell to the earth when he saw his wife and two, young children dragged forward. They were gagged and bound. The youngest one, a girl of about four years, tripped and fell headlong into a puddle. Her evil escort laughed and roughly pulled her to her feet. It was obvious that all three were terrified. Their eyes were wide, searching, and tear-streaked.

The judge turned to Amalickiah in fury, "If you hurt any of them!—"

Amalickiah cut him off, unintimidated, "The only one who will cause them any hurt, will be you, if you don't cooperate." Then he added, "And these are not the only ones who would be hurt this day because of you. This city holds many wives and children. I have no need for wives and children. They eat provisions meant for warriors. They make noises I have no interest in. In fact, all they're good for is breeding more Nephites to cause me more concern in the future. I have no need for them at all. You would be doing me a great favor to encourage me to rid the city of them."

Amalickiah narrowed his eyes as he made this final point and again sent cold chills through the judge and his men. They had the distinct impression that he was about to kill the city's women and children on the spot.

The trio was less than pleased with their predicament. At this moment, one of Amalickiah's soldiers approached bearing the city's Title of Liberty. He handed it to Amalickiah and reported, "Here's their sacred symbol, sir, just as you requested."

"Thank you," Amalickiah responded. "Burn it!"

The Nephites eyes flared with shock and anger at this, which delighted Amalickiah to no end. He inwardly hoped that at least one of them would try to stop the act. The Nephites used great restraint, recognizing that any attempt on their part would be futile. Within moments, the flag lay burning in a makeshift campfire.

Eyeing their symbol of liberty turning to flames and ashes at the hands of their conquerors one of the judge's assistants asked, "What do you want us to do?" with a bitter, yet concerned edge to his voice.

"Nothing," Amalickiah replied. "Nothing at all. I just want you to accompany me on a walk." His voice changed to include a less-than-patient lilt as he commanded, "Now!"

The three were hefted to their feet and pushed forward. Amalickiah donned the judicial robes and strutted for a moment, turning to admire himself. He pulled the loose hood up over his head and allowed the tails to trail freely behind him. He held his arms outward, letting the oversized sleeves droop downward. Although his face was nearly entirely concealed by the floppy hood, his wicked smile was still clearly discernable.

"My, my!" he said. "Don't I look official now? Just as a king should! Come on!"

Amalickiah motioned to his men; they all headed out following Amalickiah and his new entourage. They again left behind two dozen soldiers to guard the city in a fashion similar to the other conquered city.

Chapter 15

A Message for Moroni

*A*malickiah and his men marched along a lonely road. The jungle encroached heavily on both sides. Now and then long-tailed exotic birds flew across their view. Animals chattered and stirred as the army passed through and disrupted their morning solitude. Amalickiah gloated at the ease of his success.

He had the confidence of a conqueror who headed toward yet another certain victory. His men followed him with a trust and loyalty earned by witnessing his genius. Those who were on the campaigns against Ammonihah and Lehi were especially impressed. They had found a leader who could defy Moroni's impregnable fortresses.

With each step, Amalickiah imagined Moroni cringing and grieving at the loss of his beloved cities. Suddenly, he raised his hand to stop and silence his army. He motioned for them to conceal themselves in the jungle through which the road had been cut. They quickly obeyed. Amalickiah motioned for his entourage to be brought forward.

"All right, sir judge," he said. "Now you earn your keep."

"We'll do nothing to help you," the judge said trying to sound defiant, but knowing full well that his life and the lives of hundreds of women and children lay directly in Amalickiah's hands. Protest as he might, the judge feared that sooner or later he would be compelled to follow Amalickiah's orders. Even still, he did not want to make it any easier on his captor than he absolutely had to.

"I'm not known as a patient man," Amalickiah explained. "There are enough present here who wonder why you three still breathe air. Don't push me. If you want your wives and little ones to see the sunset you'll hold your peace and follow me."

As the judge remembered the terror on his own family's faces, Amalickiah added, "Besides, there are plenty of wives and children in this city as well. If you do as you're told, there will be a lot less bloodshed. Now, you wouldn't want to cause any unnecessary bloodshed would you?"

The men were beaten. They hated to admit it, but they could see no way out. Amalickiah was very persuasive. They looked at the dirty path before them and wished to be anywhere but there. They had to agree with this conquering fiend. The judge was subdued and submissive. He repeated his earlier question, "What are you asking us to do?"

"That's better," Amalickiah said with a wicked grin. "You're beginning to see the light. Good. All I want is for the three of you to walk up through the city gate, with me and two others at your rear. You don't need to say anything or do anything special."

"What if they question me?" the judge asked.

"What? After we're in?" Amalickiah said with mock surprise. "Don't worry. By then it won't matter. Your part will be complete. I just want you to walk through that gate. That's all. Understood?" He gave evil emphasis to the word "understood" implying that their lives depended on their comprehension of that word.

The captive trio nodded, comprehending.

"Good," Amalickiah concluded. Turning to Ammoron and the other soldier he said, "It's time we get dressed."

Amalickiah tossed his two men the judge's robes they had pilfered from the other city. They pulled them on around their shoulders and tied the loose belts. Amalickiah then pulled his bulky hood over his head. "You too!" he said and reached over and pulled the burly soldier's hood over his head too. "And you!" he said to his brother.

Ammoron dutifully obeyed. The real judges followed suit as well. Amalickiah shook his head at the main judge. As he reached over and yanked the hood back, he said, "No, not you, friend. These others are fine, but not you. I want them to see your pretty face clean as day. Now, let's get moving."

As they began their walk back to the road that led to the city, Amalickiah, Ammoron, and the burly soldier brought up the rear. While these six casually strolled to the city, Amalickiah's army sneaked through the jungle for closer access to the city's gate. As Amalickiah and his cohorts arrived at the gate, a watch guard saw them. Amalickiah nudged the judge to look up and be acknowledged.

He waved judiciously. The guard nodded and turned his head back toward the inner wall, it was apparent he was shouting to someone, alarmed. Momentarily, the gate was opening. Amalickiah's expression grew wickedly pleased. The burly soldier could not help letting out a snicker, which was quickly subdued by Amalickiah's warning nudge into his ribs.

With the gate open completely, the six entered the city. Amalickiah bowed thankfully as he strolled into the square's opening. Suddenly, the burly soldier leaped to the side and stabbed the gatekeeper with the knife he had concealed under his robe. He then cut the rope used to open and close the gate, instigating the need for it to be closed manually. Ammoron stabbed the guard on the other side of the gate, leaving no one in the near vicinity to quickly close the gate.

During this, Amalickiah's troops dashed from the woods for the city. Archers on the wall vainly tried to halt their progress, felling several men, but being unable to withhold the swarm. The invaders poured through the gate and into the city. Hand-to-hand skirmishes left several dead on both sides, but in the end, Amalickiah's men had a solid victory. The city was theirs. Amalickiah gave a victory shout, with his sword held high, from the city square.

Completing his shout he commanded, "Bring me their leader!" He shouted so loudly that spit sprayed the air and Amalickiah grinned in evil triumph.

Two soldiers dragged and tossed a wounded, dirtied man to Amalickiah's feet. Amalickiah continued to grin. He slowly strolled around the man, walking with his hands crossed behind his back showing casual superiority.

"Such a noble man," Amalickiah assessed. "Stand!" he suddenly commanded.

The soldiers roughly picked him up to his feet.

"Such a fine city," Amalickiah said. "I thank you for keeping it ready for me."

"What do you want?" the captive leader demanded.

"What do I want?" feigning surprise at the question. Using a level, but insistent tone he stated, "I want three of your best archers. Here. With their bows." Then with characteristically impatient harshness, he shouted, "Now!"

The leader looked puzzled, but saw he must obey. He looked to his left and nodded to one of his men who was also held captive. Amalickiah's soldier, holding the man, looked to Amalickiah who nodded approval to release him. Moments later, he returned with three, captive archers with their bows.

"Such capable looking men," Amalickiah baited, now slowly circling the three archers. "I imagine you've tagged many a human target in your day. I wonder, how many of my men are now filled with feathers sent from your bows?"

Amalickiah stopped pacing and leaned up close face to face with one of the archers. He looked the man straight in the eye, daring him to respond. After a brief, but silent show of wills, he stepped off and casually pointed out their failure to defend themselves, "No matter. We're here."

Amalickiah turned to the tallest of the three archers. He eyed him momentarily then grabbed his bow.

"Now," he said, "Isn't this a fine work of art? Did you make this yourself?"

"My father made that and handed it down to me," the archer said in a bold tone, attempting to depict both familial pride, but also a lack of intimidation.

"Well, isn't that sweet?" Amalickiah taunted, "A family tradition. An heirloom no less!" He held the bow high above his head so that all could see. His men laughed. He pulled it down again and turned back to the archer. "What a thoughtful father you had." Imitating a father and very young son, he said, "'Here son, let's go shoot some Lamanites!' 'Gee, thanks dad!'" When imitating a young boy's voice, he raised his eyebrows and let his eyes grow wide, imitating youthful enthusiasm. When he finished his mocking, he let the childish expression drop off of his face and then sarcastically concluded, "I'm all choked up." He callously tossed the bow back to its owner.

175

"This bow has only been used for defense to protect my family and my city!" the archer declared indignantly and clearly bristling, in spite of the danger he faced.

"Easy now," Amalickiah patronized him. "Besides, I guess it didn't work very well today," he added as a direct assault on his ego.

The captive city leader could handle the taunting no longer. He interrupted Amalickiah to deflect attention away from his archer. "I'm sure you're not here to discuss family traditions. What do you want with my men?"

Amalickiah turned, surprisingly not showing either anger or impatience, indicating he was up to more scheming.

"It's quite simple, actually," he stated. "Your grand city is a delightful little war trophy, but it's really not my objective. No offense intended. However, I do want to make sure that good Captain Moroni is aware of my morning's activities. Your men will have a chance to let him know that I have your city and your two neighbors' well in hand. And—that this is just the beginning."

"Why should we want to be your couriers?" the second archer asked.

"Perhaps to save your fuzzy, little necks," Amalickiah curtly replied. "If it gives you any more incentive, consider yourself as a little savior running to seek aid for your fallen home."

"Why are there three of us?" the third archer queried. "It only takes one to carry a message."

"Very good!" Amalickiah whirled around and acknowledged. "We have a scholar in our midst! I have a little game planned for the three of you."

"Game?" the second archer asked suspiciously.

"Don't worry," Amalickiah comforted him, "It's not too complicated. Do you see my archers on the city wall? Why, I believe that's precisely where you would normally be found. You've surely shot things from there before. Now you'll have the chance to see what it's like to be the target. I'll give each of you one chance to make it out of range of my archers."

Amalickiah walked a pace or two over to a campfire as he talked. He reached for a burning stick and poked a burning piece of cloth. He stirred it and wrapped the flaming fibers around the end of the stick.

"Hand me the little heirloom," he said, still holding the makeshift torch.

He reached out for the first archer's bow.

"You have until the string snaps before I give my archers permission to shoot. I might add that they're quite enthusiastic about this game, and I'm very certain you're familiar with the range they have from there. So, I suggest you better not dawdle."

Amalickiah held his torch under the bow's string. As he held it there, the archers noted that the flames were emanating from what remained of their city's Title of Liberty. Their indignation burned more intensely than the flames. They too held their retaliatory efforts for another time. Meanwhile, the bowstring caught on fire.

As his bowstring burned, the first archer was puzzled and looked to the city's leader. The leader nodded with urgency that he had better take Amalickiah seriously and depart with haste. The archer dashed out of the square, through the open gate, down the path and along the road. The others watched anxiously through the open city gateway and looked back and forth between his dashing and the burning string.

Amalickiah continued to hold the bow as wisps of smoke rose from the remainder of its snapped string. He looked up to his archers on the wall and waved the bow, signaling for them to shoot. The Nephite archer had hesitated too long and was unable to get out of range in time. A Lamanite arrow hit the fleeing victim squarely in the back. He fell forward and lay motionless. Amalickiah turned back to the other two archers.

"Well," he said, "It looks like he wasn't quite quick enough."

Amalickiah grabbed the second archer's bow. "Perhaps you are more fleet of foot—"

Before Amalickiah finished this sentence, the second archer was dashing out through the gate at great speed. Amalickiah turned to glimpse the departure, smiled, and continued to light the string on fire.

"I see this game catches on quickly," he said.

As the string burned, the captive Nephites cheered on the archer. None of them were more sincere in their urging than the third archer. By this time, he had a keen grasp of the importance of this macabre "game." He realized full well that if his fellow archer failed, he would be next in line to compete against time and Amalickiah's evil whims.

Amalickiah thoroughly enjoyed the spectacle. The archer passed his fallen comrade without being able to give any aid. The string broke as the second archer was nearly out of range. Amalickiah signaled for his own archers to take aim and let fly. The sprinting archer turned and looked back only briefly. He continued onward at a frantic pace as an arrow zeroed in on him. As if he heard it, or perhaps his instincts warned him, he turned sideways and managed to dodge and narrowly miss being hit. He regained his footing and kept up his fast pace.

"He's a nimble little fellow, isn't he?" Amalickiah acknowledged. "It looks like we've found a winner." He applauded lightly and mockingly.

The archer continued sprinting away and out of sight.

MORONI, LEHI, TEANCUM, and Helaman were in the council chamber speaking to Pahoran and the other judges.

"No," Moroni stated, "I'm not sure why Amalickiah hasn't attacked yet. He's definitely been in the area. My scouts found the remains of a large encampment not too many leagues west of here. They said their trail headed north of our city and then directly east of here. It's obvious he by-passed Zarahemla and is up to something. We just need to determine what that is."

"What do you propose?" Pahoran asked.

"Keep the city on full watch," Moroni ordered. "Meanwhile, I'll ready my men to march after him."

"You're whole army?" Pahoran asked.

"All those who aren't needed to defend the city," Moroni responded. "We'll split the army into three. Lehi and Teancum will each take a third—"

Moroni was interrupted by a modest knock on the chamber door. All of them turned to look to the door. Pahoran nodded to the guard by the door, indicating that he should open it. The guard obeyed and pulled the wide, hand-carved wooden door open. A Nephite stood behind it and entered the room in a respectful manner. He continued into the chamber and approached the clearing in front of the judgment seat upon which Pahoran sat. He stopped and bowed with dignity.

Pahoran nodded and asked, "What brings you to our court?"

"Chief Judge, I beg your pardon for the intrusion. I did not mean to interrupt your meeting, but I bear news that must be told," the Nephite responded.

"News? I trust it's not good," Pahoran replied.

"No, it's not. That much is certain. It's sad at best."

"Tell us, please," Pahoran said with a compassionate tone. He could tell from the man's eyes that he appeared greatly disturbed by the news he bore.

"It brings me no pleasure to inform you that Ammon has gone the way of all the earth and has been called home to that God who gave him breath."

Gasps of surprise escaped from those within the room. They all remained silent. Their thoughts drifted quickly to the people of Ammon. Years earlier, a much younger Ammon, accompanied by his brothers and Helaman's father Alma, had been powerful missionaries among the Lamanite people.

There were many, including their fathers who had tried to dissuade them from going. But, trusting in the Lord, they went. Each journeyed to a different part of the land. Ammon in particular had met with astounding success. He converted an entire city of Lamanites who swore the oath of peace and were forced to flee their lands.

Many of the converted Lamanites lost their lives before Ammon was able to lead them back to Nephite territory. The Nephites had granted them a generous portion of land. They strategically gave them land in the northeastern corner of their territory, so to put as much space between them and the Lamanites as possible. In addition to sheer space, the Nephite cities acted as a shield and buffer zone between the angered Lamanites and those of their number who had sworn the oath of peace.

There the converted Lamanites lived in a protected peace, with Ammon as their spiritual leader. These converted men and women chose to take on Ammon's name as a sign of respect and became known as "Ammonites."

"You may wish to know," the messenger added while bowing his head, "that he went peacefully, in his sleep, surrounded by those he loved, and who loved him in return. No man can ask for a better exit from this life."

Moroni stepped forward and put his hand on the messenger's shoulder.

"We thank you for delivering this message. Our loss is most unfortunate, for he was a man of great faith and unsurpassed deeds. Please return our love and respect to his people," Moroni offered.

After the messenger left the chamber room, Helaman turned to Moroni, "Moroni, now that the people of Ammon have lost their spiritual leader, I think it would be appropriate for me to pay them a visit."

Moroni agreed. "Give them our best wishes and help them to continue to look forward to the coming of the great Messiah. At the same time, I'm concerned that Amalickiah may wreak some form of revenge on those Lamanites who have sworn the oath of peace. Look into their safety, and ensure that nothing ill is afoot."

"Certainly," Helaman replied.

Moroni looked to his other officers, "And now we should continue making our plans for dealing with Amalickiah directly. Teancum, I'd like you to head north in case—"

At this, Moroni was again interrupted as a guard helped a sweaty, panting archer into the room. He had run the entire distance from his now-occupied city to bring word of Amalickiah. Although he tried to hide it, it was clear that he was breathing heavily. He was barely able to speak, due to his breathlessness. Sweat drenched his hair and dripped down his temples.

"Captain Moroni, Pahoran!" he panted. "Excuse me! I bring word of Amalickiah."

"Amalickiah!" Moroni said with keen interest, "What can you tell us?"

They aided the archer in getting to a chair and gave him a flask of water. He sat and drank a quick, but gulping drink before talking.

"My name—my name is Enos. From the city of Mulek," he said, gathering his composure, but still only able to speak in brief bursts of words, "I'm one of their archers—Amalickiah attacked—without warning.—He's taken the city."

"Attacked?" Lehi exclaimed, "Taken the city?! How? How'd he get passed our defenses?"

Enos, slowly regaining his breath, turned and looked Lehi in the eye. He took a deep breath, swallowed, and said quite clearly for emphasis, "He just walked in through the main gate."

"Through the main gate?!" Teancum exclaimed, "What is this?!"

"He was dressed as a judge," the archer explained as he slowly straightened himself, "And hiding among the entourage of the main judge from the city of Gid. We didn't know we were letting him in until it was too late."

"What was the city of Gid's judge doing with Amalickiah?!" Lehi asked incredulously, "Has he turned traitor?"

"No!" Enos continued, "Amalickiah took over the city of Gid this morning before attacking us."

"Gid too!?" Teancum lamented with anger.

"And Morianton, as I understand it," Enos added.

"Three cities in one day?" Moroni acknowledged, "He's certainly trying to make his point clear."

"Point? Point?! What point?" Lehi demanded, "He's just taken three cities! Three cities that *we* fortified."

"Exactly," Moroni pointed out, "He obviously wants us to know this, or we wouldn't have this brave visitor. He's trying to draw us out."

Moroni turned back to Enos, the archer, "You say he took Morianton, Gid, then Mulek?"

"Yes," the man confirmed.

"In that order?" Moroni questioned.

"I believe so. He didn't say specifically, but that was the impression I had."

"I would believe so too," Moroni mused. "I can't see him taking the judge from Gid, marching him over to Morianton and then back to Mulek. Nor do I think he would have taken Gid and then come back for him after taking Morianton. He must have attacked in that order, which means he is making a straight drive westward. At least, that's what he wants us to believe."

"What do you think he's up to?" Lehi asked.

"Throwing us off his track, obviously," Moroni said. "He may be going west and he may not. We need to anticipate his moves and work his own strategy against him."

"Sounds great," Teancum responded with a mixture of disappointment from the day's news and determination to overcome their adversary, "What's the plan?"

"Actually," Moroni began, "I believe that we need to only slightly modify the plan I've been trying to present. Lehi will take his third of the army first, heading in a direct eastward course to Mulek. I suspect Amalickiah will have sent spies who will see them leave. Perhaps his spies will see this and leave then. In case they linger, my third and I will wait a short time after Lehi's departure before we leave.

"Mine will also head east, but slightly to the south. The intent is for him to believe that we believe he's still there with the greater number of his forces, holding the city captive. I suspect if his spies see me personally leading the second wave he'll believe that's our main objective. I also suspect he's actually heading for the land Bountiful.

"Teancum, I want you to take the last third of the army northward. I'm hoping you can head him off before he gets there. If you move quickly, but quietly, you should be able to gain the edge of surprise. Don't leave until my army has been gone at least two hours. His spies won't dare linger longer than that to get word to Amalickiah. One other thing, Teancum, while you're waiting, I want all of your men indoors and silent. I want this city to look as abandoned as possible. Post the minimal guards on the walls."

"Why?" Teancum asked, meaning no disrespect.

"Just in case," Moroni said, "I want to remove any doubt that when my army has gone, everyone has gone. I don't want Amalickiah to have any chance of being alerted to your march."

"Understood," Teancum responded.

"Do you still want me to check on the people of Ammon?" Helaman asked.

"By all means, yes!" Moroni said with emphasis. "I'm as concerned as ever about how Amalickiah may try to abuse them. This has certainly been a day of ill news. We can't let that dissuade us from our cause. Our people need our leadership now more than ever. Are there any other questions?" No one responded. "Good. Lehi, how soon can you and your men leave?"

"We'll be long gone before other men are sitting down to sup this day," Lehi predicted.

"Excellent," Moroni responded, "My men will be right on your heels."

Moroni turned to the speedy archer, "I can't tell you how fortunate we are that you made it here with this news." He gave Enos a look of fatherly warmth and comfort, knowing that he could use a favorable word about now, given that a vengeful megalomaniac had just been overturned his world.

Having delivered his message, Enos sat and leaned forward on the table laying his head in his arms both to rest and out of relief. Teancum and Helaman patted him respectfully on the back before leaving.

Chapter 16

Retaliation

rue to Moroni's orders, Lehi led his army through Zarahemla's front gate. As the army marched in a uniform fashion, a man on horseback rushed out of the gate. The rider broke away from the army, turned northeast, and hurried off. Lehi's army purposely ignored Helaman as he rode off to aid the Ammonites.

The army continued heading due east. They streamed out of the gates for quite some time. When they were finally gone, the gates closed. Several moments passed. More time elapsed. Finally, the city gates slowly reopened. Moroni himself now led his army out through the gates.

All of these events had been observed and duly noted by two of Amalickiah's spies hiding in the brush not far from the city wall. As Moroni and his men continued their exodus, the first spy spoke in hushed tones to his partner, "I told you there'd be more. It's Moroni himself!" The spy was quite pleased with this vindication of his hunch.

"Well," conceded the second spy, "It looks like we've got

something big to report to Amalickiah after all. Come on, we'll need to hurry to get word to him in time."

"Wait a minute!" the first spy countered, "I say we wait around, just in case—" his words trailed off as he continued to watch the city. Its great gate had been firmly closed and remained closed and unmoving. Moroni's army had all but passed them by. The dust on the trail was beginning to settle and drift off into the trees led by the gentle, warm, tropical breeze.

"Wait around?!" the second spy wore an incredulous expression. "Are you crazy? That's Moroni, no mistake! He's got that banner of his. If we don't tell Amalickiah now, he'll have our heads." He began to rise, ready to make a hasty departure.

His partner grabbed his arm and pulled him down again. "I say we wait. There may be another trick up his sleeves."

"You wait," his unwilling companion retorted. "I have a kind of liking for my head. I want to see it preserved."

"Ok, let's make a deal."

"What sort of deal?"

"Do you see that hill and ledge?" He pointed to a steep hill to the northeast of the city.

"Yeah, what about it?"

"It's out of our way, but not by much. I say we go to it on our way to Amalickiah."

"What on earth for?" the unwilling spy demanded. So far as he could tell, his partner had been in the jungle's sun a bit too long.

"Because," the first spy explained, "I believe it's just high enough and positioned well enough that we should be able to see over the city wall."

"So?" asked the second, still not seeing any point to the climb.

"So, then we can see if there's another army in there milling about. If there is, you can bet Amalickiah would want to know about it. And, if there *is* and we *don't* find out, but Amalickiah does, we're as good as dead," the first spy explained in all seriousness, holding his knife up to his partner's chest to help drive the point home.

"I see your point," the second spy admitted. His fingers lightly touch the blade and pushed it away from him. Having agreed that the plan had a solid purpose, he now embraced it wholly, but with concern, "OK, but let's hurry. This will slow us down. If there isn't an army in there, we're losing valuable time on warning Amalickiah about Moroni."

He bent down to pick up his gear as he spoke. As he looked up, he saw that the first spy was already up and hustling away.

"Then why are you still hiding there?" the first one called back.

The second spy hurried after the first. Both took care not to be seen.

THE LAST FEW yards of their climb proved to be the most difficult as the ledge they had seen from far below protruded outward from the mountainous hillside's body in a most precarious and nearly unattainable manner. Overall, the entire climb was more laborious than it had appeared it would be from farther down. The spy who proposed the climb was the first one up. He turned and offered his partner a very dirty and sweaty hand. Once both were safely upon the ledge they straightened up quickly, patted themselves off and turned to look.

"Well, you were right," the doubtful spy concluded. "We can see right into the city."

Far below lay Zarahemla, stronghold of the Nephites. Its city wall arched around and surrounded the city. Within the wall was the city square toward the west and the city's entrance. Beyond this lay a series of buildings of various sizes and shapes. Their walls were made most commonly of stones hewn in such a way that they could be placed one atop another. Their enormous size produced the weight necessary to keep them firmly in place. Their edges were so perfectly carved that they fit snugly together without the need of mortar.

So far as the two spies could see, the entire city appeared deserted. There were tracks left behind from the many soldiers who had milled about awaiting their marching orders. Those tracks mingled in disarray and then approached the city gate. Once outside the city gate, they formed a singular and uniform telltale sign of the city's departed forces.

"And, it looks like you were also right," the first spy observed. "I don't see a soul. They must have taken every man they had."

"Surely they didn't leave the city deserted? Not their mighty Zarahemla?" even the doubtful spy could not accept that Moroni would wholly desert his most precious of cities.

"I don't know," his partner responded, looking carefully around for any sign of life, "Maybe—"

"No! Wait! I see a guard, and another," the second spy interrupted. "Yes, he's left the city guarded, but I think everyone else must be gone. See, there on the city wall."

The first spy looked to where his partner pointed. Their perch was so distant that it was difficult to gain a distinct view of something so tiny as a man standing on the wall. With some concerted peering he was eventually able to make out the figures of two men.

"I see them now," he said, still leery of Moroni's ability to strategically outmaneuver them he added, "Maybe we ought to wait just a little longer—"

"For what?! For someone to spot us? For someone to march up

here and hand us our heads on a platter? Look, I'll admit that I'm impressed that we can see into the city from up here, but your 'Wait, what about this? Wait, what about that?' is just too much! We've already lost too much time on your wild 'what if's?' The city's virtually deserted. You can see that for yourself. I'm making a straight dash to Amalickiah before Moroni beats us to him."

The first spy continued to take one, last, lingering look.

"All right, all right," he said with resignation. "I'm coming. I just wanted to be certain."

Both of the men turned away and headed down the other side of the hill as quickly but carefully as they could. When they finally emerged onto level ground they headed off as fast as they could through the jungle toward Amalickiah's present location.

FAR BELOW THE ledge, Teancum stood on the city wall, looking up toward the hill where the two spies had stood. He watched as the two spies dashed off and out of sight. The guard that the spies had seen pacing the wall walked up to Teancum.

Teancum still shook his head incredulously. He was clearly impressed. "I don't know how he does it, but he was right again," he mumbled to himself as much as to the guard. He then turned and looked the guard in the eye and gave the order, "Tell the men it's time to go!"

Teancum climbed down from the wall and headed toward the city's inner buildings. He made his way to a certain house he called home. He opened the door and entered. Sephara approached him. She had a look of strength, but also concern.

"It's time," Teancum said, looking his sweetheart in the eye. "We'll be heading out as soon as the men are assembled."

"You take care of yourself," Sephara responded.

"And you take care of our little one," Teancum said with a proud smile.

They hugged and Teancum caressed Sephara's tummy, trying to feel their little one growing within her. He felt a little kick and smiled with a touch of sadness, knowing that it was almost certain he would not be there for his child's birth.

"I'm sorry to be leaving you at this time," he said with genuine angst. "It's doubtful I'll even be able to hear about the birth until long afterwards, let alone be here for it."

"You go out there and settle this strife," she said. "Make this world free so that our child can grow up without worrying about whether or not his father will be coming home at night."

"I love you," he said, as he memorized her face, hoping to burn the image of her every detail into his mind so that he could see her in his heart while he was away. "I love everything about you. I love your hair, the way you look at me when I tease you, your—"

"Tell me when you return," she interrupted. The prolonged goodbye was tearing at her heart. With an air of forced strength buried in a shield of sarcastic grandiose she added, "You must be gone!"

Appreciating his wife's flare for concealing inner turmoil, he continued the charade of bravado, "I'm off to establish liberty for you!" then, unable to avoid the sincerity of the intent, he added, "And our little one."

At this, Sephara dropped all pretenses and earnestly vowed, "I'll count the hours until your return."

They embraced one last time and then kissed warmly and firmly. Finally, Teancum turned to leave. They continued to hold hands, but they slowly pulled apart. Sephara let her hand drop loosely to her side.

Unable to restrain himself, Teancum turned back and gave her one more kiss of farewell.

Then he reached out his hand and held her chin. With his index finger lovingly curled around the base of her chin, he gently caressed her cheek with the tip of his thumb. "I love you. Take care of yourself," he whispered. He then exited through the door and softly closed it behind him.

Sephara continued to stand in silence. She raised her hand and gently stroked her cheek where Teancum had last touched her. Her tears flowed freely. She stood there quietly for a long while, with her eyes closed, and was unaware of how long she had been caressing her expectant tummy. All she knew was that her heart full of prayers for the safe return of her child's father, and her life's love.

OUT IN THE city square, Teancum led his army through the city gate. They veered northeast, intent on cutting off Amalickiah, who Moroni had assumed was on his way to the land Bountiful. Teancum's men were large. They jogged quickly and in step, rather than marched. The jog did not appear to tire any of the men, in spite of their armor, gear, and weapons. These were large, powerful warriors with tremendous endurance. Again, they cut their way through the jungle underbrush.

ONLY A FEW days later, Teancum and two of his best officers were crouched in some undergrowth spying on another army encamped in a clearing in the jungle. A man in a distinctive, red cloak emerged from a tent, passed a campfire, and went into another, larger tent.

"No doubt about it now," Teancum stated with confidence. "That was Amalickiah. We've already caught his army!" Teancum turned to the officer on his right. "You take your third of the men around to the west." To the officer on his left he ordered, "You take your third to the east of their camp. My men will rush them straight on. When both of you are in position, give the call. Today there won't be any phases of battle. I want to rush him with everything at once, taking him completely off guard. I've grown weary of Amalickiah's tricks and want to put an end to it here and now. Understood?"

"Absolutely!" the first officer responded.

"It's high time!" the second officer concurred.

Teancum returned to his forces. He whispered orders to nine of his soldiers. They then spread out and passed the word onto their units. Teancum looked along the edges of the jungle and could just make out his two officers as they stealthily led their men into position. After a moment of impatient waiting, there was a loud snap of a tree limb on the east of the clearing. Some of Amalickiah's men looked east. This was followed by a loud snap from the left. Amalickiah's men turned their attention west, while Amalickiah himself emerged from his tent. Suddenly, the area was filled to overflowing with a horrific war shout from both the east and the west.

Teancum led his men from their lair to the south in a furious race toward their foe. All of them were screaming a unified, blood curdling war challenge. Teancum's other units emerged simultaneously from the east and west. Amalickiah's men were caught in a battle for their lives. Their army was not small, so it was a tremendous fight. The day was blistering hot. The men sweated heavily under the heat of the sun and the humidity of the jungle, as well as from their vigorous fighting.

The hand-to-hand combat continued for quite some time before Amalickiah's army was able to pierce a hole in the human wall of their foe and flee northward. Amalickiah headed the flight through the jungle. Teancum's army pursued with vigor. The race continued until sunset.

AS NIGHT FELL, the Lamanites set up a hasty camp with Teancum's army camped nearby. Both armies were exhausted, and they rested for further battle in the morning. While the night animals began to scurry about seeking their prey, most of the men were sleeping soundly, including an exhausted, disheveled-looking Amalickiah.

Teancum, however, sat on the edge of his cot. Sleep was plainly far from him. He was edgy, irritable, deep in thought, and on the verge of a decision. He stood up suddenly and called for his servant in a determined, stern voice, but not so loud as to rouse his other troops.

"Sherem, come here!" he ordered.

Sherem, whose tent was next to Teancum's, rushed into Teancum's tent.

"Yes, Teancum, how can I serve you?"

"Why are we here?" Teancum asked.

Sherem looked very puzzled. "To fight the Lamanites, sir."

"And why are we fighting the Lamanites?"

"Because they've attacked our cities, killed our people, and won't let us live in peace," Sherem responded, confused and attempting to be succinct, but accurate, hoping to alleviate his leader's questions.

"Exactly!" Teancum responded with unnerving enthusiasm, "And who is the cause for all of this?"

"Uh," Sherem stammered, "The Lamanites?"

"No!" Teancum corrected, "Amalickiah! His bloodthirsty lust for power has driven him to this. First, he wanted to be king of the Nephites. We wouldn't allow it, so he ran off, enslaved the Lamanites and became their king. Now, he wants to take us over by force. Amalickiah is the cause of this war, this killing, this waste of lives.

He must be stopped and stopped now!"

"I know, sir!" Sherem responded with encouragement, "And we'll do that first thing tomorrow!"

"No," Teancum said, "You don't understand. He has to be stopped now! Right now. Tonight!"

"Tonight?!"

"Yes, tonight! I need you to come with me and keep an eye out while I find Amalickiah's tent."

"Find his tent?" Sherem questioned, "You're going into his camp?" If Sherem had any concerns about the heat of the day affecting his leader's mind, they came to the forefront of his thoughts at this moment.

"Not just me, 'we.'" Teancum corrected, "We're going to put a stop to this, and I need you to help."

Sherem shook the confusion from his head. He realized his leader was not in a delirium, but instead had decided to take action. He summoned his warrior's courage and replied, "I see. Sir, it will be an honor!"

"Fine," Teancum replied. "Now, let's get moving—and put on some darker clothing."

Teancum grabbed a dark cloak and a spear as the two left his tent. Sherem dashed into his own tent briefly and emerged with a similar, dark cloak. They sneaked out of their own campsite full of their sleeping comrades. A guard noticed them. Teancum approached and allowed himself to be recognized, while giving the signal for silence. The burly guard appeared puzzled, but allowed them to slip out of the camp and into the jungle.

Using the dim light of the waning moon as their only source of light, they made their way toward the Lamanites. They soon arrived at the edge of the Lamanite camp. They paused only momentarily as Teancum looked about. Smoldering campfires were scattered through the camp. They lent feeble light to the scene. So far as he could tell, the entire Lamanite army was fast asleep, worn out by the rigors of the day. The heat and humidity had compounded their exhaustion. Surprisingly, no guards had been posted.

Teancum saw three, large tents in the middle of the encampment and pointed. Sherem nodded and the two made a beeline for the tents. Teancum silently peered into the first tent. He backed out and shook his head negatively to Sherem. They worked their way over to the second tent with the same result.

Teancum was now certain that Amalickiah must be in the third tent. He pantomimed to Sherem that he wanted him to open the tent flap enough for him to enter quickly with his spear. Sherem nodded comprehendingly. When Teancum nodded that he was ready, Sherem silently, but quickly, cut the cords holding the flap closed and pulled the door open widely. Teancum saw Amalickiah lying on his bed, lying on his back in the king position.

He darted in and rammed his spear directly through Amalickiah's heart. Amalickiah was dead before even opening his eyes or uttering a sound. Teancum did not linger. He exited quickly. Sherem, who had seen his master's success, knew that they needed to make a hasty retreat. They both dashed silently out of their enemy's camp.

Their race through the jungle was swift. They leaped over logs and ducked under vines with the agility of a leopard after its prey. An adrenaline rush sped their feet. They reached their guard who immediately recognized them, but remained confused about their errand. Paying him no mind, they raced to the center of the encampment.

"Men, arise!" Teancum shouted. "I have killed Amalickiah! I've killed Amalickiah! We must be at the ready in case the Lamanites attack!"

The men emerged from their tents in surprise. There was a great deal of commotion. The air was filled with Nephites questioning what they thought they had heard.

"Did he say he's killed Amalickiah?" a soldier asked.

"Amalickiah? Dead?" a second soldier questioned, "God be praised!"

"What's the plan now?" a third queried.

"The plan?" Teancum asked with unbridled enthusiasm and excitement, "We make ready to take the Lamanites at dawn!"

The men shouted in anticipation of their victory. Monkeys, birds, and other jungle animals roused from their tranquil sleep shouted back angry retorts, which reverberated in the night. Teancum longed to attack now, but knew that his men were too weary. He must give them the night to recuperate. Soon the victory would be theirs. Soon.

Chapter 17

Discovery

———◆———

An early dawn crept across the jungle undergrowth. Humid mist still hovered among the trees. Exotic flowers began to open. Monkeys rubbed and opened their tired eyes. Birds rustled in typical preparations for the day. In a small clearing of the jungle, a group of tents lay hastily pitched. These were the sleepy tents of Amalickiah's army.

The flap to Amalickiah's tent was wide open. A loud shout of anguish was heard from within. "No! No!" Ammoron's voice pierced the morning.

Inside, Ammoron bent over his brother's lifeless body, distraught.

"Brother!" he cried out, "No!"

At the sound of the shriek, Amalickiah's servant rushed to the tent. He saw the scene and stood by helpless, and at a loss for how to comfort Ammoron. Two Lamanite generals dashed into the tent.

"What?!" General Jacob demanded, "What's this shouting?"

They saw Amalickiah's body, the spear still protruding from his chest, and guessed the rest.

"Now what?!" a second commander asked with more disgust than anguish.

They both looked at Ammoron who knelt hopelessly and helplessly.

"What do I tell the men?" General Jacob asked.

Ammoron was speechless for a moment. Then he turned to them with a determined look, shouldering his new responsibility, but obviously without a sincere plan.

"We make haste like the devil," Ammoron declared. "Back to the city of Mulek!"

"Mulek?" the second commander questioned, "Why there? Why not fight?"

"Amalickiah's dead," Ammoron explained, "And so are his plans. You know he never shared his strategies with anyone but himself. Do you want to toss a plan together and contend with Teancum right here and now? I'm certain Amalickiah's death won't come as any surprise to him. I'm also certain he is right now surrounding this camp. I say we withdraw and move to a safe haven where we can plan our next move."

"Agreed," General Jacob stated. "It's our best move considering our circumstances. Let's move the men quickly."

TEANCUM LED HIS men through the jungle. Their pace was not nearly as quick as his return to camp on the previous night, but it was as fast as an army could move through such unrelenting territory. He hastened them onward hoping to catch their enemy before they managed to elude them.

They broke through to Amalickiah's camp only to find abandoned tents, equipment, and smoldering fires. Ammoron did not even wait to pack up their gear. Teancum now wished he had not waited either. They checked the place over quickly and looked for the direction of Amalickiah's army's flight. A distinct break in the thick jungle brush gave their path away to one of Teancum's scouts who shouted. Teancum saw and agreed. He sent his men into the jungle and the hunt was on.

Far ahead, Ammoron's men were on a desperate flight. They were sweaty and bore humorless, angst-riddled expressions in an obvious race for their lives. None of them spoke. They all vied for the foremost position like migratory birds struggling to be at the apex of their v-shaped configuration. Ammoron maintained that position with distinct clarity. Of all of his traits of leadership on the battlefield, retreat was by far his greatest strength.

Teancum's army maintained a steady chase. The gap between the pursuers and the pursued narrowed. Here and there Teancum's men noted a dropped weapon left lying as its former owner quickly chose not to pause long enough to retrieve it. Where the jungle had grown denser and the trees and vines provided only narrow passage, they found occasional pieces of cloth torn from Lamanite clothing.

They passed a tree where disturbed monkeys still chided the former intruders and picked up their chatter at these new invaders who scurried below them. It was difficult to be certain over the din of his own troops, especially at full stride, but Teancum began to sense that he could hear the enemy ahead. He urged his men onward at an ever-increasing pace. Ahead they saw branches and vines still swinging from being hastily pushed aside during the Lamanites' passing.

Soon, very soon, Teancum would catch up with them. Then the last battle would commence and he could return victorious to his beloved Sephara. The edge of the jungle came suddenly and without expectation. Teancum and his men burst through it like flood waters penetrating a weakened dike.

Ammoron and his men were within view. To Teancum's utter dismay, so was the Lamanite-occupied city of Mulek. Teancum shouted in rage, sprinting ahead of his army, not caring for his own safety. His swiftest officers attempted to match his speed, as Ammoron's army approached the safety of the city of Mulek. Two tower guards saw Ammoron leading the army, then Teancum's army closing in.

They shouted orders to open the city gate for Ammoron and to get archers up onto the city wall. The last of Ammoron's men were into the city as more and more archers joined in and rained ever-increasing numbers of arrows down toward Teancum's army. This first impeded, and then effectively prevented the Nephite's assault on the city. Teancum was forced to withhold attack and resigned himself to an abundantly unsatisfactory retreat. The once-haven-of-safety for the Nephites was now being used by their mortal enemies against them.

TEANCUM'S MEN OCCUPIED themselves with building a makeshift stronghold near the city of Mulek. They had their prey penned in and intended to commence a long siege until they could coax them out. Were they able to see within the city walls, they would have seen Ammoron walk into the city square and pause before a makeshift throne.

A Lamanite approached him, gingerly carrying royal garb and a crown. With the aid of two others, he placed these ceremoniously on Ammoron who sat down amid cheers. He acknowledged the cheers with a self-indulgent arrogance that he had learned from observing a now-deceased master of the art.

Teancum's army was encamped a mile or two from the city of Mulek. Tents had been erected behind the dirt and wooden walls that the soldiers were quickly erecting. Other soldiers milled about. One of them approached Teancum, who stood looking toward the city.

"Do we attack?" the soldier asked with earnest desire.

"Attack?" Teancum responded with dejected acceptance of the futility of the act, "How? Moroni himself planned the defenses of that city. We wouldn't stand a chance!"

"Well," the soldier declared, "We can't just sit and let them invade our city!"

"Oh," Teancum replied, "I'm not sitting still for this. I just don't intend to turn this into a suicide mission. We'll take them all right, but not until we have sufficient forces. I've sent word to Moroni. I just hope he arrives before more Lamanites do."

"More?" the soldier questioned.

"Certainly!" Teancum stated with confidence, "I'm afraid Amalickiah may have gotten in league with some of the other factions before taking us on. He was a clever strategist. I seriously doubt he would have come up here without planning for reinforcements. This battle is going to get a whole lot worse before it gets any better. Have the men continue their work on our wall of defense. We may be here a while and I don't want the Lamanites to be able to just walk into camp and pick us off in our sleep."

THE HEAVY PANTING and constant thumping of his feet removed all signs of stealth. The sweaty, tired, and somewhat frantic Lamanite had wholly given up on finding Ammoron and the others. He had spent the better part of the day cursing and swearing at himself for losing them. For the first time in his military career, he had gained an appreciation for his new—and now late—commander Amalickiah's strict regulations on discipline and order. Before Amalickiah, the army ignored such matters, relying heavily on maintaining oafish brutality and shear fear.

But, a misplaced pair of sandals on the morning of an unexpectedly early call for retreat had provided a disastrous impact on this day. Even as they ran off leaving him behind, he had thought for certain he would be able to track them down and catch up. He just had not counted on the Nephites being so close behind. Had they been a moment sooner, he would have still been in the clearing and unable to seek a hideaway. It was only dumb luck that allowed him to crouch down and watch them pass. Only a fool would have followed the Nephite's from directly behind.

His side trail should have enabled him to parallel the main trail, but instead it led to uncounted obstacles. Once he was forced to admit he had hopelessly lost their trail, there was no other alternative than to turn around and make his way back to the land of Nephi. At least he could comfort himself with the ability of telling the queen about their king's demise, if that could be considered a point of "comfort."

All this depended on his being able to make it there with his head still attached to his shoulders. He was still in enemy territory and, given the misfortunes of the day, safe passage back to Lamanite territory was anything but a sure thing. And so he trudged on quickly and dirty through the jungle. With his sword, he slapped at vines and snakes along his way. Birds and monkeys were startled and bolted away as he hectically cut his way through.

He paused at a large log, catching his breath while preparing to climb over. Just before he climbed, he looked back quickly to ensure he was not being followed. He hurdled the log and dashed onward.

If he really hustled, he hoped to make the land of Nephi by nightfall of the third day.

IN ANOTHER PART of the land, a large, Nephite warrior jogged at a quick and steady pace in a straight route through the jungle. He sweat from the exertion of a long jaunt, but bore a determined, indefatigable expression. He neared the edge of the jungle and entered a clearing of tents where Moroni's army was encamped. He continued his pace up to the center of the camp to where Moroni's tent was.

Moroni exited his tent as the warrior approached him. "Captain Moroni," the messenger declared, "I bear news from Teancum. He has killed Amalickiah, but Ammoron now leads the army and has entrenched himself in the city of Mulek!"

"Amalickiah dead?!" Moroni said with surprise, "What a terrible waste," he concluded, taking no delight in the death of his mortal adversary.

Moroni paused only briefly as he thought with disgust of his enemy's self-imposed, inevitable demise. Then he added, "I've already gotten word that more Lamanites are gathering in the south and harassing our cities there. Tell Teancum that I would come with haste, but I must first deal with these other attacks. Tell him to scourge the Lamanites as best he can, and if possible, take back the cities. We need that area strengthened. Tell him to use whatever means of strategy he can. I'll send half my army to the south and join him with the rest of my army shortly. I imagine we'll only be a few days behind you."

Almost as an afterthought, Moroni added, "And tell him that if he takes any Lamanite prisoners, he should keep them secure. We may be able to use them to ransom back some of our captive brethren."

"Yes, sir!" the messenger replied.

The warrior bowed, turned, and dashed off at the same quick and steady pace as before, on his way back to Teancum's camp.

THE FRANTIC AND fleeing Lamanite still struggled onward. He was even more sweaty and disheveled than before. He tripped on a vine and looked up. Through the last patch of trees and vines he could see that he was finally near the edge of the jungle. Somehow he had avoided the great hill north of Nephi and the Lamanite city lay across an open field. He raised himself on his hands and panted for a bit before going on and bursting through the last of the jungle. He stumbled across the clearing to the city. Guards opened the gate and helped him enter.

Wholly out of breath, he muttered, "The queen! I must see the queen! I have a message for the queen! Amalickiah is dead! Ammoron and the army are fleeing from the Nephites! I must tell the queen!" he repeated.

TEANCUM'S CAMP WAS already protected by a large wall of rock and dirt. His men had worked quickly, with more construction ongoing. Teancum's messenger emerged quickly from the jungle, climbed through an incomplete portion of the wall and hustled over to where Teancum stood speaking to some of his men. He bore Moroni's message. It was a message that Teancum was intent on hearing.

Teancum nodded several times while the messenger delivered his report. Finally, the Nephite took a step back and bowed as he had done to Moroni. Teancum raised his hand and placed it on the messenger's shoulder in acknowledgment of a difficult deed done well and gestured to the campfire. The messenger nodded appreciatively and headed in that direction.

Two other Nephite soldiers approached him in a respectful and welcoming manner. The one offered him an animal skin flask with water; the other, food. He nodded his appreciation and the three turned and walked away to sit together. He began to drink and eat.

Chapter 18

Second Chance

*T*he coals in the campfire burned brightly. Flames licked at the logs and offered inconstant light to the surrounding darkness. Shadows jumped and swerved throughout the campsite, especially on the nearest tent. Within the tent stood a table of ancient design. Less than a handful of men sat around it. Moroni spoke to Teancum.

"Be sure to let them keep up," Moroni advised. "We don't want them lagging behind and giving up on the chase."

"Understood," Teancum acknowledged. "You do the same." He smiled at this bit of encouragement.

The humor was not lost on Moroni, who smiled in return and added, "Yes, sir."

He put his hand on Teancum's shoulder in the traditional sign of respect, but also jostled him slightly with the warmth of comrades in arms.

"Now get some rest," Moroni ordered, "And make sure your men do too."

"Yes, sir," Teancum replied. "Good night, sir. And, it's good to see you again."

"And you," Moroni answered. "Sleep well."

ALTHOUGH IT WAS still early morning, the jungle already offered continued warmth and humidity. The main road in front of the city of Mulek had a mist that crept from the jungle on both sides and hung over the road's surface like a pale, thick blanket. It limited any view of the road only a few feet. High up in the city's tower, a Lamanite guard was nearing the completion of his watch. He was weary from a long night's duty, but alert.

His ears perked up and his eyes peered into the unrelenting mist as he heard a faint rhythmic sound. He strained his senses, but was unable to place its location or origin. He looked quizzically around. Try as he might, he could find no clue as to where or what was generating the sound. Just as it became louder and distinct enough to recognize it as the sound of a quick march, Teancum and his men, a couple hundred in number, burst through the mist on the road directly below him.

Before they were swallowed up in the mist again, he saw that these Nephites were hustling in unison right in front of the city wall, and continuing onward. The guard was at first astounded by the audacity and boldness of his foe. He was not awestruck beyond action, however. He reached for his horn and gave it a mighty, long blow.

Teancum, without breaking stride, looked up toward the city wall and allowed half a smile to breach his otherwise stony expression. He looked forward again and continued leading his men on their double-paced march.

The guard gave a triple blast on his horn. Lamanites leaped from their beds and quickly donned their gear. The Lamanite general named Jacob, who had been left in charge of Mulek, climbed the catwalk and rushed to the side of his guard.

"What's this?" General Jacob asked, "Do they dare attack us? They don't stand a chance!"

"No, sir," the guard replied, "It's not an attack. It looks more like some sort of escape or retreat. See there!"

The guard pointed and General Jacob saw the latter part of Teancum's army disappearing eastward into the morning mist.

"Well done!" the general said, "This is too easy. Call the men to arms! We'll hunt them down like dogs and make quick work of this."

The guard gave three quick blasts of his horn, followed by one long one blast and four more quick ones. He paused momentarily, then repeated the signal. The army filed into the city square, with Jacob at their head. He nodded to the gatekeepers who opened the gate to allow them to exit. They did so eagerly and began the chase.

TEANCUM'S ARMY CONTINUED to quickstep down the road. The mist swirled around their ankles and legs as they passed through it. The final soldier looked back. Through the swirling mist he was able to make out that the Lamanites were pursuing, but were quite a ways back. The soldier looked forward again. His face did not bear an expression of concern but, to the contrary, one of confidence and appreciation for having received the visual confirmation that their plan was so far successful.

Keeping in step, he spread the word forward. In classic gossip chain format, the message passed from soldier to soldier until it reached Teancum. Teancum's reaction was to raise an arm to signal stopping. He turned and faced his men.

"Men, it's working!" he declared. "So far all is going as planned. I think we shouldn't get too anxious, or we'll out pace our prey. Let's enjoy a quick rest before continuing, just to be certain."

They rested for only a few seconds then continued onward. Farther back on the road, a large Lamanite army continued their pursuit. Row after row after row of anxious warriors trotted forward eager to do battle. They had sat restlessly within the city walls for far too long to let this easy conquest slip away. General Jacob at their head was as eager as the others. He had allowed nearly all of his men to leave the city and join in the chase. He considered this a well-deserved reward for his men.

THE CITY WALL towered over the now-vacant road. The morning mist had all but burned away from the warmth of the rising sun. There were a few, scattered Lamanite soldiers gathered on the catwalk looking into the distance in the direction of the morning's pursuit. They were engaged in debate attempting to predict what was going on.

Some of the men looked confident and appeared to be indicating a Lamanite massacre of the fleeing Nephites, as they made jabbing motions with their swords and then laughing. The city square was empty. The western wall was vacated. All of the guards had moved to the eastern wall to join in the debate. They feared this vicarious verbal haranguing would be as close as they would be able to come to any real action.

With their attention focused eastward, and in fact, their very presence residing on that wall, they remained wholly oblivious to the western wall, especially to what now clung to its outer side. One peek over the rim would have revealed Nephites swarming over its surface. They had ladders, ropes, and climbing spades for digging footholds. At the very time the Lamanite guards longed for action, their mortal enemies covered their wall and were nearing its top.

The first to scale the wall's summit leaped onto the catwalk and crept silently, but with tremendous speed, along the catwalk toward the preoccupied Lamanites. His name was Enos. He was the same Enos who had once been an archer assigned to protect this very city, and whom Amalickiah had glibly sent to warn Moroni that his days were numbered. It was a distinct honor for him to lead the assault to retake his own city.

He was joined in his stealth pursuit by what seemed to be an unending tide of Nephite warriors leaping over the wall's edge and onto the catwalk. They wended their way quickly toward their unsuspecting and unprepared foes. Other Nephites poured down into the city square and made their way to the bunkhouses and other areas in which they might find Lamanites.

Although the Nephites had split up and were silently charging the Lamanites in many areas within the city, they converged on their foes all at once. In each case, the Lamanites saw their foes coming only at the last moment. They all turned and raised their swords to fend off blows just before the onslaught. This alert was thorough mainly because the Nephites all gave a roaring war cry just as they came down on their enemies.

The war cry successfully both alerted and terrorized their startled enemies. The Nephites had sneaked up on their prey with great stealth, but would not kill men whose backs were turned to them. Fierce hand-to-hand combat ensued, but with General Jacob using nearly his entire army to chase down Teancum and his men, the Nephites had a definite advantage in this particular struggle.

The city was soon theirs. The final act of the conflict was that of Lamanite prisoners of war being bound and guarded in the center of the once-tranquil city square. The freed Nephites were released and allowed to roam their city again. They were gleefully surrounding their now-bound captives. One particular bound Lamanite, evidently an officer judging by his demeanor, looked around at his captors.

"Where's Moroni?" he demanded, confused.

Enos stepped forward.

"That's *Captain* Moroni to you," he sternly corrected. Then, he added with a mocking laugh, "He's hunting down some strays."

The Nephites laughed with an enthusiasm they had not been able to in many a month. The captive officer caught the meaning, lowered his head and grit his teeth in frustration.

A proud Nephite posted a new Title of Liberty over the city gate.

MORONI LED HIS men while cutting a path through the jungle. The men looked eager and ready to do battle. Moroni stopped and raised his arm signaling that his men should stop.

"Easy men," he cautioned. "Let's not be too eager. We want to give Teancum enough time."

The men nodded knowingly. Moroni began their march again, at an easier pace.

TEANCUM AND HIS relatively small band of a couple hundred men jogged through a clearing. The Lamanites who had been trailing them for quite some time were now closing in. It was evident that they could quite possibly overtake them before they reached the other end of the clearing. Teancum and his men did not appear the least concerned, but kept right on jogging. The Lamanites increased their pace, eager to do battle in the open area, rather than the jungle.

The clearing provided a distinct gap in the dense rainforest's terrain. Teancum's men were in the lead, nearing one end of the clearing. The Lamanites filled the clearing from shortly behind Teancum's men completely to the other end. As all of the Lamanites entered the clearing, the advantage they held over Teancum's numbers became abundantly apparent. They outnumbered Teancum's men nearly seven to one. This underscored the cause of the Lamanites' eager anticipation of an easy conquest.

Teancum and his men continued to double-time their march without fear or concern in their eyes. They also subtly quickened their pace to ensure they stayed ahead of their prey. They managed to get within a few yards of the jungle on the other side of the clearing, with the Lamanites only a dozen yards on their tails. There was a sudden, enormous roar from all parts of the jungle. A large flock of exotic birds was startled and took flight directly over the clearing, adding to the Lamanites' surprise.

The Lamanites instinctively ducked as they looked up, saw the birds, then looked forward to the place from which the roar had come. The jungle facing the Lamanites from all angles was nothing but dense foliage. There was no sign of who or what made the awful roar. While the Lamanites were distracted, Teancum and his army had disappeared into the trees. Jacob and his men were left standing alone in the clearing without any sign of the Nephites. The dense jungle that surrounded them revealed no sign of humans, yet also seemed to be holding back an inexplicable flood of energy waiting to be set free. An eerie chill ran up their spines. Something was suddenly very much amiss.

The trap had been baited and set. A split second later, it was sprung. In all directions, the fringes of the clearing were rapidly filled with Nephite warriors emerging from the jungle and swarming toward the Lamanites. Lehi led his army inward, taking up where Teancum had left off. His army was fresh and vigorous having waited the morning for Teancum to lure their enemy into the trap. They converged on the Lamanites from three sides, nearly surrounding them.

The Lamanites were wholly incapable of concealing their disappointment at this unexpected turn of events. The sweat from their long chase streaked down their faces. They stood panting, no longer grinning, as fear and dread crept over them.

The Nephites continued to emerge and approach them, fully ready for the fight. The quickest Nephite warrior approached his foe. He brought his sword fully upward and swung it with crushing forcefulness upon his enemy.

The Lamanites fought fiercely, but without sincere leadership. Jacob had been the only visible leader among them. As he saw how rested and energetic Lehi's army was as well as the fact that they had the upper hand in nearly surrounding them, he signaled for his men to retreat. Word traveled awkwardly across the battleground. Jacob made his way to the other end of the clearing.

By this time, the greater portion of his army already understood the need to retreat. The army was certain of two things. They had to leave that field quickly and they had to return to the safety they believed the city of Mulek offered, not knowing it was no longer in their possession.

As the Lamanites attempted to enter the jungle on the other end of the clearing, they suddenly retreated quickly back into the clearing again. The cause was not immediately apparent until Moroni emerged at the head of his army. The Lamanites were now completely surrounded and enclosed in the clearing. In an act of combined desperation, frustration and pure rage, Jacob continued to fight with even more vigor than before.

Like a mountain cat backed into a corner, he charged and lashed out at Moroni himself. He fought with the fury of a desperate man.

His blows were wild and non-rhythmic. Moroni was on the defense, parrying the blows. As he backed up he stumbled momentarily on a fallen soldier's helmet. Moroni twisted to his right and steadied himself with his sword hand to prevent a fall. Jacob took full advantage of the moment and swung vigorously at Moroni. Moroni took a blow to the left arm, causing a severe wound, but not disarming him.

Moroni was in harm's way and fought back in full defense of his life. He managed to force Jacob backward. They struggled, fending each other's blows. Moroni's left arm flopped limply at his side, bleeding profusely. The fight was intense. Jacob delivered a massive blow that Moroni parried and then used the momentum from the first strike to swing around for another powerful blow. Moroni was ahead of him, however, and stepped to the side. Jacob was left off balance from not landing the blow and Moroni's sword caught him. Jacob was slain.

With Jacob's death, all hope of a Lamanite victory was lost. Their defenses cracked and ebbed. The potential for a Nephite victory now increased well beyond the point of feasibly to becoming a massacre of this entire Lamanite army. Moroni then raised his sword straight and high into the air, signaling the cessation of hostilities. The signal was noted and foes stepped back from each other. Lamanites cast their weapons at the feet of their victors.

The Nephites began to herd their captives to the center of the clearing. This was done quickly. Soon the Nephites stood surrounding the unarmed Lamanites. Moroni stepped to a prominent area in front of their army. As he stepped forward, it was seen that he held a bandage to his arm. One of his soldiers tied it off. Moroni was grateful, but ignored the action as he focused his attention on finding Ammoron.

"Ammoron!" he shouted. "Come forward!"

He paused, waiting for Ammoron to step forward.

"Ammoron!" he repeated. "Step forward now!"

He waited again for a moment.

"Is Ammoron slain?" Moroni asked. "Someone report!"

Teancum stepped up to Moroni.

"Do you want my men to search their dead?" he asked.

"No," Moroni responded. "Not yet. Wait."

Moroni again addressed the Lamanites.

"Is Ammoron among you—or among your dead?"

From somewhere among the Lamanites a prisoner had found the ability to taunt his foe.

"Neither!" the voice declared loudly and with defiance.

"What?" Moroni questioned. "Who said that? Step forward!"

The taunting prisoner did not step forward. Moroni drew his sword.

"Don't make me cut my way to you!" he warned. "Step forward!"

Moroni approached the captives with his sword drawn. They stepped sideways creating a break in their ranks that continued to sever its way through the crowd until it left the taunting soldier exposed. He stood facing Moroni whose sword was pointed into the human crevice.

"You there!" Moroni called. "Step forward!"

The Lamanite stepped forward through the prisoners and stood a pace or two in front of Moroni. He looked defiant and unrepentant in spite of his defeat.

"Where's Ammoron?" he demanded.

"I imagine," the Lamanite said with a smirk, "he's marching through the city square of Zarahemla by now."

Teancum stepped forward quickly.

"What do you mean?" Teancum demanded. "He couldn't have gotten that far in a day."

"In a day, no," the soldier agreed. "But, he's had much more than a day to make his trek."

"What do you mean?" Teancum asked with confused concern mingled with anger. "Speak plainly!"

"Ammoron never spent a single night in the city of Mulek," the soldier explained with pride.

Teancum's face turned ashen with shock and surprise. He stepped back, involuntarily. The taunter was plainly aware of the effect this news had on him and added with a wicked laugh, "If you thought you had our king penned up behind those walls all this time, then you've truly been guarding him in vain! He's been off free to plot and spoil for weeks now!"

Teancum turned and started to apologize to Moroni. Moroni wouldn't allow his officer to fall prey to his tormenter's taunting and did not allow Teancum to even broach the subject. Instead, he interjected his own comprehension of the situation. "That explains the news I've been hearing from the south. Helaman is likely in for more action than we had anticipated." He could not hide his concern. Then, looking back toward the defiant prisoner, he added loudly, "Still, we have a great number of prisoners now, don't we?"

He did so to make it clear that he had the upper hand and that the defiant Lamanite and his comrades were soundly beaten this day and should know their place.

"Teancum," he continued, "Make certain these prisoners are

securely guarded and escort them to Bountiful. Lehi and I will return to *our* city of Mulek."

Moroni emphasized the word "our," giving clear indication that it was now back under the control of the Nephites. He also gave this assignment to Teancum to reinforce his confidence in him, at a moment when Teancum had begun to doubt himself.

"Be sure to have the prisoners bury the dead before you march," Moroni added. "Come as quickly after securing the prisoners as you can."

"Yes, sir," Teancum responded.

Chapter 19

The Art of Proper Negotiation

⟁◈⟁

*R*eturning to Zarahemla to review on-going strategy simply was not practical. Moroni and his officers needed a place closer to the action. Having freed the city of Mulek, Moroni made it his headquarters in the front. There was a moderate-sized records room around the corner from the city's council chamber that was ideal for converting into a strategy room. It already contained a large table, chairs, and even renditions of several of the maps that Moroni had used previously back at Zarahemla.

Moroni, Teancum, and Lehi sat at a table discussing matters of war and strategy. Ammoron's escape had laid a frustrating blow on them all, but they refused to let it deter them. To the contrary, they became more intent than ever in tracking him down and removing him from power.

While they were in deep discussion, a Nephite soldier requested leave to enter the room. When permission was given, he entered with a Lamanite messenger.

"Captain," the Nephite soldier announced, "This man claims to have a message for you from Ammoron."

"*King* Ammoron," the messenger corrected the soldier and gave him a glare while attempting to establish dignity.

"A message from King Ammoron," Moroni mused. "Sounds intriguing."

"It's probably a trick," Teancum muttered suspiciously.

"Probably so," Moroni conceded. "But, I'm interested nonetheless. Never let distrust keep you from gaining the advantage of knowledge." He turned to the messenger, "What is the message?"

The Lamanite messenger stepped forward and held out a bamboo canister sealed at both ends with leather skin. There was a long, leather strap attached to both ends of the canister. The strap was looped around the messenger's shoulder. He pulled the canister forward to offer it to Moroni. He quickly pulled it free from his shoulder as he did so.

"This contains a message written directly by the hand of King Ammoron," the messenger stated with pride.

Moroni offered his enemy's messenger sincere respect as he took the canister.

"I see. I appreciate your diligence in bringing it to me. Please wait outside, as I will likely have something for you to deliver to your king in return. My men will see to it that you're made comfortable."

Moroni nodded to the soldier who brought him in and the messenger was ushered out with all the respect that Moroni's nod intended to convey. As Moroni returned to the table and began to sit, he sensed Teancum's confusion and concern about the respectful manner in which he had treated the Lamanite.

"Sir, he's—" Teancum began.

"He's a member of the enemy camp. Yes, I know," Moroni

interrupted. "But, that's no reason to treat him without the utmost civility. In fact, that's all the more reason to treat him personally as a king. If we can get the soldiers themselves to disbelieve the lies their leaders tell about us, we'll have a greater chance of currying their favor and converting them to believe that we're not such a loathsome people after all."

Teancum began to nod comprehendingly, and gained an increased appreciation for Moroni's wisdom. Moroni turned toward the table.

"Now," he said, "Let's see what Ammoron has to say."

Moroni opened the canister and slid out the scroll. The message read:

> *Moroni, I am Ammoron, king of the Lamanites. I write this epistle to you that I may convince you to exchange prisoners with me. Behold, I have many of your people and I find them loathsome and a burden. I propose exchanging your men for my men. Surely you have enough honor in your soul to grant this small request. If you do not agree to this, I will come upon you with fury to atone for the wrongs you have made against my people. I await your word. King Ammoron.*

"A prisoner exchange!" Lehi exclaimed. "That could be very beneficial. We can use our men back to strengthen our army."

"Yes," Moroni stated. "And so could the Lamanites. However, I would rather see our provisions go to feeding our own people, instead of our prisoners. I believe a trade is in order, but not necessarily on the terms that Ammoron has in mind. He wouldn't have initiated this deal if he didn't have a personal need. My guess is he's either low on men or low on supplies. It's probably the latter. Let's see about a reply—"

Moroni grabbed a charcoal pencil and scroll and began to write. Lehi and Teancum moved to stand behind him so that they could read over his shoulder as he wrote. They occasionally nodded approvingly to each other.

Upon its completion, the Lamanite messenger was ushered in and given the letter. He returned to Ammoron's camp and delivered the message to his new king. Ammoron began to read the message with interest:

> *Ammoron, I write to you somewhat concerning this war that you have waged against my people, or rather that your brother has waged against them, and that you are still determined to carry on after his death. Behold, I would tell you somewhat concerning the justice of God, and the sword of His almighty wrath, which hangs over you except you repent and withdraw your armies into your own lands, or the land of your possessions, which is the land of Nephi.*
>
> *I would tell you these things if you were capable of hearkening to them. I would tell you concerning that awful hell that awaits to receive such murderers as you and your brother have been, except you repent and withdraw your murderous purposes, and return with your armies to your own lands.*
>
> *But as you have once rejected these things, and have fought against the people of the Lord, even so I may expect you will do it again. And now behold, we are prepared to receive you. I warn you that except you withdraw your purposes, you will pull down upon you the wrath of that God whom you have rejected, even to your utter destruction.*

As the Lord lives, our armies will come upon you except you withdraw, and you will soon be visited with death, for we will retain our cities and our lands. We will maintain our religion and the cause of our God.

But, I suppose that I talk to you concerning these things in vain. For I suppose that you are a child of hell, therefore I will close my epistle by telling you that I will not exchange prisoners, save it is on conditions that you deliver up a man and his wife and his children, for one prisoner, and you withdraw your intention to attack my people. If this is the case, I will exchange.

If you do not agree to this, I will come against you with my armies. I will even arm my women and my children, and I will come against you, and I will follow you down into your own land, and it will be blood for blood, and life for life. I will give you battle until you are destroyed from off the face of the earth.

Behold, I am in my anger, and also my people. You have sought to murder us, and we have only sought to defend ourselves. If you seek to destroy us more we will seek to destroy you, and we will seek our land. Now I close my epistle. I am Moroni. I am a leader of the people of the Nephites.

As Ammoron read Moroni's letter he grew visibly upset. By the letter's end he was standing enraged. He crumpled the letter in his hand. He picked up and threw a chalice, nearly hitting his messenger. The messenger ducked and avoided it, but straightened to attention after it passed, without complaint.

"Wage a war!" Ammoron muttered with contempt. "Child of Hell!

Who docs hc think hc is?! Bring mc my scroll!"

An aid rushed in with writing materials. Ammoron sat down to write. His eyes were ablaze with fire and indignation. He pressed so hard with his writing implements that he nearly tore the manuscript. Once completed, he shoved the message into the canister. He pressed the message canister into the messenger's hands and demanded he return it to Moroni.

"Take this back to that Moroni!" he commanded fiercely. "And be quick about it!" he added in a threatening tone as he nearly pushed his messenger out of the room.

The messenger did his bidding and soon arrived at Moroni's camp. He was ushered into Moroni's presence. Once there, he was shown the same civility as before. With the message handed off, he was sent from the room to await Moroni's reply.

Moroni, Lehi, and Teancum were eager to find out the contents of the reply. Moroni read it aloud:

> *I am Ammoron, the king of the Lamanites. I am the brother of Amalickiah whom you have murdered. Behold, I will avenge his blood upon you and I will come upon you with my armies for I fear not your threatenings. And now behold, if you will lay down your arms, and subject yourselves to be governed by those to whom the government rightly belongs, then I will cause that my people will lay down their weapons and there will be no more war.*
>
> *You have breathed out many threatenings against me and my people. But, we fear not your threatenings. Nevertheless, I will grant to exchange prisoners according to your request, gladly, that I may preserve my food for my men of war, and we will wage a war*

that will be eternal, either to the subjecting of the Nephites to our authority or to your eternal extinction.

And as concerning that God whom you say we have rejected, behold, we know not such a being, neither do you. But, if it so be that there is such a being, we know not but that he has made us as well as you. And if it so be that there is a devil and a hell, behold will he not send you there to dwell with my brother whom you have murdered, whom you have hinted that he has gone to such a place? But behold, these things matter not. I am Ammoron. I am a bold Lamanite, and this war has been waged to avenge their wrongs and to maintain and to obtain their rights to the government. I close my epistle to Moroni.

Moroni placed the letter down on the table in front of him. All three were angered.

"He lies!" Lehi declared. "He lies!"

"Yes," Moroni said, "And he knows he lies. He has a perfect knowledge of his fraud. He knows full well that his is not a just cause. I'll not exchange prisoners until he withdraws his purpose to attack. I'll not grant him any more power than he already has. Since he ignored my terms, I'll keep my own word and go against them until they sue for peace."

Moroni rose, paused, and then added, "We know that most of our prisoners are being held captive in the city of Gid. Search among our men. Find a Lamanite. Surely we have one among our ranks who believes in our cause."

MORONI AND THE others were in the same room as before. A Nephite soldier entered with a Lamanite.

"Welcome," Moroni said. "Sit. What is your name?"

"My name is Laman," the Lamanite stated. "I was a servant of our king, until Amalickiah's men murdered him and tried to blame me and the king's other servants. I'm ready to help you bring down Ammoron in any way I can."

"Excellent!" Moroni responded with a smile.

Moroni and the others sat down and began speaking with Laman. Laman's face lit up with a smile of enlightenment as Moroni unfolded his plan to him.

THE JUNGLE TRAIL was dark and treacherous. Five men hustled along its seldom-used path. They kept close together and carried objects that they held close to their bosoms. As they broke free of the jungle trees and began a quick dash toward a city gate, the rays of the full moon made the leader's face visible. It was Laman, the same Laman who had met with Moroni earlier. He traveled quickly with four other Lamanites.

As they neared the gate, the Lamanite guards noticed the five approaching them at a quick pace and snapped into an attentive, leery state.

"Who goes there?!" the Lamanite guard demanded.

"Be at peace!" Laman reassured him. "I am Laman, a Lamanite like yourself. We've escaped from that wretched Moroni while his guards slept. And, we managed to swipe some of their fine wine before we left!"

"Wine?!" a second guard said with a touch of excitement. "Splendid! Let's drink to celebrate your escape!"

"No, no!" Laman said. "Not yet. Let's save it for when we go to battle against the Nephites."

"Save it?" the guard replied. "It's going to be a long night, let's drink it now!"

"No," Laman repeated. "Let's wait," purposefully egging on their thirst.

"He's right," the first guard countered. "We've got a long night ahead of us and we're already weary. We'll get more wine for our rations. We can drink that when we go to battle."

"You may do as you wish," Laman relented.

Laman handed the men the flasks, feigning reluctance. They began to drink. Laman and his men suppressed smiles as they nodded to each other.

THE MOON HAD slipped behind thick clouds. The flasks of wine were nearly drained. The last of the now-drunk guards to hang onto consciousness held a drained flask flimsily in his hand. He leaned forward, barely able to keep his eyes open.

"To Laman!" he slurred in praise of his newfound friend.

The guard collapsed. Laman paused, looking at him for a moment. Then he went up and nudged the guard. His men checked the other guards. They all nodded to Laman. He then pointed to two of the five and then to the jungle, indicating it was time for them to begin the next phase of Moroni's plan. They dashed off.

Laman's guards entered the jungle. Moroni and his men were there to meet them.

"Captain Moroni!" Laman's man announced in a hushed, but excited tone. "It's all gone as planned. They're all out cold. The city is yours for the taking!"

"Good work," Moroni congratulated the Lamanite. "Your former king should feel avenged tonight."

Laman's man was taken aback by Moroni's words and beamed with pride, as he stood tall, and unable to respond. Moroni led his men on a silent assault on the city. They reached the area where Laman and his other men waited. Moroni's men bore many bundles of weapons wrapped in animal skins. They began passing them to Laman and his men.

One particular batch of swords was passed from one of Moroni's men, to Laman's man, to another of Laman's men who then took it through the small guard's opening in the wall that led into the main part of the city. He silently crept to an inner building and opened the door. Captive Nephites lay inside, sleeping.

Laman's man put his bundle of weapons on the floor in the center of the room. He unwrapped the skin and revealed the pile of swords and knives. He then put his hand over the mouth of one of the sleeping Nephites and began whispering in his ear. The Nephite awakened with a start.

He initially began to struggle, but calmed down as Laman's man continued to whisper and pointed to the weapons on the floor. The Nephite saw the weapons at his disposal and nodded. Laman's man took his hand away and left as the Nephite began to quietly awaken the other prisoners.

This dispersal of the weaponry was repeated several times. As the flow of weapons continued, Moroni had his other men surround the city from outside. They began scaling the city walls. As they finished gathering onto the city wall's catwalk, as well as standing outside all of the entrances to the city, a red sunrise began to streak across the sky. Moroni stepped onto the catwalk at the center of the city wall.

"Surrender this city or forfeit your lives!" Moroni shouted.

He paused knowing his first shout would just awaken his foes.

"Surrender this city or forfeit your lives!" he repeated forcefully.

The Lamanites woke up suddenly and went for their weapons. As they rushed to the city square, they saw Moroni's men surrounding them on the walls above. The Nephite prisoners dashed out of their holding buildings fully armed.

"Surrender this city or forfeit your lives!" Moroni repeated for the third time.

A Lamanite warrior in the center of the square, evidently the leader, looked around and saw the hopelessness of his cause. He looked at his men, then Moroni, and then lowered his sword and tossed it to the ground, toward the clearing below Moroni's perch. He motioned to his men to do the same. They did. The Nephite prisoners cheered, as well as Moroni's army. The occupied city of Gid was retaken without a single blow. Moroni had regained his prisoners. The Title of Liberty again flew freely over the city's main gate.

Chapter 20

The Value of the Oath

———◁◆▷———

Moroni, Lehi, and other commanders sat around a wooden table. Scroll-like maps made of animal skins were laid out on the table. They were going over their strategy.

"My scouts have seen the Lamanites," Lehi began, "sending wave after wave of provisions to the city Morianton."

"They must be making that their stronghold," Moroni said. "We'll need to focus our efforts there for a while."

Moroni was interrupted by a messenger who came in suddenly, but showed respect.

"Yes," Moroni asked. "What is it?"

"I have a message from Helaman," the messenger stated.

"Helaman?!" Moroni exclaimed with interest. "Let me see it."

The messenger took the leather strap that held the customary message flask from around his shoulder and gave it to Moroni. All those in the room were anxious to hear what the message contained.

Moroni sat and opened the bamboo canister. As he read, those in the room bore solemn expressions.

The message unfolded the tale of Helaman's efforts among those Lamanites who had sworn the oath of peace and were now concerned about this long and weary war.

The message began:

> *My beloved brother, Moroni, in the Lord as well as in these tribulations; behold, I have somewhat to tell you concerning our warfare in this part of the land.*
>
> *I wish to tell you of those aging Lamanite men who swore an oath of peace in the days of Alma, my father. According to the covenant that they made, they should not take up their weapons of war against their brethren to shed blood. However, when they saw our afflictions and our tribulations in their behalf, the men were about to break their covenant and take up their weapons in our defense. But I would not allow them to do this—*

THE COUNCIL HALL was full to overflowing with Lamanite men. Each seat was occupied. The benches were packed beyond capacity. More men stood along the aisles many rows deep. The doors were open with countless bodies crammed into their frames and spilling into the area beyond. Helaman was the only Nephite present. He sat in the judge's seat out of custom, not position.

He had come to confer with these converted Lamanite brethren. He found that they were saddened at the passing of Ammon, but were coping well because of the great faith in the coming Messiah that

Ammon had helped them foster. They knew that he had gone on to his eternal reward and that one day they would follow.

Somewhat to his surprise, he found that they were very inquisitive concerning the status of the war with Ammoron. As they learned of the current struggles, a great number of them had voiced interest in joining this war waged by their ambitious and angry former brethren. This was the issue that now filled the chamber. They were eager to put an end to the abuses to both societies that were being perpetuated by Ammoron, the Nephite turned bitter traitor and self-proclaimed Lamanite king.

"No man among you understands how greatly I appreciate your willingness to serve in this way," Helaman stated to the assembled throng, "But I cannot allow you to break your sacred oath."

Shimlon, a Lamanite in his late fifties, rose from a front bench. The eyes in the room watched his approach to the judge's chair. He stood tall with an air of honor, dignity, and humility. The room grew silent awaiting his words. Helaman respectfully nodded.

"Your people, the Nephites, have treated us well," Shimlon began. "You have not just treated us as friends, but as brothers. We have grown to love and appreciate the warm bond between us. We will never be able to repay the debt we feel toward you for saving our souls by bringing us an eternal light.

"We swore the oath of peace when this light was brought into our souls by your father's companion, Ammon, many years ago. Since that time, we have learned to rejoice in the coming of the blessed Messiah. We praise his holy name and look forward to His coming. We cannot number our blessings, both spiritual and temporal, that this knowledge has brought to us.

"All this while, your people, the Nephites, have been our teachers and our protectors. You enlighten our minds with the spirit of truth, and have not hidden from our knowledge the goings on of our former people. We know that they now wage a war of hate against you. We know that their numbers are many. We know that their hatred runs deep, as deeply as it once ran in our own veins.

"We are men who have known a warrior's way. Though the years have passed, we remember the warrior's way still. Please, allow us to now repay a portion of our debt. Let us now take up arms and aid you in this grueling battle. We do not renounce the Messiah by doing this. We remember Him still. But, we also know that we are needed if your quest is to prevail. If it fails, the freedom to worship the Messiah will be lost. Surely the Lord understands that the right to worship the Messiah must transcend the need to keep our oath at this perilous time."

The room erupted with shouts of approval from the other Lamanite men who filled the seats and aisles. Even the oldest men banged their walking sticks on the stone floor. The din was heard throughout the city. Helaman looked about him at the earnestness in their faces. He did not doubt their loyalty or their sincerity. He was not disturbed at the outbreak.

To the contrary, he was moved within. He rose slowly. Upon this, the room began to silence. The warriors from days gone by had a keen interest in knowing how their new spiritual leader was going to respond to their pledge of action.

"You are a remarkable people," Helaman said with emotion. "A remarkable people indeed. I see why it is that my father and his companions grew to love you so dearly. I look into your faces and I see into the years that have now faded. I can see Ammon preaching to your King Lamoni of the promised coming of the Messiah. I see your king's love for Ammon. I see how completely your entire city was converted to the truth."

Helaman paused, swept up with the spirit of the moment. His pause was met with utter silence as the men recalled with vividness the times that he described.

"I do not doubt," Helaman continued, "that you remember the warrior's way, for you were indeed mighty warriors. I also do not doubt that you also remember the teachings of Ammon and my father. You were moved by the spirit to renounce the ways of evil and death. Your swords and shields lie buried deep in the earth as a token of your oath of peace. You, the fiercest of warriors, were touched by God's spirit of love and have from that day forward kept your oath of peace.

"It is true that we are in the midst of a terrible battle. It is true that we are in need of as many able warriors as we can possibly muster at this time. You perceive correctly that our rights and our liberties are at this time being threatened by evil and conspiring men. We need to defend ourselves, or we will lose our liberty. We need men who can fight for our liberty. But, we also need men who are true to their word, true to their God, true to themselves.

"If we cannot keep our oaths to God and our pacts within our own society, then we will have truly lost our liberties; not to these treacherous foes, but to ourselves. I cannot believe that God will let us perish for keeping our word. I cannot believe He will allow us to conquer by revoking it. I cannot with good conscience let you break your oath and take up arms. I simply can't. I believe we will find the strength we need from somewhere."

Helaman stopped speaking. His arms ceased their broad sweeps of emphasis and drifted down to his sides. His head unintentionally drooped as he searched for more words. He sensed he was on the verge of an answer, but was searching within to find out what it would be.

The men all knew that he had spoken truthfully. Their hearts and minds had been brought to a remembrance of why they swore the oath and the glories of enlightenment. They, too, sat with bowed heads, caught in a struggle between wanting to act and knowing they must use restraint.

A teenage boy had sneaked into the assembly. Silently, but steadily, he pushed his way forward. Few paid him any heed until he had worked his way through the crowd that pressed against the walls and was nearly to the front of the room. Still working his way forward, and still hidden by the crowd, he was unable to retain his silence.

"I haven't sworn the oath!" he declared with the boldness of youth. "Let me fight!"

Helaman looked up, but was unable to see the lad. "Who said that?" he queried.

The boy pushed forward. The crowd gave way. As he stepped into the scant clearing between the benches and the judges' seats, Helaman and the others saw his youthful stature.

"I did. My name is Jershon, son of Lemuel. I haven't sworn the oath," he repeated. "I was just a baby when my father swore it. Let me fight and I know that the Lord will protect me."

Before anyone could respond, the room was filled with shouts from all corners of the room. The windowsills, the doorways, and all along the walls were filled with teenage boys. Each confirmed that which the first boy had declared.

"I haven't sworn the oath. Let me fight!" they called out one after another. Then in unison, with great enthusiasm and volume, they pled, "Let us fight!"

The room remained filled with emotion. Before Helaman could reply, the boy in the clearing took another step toward him and said, "Helaman, my mother taught me that when your father and his companions asked permission to come into our land and preach the Gospel, there were many who objected. But, when their king prayed about it, the Lord said to let them go, that their lives would be preserved, and that a great good would come of their efforts. Was this not so?"

"Yes, it was so," Helaman nodded.

"We here today are a portion of that good that came of their efforts. Are we not?" Jershon continued, turning and gesturing to the multitude with his outstretched arm.

The Lamanite men sat straight and true with sincere determination in their eyes. Helaman looked over the crowd and could not help but be impressed and moved by the point that the young Lamanite made.

"Yes, you most certainly are," Helaman agreed.

"Our mothers have taught us that if we believe in the Lord and walk in His ways, He will prosper our efforts, just as He did with your father, Alma, and Ammon. Do you believe this?" Jershon asked.

"Yes, I do."

"We don't doubt that our mothers believe this. We have learned from their faith and gained our own. We also believe that the Lord will be with us. Please, let us go forward and defend our homes. Let us go forward and fight the battles our fathers cannot. We will stand and we will conquer, for the Lord will be with us!" Jershon declared with triumph in his voice.

Once again the room echoed with the shouts of those swept up with the emotion of the day. All of them wholly agreed that the boy had spoken truthfully. Helaman allowed the shouts to continue for a time. The people deserved this moment. Finally, he raised his hand for silence.

As the cheering finally ebbed he added, "Once again, I am forced to say, you are a remarkable people. Truly remarkable."

Helaman's countenance beamed. The would-be teen-warriors smiled with confidence. Their fathers' souls shined and their eyes were moist with tears of pride at their sons' display of faith and obedience.

"Yes," Helaman stated, "I believe you are correct. You have not sworn the oath of peace. And, I believe your mothers are correct. The Lord will watch over those who follow in His ways. I can think of no people more worthy of His watchfulness than those I see here today. I would be honored to lead you to battle, if you will have me for your commander."

"We will!" Jershon shouted, "To commander Helaman!" He urged his young brethren on. They all shouted their acceptance. On this day, an army, a very young army, was born.

HELAMAN WAS ON horseback. He sat tall and in full armor. Before him marched a row of teenage Lamanites in the splendor of their new uniforms. Thick leather was girded about their arms, thighs, and chests. Shiny, newly forged swords hung from their sides. Sharpened spears rose high above their heads. All except the center soldier, Jershon. He proudly bore the Title of Liberty. Following Helaman were row upon row of young warriors marching to their first battle, intent on preserving the liberty of their fathers and their Nephite brethren.

Some two thousand of these stripling warriors marched with Helaman on their way to the far off city of Judea. It proudly bore a name from the Old World, lest the people forget their roots. They went to aid Antipus who Moroni had appointed as the military leader of the people in that part of the land. Helaman knew that this area was far from Moroni and could seek reinforcements from no other source.

He also knew that the march would be a long one, for it was in the southeastern section of their land. Although the march was long, it was also uneventful. For the young warriors, it was their first venturing out from their protected homes. They were wide-eyed and intrigued with every city they passed on their way southward, crossing the majority of the entire Nephite nation. Days later, they neared their goal.

As they approached the city, the tower guard spotted the Title of Liberty. The good word spread quickly. As Helaman and his "young sons," as he often referred to them, neared the city gate, it opened from within. True to his prompting, Helaman was welcomed with unbridled enthusiasm.

"Come! Quickly!" Antipus himself was the first to usher them within the walls.

Soon, the army was within their first fortress. Antipus ordered his officers to find quarters and rations for Helaman's men. Antipus added, "Once they've had a good meal, put them to work on the wall."

"Yes, sir!" his officer responded with relief in his eyes.

OVER A PRUDENT meal, Antipus and his officers conferred with Helaman. In spite of the ever-decreasing rations, Antipus beamed at Helaman, "I can't tell you what a welcome relief your forces are!"

"They're young, but I believe they'll pull their weight," Helaman said, hoping to gain acceptance for them in spite of their inexperience at life, let alone warfare.

"Oh, that doesn't bother us! We'll take them any way we can!" Antipus said with enthusiasm. "This is as an answer to our prayers!"

"I take it you've been having a rough time," Helaman observed.

"Rough?! We're lucky to still be breathing! To be able to eat these far from bounteous rations!" Antipus replied. "These blasted Lamanites are unrelenting!" His face grimaced a moment and he added, "Uh, no offense to your men."

"None taken," Helaman reassured. "They fully understand. That's why we're here." He added, "What's your status?"

"Nearly dead on our feet!" Antipus offered. "I tell you I've lost nearly half of my men so far. And when I mean lost, I mean lost. Dead. Gone. The Lamanites here don't take prisoners, unless it's a high-ranking officer. All others are put to death either in the heat of battle or in the most appalling and tortuous means after being taken captive. We can hear their shrieks and cries until late in the night, but we can do nothing to help them." Lowering his voice and leaning toward Helaman, he added, "The men fear being taken alive more than a swift death in the field."

"I'm very sorry that we could come no sooner," Helaman replied.

"Yes, well, we can console ourselves in this point," Antipus stated, "They have died in the cause of their country and their God. But, we have to stop this, before any more cities fall."

"Which cities have fallen so far?" Helaman asked.

"Far too many," Antipus replied." The cities of Manti, Zeezrom, Cumeni, and Antiparah. And we're struggling desperately to maintain this one. We fight in the field during the day and toil through the night to refortify the city walls. They just keep pecking at us like a hungry bird and tearing us apart bit by bit. My men are nearly drained both in body and spirit. You can't imagine the afflictions we endure. But, we've decided to make our stand. We will either conquer here, in this place, or die! Your men give us new hope that perhaps we will conquer!"

"We will do all that is within our power to see that it is so,"

Helaman confirmed. "Still, I don't see how we can long withstand their advances."

"We'll simply hold them off as long as we are able," Antipus concluded.

Chapter 21

A Time to Decide

━━━━◆◆◆◆━━━━

*D*eep within Nephite territory, surrounded by occupied cities, Ammoron was housed in a temporary headquarters. He had taken up residence in the city of Manti, which his army had recently overpowered. From here, he guided his war on two fronts, the first was an assault on the nearby cities; the second was in the remote areas that Moroni now defended. His greatest successes were here in the southwest, as Antipus had attested.

Ammoron sat at a table reviewing maps and planning his next conquests. He had learned much from his fallen brother and gloried in his successes. He had awakened a beast from deep within himself that had produced a hunger for battle that he had never before realized. To him it was as if being born anew. Under his oppressive brother, commands seemed doleful and tiresome. Now, with the power of life and death over his own soldiers he felt vibrant and reveled in each new day. He longed to hear that his foes quiver at his name.

A Lamanite soldier had approached his war room and requested permission to enter.

"Come!" Ammoron commanded.

The soldier opened the door and entered. Once inside, he straightened then took two steps forward and stood at attention before Ammoron's planning table. He silently awaited his orders.

"Yes," Ammoron demanded, "What is it?"

"Sir," the soldier stated with militaristic precision, "I bring word from my spies."

"*Your* spies?!" Ammoron questioned with more than a mere hint of accusation and correction in his voice.

"Excuse me, sir," the soldier quickly corrected. "Your spies have news that I believe you should hear."

"What news is this?" Ammoron asked, again pleased with himself and the inherited hold he had on his men.

"Sir," the soldier said, "They have seen an army of Lamanites being led by a Nephite."

"An army of Lamanites?!" Ammoron questioned, "Led by a Nephite! Are you certain?"

"Yes, sir," the Lamanite added, "Quite certain. They said the Nephite was on horseback and before him a standard bearer bore the Title of Liberty. They said there was no doubt of this."

"Where are they going?" Ammoron asked, "Are they encamped nearby?"

"Not exactly, sir," the soldier replied, "They have entered the city of Judea. We believe they have joined forces with Antipus. We assume Moroni has sent them as reinforcements."

"How many are there?" Ammoron asked.

"I do not have a precise count, sir," the soldier replied. "My sources estimate that it is at least a couple thousand."

"A couple thousand?" Ammoron pondered. "That's a healthy contribution to an ailing army." He began to pace as he thought on his feet. "I had thought that we could have taken Antipus' men within a week. But, this should bring them new life. I don't think it would be wise for us to continue our assault there for now. Tell the men to maintain the cities we have taken, but withhold their attacks on Judea until further notice."

"But, sir," the soldier questioned, "We still greatly outnumber them! We could—" the soldier cut himself off, realizing with a small degree of horror that he was questioning his impassioned king.

Ammoron eyed him carefully and with a blazing glare. Still at attention, the soldier spread his legs and bowed his head. He concluded with, "Yes, sir. Right away, sir. I will go and tell the men." He turned quickly and exited the tent relieved to be able to stand on his own feet after his near fatal faux pas with his volatile commander.

ANTIPUS AND HELAMAN sat in the city's war room reviewing plans. The room contained an archive of critical maps and drawings shelved in wooden bookcases that spread from floor to ceiling and completely filled one wall. The majority of them were covered by a multi-colored cloth curtain draped in front of them. The room was lit by torches set in canisters attached to three of the four walls. No torches were within five feet of the archive wall. The center of the room had a large table with several chairs around it for planning sessions. Helaman and Antipus were the only ones in the room.

A soldier knocked on the door with the request to enter and give his report. Antipus gave him leave to enter. The soldier entered and stood at attention at the head of the planning table.

"What is your report?" Antipus asked, placing a flask and his knife on either side of a large map to keep it from curling up on the table.

"Sir, we have now finished our repairs on the west wall," the soldier stated. "With this complete, we now feel that the city is again secure. We owe much to these young Lamanites. They are a hardy people full of energy and skill," the soldier nodded to Helaman.

"Thank you," Helaman replied, "I'll pass your compliments to the men. They'll appreciate that."

"Sir," the soldier continued, "The men are now rested and eager for battle. We feel we are prepared to take on these other Lamanites." He was careful to distinguish between Helaman's soldiers and Ammoron's, lest any insult be given unintentionally.

"That is simply excellent news," Antipus replied, "I hoped as much. We've had several weeks now without an assault from Ammoron." He turned to Helaman, "I guess word spread quickly about your reinforcements. Though I'm surprised at the result."

"It surprises me as well," Helaman replied. "These are good, young men, but I must confess that had they attacked the day we arrived, I don't know that we could have held them off. I count Ammoron's reluctance as another blessing from the Lord."

"Yes," Antipus said, "I agree, but we can't just sit here waiting for them to finally attack. I would have thought they would have tried to attack other cities, but our spies have yet to find them on the offensive. They seem content with the cities they have. If we could catch them on a march, we could take them, but so far they seem to be staying put."

"Somehow," Helaman added, "We need to draw them out so we can take them on outside of their strongholds."

HELAMAN WAS ROUSED from his sleep by a sound he had not heard in many, many days. It was the sound of Nephites cheering. He left his bed, donned his garb and made his way to the city square. All the while, the cheering had continued. Nephite soldiers hustled to the city wall and up to the catwalk to see what the excitement was about.

Helaman joined them. As he peered down from the city wall, he saw soldiers bearing provisions. The city gate was opened and the soldiers were welcomed into the city. They bore fruits, vegetables, and wild game killed for meat. Their sacks bulged with the foods. Their leader stepped forward.

"These are sent from the land of Ammon," he announced. "Presents from the fathers of the young Lamanite lads who have come to aid the Nephites! I'm told that there will be more sent along at regular intervals! So long as their crops and game hold out, we should no longer want for food!"

Again, the cheers rose in a crescendo of enthusiasm and echoed through the hills. Ammoron's spies, hidden nearby, took note and sent word to their master. That night the Nephite army enjoyed a splendid feast. Once again, Helaman's band had earned the gratitude of Antipus and his army.

ONLY TWO MORE days passed when the city again erupted with more good news. Reinforcements from Zarahemla had been spotted less than a day's journey away. Two thousand men marched bearing provisions for Antipus and his men, but also for their wives and children who shared in the protection of the high city walls.

Ammoron's spies again took note of the comings and goings in Judea. They were less than pleased and quite certain that their master would agree that this did not bode well for their ill-intentioned plans of siege. They hurried to Manti to meet with their king and deliver their news.

The king's guards had learned to ask no questions when the dark, shrouded scouts returned to the city. They simply opened the gates and allowed the two to march without an escort directly to the king's chamber. They knocked a coded knock and entered without waiting for an invitation. The king knew which visitors the signal represented. Ammoron sat with his back to the door, hunched over a table full of maps and scrolls bearing various plans and writings.

"Great king," the first spy reported, "We bear more news."

"So soon?" Ammoron responded, without turning around. "What news could this possibly be?"

"Antipus has received more provisions. And more troops," the second spy stated.

"More troops?" Ammoron said with a bit of surprise. "How many dozen?"

"We did not count them by the dozens, great king," the first spy offered. "We numbered them by the hundreds."

"Thousands, actually," the second spy corrected. "Approximately two thousand."

At this, Ammoron's temper reached a pique. He still sat with his back to the spies as he slammed his writing utensil firmly onto the tabletop with his right palm. His drinking flask jumped. The utensil snapped in two. His spies did not flinch.

"Thank you," Ammoron responded in a regained, level tone, still sitting with his back to the men. "Bring me word of any more such developments. Inform Zerom that I'd like to have a word with him and his officers, before you return to your duties."

"Yes, your majesty," the spies responded in unison. They turned and left while Ammoron still sat with his back to the door.

ANTIPUS AND HIS officers met in the war room with Helaman. They continued to discuss their next steps.

"The Lamanites continue to try to stop the shipments," an officer reported, "But, the provisions are making it through nonetheless. I'll add it's becoming more and more risky, however."

"Yes," another agreed, "I think they're getting edgy. They see these provisions and reinforcements coming and they know we can last even longer with each arrival."

"We should pit their uneasiness against them," Antipus surmised.

"How so?" Helaman asked.

"Do you remember our earlier discussion where you said we needed to draw them out?" Antipus asked.

"Yes," Helaman answered.

"I think I know how we can accomplish it now," Antipus said. "You and your young soldiers need to go on a march—"

THE SHADOWS OF night were still fading and the dew still collecting as Helaman and his young warriors set out on their march. Their arms were laden with bundles. Soon, word from Ammoron's spies would reach their master that now Antipus was attempting to share his surplus provisions with a neighboring city near the sea. Helaman, like his men, was on foot.

Helaman ensured that their march took them in a path near the city of Antiparah. News of their passage had leaked from the spies' report to other guards. Word spread quickly. Soon, the entire city was alerted to the foolhardy Nephites who thought they could sneak past the stronghold of the Lamanites.

Giddoni, the commander Ammoron had personally chosen to guard this captured city, was among those who stood on the city wall vainly listening for any distant sounds that would confirm this blatant show of defiance, which was hidden from sight by the dense jungle. He knew they were out there, and he simply would not stand for this. He knew he had to quell this show of resistance quickly or risk the wrath of his supreme commander.

Ammoron had spoken to him personally of these traitorous Lamanites with nothing but ill contempt. Ammoron had made it clear that he wanted to stop this band of would-be soldiers particularly because of their Lamanite heritage. He was, after all, king of the Lamanites. In his mind, that included *all* Lamanites.

From high atop the city wall, Giddoni turned and faced the city square. He shouted the command to his officers, "Round up all your men! We'll put a stop to this little escapade here and now. Keep the night guards on duty. I want my best soldiers to be ready to leave immediately! Sound the battle horn!"

A tower guard gave three, quick blasts into the horn, followed by two, long, slow ones. The sequence was repeated three times. Before the signal was complete, Giddoni's army had assembled in the square. Giddoni stood on the wall and addressed his men and officers.

"You men are called upon to put down a treasonous act of defiance!" he declared. "Word has reached us that an army of your brethren have turned traitors and marches nearby. You men are to catch this army and make a proper example of them!"

His meaning was clear. The men cheered with anticipation. The city gate opened and Giddoni and his men flooded outward after their prey. The weary night guards received temporary energy as they watched row upon row of the strongest Lamanite army in the region hit the trail, eager to do battle.

The departure of Giddoni's army was observed by more eyes than just those of his remaining guards. This city backed up against the dense jungle growth with only a few dozen yards of clearance. On the far side of the city, Antipus and his men awaited word from their scouts. A shrill birdcall broke through the morning air. Antipus' scouts announced the anticipated departure.

Antipus signaled his officers. It had been their design to ensure that the Lamanites took the bait. Now they intended to catch the Lamanites from behind. If all went well, they would be able to come off the conqueror. The trick would be allowing the Lamanites to gain enough distance from Antiparah so that no more reinforcements would be able to aid them. If they attacked too soon, then other Lamanites could sneak up on them from behind and cause the same damage they intended to do to their unsuspecting target.

HELAMAN AND HIS young band continued onward, northward, farther and farther away from Antiparah. Two young scouts, who had lingered behind, dashed up to him. Helaman ordered his troops to halt while he listened to their report.

"Helaman," the first reported, "It's just as you had hoped. Giddoni and his men have fled the city in search of us. It appears to be their entire army!"

"They're making good time," the second added, "We'll need to be quick if we want to stay ahead of them."

"Very well," Helaman responded, "Good work, my sons." He stood and raised his arm, "Onward!"

The army was again on the move. Northward.

"GIDDONI!" A VOICE shouted, "Giddoni! We've spotted more Nephites!"

Giddoni signaled his army to halt. He turned to the voice, "What is this?! What do you mean more Nephites? Where?"

The messenger caught up to where Giddoni waited. He caught his breath a moment, standing in place panting and sweating, attempting to be at attention. Giddoni asked, "Are you going to answer my questions or stand there and breathe on me?"

The messenger raised a hand slightly to calm his commander and acknowledge that he had more to say. Finally, he blurted out between great gasps for air, "More Nephites—Behind us—We believe it's Antipus."

"Antipus?!" Giddoni exclaimed. "It appears we've been had. We better move quickly, if Antipus catches us while those illegitimate Lamanites are still ahead of us, we'll be surrounded. We'll stand a much better chance if we can finish them off before we engage Antipus. Forward!"

"ANTIPUS!" THE ADVANCE guard shouted. "Antipus!"

Antipus hurried and met the guard who was charging back to rejoin the army. "Antipus! We've been spotted! Giddoni and his men are now tailing Helaman with vigor! We'll need to hurry if we're to catch up with them!"

"Very well. It appears we were wise to send you on ahead," Antipus turned and ordered his men, "Make haste! Helaman's life depends on us!"

They hurried onward; trying to make up for the time lost watching the city to ensure their prey took the bait. Their journey lasted until nightfall, when all armies managed to take a much-needed rest.

THE FOLLOWING DAY, the chase continued. Giddoni and his army remained on the heels of Helaman and his men. Helaman chose to lead his men through the wilderness in hopes that his youthful troops could negotiate the rough, jungle terrain more nimbly than the older Lamanites. Although he was correct, it slowed his progress nevertheless. Worse, Giddoni benefitted from the path they cut. Helaman was unable to keep far out of reach of his pursuers.

Antipus and his men continued to race at double speed hoping to catch Giddoni, before Giddoni caught up with Helaman. On the morning of the third day, the race was nearly over. Helaman's army awakened to find Giddoni's army nearly upon them. The alarm went off throughout the camp and soon Helaman and his men were again on the run. Their first concern was to get a lead.

To their credit, Helaman's army moved quickly and again outdistanced Giddoni's men. They continued the race, knowing that they could not possibly prevail against Giddoni's superior forces. It was critical that they fight only with Antipus' support.

It was not long before Helaman's rearguard took note of something peculiar. The guard raised and waved his warning banner to attract the attention of the others. Soon the army stopped. Helaman made his way to the back and approached the rearguard.

"Limna," Helaman asked, "What is it?"

"I'm not sure," Limna replied, "I can't make out any signs of Giddoni's pursuit."

"Well," Helaman pointed out, "We've been trying to outrun them."

"Yes," Limna agreed, "I know, sir. But, it doesn't seem right. Before, I've been able to make out traces of sound. But, now there's nothing. It's like they're no longer back there. It's just not the same."

"No longer back there?" Helaman pondered, "I wonder if Antipus has finally caught up with them. If so, he'll need our support. But, if this is a trick, they could be luring us back—" Helaman thought a moment then shouted to his men, "Call the officers! I want to meet with my officers! Have them report here, now!"

The officers assembled quickly. Helaman paced before his men, waiting for the last officer to report. His brow bore a serious furrow. When the last of them reported, he stopped and faced his men. He looked into their teenage eyes. He did not see fear. To his relief, he did not see naïveté either. He saw looks of determination, honesty, and courage.

"My sons," he began, "We have a decision to make. This is perhaps the most important decision any of you have had to make until now. Giddoni and his men have halted in their pursuit of us. We don't know if this is because Antipus has overtaken them, or if they are laying in wait to catch us in their snare. If this is a trap, they can surely overcome us with their great numbers. But, if this is not a trap, and Antipus has overtaken them, I fear for Antipus and his men. They have had to run great speeds over long distances to catch up. I fear that this will have tired their men and give Giddoni's army the edge."

"So," Helaman concluded, "What do you say, my sons, will you go against them to battle?"

Helaman was not given time to await an answer. The tallest of the youthful leaders immediately stepped forward. It was Jershon, the lad who had stood before his people and declared their readiness to defend their liberty. The other young men nodded approvingly, anticipating his words.

256

"Father," he said symbolically, "Behold our God is with us, and He will not suffer that we should fall. Let us go forward. We would not slay our brethren if they would let us alone and live in peace, but they will not. They seek to take our cities, our homes, our liberty and our lives. Let us go after them, lest they overpower the army of Antipus."

The other officers cheered, "Forward!" "To battle!" "For liberty!"

The standard bearer stepped forward waving the Title of Liberty. Soon, the entire army was cheering and waving their swords and spears in the air. Jungle animals scurried about startled by the din. The answer was clear. Helaman smiled and nodded his head incredulously at the faith of the young men.

He turned toward the jungle path they had just cut. He raised his sword and pointed it toward the way to battle and shouted, "Forward!"

Chapter 22

Tried in the Heat of Battle

*H*elaman and his band of two thousand stalwart youth rushed back through the jungle toward those who had pursued them. They had never fought, nor had they even seen battle, yet they were about to engage one of the Lamanites' strongest forces. Inexperienced as they were, they had trust and faith in God. It was a faith taught to them by their mothers. They had been taught that if they remained true, they would be preserved. With faith in their hearts and weapons in their hands, they charged toward battle wholly unafraid.

Their course was straight and speedy. They leaped over logs, branches, and vines cut down short moments before as they passed in the other direction. Each warrior kept a constant pace as he ran. Heads sank into their shoulders, hunched in an effort to maintain balance as they ran and leaped over the obstacles at a surprising pace. The entire army was one long line of racing soldiers, several men wide.

Though they were individuals, they ran in unison. One entire row simultaneously leaped over logs or holes, followed by succeeding rows maintaining the pace. The army as a whole gained a rhythm to their charge as if they were all a part of a singular chain, each man representing an integral piece in this war machine on feet. They snaked their way over the terrain like a mighty python bearing down and ready to strike at first sight of its unsuspecting prey.

Their cheers had stopped, not out of lack of enthusiasm, but from concentration on their goal. All eyes and minds were focused forward, anxious for the moment when they could reach their target. The farther they ran, the more anxious they became. Adrenaline coursed through their veins in anticipation. Only the sounds of their running feet, the snapping twigs and the rustle of swords against cloth could be heard. Nearly imperceptible at first, another sound was introduced.

It emanated not from the charging warriors, but from ahead. It grew louder and more distinct. Soon, each of them could clearly hear the sounds of metal clicking against metal. They heard the war cries of the defiant and the woeful groans of the vanquished and dying. The sounds filled the jungle, filled the pathway, filled their ears. It was the prelude to the harsh reality they so enthusiastically charged toward.

The sounds did not diminish, nor did they deter the intensity of their determination. To the contrary, they heightened their desire to conquer. They knew not what to picture, having never fought, but they gained a vision as they charged, of their ruthless enemies cutting down weary men who had risked all to catch and aid their youthful comrades in arms.

Suddenly, the jungle parted and Helaman's army lunged into an expansive clearing filled with warring men. Antipus and his men had indeed engaged Giddoni. As feared, Antipus and his men, weary because of their long march in so short a space of time, were about to fall into the hands of the Lamanites. Antipus himself lay lifeless on the battlefield, fallen by the sword. Many of his leaders had suffered the same fate. The army was crumbling under the crush of the ruthless Lamanites.

As the stripling warriors engaged their foes, the Lamanites were taken off guard. Their entire attention had been focused on the rout taking place on the far side of the clearing. Antipus' well-intentioned rescue party managed to do damage to the Lamanite horde, but was unfortunately falling back. The Lamanites took courage and were in the midst of pursuing them just as Helaman and his army came upon them from the rear.

Helaman's young soldiers fought with honor and vigor. They unleashed their righteous indignation at their foes. Their swords swung swiftly and forcefully. They took the Lamanites wholly unaware. The Lamanites had no anticipation that this youthful troupe that they had pursued had such strength and determination. Many a surprised and impressed Lamanite soon lay lifeless on the battlefield ground.

The stripling warriors continued to fight in hand-to-hand combat against a people who should have been their brothers if only they had not turned to evil ways and accepted a traitorous king as their leader. Recognition of the fighting in the rear soon reached the front ranks. The Lamanite army gave up on its frontal assault on the failing and fleeing army of Antipus. As one, the whole army of Giddoni turned and focused on Helaman's army.

The decision to turn had become a matter of survival for the Lamanites, and because of their turn, the same could be said of Helaman's army. The young men were outnumbered, but did not give in, give ground, or give up. They continued to fight as if with the strength of angels. There was no fear in their eyes. Blow after blow by the Lamanites was fended and counter blows were returned with increased force. The Lamanites continued to drop a dozen at a time as two thousand spirited soldiers fought to preserve their lives, their homes, their religion, their freedom, and their way of life. Their fathers could not fight, so they fought in their behalf. Their success was beyond anticipation.

The fleeing people of Antipus, who had lost all hope of seeing another day, took note that their pursuers had withdrawn. Looking back, they saw that the army of Giddoni had turned to take on the young warriors they themselves had originally planned to protect. They saw the heroics of Helaman's men and took courage. Still ignored by their enemy, they gathered their ranks together and charged the Lamanites, giving a fierce, ear-piercing battle cry that was even heard above the din of the clashing swords and the groans of the wounded and dying.

The stripling warriors heard the cry and looked up from their hand-to-hand skirmishes just long enough to see Antipus' army rejoining the fray. Jershon cried out, "Liberty! Liberty! Liberty!"

Several of his fellow soldiers took up the cry. Antipus' men also joined in. The cry became a rhythmic chant. They slung their swords in unison to the rhythm. Soon, the Lamanites found themselves wholly surrounded by an army that now fought as one, chanting and swinging and gathering courage and strength with each swing and each cry of "Liberty!"

The awesome power and unity of their foe was too much for them. Giddoni, the Lamanite officer in the center of the field cried out, "Peace! Peace! We will have peace!" and waved his sword high above the horde.

Helaman saw and heard the cry of submission. He raised his sword as the token to cease the battle. Almost immediately, all of the men disengaged and the warring parties took steps back from each other. The Lamanite men threw down their weapons of war and knelt.

Youthful hands retrieved the sweaty, instruments of death. This particular Lamanite army was defeated and captured. This, one of the strongest of the Lamanite armies, who had only a few days previously thought they could teach the Nephites a lesson, now found itself prisoners of war, at the mercy of men half their age.

The Lamanite arms were piled up near Helaman. Helaman called out for the Lamanite commander to step forward. He worked his way to the Nephite leader, who asked, "Do you now give up this battle this day?"

Giddoni responded to Helaman, "Yes, I don't know where you found these demons from Hell, but we see that we're no match for them. We will not fight a war we cannot win. We give up our arms to you."

"Do you also swear the oath of peace?" Helaman asked.

"We do not!" Giddoni retorted. "We give up this day, but we will not swear the oath of peace. Do with us what you will, but when we have our wits and our weapons back, and we see that you no longer have these demons at your command, we will fight again, and we will prevail!"

"Very well," Helaman replied. "Breathe out whatsoever threatenings you will. But know this. This day you have become our prisoners. You are defeated, and you are in our power."

Helaman called to the men of Antipus. "Is there a leader among you who still breathes?"

From across the field, a tall Nephite turned and raised his sword. "I am here."

"Come!" Helaman ordered, "Gather your men and take charge. We must secure these prisoners!"

As the Nephites surrounded the weaponless prisoners, Helaman turned to his own men. "Jershon, come here!"

Jershon straightened and walked with pride to his fatherly leader. When he stood within a few paces, he paused awaiting his orders. Helaman beckoned with his hand for him to come closer. Jershon came to within a couple paces of Helaman. Helaman beckoned him even nearer and let Jershon realize that he wished to tell him something in private, out of earshot of their captives.

"Jershon," Helaman said with his hand on Jershon's shoulder, pulling him even closer, "You and your brothers have fought boldly and bravely today!"

"Thank you, father," Jershon responded with gratitude. "We believe we have proven our mothers right. If we are faithful, they said, God would help us prevail."

"Yes," Helaman smiled. "And you have been faithful! I am concerned to know of the safety of your brothers. I want to know how many have fallen or need assistance."

Jershon's demeanor darkened at the realities of combat. He nodded with understanding.

"Call the officers," Helaman continued, "without letting the Lamanites overhear, have them make an accounting of their men. Bring me word of how many have fallen."

"Understood," Jershon responded and quickly dashed off.

Jershon went to each officer, who in turn made a headcount of his men. During this, Helaman spoke again with the Nephite officer. "We have no place for these prisoners. Take command of them. Take as many of your men as you feel you need to safely control their march to the land of Zarahemla. Surely, they will have a holding place for them there. The remainder of your men can join us as we return to the city of Judea."

The Nephite nodded obediently and did as Helaman commanded. As they completed selecting men to guard the prisoners, Jershon returned to Helaman. He was smiling broadly.

"Helaman," he said, "Not one soul has been lost! We all still stand and breathe!"

"God be praised!" Helaman said, grabbing Jershon's shoulder and shaking it vigorously with a smile that could not be hidden. "God be praised!" After a pause, he added, "Jershon, gather your men. It's time to return to Judea!"

"Yes, sir!" Jershon obeyed.

THE CITY OF Judea had opened its doors to some unlikely heroes. Helaman and his young army returned victorious. It was the first solid victory the people of this war-ravaged area had been able to celebrate in many, many days. The mood distinctly shifted to a more positive realm.

On the heels of this victory, the Nephites awakened early one morning to a signal from a tower guard. Helaman was among the first officers to climb the wall and join the guard.

"What is it?" he asked the guard.

"I saw someone," the guard replied.

"Where?" Helaman asked.

"Down by the main road," the guard said. "Straight in that direction," the guard pointed a muscular arm in the direction of the road that led to the main gate. Most of the road was obscured by the thick morning fog that rolled in from the humid jungle and often lingered until the warm sun burned it away. It did not cover the entire road, as portions here and there were vaguely visible.

"I'm afraid I don't see anyone," Helaman added.

"Keep watching. You'll see him," the guard replied. "I'm certain it wasn't a trick of the eyes."

Helaman continued to watch. All he saw was the swirling fog being torn and twirled by the gentle jungle breeze. Then as if stepping from within his imagination he caught the vague glimpse of a shape moving through the fog. Just as suddenly, it was gone again. It never managed to become distinct, just the hint of a shape, without solid color or form moving within the vaporous blanket.

"Did you see him that time?" the guard asked.

"I saw something," Helaman conceded. "But, I wasn't able to make it out."

"I'm certain it's a man," the guard concluded. "And I don't like it. It isn't normal."

"I'll agree to that," Helaman responded, "But, then, what *is* normal these days?"

They continued to watch. The shape came into existence and faded again, but was as difficult to track as sighting whales between the waves of the sea.

"There's definitely someone there, alright," Helaman said. "The question is who. And why. This should prove interesting."

The shape appeared again with distinctness when it was within a few dozen yards of the city gate. The fog shifted and whirled away revealing him with clarity.

"It's a Lamanite!" the guard shouted. "I knew it! It's a Lamanite!"

"Hardly enough to pose much of a threat," Helaman calmed his excited brother in arms, "I don't see any weapons. Most likely he's a messenger."

"I knew there was someone out there," the guard repeated.

"Yes, you did," Helaman comforted the weary man who had spent the better part of the night peering into the blackness trying to diligently foresee any signs of danger. Helaman knew that this vigil was repeated night after night, and that the man's efforts were now rewarded with finally seeing something more than a wild cat or swinging set of monkeys scampering between the trees. He deserved the acknowledgment.

"I better get down to the gate," Helaman continued. "I want to meet this visitor. Good work, brother."

"Thank you, sir," the guard replied, "Just doing my duty."

The guard looked out over the wall again with an air of pride at a job well done. The Lamanite had stopped within half a dozen feet of the gate and stood wordlessly waiting. He knew that by now he had been spotted and it was only a matter of time before he could perform his errand.

Helaman climbed down and approached the gate. He instructed the gate guard to open the city gate. The guard dutifully responded and swung the gate wide open. There, Helaman saw the Lamanite standing, facing him. He stood tall and proud with the majesty inherent to the mighty Lamanite people. Helaman saw a message flask secured to the man's shoulder, confirming his suspicion.

"Won't you please come inside?" Helaman beckoned.

The messenger gave a slight nod and without speaking, stepped forward and entered the Nephite city. Once within its walls, the city gate was closed and secured. The Lamanite was now soundly within his enemy's fortress. He followed Helaman who led him to the building that housed their council chamber. Helaman led the messenger directly into the war room. The other officers, including Jershon, were already assembled and waiting. They rose as Helaman entered.

"Be seated," Helaman commanded. "It seems we have a message

to ponder." He turned to the messenger, "May we have it now?" He held out his hand.

The messenger quickly removed the strap holding the message flask from around his shoulder. "This was written by the hand of king Ammoron," he declared and held the flask out to Helaman. Helaman reached for the flask and took it.

"Thank you," he responded. "Please wait outside. Our guards will make you comfortable and find you some nourishment after your morning's journey." Helaman had learned from his friend and mentor, Moroni how to treat an enemy courier.

The messenger gave a slight nod of understanding, but his eyes belied his confusion at the polite treatment. In spite of this, he turned and followed the guard out of the room. Helaman withheld a knowing smile and turned back to the business at hand.

"Well, now," he stated. "Let's see what Ammoron wishes us to know."

Helaman untied the leather band from one end of the flask and removed the leather end cap. He turned the flask upside down and emptied its contents into his hand. The rolled paper tumbled out. He untied the string that held it bound and it began to uncurl in his hand. Using both hands, he unrolled it completely and read his mortal enemy's message:

> *Behold, I am Ammoron, king of the Lamanites. I address this to Helaman whom my men know is now involved in this work of destruction that you wage against me and my people whom you have wronged. You have now taken many of my noble men captive. I would that you should return them. I know that you will not do this without a price being paid for them. They are a good people whom I esteem as great.*

Therefore, I will make for you this offer. If you will deliver up those prisoners of war whom you have taken, I will deliver up the city of Antiparah to you. This is a grand price that I am willing to pay for a people whom I love. I await your word. I am Ammoron, king of the Lamanites, and I make an end to my epistle.

Upon completion of the reading, Jershon was beside himself with fury. "He lies! He said that we're waging a war against them! We're only defending ourselves! He's the one waging the war!" Jershon was nearly shaking with anger.

"Yes, I know," Helaman turned to Jershon and replied soothingly, "I've seen such notes before. You mustn't let them rile you. He's trying to pit your emotions against you to force you into making a rash decision and a tactical mistake. We won't be drawn in."

Helaman shifted in his seat, looking back at the message from the traitorous king. He rubbed his chin, pondering. He put the parchment down on the table and turned to the others.

"Let's see about crafting a suitable reply. Hand me the writing utensils," he stated.

One of the officers slid the implements to Helaman. Helaman put the charcoal pencil to work on a clean sheet of parchment. The other officers watched approvingly as they read his words. After a time of writing, Helaman sat up and reread the message to the others aloud.

The epistle read:

I am Helaman, a leader of the people of Nephi, whom you have chosen to inflict with the many atrocities of war. I have received your epistle and have considered it carefully. You have asked that we deliver up to you our many Lamanite prisoners of war in exchange for the city of Antiparah. We believe that if we should do such a thing, we should consider ourselves as unwise. We believe that we have depleted your men in this great city so sufficiently that we could take the city without too great effort.

This is a belief for which we shall soon demonstrate its validity. We are interested in an exchange of prisoners, however. We are as willing to see our own men returned to us as you are to receive yours back into your fold. If you will deliver up a Nephite for each Lamanite we return, we will exchange prisoners with you. Otherwise, we will thank you to put an end to this senseless war so that we may all return to our homes in peace and the worship of our God in a manner fitting His children. I am Helaman and I close my epistle to Ammoron.

"I believe even Moroni would agree that this is a suitable reply," Helaman said confidently. "Call in the messenger and let's have him complete his delivery."

MANY DAYS PASSED. With each day, Helaman's initial suspicion deepened into a searing conviction that Ammoron would pay no heed to his message. His scouts began returning word of people leaving the city of Antiparah in the night, with their goods. They suspected that these citizens were fleeing to neighboring cities out of fear from Helaman's implied threat.

Finally, the Lamanite messenger was again spotted on the road to Judea. The city gate was again opened and the messenger was taken into the war room to meet with Helaman and his officers. He delivered the message flask and was taken out to await a reply.

Helaman unrolled the message and read:

> *I am Ammoron I return your words to you. I am not pleased, nor amused by your threatenings. Our army is sufficient to withstand your paltry efforts. We will not exchange prisoners with men such as you who will not accept my magnanimous offer. I close my epistle to Helaman.*

Helaman tipped the flask again and noted it was not empty. He tapped the open end on the table. A clump of torn paper tumbled out. He picked it up and smoothed out a couple of the crumpled pieces. He recognized it as his previous message.

"It appears Ammoron is sincere," Helaman commented calmly. "Very well. It's time he learns to believe. Prepare your men. We're taking Antiparah back!"

The men cheered their leader. The excitement and enthusiasm in their eyes was palpable. They called for the guards to bring the Lamanite messenger back into the room.

He returned and eyed his enemies with a stern expression, but was unable to wholly mask the confusion in his eyes. Helaman handed him the message flask. The messenger noted that it had been left open. He also noted that it remained empty. He looked to Helaman.

"Do you have a reply for king Ammoron?" the messenger asked, puzzled.

"Yes, I do," Helaman replied.

"Then may I have it?" the messenger asked.

"Oh, Ammoron will receive it soon enough," Helaman said. "And we'll deliver it personally," he smiled. "You are more than welcome to let him know that."

Helaman motioned to the guard to escort their visitor out of the room and out of the city. The guard obeyed as the messenger continued to question, but ultimately, when he found himself standing outside the closed city gate, he had to accept the minimal answer that Helaman had offered him. He returned to Ammoron with nothing more than confused speculation.

Upon receiving his report, however, Ammoron was not confused, nor was he pleased. He was even less pleased when word reached him a few days later that not only had his people fled Antiparah in droves, but Helaman's men marched in and declared it theirs without so much as a skirmish.

Chapter 23

Maintaining the Advantage

The Nephites traditionally reckoned their time by accounting for the number of years that had passed since a significant event. The most recent significant event in their civilization's history, at this point in time, was the shift from being ruled by a single king, to being ruled by an organization of judges. The Nephites referred to this change in government simply as the "reign of judges."

In the beginning of the twenty-ninth year of the reign of judges, Helaman's army received a bounteous supply of provisions and reinforcements from the land of Zarahemla and other Nephite-controlled lands in the near vicinity. These reinforcements numbered some six thousand soldiers.

In addition to these men and provisions, sixty more strong sons of the Ammonite men whose fathers had sworn the oath of peace arrived in Judea. They brought with them more provisions and, more importantly, word from home to many young men who were away on their first solo excursions from their families. The news and encouragement they brought greatly bolstered the young soldiers' morale.

The provisions and reinforcements gave so much added confidence to Helaman and the other officers that they decided that they should now wage an offensive against another of Ammoron's occupied cities. After only a brief debate, the officers unanimously chose the city of Cumeni. It was the nearest to Antiparah and, logistically, it was the most obvious choice.

"As I see it," Helaman pointed out, "We have two strategic options. On the one hand, we can attempt to combat them man to man by either charging in, or luring them out. Or," he added with an emphasis that allowed all of those present to realize that he was about to reveal his true recommendation, "We can try something a bit more subtle, which I believe will give us the same result in the end, while sparing our own men from harm."

"This sounds intriguing," one of his officers replied. "What do you have in mind?"

"We know that Cumeni, like most cities, is not self-sustained," Helaman said.

"Yes, I agree," the officer acknowledged.

"Just as we depend on supplies sent to us from other cities, Cumeni depends on shipments as well." Helaman continued, "Our scouts have confirmed that supplies arrive on a fairly regular basis, typically under the cover and protection of night."

"And—" the officer coaxed, not quite certain he followed the full line of reasoning.

"And," Helaman finished, "If we lay siege to the city and intercept these shipments, Cumeni would eventually be in great need. I believe we could more easily take them."

The officers looked around the room. The plan appeared sound enough.

"I'll add this," Helaman said, "We've just recently coaxed them out of one city to their great loss. I don't believe we'll have much luck trying that again any time soon. Also, if we wage a direct assault on their city, with their great walls and guards, I fear we would lose a tremendous number of men if and when we succeeded. I believe this siege will cost the least number of lives, on both sides of this war."

"Helaman's points are good," Jershon, the youthful officer concluded, "I say we put them into action. I volunteer my men to stage the siege."

"Are there any opposed?" Helaman asked.

He looked around the room. No one spoke negatively. To the contrary their eyes and expressions implied they were in complete consent.

"It's done then. We begin the siege tonight, under the cover of darkness. When the Lamanites awaken, we'll be right there keeping them company," Helaman concluded.

"STOP! PUT OUT your torches!" Jershon commanded in a hushed voice, "Pass the word. All torches are to be put out! We're nearing Cumeni!"

The army obeyed. Torches were quickly snuffed out on the dirt path. For a moment, all eyes were blind and the march was forced to come to a complete halt. Some form of large bird flew across the path overhead. None of them could see it as it made its way from one set of trees to another. They could only hear its feathers beat and stir the warm, jungle air. The timing of its action at the moment of lost light, lent an eerie aura to their situation.

Bit by bit, obscure shapes were becoming visible as their eyes began to adjust to the darkness. Within only a few short moments, the shapes were becoming discernable, most notable were the clouds high overhead, with the moon peering out from between openings. The tall jungle trees that encroached closely on both sides of the path were the next shapes to take on recognizable form. Gradually, the soldiers were able to see the moonlight shining on the arms, breastplates, and helmets of their fellow comrades. The path slowly became visible again.

"All right, it's time to move on!" Jershon again commanded, keeping his voice low. "Be sure to keep silent."

The army moved again, making its way down the road that led to their enemy's lair. Those soldiers, whose sight had not yet fully adjusted to the darkness, followed closely behind or beside fellows who appeared more capable of discernment. It was not long, however, until all of them had regained their night vision. Their pace quickened.

The silent army wound its way around the last bend and again halted.

"There it is, the city of Cumeni!" Jershon exclaimed in a hoarse whisper.

Jershon signaled for his officers to come forward. The youthful army began to bunch up as the soldiers pushed closer to catch a glimpse of their target, but stayed behind the officers. Jershon gave the orders.

"Let's go over this again so everyone is clear. We want to totally surround the city, and keep our best guards nearest all entrances. Our point is to be able to stop and capture any man attempting to bring supplies to the city. We don't know where these will come from, so we have to be on our guard at all times and in all directions.

"We also don't want to become easy targets for their bowmen.

Keep a fair distance. Also, remember that your first task will be to dig an embankment to protect yourselves from their arrows, rocks, or anything else they may decide to fling at us," Jershon explained.

"We understand," Omner replied. "Let's get in position."

"Good," Jershon said, "But, does everyone remember where that is?"

Jershon looked at his young officers. All of their heads were vigorously nodding affirmatively.

"Does anyone *not* know where their position is?" Jershon asked.

None of them admitted to this. Jershon scanned their faces for confirmation.

"Jershon, we've been through all this," Omner, Jershon's lifelong friend and junior officer stated. "We appreciate your diligence, but we're losing time in building our embankments. We need to get moving."

"I know, I know," Jershon said. "I just don't want anyone to get hurt for lack of understanding the plan. Move your men into position. And, keep them quiet!"

An hour later, the people and soldiers within the walls of the city of Cumeni continued to sleep. They were unaware that they were now completely surrounded by a very determined, very patient, very obedient and very protected enemy force. Each platoon had dug a trench long enough and wide enough to house its troops.

The dirt from the trenches had been pushed into a horizontal, bulging, long pile between the trench and the city wall. The dirt was propped up and supported by logs, branches, and thick, wide leaves and ferns scavenged from the surrounding jungle and tightly bound together by ropes and vines. It offered substantial protection from whatever projectiles the city guards may have hoped to send their way.

The youthful soldiers slept content and safe, but with their swords by their sides in case of sudden attack. Guards at either end of each trench kept an alert watch, and were within visual range and earshot of the guard in the neighboring trench.

These trenches continued around the city from one end to the other. It was estimated that an order could be voiced and passed on from one trench to the next and reach its way back to the originating trench in less than two minutes. The siege had begun.

MORNING BROUGHT THE warmth of the sun, the familiar calls of birds, and the chattering of the rainforest animals. The people of Cumeni, and even the soldiers protecting the city, had come to expect, appreciate, and eventually ignore these commonalities. With the dawning of the rays on this particular day, however, the tower guards were the first to note something highly uncommon. All about them, they saw a strangeness in the earth.

From their vantage points inside the city, all they saw were the protective mounds that stretched and arched around the city. Their sandy, dirt heaps were nearly invisible in the early morning light. But then first one, then another, was noted until it was discovered that they continued around the city's full circumference. The tower guards saw no people, however, and began to speculate and discuss what this phenomenon might mean. One, bright guard ignored the discussions and simply sounded the alarm.

The horn still vibrated against his lips as the commanding officer charged up to the catwalk and stood by his side. In response to the officer's question, the guard simply pointed to the outer area.

"What nature of evil is this?" the officer, Himner, asked rhetorically.

"I know not, sir. They became visible with the rising of the sun," the guard offered.

"You saw nothing in the night?" Himner asked pointedly. The guard shook his head.

"You heard nothing?" The guard again shook his head.

"You were awake, were you not?" Himner demanded.

"Sir! Yes, sir! I was! And, all of the other tower guards! We were all awake and alert throughout the entire shift!" the guard insisted with alarm.

Himner looked out again at the embankments. "Well, then, what are these? What's the point?—"

He cut himself off. For the first time, he saw some form of movement. At first he was uncertain, as the distance was fairly substantial. Then he distinctly saw a man walking behind the embankment. The man stepped keenly into view. The figure turned and faced the city. It was evident he intended to make himself seen. It became apparent the figure also intended to make himself heard. Himner, the tower guards, and the others, who had joined them on the catwalk, strained their ears to hear. The unidentified figure already had their complete attention.

"We have you and your fair city surrounded!" Jershon, the unknown figure, declared in a booming voice that echoed through the trees. "We give you this opportunity to surrender without bloodshed before we make an end of your stronghold."

"You have us surrounded?" Himner retorted attempting to sound unimpressed. "You and what army? Who is this 'we?' I see only one man!"

Jershon turned for a moment to give word to his officers. They spread the word quickly from trench guard to trench guard.

"I and this army!" Jershon declared.

At his word, the group behind his trench climbed out of their trench and backed away from the city, revealing themselves on the far side of their embankment. Just as they reached the apex of their revelation, the groups from the two trenches on either side did the same. The groups in the next two trenches also backed out. The revelation continued in a wave that went both ways around the city until all of Jershon's men were revealed, standing boldly and strongly within clear view.

The effect was calculated to strike a moment of terror and despair in the hearts of their proud enemies. For that moment, its impact was complete and successful. It did not generate a surrender, however, nor was it truly expected to.

"Archers, mount the wall and take aim!" the Lamanite commander shouted. "Rid us of these troublesome mites."

Jershon signaled his men to take cover. Those among them who could hear Himner's order knew the need to move quickly. Those who could not, rightly guessed the cause. By the time Himner's archers were in place, Jershon's entire army was securely hidden behind the protective embankments.

Arrows flew at an unseen foe. The distance was great enough to detract any aim or force. The projectiles fell to the earth striking the embankments, the ground, or flew beyond the trenches, but none posed any form of danger to the Nephite army.

The arrows continued to rain for several minutes out of sheer frustration on the part of the Lamanites. When the torrent gradually subsided and then died entirely, Jershon again stepped out from his cover.

"I am Jershon. You see that your arrows have no effect on us. I give you one more chance to surrender!"

"And I am Himner, a bold Lamanite! I neither fear you, nor heed you! We will not surrender!"

"Very well," Jershon responded, "But, I must thank you!"

"Thank me?!" Himner was puzzled. "For what?"

"For giving us an ample supply of arrows! We wondered if we'd packed enough. Now I doubt we'll even need to use those that we brought!" Jershon laughed and motioned to his men.

The nearest arrows were quickly retrieved by men that darted out from trenches on all sides, and then disappeared again before Himner or any of his men could react.

"Sir! They're taking our arrows!" an archer called out, quite disturbed.

"Yes, I see that. What do you want me to do, tell them to stop?" Himner retorted with disgust.

Jershon laughed again, soon the laughing spread from trench to trench. The infectious laughter of the hidden army echoed out from behind their embankments. It grew in volume until all within the city could hear it. It had an unnerving, stifling effect on the spirits of the Lamanite populace. For the first time, their city began to take on the aura of a prison.

Himner was neither impressed nor depressed. He ordered his men into action. The city gate opened and soldiers began to storm out after Jershon's men. The first one out took no more than a dozen steps before being felled by newly acquired Lamanite arrows shot from Nephite bows. The youthful archers remained safely behind their

281

embankments that had been constructed to include angles that allowed for just such occasions.

More Lamanites made the attempt, but stumbled over dead and dying comrades as they became targets themselves. Without needing orders from above, the Lamanite soldiers recognized the hopelessness of their charge. Himner himself finally called it off and the great city gate was closed.

Himner shifted his tactics and sent men out the back pass, but they received equivalent greetings. Himner was forced to reluctantly accept the fact that the siege was effective. Their peaceful morning had turned into an oppressive day that lingered well beyond the night.

As the days passed, Himner continued occasional assaults on the determined Nephite army. He tried varying numbers of troops, various exits from the city, inconsistent times of day and night, but in all cases the Nephite army maintained the advantage. In a fit of frustrated pique he rained more arrows blindly at the encircled horde, only to be met with more taunting laughter and cries of thanks for restoring their depleted supplies.

Jershon's men maintained a positive mood. They were anxious to bring the siege to a successful conclusion and they knew that each day brought more despair to their captives. They also knew that the city's supplies were becoming more and more in need of replenishment. The supply convoy would surely come soon.

LATE ONE NIGHT, it finally arrived. Under the cover of darkness, the Lamanite convoy planned to enter the city. They were cautious by habit. They remained unaware of the situation they were walking into. Jershon's scouts had already spied the convoy. Jershon and a handful of his officers went beyond the trenches away from the city and met them before they approached the city.

The convoy saw Jershon's Lamanite appearance and saw nothing awry.

"Hoy there!" Jershon called to the convoy. "My men and I have been waiting for you. We're all anxious for your supplies."

"Yes, we've come as quickly as we could," the convoy's leader replied. "We ran into some Nephites a ways back, but we're here now."

"Well, we'd be happy to give you a hand," Jershon replied.

"We'd appreciate that. We've traveled far."

"Just come with me," Jershon offered.

He led them directly to his main trench. By the time the puzzled convoy realized something was amiss, Jershon's men had them completely surrounded.

"And now, kind sir, I ask that you hand over your weapons of war," Jershon announced with a smile.

"What? But? What is this?" the confused, new captive sputtered.

"This is a great night for the Nephite army, that's what this is!" Jershon declared.

MORNING BROUGHT AN enthusiastic Jershon calling out to the Lamanite city.

"Hoy! You there! Oh, great Lamanite leader! It's me, Jershon! Come forward, please!" Jershon taunted with youthful exuberance.

The Lamanite guards were well aware of Jershon's all-too-frequent and all-too-vexing calls. They tried to ignore him, but could not keep their eyes from drifting toward him. Some of them vainly attempted to shoot him full of arrows, but the young leader deftly dodged those that managed to clear the gap. Given the distance, he had plenty of time to see them and plan his move. Finally, reluctantly, Himner stepped into view atop the wall.

"Oh, there you are! Thanks for coming forward!" Jershon called.

"What is it you want!" Himner called back with disgust.

"I just wanted to let you see something. Or someone. Actually, it's both a someone and a something!" Jershon said with glee.

"What is it?! I have no patience for games!" Himner declared.

"Oh, this is no game, great leader!" Jershon assured him. "This is life. Real life. I just wanted you to see what I picked up last night!"

Jershon motioned to his men. They escorted the bound Lamanite convoy into full view. Himner retained his look of disgust and dismay, not wholly clear on what the captives represented. After all, there were many Lamanites that wandered the wilderness. These could be from anywhere.

"These nice men brought us gifts last night," Jershon continued. "But, we have plenty already. We have no need for more."

Jershon motioned for another group of his men to step into view with the food supplies. The effect was inescapable. An audible gasp came from those on the wall. Himner closed his eyes and took an unexpected deep breath at the sight of the much-needed provisions in the hands of his enemy.

"Like I said," Jershon repeated, "We have no need for these things. So, we're sending them back to the city of Judea. Perhaps they can find a use for them."

The group of Jershon's men with the supplies made a hasty retreat for the road back to Judea purposefully remaining within view of all atop the city wall. They were pretty much out of range already, but within a few paces, they were completely and hopelessly beyond the reach of the city's archers. This act of toying with and then sending away food supplies in the face of an army on severely limited rations had a highly demoralizing impact.

Without warning the city gate opened and several Lamanites charged out intent on retrieving the goods. They were quickly shot full of arrows.

"Now, now, please don't do that. We don't want to kill any more of your men," Jershon said with sincere regret. "We give you this opportunity again to surrender. We have your city. We have your convoy. We have your food. We have you. I highly recommend you give us your weapons."

"We most certainly will not!" Himner replied with inborn stubbornness.

"Then you and your fine soldiers will slowly die!" Jershon retorted. "We have plenty of supplies ourselves. We wouldn't send away your food stuffs if we didn't. Our own convoys come and go as they please. We can stay here for a very, very long time."

"And you will find yourselves very, very bored!" Himner called back defiantly.

He turned away, his face red with anger, and left the city wall to return to his quarters. Jershon shook his head and returned to his trench. He approached his men who still held the captive convoy.

"Take these prisoners to Zarahemla. I have no need for them here," he commanded.

"Yes, sir," his men replied and led the prisoners away.

High up on the city wall, many anxiously concerned eyes watched their would-be saviors disappear down the dusty trail. None of them dared to speak, however, lest they incur the wrath of their determined leader. His boiling countenance gave clear indications of his ill mood. There was not one among them who wanted to offer him an opportunity to vent his pent-up anger.

Chapter 24

The Weight of Success

The days continued to pass. No convoys made it to Cumeni. No Lamanites made it out of the city alive. No arrows from the city walls made their mark. Jershon and his army continued to hold and taunt the Lamanite city. Even from the great distance, Jershon's men could see the depleted morale of the guards on the wall. Those guards who looked out at their tormenters did so with hopes that were faltering absolutely. Some guards refused to face outward at all, unwilling to perpetually face their indefatigable assailants.

Finally, the day came that it was Himner who called out to Jershon. He stood upon the wall trying to maintain his dignity and pride, but he was clearly beaten. He initially had a hint of irritation in his voice.

"Jershon, this is Himner, leader of the Lamanites. I wish to speak with you."

Himner watched carefully. There was no reply and no sign of movement from Jershon's trench. Himner fidgeted. It was difficult for a leader to maintain an air of dignity when he spoke and no one responded.

"Jershon, I am Himner. I wish to speak with you!" he repeated.

Finally, Jershon walked into view.

"I am Jershon, a leader of the Nephites. I am ready to hear your words. What is it you wish to tell me on this fine morning?"

"My people suffer much from your siege. We lack food and supplies. We wish for this to end."

Jershon did not reply. He let the air hang heavy with silence, forcing his adversary to continue.

"We wish—" Himner began, but stopped, regretting the words he was forced to speak. He closed his eyes and sighed. Then he straightened up again. He called out with as much boldness as he could muster, "We wish to surrender!"

Himner's own soldiers were more relieved than shocked. The hopelessness of their situation had weighed heavily on their souls. Many had longed to hear their leader speak these words so that they could be relieved from their misery. Several of Himner's officers had spent the better part of the night pleading the hopelessness of their situation and begging him to say these words. Himner saw this as the lowest moment of his life, and certainly of his military career, but one he was wholly incapable of avoiding.

"I accept your offer!" Jershon shouted back. "Your people have proven themselves worthy adversaries. We are pleased to end this ordeal for you and for them. Throw out your weapons, then open your gate, and we will end this siege!"

Swords, spears, arrows, bows, scimitars, shields and all manner of weapons of war flew over the city wall, descended through the air, and landed at the base of the city wall, forfeited by their defeated owners. Once the dispersal was ended, Jershon's men rocked the trees and hills with their shouts of triumph. Cumeni was theirs.

MAINTAINING A SIEGE was one thing. Maintaining prisoners was something else entirely. In a siege, one could taunt, harass, demoralize, and threaten. One could also keep one's distance and not only abstain from any responsibility toward the welfare of their captives, but actually made it a point to withhold and deprive their captives of any possible sustenance.

Once captives became prisoners instead of enemies boldly holding out under adverse conditions, the conquerors gained a responsibility that included much more direct involvement and intervention than a siege required. Suddenly, the duty to provide supplies and sustenance shifted to the forefront and became a major responsibility of the victor. The captives no longer whiled away their time in a waiting game, but turned to plans of escape. The victors had to post guards who now played their roles on a much more individual nature.

Such was the case with Jershon and his men. The faceless city, hidden behind a towering, inhuman wall, had now been replaced with countless mouths to feed and numerous, angry, defiant, and individual captives bent on escape. Again and again, the weaponless captives rushed their guards, hoping to overpower them.

The Lamanites did not take well to captivity. They seemed to have no care for life or limb, including their own. Their tactic was to swarm their guards as a group in hopes that one or two could break free and flee to the jungle. Jershon's men were forced to wound or kill many, many dozen as the days progressed. The Nephite warrior's hearts sickened at the needless deaths.

Adding an increased complexity to their situation was the need to feed the masses. No more Lamanite convoys came bearing food. The city's storehouses were all but depleted. That was, after all, the main tool of the siege. Jershon's supplies were plenty when designated for his own men, but made meager rations when spread so far. Judea could hardly support itself, adding to it the captive city of Cumeni; the rations soon proved to be much too short in supply.

The only items of abundance were the hungry mouths and the realization that these captives needed to be taken elsewhere. Jershon sent word to Helaman that something must be done soon if all were to survive. The next day, an officer named Gid arrived with a large army of men. Jershon met him outside the city.

"I am Gid. Helaman has sent me and my men to relieve you of your prisoners and this city."

"Gid, I welcome you and the relief you offer. I and my men are weary," Jershon replied. "What will you do with so many prisoners?"

"Helaman has ordered that I leave half of my army here to guard the city and use the other half to march your prisoners up to the land of Zarahemla," Gid replied.

"I don't envy you the task. It should be a daunting feat to march so many unwilling prisoners through such rough territory. They've been harassing and attacking my men as often as they saw even the slightest opportunity. You'll want to be on the watch at all times," Jershon said.

"Thank you, we will," Gid responded.

"God speed," Jershon added.

JERSHON AND HIS men made their way through the morning mist on their return to Judea while Gid divided his army in half. The one maintained Cumeni. Gid personally led the other half on a march with swords in hand, and prisoners well guarded, toward the grand city of

Zarahemla. The march, however, proved to be much less than grand. The Nephites quickly found the wisdom in Jershon's warning. They could not put down their swords for an instant. They did not just guard their prisoners; they guarded their very lives.

At every turn, at the slightest of opportunity, the Lamanite captives massed together and rushed their guardians. The farther into the wilderness the troupe marched, the more frequent the attacks became. The trail became riddled with the bodies of would-be escapees, who met cold steel and succeeded in escaping to an eternal rest.

Before the procession had managed to march more than a couple leagues on the first day, Gid heard a signal from behind. He immediately recognized it and called for a halt. All attention was on Gid, whose attention was now behind him. Gid's eyes were not on the path behind him, but on the jungle to the side. Other eyes peer into the rainforest and saw only dense, tall trees, vines, heavy undergrowth, and exotic birds.

A moment later, two Nephites leaped out of the dense undergrowth and onto the path. They were two of the Nephite spies who had been sent out to watch the Lamanite camps in hopes of learning their movements and plans. Seeing them was never a good sign. They rarely bore favorable news, especially when they traveled in pairs. Gid knew this all too well and mulled over the possibilities in his mind as they approached him. They spoke in hushed tones, but the intense expressions on their faces made everyone nearby extremely curious and interested in learning their words.

"Gid, we're fortunate to have caught you," Joseph, the taller of the two, exclaimed.

Gid clasped each spy's hand in the token of welcome, then asked, "Joseph, I can't quite say I'm excited to see you, though I am pleased to see that you're well. What is your news?"

"I fear it isn't good," Joseph responded. He looked at his comrade, who silently nodded agreement. He glanced over at the captive Lamanites who watched him closely and expectantly. He saw the armed guards who held the prisoners in check.

"We've just returned from a Lamanite camp. We've learned that they are planning an attack on Cumeni," Joseph said.

"Cumeni! So soon?!" Gid's voice was unfortunately a bit too loud. The nearest prisoners had heard his words and quickly guessed the rest. They muttered the message to the rest of the captives.

"Yes, I believe they plan to retake it," the second spy added.

"I thought I would have time to return from Zarahemla before their first assault! This is not good. This is simply *not* good. And it puts me in a very awkward position. If I take these prisoners to Zarahemla, Cumeni will be left with too few. Yet how am I supposed to return and wage a war with this many unwilling participants?! The timing couldn't possibly grow worse than this!" Gid lamented.

Gid was given only scant moments to ponder his dilemma. The Lamanite captives who overheard the report took courage at what they saw as a wonderful opportunity. They spread the word like lightning and massed an affront on the Nephites that was entirely overwhelming.

These were angry people. They would sooner die than arrive in Zarahemla as prisoners. As one, their cries pierce the air. Startled, monkeys, birds, and other wild animals jumped with fright. The Nephites put up a good resistance, but when the entire army rushed their guards with sticks, stones, and handfuls of dirt to fling at their eyes, there was no restraining them. They ran upon the Nephite swords.

A tremendous number were slain, but the remainder broke free. The liberated Lamanites did not linger to contend with their former guards. They simply charged into the jungle to join their brethren on a more grand assault against the Nephites. Some of Gid's men began to charge after them.

"Halt! Men! Stop!" Gid called to his men. "Don't bother men! We have a more important task before us! Cumeni will soon be under attack. We must return to aid our brethren. Hurry!"

Gid and his men turned and made a hasty return to Cumeni in hopes of arriving before the Lamanites.

THE FOLLOWING AFTERNOON, to the surprise of Helaman and others, Gid and a good portion of his army made a welcome return to the city of Judea. Although there was a myriad of questions as to why these great men were not on the road to Zarahemla, there was not time to ask for details. Nor was there interest in asking these types of questions at this particular time. All of them were simply greatly encouraged at the return of Gid and his men, for Judea was under attack.

Ammoron had sent a new and vigorous army from the city of Manti with supplies to aid his army in Cumeni. They were too late to save that city, and had instead set their sites on taking Judea. Revenge can be a powerful weapon, especially when wielded by fresh troops. Helaman and the rest of his army were dangerously close to falling before the onslaught. The return of Gid's captiveless troops could not have come at a more critical juncture.

They leaped into the battle. Swords beat upon swords. Orders could not be heard above the din of the war cries, shouts, and clanging of shields. The battle raged for the better part of the day. Men on both sides fought for their lives. Many lost that battle and lay lifeless on the ground. More lay motionless or reeling with wounds, trying to stay out of the way of the many legs and feet that dodged in and out among them while healthy soldiers fought hand-to-hand.

The most courageous of all on the field of battle were also the youngest. The contributions of Helaman's stripling warriors again shined brightly on this bitter day. They refused to be beaten either in body or spirit. They brought to the Nephite warriors a vigor and vitality that lent encouragement to troops who would otherwise have resigned themselves to defeat, captivity, or death.

Jershon and his men called out to each other. Unable to communicate with tangible words in the fierce and mobile heat of battle, they encouraged each other with grunts, groans, senseless shouts, and whistles. They did anything they could to let their comrades know that they too stood nearby fighting without fear. They managed to glance at each other in between exchanging blows with the Lamanites. In these brief half-moments of time, in which eyes met across the battlefield, they shared the electricity of their souls. Each of these young soldiers took courage from the courage seen in the eyes of his brothers.

They shared and spread this among themselves, wordlessly encouraging each other to greatness and victory. Their faith in the protection of their God guided their limbs and actions. Each fought with a strength and agility that exceeded their natural bodies. The other Nephites felt and shared in this force of purpose that these boys shared among themselves and also gained the strength to overcome. They looked at the young comrades with wonder and awe.

The Lamanites felt the force as well, but gained a quite different perspective. They saw these impertinent whelps as being invincible and feared them because they seemed to fight with the power of God himself. Their enthusiasm diminished in equal proportion to the Ammonites' courage.

It was as if their will to conquer and overcome was being tapped out of them and pumped into their young Nephite enemies. They marveled at how even when their blows struck flesh, the Ammonites continued to fight, twisting and turning as they engaged and parried blows from soldier after soldier. They truly seemed unstoppable.

As the battle drew on, the Lamanites eventually gave ground. At first it was difficult to distinguish the progress of the Nephite army. When that progress was finally noticed, it was noted by both sides. Like a wave held back through high tide, the entire Nephite group swelled together and then unleashed their fury on their hapless foes. They pushed them back soundly and without question. The Lamanites fled away from Judea and returned to Manti much less than victorious. The day belonged to the Nephites, and most particularly, the sons of Helaman.

WITH THE ENEMY repelled, the Nephites were left with the unfortunate task of treating the wounded and burying the dead. A clearing was made to the south of the city and the dead from both sides of the battle were to be interned in the freshly dug earth. Helaman's attention focused on the many bodies lying on the battlefield. Although leaders were concerned about all men under their command, Helaman was most concerned about the welfare of his young sons.

"Jershon!" he called across the field, "Jershon! I am glad to see you yet alive!"

Jershon rushed to his mentor and friend.

"Father!" he called back as he neared him. "And I am relieved to see that you will yet see another sunset too!"

"Jershon, I want to know the fate of my many sons. Gather your men and search among the dead and wounded. Please, give me an accounting as quickly as you can!"

"Yes, sir. We will," Jershon promised and set about the task.

A GROUP OF five men approached Helaman who still helped with the wounded. The men were the scouts Helaman had earlier sent to Cumeni to check on conditions there. When he noticed their return, he gained an immediate and active interest in their report.

"Brethren, what have you learned?" he asked.

"Cumeni is still under the protection of the Nephite army. The Lamanites who fled before us have not attacked, but have bypassed it and returned directly toward Manti," their leader replied.

"Splendid! God be praised!" Helaman responded.

As he spoke with them, Jershon approached. Helaman turned his focus to the news that this young leader bore.

"Father! I have excellent news!" Jershon beamed.

"Yes? What is it?!" Helaman asked.

"We found many of my brothers among the dead," Jershon related. "At first we feared that they were dead themselves. But, in each case we learned that they still breathed the breath of life. They were severely wounded and many had fainted for loss of blood, but they live! My men are tending to them at this time. Helaman, sir, not one soul of us has been lost!"

"Not one?!" Helaman exclaimed. "So many hundreds lie dead and yet you who I call my sons all live. This is purely astonishing."

"Yes! Our mothers have taught us to believe in the protection of God, yet work toward those things that we truly desire and He will prosper our ways. We knew that God would protect us if we remained true and valiant! And He truly has preserved us this day!" Jershon declared.

"Yes, Jershon, He truly has!" Helaman agreed. "This is certainly a day with good news mingled among the sad." Then he added, "Your mothers have taught you well. Faith in God is never a failing act."

Helaman had seen many miraculous events in his day and heard his father teach him of even more. The valiance and survival of his two-thousand-sixty young warriors, when so many seasoned warriors had been slain, now numbered among some of the most impressive miracles of his reckoning.

The others in the army also remained astonished at the fact. The tale of the brave, youthful soldiers saved by the miraculous power of God because of their great faith, would undoubtedly be retold many times over the next several generations.

Chapter 25

Leadership

———◄◆►———

*T*he latest skirmish was now history. Helaman met with his officers in the war room of the city of Judea. Those seated with Helaman included Jershon, Gid, and Teomner. Teomner had remained behind with his men to aid Helaman in defending Judea when Gid set off to relieve Jershon of his captives at Cumeni. The Nephite race was tall and muscular, but Teomner was unusually tall and well built, even for a Nephite. He had about three inches on Helaman and his men perpetuated the rumor that he could bend and re-string his bow using just one hand.

The discussion of the day focused on the recent successes against the Lamanites. While grateful for Gid's assistance, Helaman was still curious as to why they were able to render it when they should have been well on their way to Zarahemla. Gid had now recounted the experience on the road and how the Lamanites revolted and freed themselves, only after suffering heavy casualties.

He had also given details of the Lamanite attack on Cumeni. Gid explained that his men had made it within the city gate only moments before the Lamanites. In fact, the last few yards were basically a race between the two armies and was run under a shower of arrows from the tower guards. The gate was barely secured when the Lamanites began to beat against it. The resulting attack, however, was surprisingly halfhearted.

Although it lasted until nightfall, when morning came, the Lamanites were quiet. Gid first suspected that the Lamanites had taken refuge in the trenches left behind from Jershon's siege. He and his men kept a wary eye on them from sun up. When two hours of daylight had burned away and no sign of movement, or threatening oath had been heard, Gid sent some scouts out to survey the area for any sign of the Lamanites.

Fearing it was a trap, the scouts were leery and cautious. They chose the trench by the main gate first, assuming that this strategic spot would be their most likely lair. Under heavy cover offered by the best archers, one scout silently dashed out and peered into the trench. For what seemed like far too long, he disappeared behind the embankment. When he finally came back into view, he faced the city in a relaxed stance that indicated no concern for his safety.

He shouted that there were no signs of the Lamanites and that their campfires were long cold. Gid shouted orders down to the other scouts to check the other trenches and the perimeters of the jungle. The scouts dashed out to the far side of the embankments and ran off in separate directions circling the city, viewing the insides of the trenches as they ran. Gid and others on the city wall ran along the catwalk to the far side. The two scouts met at the back and both confirmed that the trenches were empty. The Lamanites were long gone.

"I concluded that the Lamanites' true objective must have been Judea," Gid added. "I gave orders to keep Cumeni guarded, but that the rest of us should return to Judea in case there was an attack. I was fearful that we'd be far too late. Praise be to God that we made it in time."

"Yes, your return gave us the added strength we needed at a time when both morale and the advantage were leaning toward the Lamanites," Helaman confirmed. "If it weren't for your return and the fiery example of Jershon's men, I don't think we would have been able to hold our ground. It appears God has preserved us again that we might continue to seek the liberty of this people. But, it has come at the expense of many valiant souls. I trust those who have been slain have entered into the rest of their God."

"I, too, am greatly pleased that we have this opportunity to sit in this peaceful room and discuss the blessings we've received from a loving God," Teomner began. "I'm still very concerned, however, at how we can win not just the battles, but this war for our freedom. I have a wife and family who I want to raise in peace. What's our next move to rid ourselves of the scourge of Ammoron?"

"Teomner, you speak the thoughts of all of us quite well," Helaman acknowledged. "Today we have won a narrow victory, but we must put an end to this fighting."

"I believe our first move is to find out just where our enemy has gone. Perhaps then we can either draw him out or at least guess his next move," Gid suggested.

"I agree, but I doubt we'll have much luck drawing him out with a small number of our army again," Jershon said. "It worked once, but I doubt he'll fall for it again."

"Yes, I'm afraid I have to agree," Helaman said. "We'll have to come up with some other form of stratagem. Teomner, can you send your scouts out to Manti to see how things fair there?"

"Yes," Teomner responded.

"Good, Gid, can you check on the city of Zeezrom?"

301

"Certainly."

"Jershon, I'd like your men to run regular reconnaissance between here and both Antiparah and Cumeni, so that we can ensure that the cities we have freed remain free. Make us aware of any Lamanite activity."

"Yes, sir."

"Meanwhile, I'll write to Pahoran in Zarahemla and see about getting ourselves more provisions and more reinforcements. We lost far too many men this day to expect to be able to defend these cities, and take on the Lamanites, without receiving considerably more men. You men know your duties. And I know I don't have to remind you of how critical it is that we be able to count on you to fulfill them. Keep us posted of any new events. Warn your men to watch themselves in their journeys, and may God watch over the faithful!"

The meeting adjourned.

MONTHS LATER, THE same officers again discussed strategy and the latest information they had managed to gather. They had held these meetings regularly over the intervening time. Each time, news of the Lamanites was both cryptic and ominous. It was clear they were up to no good, but it was not clear what their full intention was.

"I tell you I don't like this one bit!" Gid began. "They've simply abandoned the city of Zeezrom. There was no fighting, no threatening, they simply abandoned it. I don't like this at all. It's not like them. I fear they have some sort of dark plan in the works!"

"I agree with Gid," Teomner added. "Based on the timing of the report, I'd have to say the army that was at Zeezrom has now joined with Ammoron's men in Manti. They've now massed all of their men in this region in one stronghold. We wouldn't stand a chance should we try to attack them straight on!"

"Certainly not with the meager provisions and reinforcements Zarahemla has sent to us," Helaman lamented. "Were we one army in one city, perhaps it would have been sufficient. But, it's hardly noticeable when spread between four cities. I just don't understand why they sent so little to begin with, and why more hasn't arrived since. Surely they understand our plight. I made it plain in the messages. Yet all they send is a token amount of provisions and men. This is not good. Not good at all."

"My men report that the Lamanites are receiving greater strength on a regular basis. Both provisions and men," Teomner pointed out. "Soon, they'll be so strong that we won't be able to stop them at all. Already they seek to entice our men to battle."

"Yes," Jershon added, "They come in groups and taunt the men."

"And when we do respond," Gid said with a bitter edge in his voice, "They just retreat back to their strongholds before we can do anything about it!"

"They're just trying to draw us out and make us choose foolishly," Helaman replied. "Don't let them get the better of you or your men."

"Meanwhile, we slowly deplete our stores and risk starvation," Teomner said.

"Men, I need you with me. I need you to be strong," Helaman answered. "These hardships could be a result of the Lord trying our faith. Perhaps we, or our people, are beginning to slacken our faith. If so, we have cause to mourn and to fear. For the Lord will not suffer that his people dwindle into disbelief. We must take on the armor of God and exercise our faith before we can expect the Lord to prosper us in our ways."

"Helaman, father, I see the power in your words," Jershon

responded. "I feel the spirit move within me that tells me you speak truly. What do you propose we do?"

"We don't know if the lack of support from Zarahemla is because of disabilities to respond, or if it is a means of bringing the judgments of God upon us," Helaman replied. "I believe it behooves us to ensure that it's not due to our forgetting our God. I propose that we pour out our souls in prayer to God, that we ask Him to strengthen us and help deliver us out of the hands of our enemies; that He give us the strength we need to retain our cities, our lands, our possessions, and our freedom."

"I too feel the power of your words," Gid responded. "I see that this is a wise move."

"How do we help?" Teomner asked.

"Go to your men. Remind them of the cause for which we fight. Prick their hearts with the message of the Title of Liberty. Call to their minds the promises to our fathers that God has chosen this land to be a land of promise for all people who dwell on it in righteousness. That only those who live in accordance to God's ways will prosper in the land.

"Instruct them to pray earnestly for deliverance and for the knowledge of what actions we must take to make this deliverance become a reality. Remind them that with faith, all things are possible. We must believe in our cause, lead by example, and point the people in the right course if we're to expect the Lord to help us in our battles. Prepare your men. This coming Sabbath will be a day of prayer, so that we may receive the guidance we need to prosper in this cause!"

All of the men present agreed with Helaman's recommendation. The meeting dismissed and the officers spread the word to their men and called to their remembrance the purpose for which they were there. They intended to remove from them the worries of their plight and focus on the power of the Lord and the glories of His righteous purposes. As parched flowers take to a desert rain, the men responded willingly and with eagerness to the call.

THE EVE BEFORE the Sabbath, Helaman stood upon the catwalk of the city wall looking outward at the land. He chose the area where the wall was nearest the tall, lush rainforest. He leaned forward with his elbows on the wall, admiring the colors of the trees. On the edge of the jungle, a small family of monkeys could be seen perched high above the ground. Helaman thought of his own family whom he had not seen in far too long. Multicolored exotic birds flew and cawed with a myriad of voices. The warm, jungle breeze brushed against his cheeks and carried with it the sweet aroma of intricate flowers.

The setting sun began to offer a brilliant orange hue to the area. Helaman's face and body shone with orange and red. The strife between nations was laid aside for the moment and he was at peace again with nature. A soldier approached slowly from his right, unwilling to disrupt his commander's tranquil respite. The soldier paused a moment in hesitation, then continued his approach with calculated stillness. When he stood beside his leader, he spoke gently.

"Helaman, sir," Jershon said. Helaman did not turn at first, still locked in his thoughts.

"Father, sir," Jershon tried again.

Helaman blinked and turned. When he saw Jershon standing beside him with a solemn look, he straightened and turned to him with a paternal smile.

"Yes, Jershon, what is it?" he asked.

"Sir, I, uh—" Jershon hesitated.

"Jershon, is something the matter?" Helaman asked with concern.

His brow furrowed and he placed his hand on Jershon's shoulder to offer comfort. "Please, let me know how I can help."

"I'm concerned about your earlier words," Jershon offered.

"In what way?" Helaman asked.

"You spoke in a way that implied that there are those among the Nephites who do not believe in the ways of God. And that because of them we may fail. Is that truly what you meant?" Jershon asked.

"In a way," Helaman responded. He stopped and looked into the questioning youth's eyes. This teenager had now seen more of life than most men ever should. What impact was it having on the lad, he wondered, especially as he struggled to understand life and his role in it?

"Tell me, Jershon, what troubles you most about this? Is it the concept that doubting men can lead a nation into destruction?" He watched Jershon shake his head affirmatively. Perceiving the youth's innocence he added, "Or, is it simply that there are Nephites who are capable of doubting?"

"I—I was going to say it was the former, but I have to admit, I find any doubts among the Nephites as troubling. I don't understand how they *can* doubt. They're the ones who brought the truth to my people, to my parents—to me," Jershon looked down after having verbalized his concern.

"Jershon, you've just touched on one of the grand keys of wisdom. Knowledge alone is not wisdom and cannot save a people, nor can a glorious past guarantee a brilliant future," Helaman explained. "It's true that a people's roots are in their past. And it's true that a firm foundation can provide a marvelous building block upon which to sculpt grand ideals. But, it must be wholly understood that a society is only as strong as its current disposition and inclination to act on the ideals of righteousness.

"Regardless of the faith of one's forefathers, if the current people doubt the need for, or ignore, the workings of the Spirit of God in their lives, in their laws, and in their leaders, then there will one day be an unfortunate accounting. And in that day, those who fail to stand on the side of righteousness shall crumble."

"I pity most those who fail to lead, and instead choose to allow their society to fail and fall," Helaman continued. "For on their shoulders is the greatest responsibility to lead by example and set a noble tone. If all they see is glory and power, such as with Amalickiah and now Ammoron after him, and countless other Nephites who have gone after such vanities, then they will meet a disappointing and bitter end. Others may be privy to their demise, but not necessarily. Their demise may prove to be very private."

"In the quiet moments of the soul, one day these false leaders will look inwardly and see beyond their vain ambitions. They will see themselves for what they've allowed themselves to become. They will see a hollowness and an emptiness of stature. When they see the good they could have done for society as a whole, and weigh it against how they manipulated position for personal gain, glory, or fleeting pleasure, they'll see for themselves that they come up lacking. And oh, the bitterness of such wanton waste of potential. Hell itself can offer no more bitter pains."

"But, what of the people?" Jershon asked.

"The people? The people?" Helaman responded. "That is an astute question, my young warrior friend. What can we say of a people who will allow themselves to be led by men who seek after vain ambitions instead of dignity and honor? Of a people who will put a blind eye and a deaf ear to wicked and perverse leadership? Of a people who will set themselves above the needs of divine inspiration? Of a people who believe that the wisdom of men supersedes the need for the guidance of the Spirit? Of a people who believe that they have advanced in knowledge to the point that they no longer require humility and grace? Such a people are like sheep.

"No, they are worse than sheep. For sheep will follow only blindly. Such a people as this will knowingly allow the subtleties of soothing, evil words to lull them into passive submission. Such a people will gradually, but freely relinquish their rights of exactness and honor in themselves and eventually their leaders. They will heap to themselves men who say words that do not offend the slovenly. They will withhold scolding of those who pervert the greater good, out of fear of offending the offensive. They will call evil good, for fear of calling anything evil.

"Beware of those who cannot declare things as they truly are; those who fear saying words of proper chastisement, which the heart knows is right, Jershon. They can't be trusted to do you any lasting good. Nor do they truly care about your good. Their greatest concern is instead focused on themselves, their reputations, their vain glory, and their petty ambitions."

Jershon had a somber and solemn look on his face. Helaman could see that his words had a powerful effect on him. Jershon turned and looked toward the city square. He saw Nephite soldiers mingling about, some on duty, others simply mingling, going in and out of buildings, visiting with each other, and otherwise passing the time.

"Do you feel that there are many of these people here who feel this way, sir?" Jershon asked.

"Here? In Judea?" Helaman asked rhetorically. "No, I don't. At least not half so many as may be found in Zarahemla."

Jershon looked back to Helaman with surprise.

"No? How so?" Jershon pursued.

"It's unfortunately quite a simple answer, Jershon. You see, these men here—" Helaman motioned with his arm and pointed in a sweeping generalization to all of the men within the walls of the city, "these men are fighting for their very lives. They're also fighting for something even more noble. They're fighting for liberty, freedom, and the many things that the Title of Liberty that flies boldly over our city gate represents not only for themselves, but for their wives, children, friends, and neighbors. They're even fighting for the liberty of men and women they don't even know. That is true sacrifice, Jershon. That's what the Title truly represents."

Helaman pointed to the Title and Jershon looked over at the flag that he had seen every day since he arrived at Judea. He nodded.

"Men who are actively engaged in a fight for a worthy cause have the advantage of focusing their lives, their minds, and their hearts on the noble things of the soul. Liberty is more than a word to them, it's an ideal that must be won, cherished, promoted, and protected. You and your brave brothers know this as much as any other man here. You're not here to seek position in society. You're here to preserve society. Period."

Jershon nodded in agreement.

"You're here to ensure that your children can grow up believing in and worshiping the God who has freed your soul from the pains and pitfalls of the mortal world. Am I right?"

"Yes, sir!" Jershon acknowledged. "Although, I've never really thought of myself as doing this for my children. I haven't thought of myself as a father. That's all so far away."

"No, Jershon, it isn't. It will be sooner than you think. Someday you'll look back and see how time flies by, and you'll wonder where your youthful days have gone. Life seems long, but only to those who haven't lived it yet. Those who look at it from the other end wonder where it went and what it was they did with their time. This is why it's critical to spend your time pursuing the best activities and causes. Someday, you'll speak to your grandchildren with pride of what you have done to perpetuate the freedom of the Nephite nation."

Jershon smiled at the thought of his being a grandfather. He mused the thought for a moment, his face brightened. Then his countenance turned sour again.

"What is it, Jershon?" Helaman again asked.

"You say the men here are focused on the ideals of liberty. You also said that they are more focused than the people in Zarahemla are. Zarahemla is the Nephite capital. How can they lose sight of liberty?" Jershon asked.

"Jershon, they're the ones most at risk for this. They sit in a city on a hill, literally. Its massive walls have so far proven invulnerable to Lamanite attack. And, indeed, most fighting is taking place far from its walls. So, the people there live outside of fear for mortal safety. They live in comparative ease and comfort. What's more, the power to rule our society resides with those within the city's walls.

"Power and comfort are two blessings few people can tolerate. They tend to form an inexplicable trend toward self aggrandizement and overbearing, short-sighted directives that are focused at reinforcing or expanding their personal power and authority, rather than for promoting the greater good of society as a whole.

"And that, Jershon, is what I fear may be the cause of our not receiving more men and supplies from Zarahemla. I fear the leaders may have fallen into petty power feuds, rather than looking out for those who are seeking to preserve this nation's very liberty. That is the chief cause of my day of prayer. We must show our God that we still believe that He watches out for us, we must seek His guidance, and pray that He will inspire our leaders to lead this people in righteousness. When you pray tomorrow, I want you to open your heart and truly listen to what you feel the Lord is trying to make known to you."

"I will," Jershon said. "Thank you for taking the time, Helaman."

"Not at all, Jershon, that's what I'm here for," Helaman said with a smile.

Chapter 26

Returning in Kind

he day following the Sabbath, Helaman and his officers were again gathered in the war room to discuss their strategy. The men were in a somber, quiet mood. The routine chatting and tossing about of strategic opinions was noticeably absent.

"I thank you all for coming. I trust yesterday proved to be of benefit to you," Helaman stated.

The room remained silent for a moment. The men did not make eye contact with each other. It was not a matter of shame, but of awe. Jershon was the first to break the silence.

"Sir, I, uh, I don't know how to put this into words," Jershon stammered.

"That's fine, try whatever you feel is appropriate," Helaman encouraged.

"Well, sir, I prayed as you suggested. I listened with my heart. But, I heard no words," Jershon admitted.

"You heard no words?" Helaman asked.

"Yes, sir," Jershon confirmed.

"Words aren't necessarily the answers to prayer," Helaman offered. "What did you feel?"

"Feel?"

"Yes, what did you feel? Did you feel confusion?"

"Confusion? No, sir! I actually felt good."

"Good in what way?" Helaman asked.

"It was kind of a warm feeling inside," Jershon answered.

"And did that warm feeling make you think you were in a doomed situation?"

"Doomed?! Oh, no! It was a very good feeling. If anything, it was a feeling of hope!" Jershon stated emphatically.

"There's your answer then, Jershon," Helaman explained. "Answers don't just come from angels suddenly appearing and blowing a trumpet, most often they're much more subtle, such as the warm feeling in the breast that confirms that what you're praying about is right. What did you ask in your prayer?"

"Well, I asked if we would be able to overcome the Lamanites and win our fight for liberty," Jershon explained.

"And this warm feeling, did it come shortly after you asked this?" Helaman asked.

"Actually, it came *while* I was asking it. It was so strong that I found myself stopping, and just sort of feeling it. It was such a good feeling that I wanted it to last and last," Jershon answered.

"That, Jershon, was the Holy Spirit confirming to your soul that what you were praying about was true. I'd say you just received a personal witness that our cause will prosper!" Helaman said with a smile.

"Did anyone else experience anything like this?" Helaman asked the others.

The other officers had eyed Jershon closely, expectantly. With a degree of surprise, they confirmed that Jershon had pretty much summed up their own experiences. Helaman, still the spiritual leader of the Nephite society, pursued this teaching moment further.

"I dare say we have our assurance from God that He will deliver us. I too have felt Him speak peace to my soul. I feel that warm feeling returning even now as we speak of this great thing. I for one feel my faith increase. I don't know how we'll be delivered, but I now feel quite confident that if we trust in the Lord, He will be with us to ensure that our efforts succeed!" Helaman concluded. "Now, what do we want to do?"

Gid sat up tall and spoke with confidence, "Helaman, first, I want to thank you for bringing us to the remembrance of our God. Yesterday's experience was unique and one that I wish I would pursue much more often. I, too, feel good about this meeting. As to our next move, I think we should simply gather our forces and march to Manti and take on Ammoron and his army now, while the men are at a spiritual high. I don't anticipate any more forces coming from Zarahemla. We should make due with what we have and go forward."

"I agree with my comrade here," Teomner added. "I believe our men have been inspired and we should make our move while our men are still enthused. I also want to point out that, as I see it, we need to draw out Ammoron's army from behind their mighty walls. I don't believe we can do this with anything less than our full force, not after Antiparah. If we can lead them to believe we're making our last stand, then I think they'll come out."

"If we do draw them out," Gid stated, "We may want to double back with a small group and see who is left behind to guard Manti."

"Your point is well taken, Gid," Helaman replied. "Is there any opposition to this plan?"

None of them voiced a negative vote.

"Gather your men, then. We'll set off in the morning," Helaman declared.

IT TOOK THREE full days to march the army near to the city of Manti. This was actually a credible feat for an army of several thousand. Before nightfall of the third day, Nephite tents were pitched. They had purposely allowed their presence to be made known. They had chosen to pitch them on the side of the city nearest the wilderness, and far enough away that the Lamanites could not gain a good feel for the enormity of their force.

Ammoron's men had sent him word of the Nephites' movements. His officers warned him that it could be another trap to lure them out.

"I'm not going to fall for their petty little traps again!" Ammoron loudly decreed. "I want to know the size of this army before I make any decisions. Where are my spies?!"

"HELAMAN," A GUARD reported. "I've gotten word of Lamanite spies in the vicinity. What do you want us to do with them?"

"By all means, leave them alone and don't let them know you're onto them!" Helaman responded. "Let them scope out our forces and return to Ammoron. So far, this is just as we would wish it to be."

THE TWO SPIES returned to the great city of Manti. They were passed through the city gate and made their own, unescorted way through the city square and to the council chamber that had been modified into a throne room. The throne room guards allowed them in to report to an anxious and impatient king. When Ammoron saw them, he stopped pacing and whirled around to face them.

"Well?! What have you learned?!" he demanded.

"Oh, great king," the taller spy began, "We have seen that it is true, the Nephites are encamped nearby."

"I knew that! That's why I sent you!" Ammoron spit out. "How big is their force?!"

"Big," the second spy said succinctly. He had a well-earned reputation for being short on words.

"Big? Great. How big?" Ammoron pursued with increasing impatience.

"I'd be tempted to say that they seem to have collected every Nephite from every city in this area and have massed them into one, large army. That's how big," the first spy explained.

"One, large army?!" Ammoron was visibly surprised. He pondered the implications. "One, large army? How large is this army? Is it as large as ours?"

"Hardly!" the second spy offered with a sneer.

"What on earth can they be up to?!" Ammoron thought aloud, "Surely they don't think they can overpower us with an inferior army. Or, have they grown desperate?" he paced as he pondered, "No, wait, I think I know! They're planning another siege! They're going to cut off our supplies, just like at Cumeni! I won't stand for it! We've got to wipe them out before they have the chance to dig themselves in!" He faced his guard, "Call my officers, we're going to hit them with every soldier we have!"

"HELAMAN, OUR SPIES have reported significant activity within the city. It appears the Lamanites are preparing to move!" Gid reported.

"Excellent! If we do this right, this will be a great day for the Nephite army," Helaman responded. "Gid, move two dozen of your men to the far side of camp and secure yourselves in the forest to the east. Teomner, you take two dozen men and secure yourselves to the west. Regardless of all else, don't allow yourselves to be discovered. We'll take care of ourselves, no matter what. Understood?"

"Yes, Helaman," Gid and Teomner both respond.

"MOVE ON OUT men! Stay together!" Ammoron shouted.

The Lamanites marched out of Manti's grand gate row upon row upon row. They were tall, muscular, bronze warriors with breastplates, shields and swords. Their stone faces looked straight ahead in the direction of their enemy. Ammoron himself led the march. He had a cocky air of unconquerable power and vengeance about his persona.

As the Nephite camp came within sight, they could see the Nephites gathering up and preparing to move.

"Those cowardly fools!" Ammoron bellowed, "They fear even making a stand! Hurry men, before they escape!"

The Lamanites eagerly sped up their march. The Nephites did the same. Soon, their camp was vacated with the Nephites making a hasty retreat directly into the wilderness. The Lamanites trudged through the temporary camp intent on overtaking its former occupants. None of them noticed four dozen pairs of eyes surreptitiously observing their passing. As the armies continued on their way and disappeared into the woods, Gid and Teomner signaled their men to still stay low.

They were puzzled, but they obeyed nevertheless. The answer came along quickly enough. Ammoron's trailing spies came into view. As they entered the abandoned campsite, they searched among the remains, attempting to assess anything of note.

"Now!" Gid gave the order.

His men rushed from their hiding places toward the spies. As the Nephites charged, the spies' first instinct was to turn back toward Manti. They ran face to face with Teomner's men. The startled spies were effectively surrounded and taken captive by the Nephites.

"You're not going anywhere!" Teomner declared. "At least, not without plenty of new friends. We'll also take your weapons, thank you."

The two spies saw the hopelessness of the situation and dropped their swords in disgust.

"Ok, move it!" Gid ordered. "We're heading back to Manti to pay a little visit to whoever didn't get invited to your master's hunting party."

"Too bad you two won't be able to let them know we're coming. I'm sure they'd rather have a little surprise in store for us," Teomner added.

"Nice," the second spy commented as Gid's men bound his hands and then gagged his mouth.

The small band hurried back to Manti, staying out of sight until they neared the gate. The guards, not expecting anyone to return so quickly, had failed to properly secure the gate. The Nephites forced the gate open and entered the occupied city.

Ammoron, in his arrogance, had taken virtually his entire army with him. The few guards who had been left behind were easily overpowered. The mighty city of Manti returned to Nephite control in one of the briefest and smallest skirmishes of the ongoing war.

"KEEP THE MEN moving! Keep them moving!" Helaman ordered as

he stood and let the men rush past him.

He wanted a feel for how his march was going and a personal view of how far ahead they were keeping from the Lamanites. As the last men passed by, he looked through the wreckage of the rainforest caused by their passing. It did not take long before he heard signs of Ammoron's men in hot pursuit. He turned and ran back toward his army and made his way back toward the front line.

The men in the front went through a swift series of replacements, for the first row of men owned the task of swiping the vines and pushing aside the occasional long, skinny fallen trees that lay across their path, so that others could pass. They moved quickly and churned the forest as they went.

As one set hacked away at the vines or tossed logs aside, others stepped up to take on the next obstacles. Fortunately for the Nephites, the jungle was somewhat less dense in this area than in others and even opened up to occasional clearings. These respites served to help the men maintain their energy and their lead.

Helaman caught up to the front lines. The light of day was now beginning to wane.

"Well done, men. It's now time to veer directly northeast. That way!" he pointed.

The forward men dutifully adapted to the course correction. They continued to progress at a pace that was nothing short of miraculous. As if fulfilling scripture, they literally ran and did not become weary. The path they cut was clear and distinct. With the branches and lush foliage of the tall jungle trees joining directly overhead, it resembled an arboreal tunnel more so than a path. The Lamanites, to the surprise of all, did not manage to gain on them.

"CURSE THEIR PALE hides!" Ammoron spit out. "How do they move at such a speed?! You men, pick up your pace! I'll not lose these fools because of your laziness!"

At about this time, Ammoron's force came to a point in the still vibrating path where the course shifted to the right. It was a strikingly obvious deviation, as the path had remained remarkably straight until this moment. Looking forward, they could see that it continued in a straight path, but the glowing, orange light of the setting sun that penetrated the jungle growth revealed that it now headed toward the northeast.

"Halt!" Ammoron shouted and raised his sword above his head to make his point clear.

"What is it, my king?" one of his nearby officers shouted to him.

The entire army stood, curious, panting, and sweating from the heat of their march.

"I don't like this!" Ammoron stated. "I don't like it at all."

"Why, my king?" the officer questioned.

"Unless I missed my guess, they're now on a direct course for Zarahemla," Ammoron surmised. "I should have known better than this. They're leading us into another trap. They'll lead us on and on until right before we overtake them some massive horde of Nephites from Zarahemla will double back and surround us. Typical strategy. I'm not going to play that game. They're just going to have to come up with a better ruse than this. We're heading back to Manti."

"Now, my king?" the officer questioned. "It will soon be dark."

"No, you're right. Let's pitch our tents here for the night. The Nephites have got to be weary from their march. We'll break camp early in the morning and be back in Manti before the Nephites have a chance to notice we're no longer pursuing them. Pass the word! Set up camp!"

"HELAMAN, I COULD detect no sign of the Lamanites to our rear, so I doubled back and saw that they had pitched their tents. I drew near, but remained in hiding, and could overhear the soldiers speaking. They sounded confused. One of them was questioning orders to return to Manti. I believe they intend to return in the morning," Helaman's scout reported.

"Good work!" Helaman encouraged him. "It appears the ruse about returning to Zarahemla has taken affect."

Helaman was sitting in council with his officers. He turned to them and gave new orders.

"Tell your men to not set up camp. We'll not be resting here tonight. I intend to be there to greet Ammoron when he arrives at Manti tomorrow."

THE NEPHITE ARMY moved swiftly, but stealthily through the jungle, staying clear of the path they had cut previously. Their forward scouts kept a lookout for the Lamanites. When they had successfully passed by where their enemy was encamped, they returned to the path they had cut earlier in the day. The going was much easier this time around. They picked up their pace.

Eventually, the path disappeared and opened up to a very large clearing. The jungle itself gave way before them. Across the clearing they could see the light of the moon shining on the tall walls of Manti. Their goal was now within reach, if Gid and Teomner had been successful. Helaman called the men to a halt in the clearing before the gate, well out of any archer's reach. He motioned to his guards.

A torch was lit and a guard waved it in arcs high above his head. He continued to wave it while Helaman and the army watched the black, featureless wall in the distance with interest. Finally, the small silhouette of the tower guard's head could be seen. Then a torch was lit and arched over the tower guard's head. The return signal had been given. Helaman had his confirmation that Manti was under Nephite rule.

He smiled broadly and motioned his men forward. As they approached the city gate, it opened from within. Gid and Teomner were the first two to come out and greet the returning soldiers.

"Welcome home!" Gid said with a broad smile.

"Thank you. It's good to see you again, especially here!" Helaman responded and gave his officer a warm slap on the shoulder.

"Your men are doubtless exhausted," Teomner offered. "We've already made arrangements for them. My men will show them in and we'll wake you in plenty of time to join in on the morning's festivities."

"And, thank you. That's most thoughtful of you," Helaman responded with a touch of uncharacteristic teasing.

"Think nothing of it. It's the least we can do," Gid added. "Sleep well, my friends."

The Nephites marched triumphantly in and found their lodgings. The remaining night was short, but they all slept soundly after a long, tiring, and eventful day of cat and mouse.

AT THE FIRST possible hint of dawn, the Lamanites arose. They expected that the Nephites were still far ahead and fast asleep. They felt vulnerable outside of the massive city walls they had grown accustomed to and dependent on. Ammoron gave the word and the army was on the move, back to their sanctuary.

The hike back was easy and uneventful. The path remained well marked. Soon, they were in the clearing between the dense jungle and their city. Morning mist still hovered on the damp grass. Ammoron, pleased with himself for detecting and avoiding another Nephite trap, walked nonchalantly at the lead. He looked ahead and saw the Lamanite tower guards watching them from high above, not realizing that one of them went by the name of Jershon.

They were well beyond the halfway point when several Lamanites took note of a banner being hoisted directly over the city gate. It bore distinctive writing that revealed it to all as the Title of Liberty and commanded the attention of friend and foe alike. As if hit with an overpowering wind the entire Lamanite army came to an abrupt and involuntary halt at the sight.

Dispelling all doubt, but raising a myriad of questions, Helaman clearly stepped into view next to the Nephite symbol of freedom.

"Surrender your arms, or meet your maker!" he shouted down to them.

Gid and Teomner stepped up to flank their leader. The Lamanites were thoroughly disturbed by this phenomenon. They questioned among themselves, none of them addressing any one individual directly. They all wondered how their foe in the woods had suddenly vanished and reappeared in their last remaining stronghold within this region of Nephite territory.

"Surrender your arms, or meet your maker!" Helaman repeated.

The Lamanites shouted questions to Ammoron. Ammoron was as confused and confounded as those around him. He could not understand where he had gone wrong. As he played the events over in his mind, he heard an audible gasp from his men. He looked up and the entire facing wall, from end to end, was full of both Nephite and

Lamanite archers with their loaded bows trained down on him and his men.

"Surrender your arms, or prepare to die at our hands!" Helaman repeated more loudly and resolutely than before.

The demand had a much more compelling impact this time. They all realized that they were clearly within range of the hundreds of arrows waiting to take flight toward them. Not a few began to panic and squirm, but none of them fled.

"I'll never surrender to such as you!" Ammoron defiantly replied.

"Very well. Archers!" Helaman declared.

The air was pierced with hundreds of arrows simultaneously released on the staggering Lamanites. The arrows fell on all sides, surrounding the Lamanites. From their view, there was no direction to run. No one in the field noticed that the arrows did not hit human targets, as Helaman had given orders to merely intimidate.

Helaman had his archers fire in successive rows. As one line of archers let fly, the next would be setting another arrow to their bows. The effect was complete, as there seemed to be no end to the arrows that rained down on the hapless, wondering lot.

In one, quick moment the invading army's safe haven had turned into a menacing threat. The individual Lamanites were attempting to deal with a tremendous number of mentally difficult and emotionally distressing factors all at once. The army they had chased had somehow appeared behind them. The city they had held was no longer theirs. The safety they anticipated was nowhere to be found. Of uttermost concern, death flitted by on every side.

It was too much for some of the soldiers. They began to bolt and flee to the wilderness for sanctuary. It began with a few, but quickly turned into many. Ammoron saw the panic in his men as they fled the field of battle. He barked hateful threats at his army. In the confusion and shouting, his threats were inaudible to most and ignored by the rest. Confusion turned to panic. The arrows continued to fall.

The Lamanite army began to retreat without any sense of uniformity. They acted as individuals and began making their own, separate ways toward the wilderness. Ammoron decided to attempt to maintain some degree of leadership. He chose to lead his army's retreat. He gave one, last, leering glare at Helaman on the wall. Through the shower of arrows, and across the field of battle, Helaman's eyes met Ammoron's. For a moment in time, those of the Nephite spiritual leader and those of the Nephite traitor held each other's glare.

Ammoron's were consumed with ultimate hatred, while Helaman's belied the compassion within his soul. Ammoron's eyes narrowed and his brow furrowed to a threat. Helaman's eyes softened. A smile crept upon his face. He nodded to his adversary. Ammoron cursed and then raised his sword and shouted as he ran in the direction of the land of Nephi. His army caught hold of the concept of returning to the safety of their own land. Once again, they followed their leader and disappeared out of this quadrant of Nephite territory.

Helaman and his army saw the retreat. The arrows continued to fly toward the fleeing Lamanites and struck the ground at the heels of those who ran all the way up until the last man emerged into the safety of the dense jungle. Finally, they stopped. Helaman's army cheered. It was a great day for the Nephite army. The Lamanites had finally been driven out of this entire portion of the land.

IN THE QUIET that followed the celebration, Helaman decided to write to Moroni, in hopes of securing more assistance. His letter began with the account of his brave young, Lamanite soldiers whose fathers had

sworn to live peaceful lives. It concluded with the following summary:

> . . . *And of those cities that had been taken by the
> Lamanites, all of them are at this period of time in our
> possession. Our fathers and our women and our
> children are returning to their homes. But behold, our
> armies are small to maintain so great a number of
> cities and so great possessions.*
>
> *But, we trust in our God who has given us victory
> over these lands, insomuch that we have obtained
> those cities and those lands, which were our own. Now
> we do not know the cause that the government does
> not grant us more strength; neither do those men who
> came up unto us. We do not know but what you are
> unsuccessful, and you have drawn away the forces into
> that quarter of the land, if so, we do not desire to
> murmur.*
>
> *If it is not so, we fear that there is some faction in
> the government, that they do not send more men to our
> assistance, for we know that they are more numerous
> than that which they have sent. But, it mattereth not,
> we trust God will deliver us, notwithstanding the
> weakness of our armies, and deliver us out of the
> hands of our enemies.*
>
> *Those sons of the people of Ammon, of whom I
> have so highly spoken, are with me in the city of
> Manti; and the Lord has supported them and kept
> them from falling by the sword, insomuch that even
> one soul has not been slain. But, they have received
> many wounds; nevertheless they stand fast in that*

liberty wherewith God has made them free. And they are strict to remember the Lord their God from day to day and observe to keep his statutes, judgments, and commandments continually. Their faith is strong in the prophecies concerning that which is to come.

Now, my beloved brother, Moroni, may the Lord our God, who has redeemed us and made us free, keep you continually in his presence. May He favor this people, even that you may have success in obtaining the possession of all that which the Lamanites have taken from us, which was for our support. And now, behold, I close mine epistle. I am Helaman, the son of Alma.

Chapter 27

Zarahemla

———⟫◆⟪———

*M*oroni and his officers were still gathered in their makeshift strategy room in Mulek. When Moroni finished reading aloud the message from Helaman, he tossed it onto the table in front of him. He sat back with a thoughtful look on his face. The others sitting around the table remained motionless, impressed with the account they had just heard. Moroni broke the silence.

"Extraordinary! Simply extraordinary," was all that he could say as he stared at the message on the table with an impressed feeling of awe.

"Agreed," Lehi added.

"We need to make this tale known throughout this region," Moroni declared. "I think the people will take heart at hearing of their success. They could do with some good news such as this. Meanwhile, I'll write to Chief Judge Pahoran and encourage him to send reinforcements and provisions to Helaman. It will certainly be easier for them to maintain their cities than to have to retake them again."

MONTHS HAD PASSED. Again in the strategy room, Moroni was pacing the floor impatiently. A Nephite scout entered the room. Moroni turned to him expectedly.

"Any word from Pahoran yet?" Moroni asked with keen interest.

The scout shook his head negatively. In frustration, Moroni turned away from the scout and paced back to the table.

"Blast! How can they ignore our needs?" Moroni exclaimed, pounding his fist onto the table in an uncharacteristic show of anger. "What's the point of regaining territory if they simply let it slip back into Lamanite hands, while they sit on their pleasant cushions, drinking wine and growing fat?! Meanwhile, Ammoron has stepped up the Lamanites' attacks—"

"Sir, I have more news," the scout offered.

"More?" Moroni asked as he turned to face the scout who had not yet delivered his message.

"Yes, sir, and it isn't good," the scout said with an air of apology.

"Tell me," Moroni stated with an even temper.

"The city of Nephihah has fallen," the scout announced.

"Nephihah! What?! That's precisely where the reinforcements from Zarahemla were to go!" Moroni lamented.

"Yes, sir. I know, sir," the scout replied regretfully.

"Blast those pious judges!" Moroni called out. Then the anger subsided and drifted into concern. "Maybe we weren't meant to win this war after all. How can a people stay righteous if their leaders can't live proper examples? A people can only be as strong as the ideals their leaders portray. How can a government become so indifferent to matters concerning the freedom of their country?"

Moroni paused and then added with determination, "Bring me my writing utensils!"

Moroni wrote furiously. If the leaders of the Nephite society had turned to ill dealings and false ambitions, then he was not going to sit by and allow it to continue. He prepared the following epistle:

Behold, I direct my epistle to Pahoran, in the city of Zarahemla, who is the chief judge and governor over this land, and also to all those who have been chosen by this people to govern and manage the affairs of this war. I have somewhat to say by way of condemnation, for you yourselves know that you are appointed to support these efforts, yet you sit back and allow our people to go without provisions and support. I and my men, and also Helaman and his men suffer greatly from hunger, thirst, fatigue, and all manner of sickness and afflictions, yet you have done nothing to render aid.

Do you think you can sit back on your thrones in a state of thoughtless stupor, while your enemies are spreading the work of death around you and murdering thousands of your brethren? Men who have looked up to you for protection and have placed you in these positions of trust?

You could have sent armies to them, to strengthen them, but you have withheld your provisions from them, insomuch that many have fought and bled out their lives because of their great desires that they had for the welfare of this people, all the while they were about to perish with hunger, because of your enormously great neglect towards them.

331

I tell you that the blood of these thousands shall come upon your heads for vengeance, for God knows all their cries, and all their sufferings.

And now I say to you, I fear greatly that the judgments of God will come upon this people, if we allow your great wickedness to continue. For were it not for the wickedness that first commenced at our head, we could have withstood our enemies that they could not have gained any power over us.

Had it not been for these king-men who sought power and authority and caused so much bloodshed among ourselves, we would have been united in the strength of the Lord and prevailed against the Lamanites. But, we were weak as a people and have allowed them to come upon us and take possession of our lands and murder our women and children and inflict all manner of oppression.

But, why should I say much concerning this matter? For I know not but what you yourselves are seeking for authority. I know not but what you are also traitors to your country.

Or, is it that you have neglected us because you are in the heart of our country and are surrounded by security, that you don't send food to us, and also men to strengthen our armies?

Have you forgotten the commandments of the Lord your God? Do you suppose that the Lord will still deliver us, while we sit on our thrones and don't make use of the means that the Lord has provided for us? Will you sit in idleness while you're surrounded with thousands of those in the borders of the land who are falling by the sword, wounded and bleeding?

Do you suppose that God will look on you as guiltless while you sit still and behold these things? I tell you, nay! The Spirit moves within me to declare that if the leaders of this great nation do not wake up and arise to their sacred trusts, they will be removed from office, by word if possible, or by sword if necessary.

Now, except you repent of that which you have done, and begin to be up and doing, and send food and men to us, and also to Helaman, that he may support those parts of our land that he has regained, and that we may also recover the remainder of our possessions in these parts, I will leave a part of my freemen to maintain this part of our land, and I will come to you, and if there be any among you that has a desire for freedom, even if it's just a spark of freedom remaining, I will stir up insurrections among you, even until those who have desires to usurp power and authority shall become extinct.

I wait for assistance from you; and, except you administer to our relief, I will come after you, even to the land of Zarahemla, and smite you with the sword, insomuch that you can have no more power to impede the progress of this people in the cause of our freedom.

Behold, I am Moroni, your chief captain. I seek not for power, but to pull it down. I seek not for the honor of the world, but for the glory of my God, and the freedom and welfare of my country. And thus I close my epistle.

THE SUNRISE WAS brilliant and beautiful. Morning mist still hung on a peaceful, open field. The field butted up against the dense jungle. The jungle animals and exotic birds were just awakening to the new day. A baby monkey snuggled up to its mother, high in the trees. From this perch it heard a noise and looked down to see a Nephite messenger running through the jungle far below. The messenger passed directly beneath and then continued onward.

The messenger burst through the jungle and into an open field. He dashed through it without slowing his pace. Ahead, he finally saw the city wall. His destination now lay within his reach.

MORONI AND HIS officers sat at a wooden table reviewing maps and strategy. There was a distinct knock at the door.

"Enter!" Moroni acknowledged.

The Nephite Messenger opened the door. Other than beads of sweat that had formed on his forehead, he showed no sign of fatigue from his long journey back from their capital city. He wore light-weight clothes consisting of a shirt and skirt, with only a leather breastplate and strips of leather that dangled down across all areas of the skirt, for protection. His feet were shod in sandals that had straps that intertwined up his shins. Around his shoulder was a leather strap that held the message flask firmly to his side. He entered the room and once in, stood respectfully at attention.

"I bring word from Pahoran," the messenger announced.

"Pahoran? At last a timely response. Bring it here, please," Moroni responded with deep interest.

The Nephite messenger stepped forward and removed the message tube from his shoulder and dutifully handed it to Moroni.

"Thank you. You may wait outside," Moroni replied.

The Nephite messenger nodded, while still standing at attention, keeping his arms straight down along his sides. He then turned and left, closing the door behind him. Moroni opened the message tube and unrolled the message. The message was written in Pahoran's handwriting.

He read the message aloud for the others to hear:

> *I am Pahoran, the chief judge of this land, and send these words to Moroni, the chief captain over the army. I say to you, Moroni, that I do not joy in your great afflictions. They grieve my soul. But, there are those who do joy in your afflictions, insomuch that many have risen up in rebellion against me, and also those of my people who are freemen.*
>
> *Those who have sought to take away the judgment-seat from me have been the cause of this great iniquity. They have used great flattery, and have led away the hearts of many people, which will be the cause of sore affliction among us. They have withheld our provisions, and have prevented our freemen from coming to your aid.*
>
> *They have driven me out of Zarahemla, and I have fled to the land of Gideon, with as many men as it was possible for me to get. I have sent a proclamation throughout this part of the land seeking those who are friends of liberty. The people are flocking to us daily, with their arms, in the defense of their country and freedom.*

We've gathered enough forces that those who have done this great evil fear us and don't dare come against us in battle. But, they have possession of the land, or the city, of Zarahemla. And, they've appointed their most vocal leader, Pachus, to be a king over them. I have learned that he has written to the king of the Lamanites. He has joined an alliance with him in which they have agreed to allow him to maintain the city of Zarahemla, in return, they anticipate that it will enable the Lamanites to conquer the remainder of the land.

In your epistle you have censured me, but it doesn't matter. I'm not angry, but rejoice in the greatness of your heart. I, Pahoran, don't seek for power, save only to retain my judgment-seat that I may preserve the rights and the liberty of my people. My soul stands fast in that liberty in which God has made us free.

We will resist wickedness even unto bloodshed. We wouldn't shed the blood of our brethren if they wouldn't rise up in rebellion against us. But because they do rebel, I fear that this is necessary. Therefore, my beloved brother, Moroni, let's resist evil, and whatsoever evil we cannot resist with our words, such as rebellions and dissensions, let's resist it with our swords, that we may retain our freedom, that we may rejoice in the great privilege of our church, and in the cause of our Messiah and our God.

Therefore, come to me quickly with a few of your men, and leave the remainder in the charge of Lehi and Teancum. Give them power to conduct the war in

*that part of the land, according to the Spirit of God.
I have sent a few provisions to them, that they won't
perish while you come to my aid.*

*Gather whatsoever force you can during your
march here, and we will go speedily against those
dissenters, in the strength of our God according to the
faith that is in us. We'll take possession of the city of
Zarahemla, that we can obtain more food to send to
Lehi, Teancum, and Helaman. We'll go against these
dissenters and this mock king in the strength of the
Lord to put an end to this great iniquity.*

*Now, Moroni, I joy in receiving your epistle, for
I was somewhat worried concerning what we should
do, whether it should be just in us to go against our
brethren. But you have said, except they repent the
Lord commands that you should go against them.*

*See that you strengthen Lehi and Teancum in the
Lord. Tell them to fear not, for God will deliver them,
and also all those who stand fast in that liberty wherewith God has made them free. I now close my epistle
to my beloved brother, Moroni.*

As Moroni finished reading, he placed the message down with a
look of grateful pride in his eye.

"Well now, at least Pahoran has not turned traitor on us," Lehi
commented.

"Yes, it does my heart good to know that he's still true to the
cause of liberty," Moroni confirmed. "But, I'm greatly distressed at
those puffed up king-men. I fear that their desire for glory, wealth, and
power will be the ultimate downfall of the entire Nephite nation.
You'll note that it's not the Lamanites who break the peace with us,

but traitorous Nephites who fill them full of lies and prod them to war."

"Those pompous braggarts!" Teancum said in disgust. "Men are dying and they sit and quibble over whose robe looks more regal! Someone has to put a stop to this!"

"Yes," Moroni agreed, "And that someone is me."

"You? You're going personally?" Lehi said with a start.

"Certainly. I told Pahoran I'd come down and make him taste liberty if I learned he weren't true to the cause. I'm glad to see I don't have to for his sake, but I'm not going to sit here another day while these arrogant king-men quote their genealogies at me as if it gave them some sort of exemption from personally preserving the liberty of their country and fellowmen. I'm going to bring them down and for good," Moroni added.

"Will you be taking your army with you?" Lehi asked.

"No, I'll leave the majority of my men with you and Teancum. You two need to tend to the real war. Don't let Ammoron and his Lamanite horde gain any more ground," Moroni answered.

"Then how will you take on these king-men?" Teancum asked with both concern and confusion in his eyes.

"I'm going to do just as Pahoran recommended and stop by every city and village on the way to Zarahemla and seek out any true and loyal men who will flock to the cause of liberty and bring them with me. These people's leaders may be dwindling in wickedness, but I have faith that the people themselves are still good and wise," Moroni declared.

"And if you can't gather enough people to help you dethrone Pachus?" Lehi asked.

"Then these people will deserve him as their leader and the

destructive fate that will bring with it," Moroni had an unnerving look of stern sincerity in his eye.

Teancum had become contemplative. He began to approach Moroni, then stopped himself. Moroni noticed.

"Teancum, what is it?" the leader asked.

"Sir, it's nothing," Teancum responded turning his head away.

"It doesn't look like nothing. What's troubling you?" Moroni asked with a softening tone.

"Truly, I shouldn't bring this up," Teancum sidestepped.

Teancum now wished he had not initiated this exchange. But, he had now managed to gain Moroni and Lehi's full attention. He looked up and saw that this was the case, and realized he could not let the issue drop.

"To be quite honest sir, I wish I were going with you," he stated.

"I can handle this on my own, Teancum," Moroni replied.

"Yes, sir, I know this," Teancum said.

"And in my absence, I need to be able to rely on you back here more than ever before. The men need leaders such as you that they can look up to," Moroni added.

"Yes, sir, I know, sir. And I thank you for your confidence," Teancum responded.

"Then what is it?" Moroni asked.

"It's a personal matter sir," Teancum admitted.

Moroni paused. He had been so bent on strategies and conflicts at the moment that he suddenly realized he had forgotten the personal lives and interests of his men.

"This is about Sephara isn't it?" Moroni asked.

Teancum looked down and the great warrior became momentarily meek.

"Yes, sir. It's been a very long time," Teancum acknowledged.

"We've all left sweethearts at home, Teancum. All the more reason to end this conflict quickly and return home to them," Moroni responded with a mixture of directness that was not void of softness.

"Yes, sir. I agree. It's just that our child should be over a year old by now—if all went well. I haven't even received word that the child lived," Teancum explained.

In an understanding and somewhat fatherly tone, Moroni responded, "Teancum, I understand. I promise to look in on Sephara and give her your love and well wishes."

"I don't know if it's a boy or a girl, but I want to at least give the child something to remember me by while I'm away," Teancum stated in response to this unexpected opportunity.

Teancum fumbled through his clothing and finally pulled out an ordinary cloth handkerchief.

"Can you give my child this? It isn't much, but it's probably a better choice than a knife or an arrow," Teancum asked with gratitude.

Moroni took the cloth, folded it respectfully, and put it in his pocket.

"I'd be honored to," he replied.

Chapter 28

The Awakening

*M*oroni began his march at the head of the dozen warriors he was taking with him. His flag-bearer proudly bore the Title of Liberty and marched directly behind Moroni. The march was a quick-paced one. They intended to cover ground in a hurry.

They approached a Nephite city and marched in through the main gate. Moroni stood in the city square holding the flag. He spoke loudly, boldly, and with purpose. As he spoke, the crowd continued to grow in size.

"You Nephites of this great city!" he called out. "You fine people who understand the call of liberty in these troubled times! You must hear my words! Once again the king-men seek to destroy our fair society. Our leaders have been pushed aside by vainglorious king-men who seek an alliance with our enemies to protect their own supposed kingdom! They seek for power and glory, and they build their false empires on the backs of many a dead and dying patriot.

"We can't allow them to destroy all that God has blessed us with; all that we have fought and struggled for to make this a prosperous land. Those of you who understand the true meaning of liberty, who seek the protection of your homes and the lives of your loved ones, now is the time to stand forth and defend your country. Now is the time to rid ourselves of these king-men and show them that Nephites stand for liberty, not suppression. If you're in favor of liberty, now is the time to come forward and be counted!"

Moroni himself held the flag before him and waved it to emphasize his call to arms in the support of liberty. Men dashed to their homes to grab their swords and soldier's garb and returned to follow Moroni.

The scene was repeated multiple times. Moroni and his ever-growing army marched onward and forward with determination and righteous indignation in each step. Word of his approach preceded him at neighboring cities and men already stood at the ready by the time he approached. The Nephite leader, who had begun with a dozen men, now marched at the head of an army of soldiers that was several soldiers wide. It had grown beyond hundreds to become several thousand soldiers strong. They approached another city. Moroni stopped and raised his hand for the army to do the same.

"This is the city of Gideon where Pahoran said that he and his men have taken refuge," Moroni announced.

Moroni entered the city of Gideon and as he approached the city square, several soldiers came forward and met him. Two, tall and particularly handsome ones stepped forward. Moroni recognized them at once.

"Why, Corianton! Shiblon! You're here?" Moroni said with a smile.

"Certainly! We couldn't stay back with those foul king-men," Corianton said in a jovial way, but with strong sincerity.

"Tell us, what do you know of our brother, Helaman?" Shiblon asked with concern.

"That's part of the reason why I'm here. He's in the south—low on both reinforcements and provisions, which is why I wrote to Pahoran—" Moroni was cut off by a familiar voice.

"Moroni! Welcome and greetings!" Pahoran announced as he hurried in to the square. "We got word of your march and have been expecting you with gratitude and anticipation! We are eager to join with you in going up to Zarahemla."

Corianton and his brother nodded and mouthed that they would talk to him later, then turned to go so Moroni could talk with Pahoran.

"Pahoran, I remain grateful to know that you're still a friend to liberty," Moroni responded. "Let's make short work of Pachus so I can get back to defending the borders of our lands and you can return to the judgement seat and defend our laws."

"Well put, Moroni. Come, join us. We'll feed you and your men," Pahoran announced.

"I thank you, Pahoran. My men will appreciate your hospitality. I have an errand before I may join you, though," Moroni responded.

"An errand? What might that be?" Pahoran asked.

"You remember Teancum, no doubt?" Moroni said.

"Yes, quite well. He's a brave man, and a good leader," Pahoran replied.

"That's the man. Do you remember his wife, Sephara?" Moroni asked.

"Sephara? Certainly!" Pahoran said, his eyes lighting up. "She was actually quite vocal when the king-men began their uprising. While I appreciated her support, I cautioned her. I began to fear for her safety."

"She is safe then?" Moroni asked with genuine concern.

"Certainly, certainly! I've made sure of that," Pahoran reassured him. "She traveled with my group, and I personally found her a place to stay just around the corner from my own. She's a good woman, that Sephara. A fiery spirit and a solid head on her shoulders. She knows what's right and makes no bones about it."

Moroni smiled. "Yes, that sounds like the same woman. I still vividly remember the first time I met her after she'd escaped from the clutches of Morianton. She nearly took out my best guard."

They both laughed briefly.

"At any rate, Teancum asked me to look in on her. If you don't mind, I'd like to do that first thing," Moroni said.

"I understand completely. Teancum—and Sephara for that matter—deserves no less. I'll personally lead you to her where she's staying," Pahoran replied.

MORONI AND PAHORAN walked down a nicely kept walkway between buildings. They rounded a corner, approached another small home, and stopped. Pahoran gestured to a door on their right.

"She's in there. I'll leave you to meet with her alone. I'll be in the main chamber hall when you're through. I believe you're familiar with its location," Pahoran said.

"Yes, sir. Thank you again. And, it's good to see you in good health, Pahoran," Moroni replied.

"And you," Pahoran said, patting the military leader's shoulder.

Pahoran turned and left. Moroni knocked on the wooden door. A voice called out from inside.

"Yes, who is it?" Sephara called out.

"A friend on an important errand," Moroni replied.

Sephara's voice grew louder as she rushed to the door. "Moroni?! Is that the captain's voice?" She pulled the door open. "It is! Welcome, welcome, come on in! How good it is to see you! How's my Teancum?"

Moroni stepped into her home and Sephara closed the door and gestured for him to sit on a wooden chair handcrafted from rainforest wood and bound together with leather thongs.

"He's doing quite well. He very much wanted to come himself, but his duties wouldn't permit," Moroni explained.

"I understand," Sephara replied.

"I must confess that he very nearly convinced me to let him come, but I really do need him back at the front. With me gone, he and Lehi are the only sound leadership those men have. He's a very important man, your husband," Moroni added.

Sephara seemed to take pride in his words.

"Yes, in more ways than one. I miss him terribly," Sephara confessed.

"Yes, well, he asked me to give you this for your child," Moroni said.

He reached into his pocket and pulled out the folded cloth he had kept safe from the time Teancum gave it to him until then.

"He said he knows it isn't much, but he wanted your child to at least have something of his to remember him while he's away," Moroni explained.

Moroni handed the cloth to Sephara. She took it gingerly, looked at it, and pulled it to her cheek, to the same place that Teancum had last touched her. She closed her eyes for a moment in remembrance of their last parting. She spoke with her eyes still shut initially.

"It's been such a long time," she sighed slowly, paying heavy emphasis to the word "long."

"Yes, it has. Hopefully, we'll be able to put an end to it soon," Moroni added trying to be of comfort.

His thoughts could not help drifting to the memory of his own wife who waited for him with longing. His thoughts were interrupted as a wobbly one-year-old boy stumbled his way into the room. Both turned to see him.

"Well, this can't be the little one is it? Look how big he's grown!" Moroni smiled.

The boy saw Moroni and smiled back with a glowing look of honest innocence. It was a look that this seasoned soldier had not seen in many, many months. The toddler held his hands out and began walking quickly toward him. With the characteristic difficulties of all toddlers, he spoke a word his mother had been teaching him.

"Pa-pa!" the boy uttered with a degree of concentration.

Sephara smiled and corrected her son. "No, no, Nephi, this isn't your papa. This is Moroni, a very brave man who is a good friend of your papa. And he's brought a gift to you from your papa. Come here and see this, Nephi."

Moroni rose and picked up the boy. The boy hugged him affectionately and Moroni returned the hug. He then gave the boy to Sephara, who handed him the cloth.

"See, Papa gave you a handkerchief to wear," she said.

She wrapped it around his neck and tied it off. Moroni still stood, watching the mother and son.

"It's been a long time since I've seen my own boys. They must be growing too," Moroni said.

Sephara looked to Moroni.

"Moroni, just do what you can to put an end to this senseless bickering and fighting so we can all be with our families again. I've been telling Nephi all about his brave father, but he needs to see him for himself. He needs to feel his warmth and love, hear his voice, and learn from his wisdom." She paused, being strong and holding back tears. Then added a bit more silently, but still audibly. "I do too."

Little Nephi wobbled about the room proudly wearing his father's gift.

THE COUNCIL CHAMBERS in Zarahemla had been converted into a throne room. The newly self-crowned King Pachus sat on his throne enjoying his new power. He was flanked on each side by several of his loyal supporters who he had rewarded by making them stewards of the kingdom. They sat in the chairs of the former judges who they had chased off to make room for themselves.

A messenger rushed in with news. The messenger was in great haste and anxiety. He was caught between wanting to rush up to the king and blurt out the news, and knowing that he must follow the recently instituted platitudes of the throne room lest he suffer the dire consequences of the king's wrath. He controlled his rush and bowed ceremoniously half a moment before the king's patience was taxed.

"Oh, mighty, wise, and powerful king, I have news that must be heard," the messenger offered.

"What news is this that intrudes upon my day?" the king snidely demanded.

"In my journey in your fine kingdom this day I saw Pahoran leading a large group of men this way," the messenger stated.

"Pahoran? Is he coming to admire my kingdom?" King Pachus arrogantly asked.

"With all due respect, great king, I don't believe that is his intent. The man who marches by his side bares a strong resemblance to Captain Moroni and—" the messenger was interrupted.

King Pachus rose abruptly to his feet.

"Moroni!" he said with concern, "I thought he was occupied with the Lamanites to the north? Are you certain?"

"Yes, sire, nearly certain. The man behind Captain Moroni bore the Title of Liberty. They looked very determined and are coming at a quick pace," the messenger replied.

The king remained standing, puzzling what to do next. One of his advisors, who secretly wished for the crown himself, broke the silence.

"What an excellent opportunity for our new king to prove his leadership by meeting Captain Moroni and Pahoran and ridding them from our land," the advisor slyly unfurled his words. "When you do this, your majesty—when you lead this people to victory over our old foe—they will see your natural leadership and embrace your reign with the support and loyalty that your regal lineage warrants."

King Pachus was still enveloped in his thoughts, but had heard these words, as had all in the court. It was clear that he had no choice, but to lead the attack. Anything less would be a tremendous loss of face and lead to an internal strife, as those contending for the throne would try to determine who should rightfully replace a cowardly king. In the advisor's mind, that choice was already clear.

"Yes, yes, of course," the king acknowledged with distraction. "Sound the alarm and rally the troops. We'll rid ourselves of this scourge Moroni once and for all." There was no enthusiasm in his voice.

MORONI AND PAHORAN led their troops. They were within sight of Zarahemla.

"Do you believe Pachus will see reason and give himself up, or will there be trouble?" Moroni asked as they came within a few leagues of the city gate.

"Based on the boasting and threats he gave when he ousted me from the judgement seat, I'd say we need to consider him a very serious threat. My men and I were fortunate to get out of Zarahemla with our lives," Pahoran warned.

"What a pathetic waste of potential. He could have made a great leader had he not sought so passionately after power," Moroni lamented.

Just then, Zarahemla's city gate burst open. A flood of Nephite soldiers poured out toward Moroni and Pahoran's troops. They dashed madly across the field. Pachus was in the lead. He lunged directly at Moroni who parried his blow. Pachus turned to fight more, but tripped on his own regal robes that he had worn over his armor and fell upon his own sword. The skirmish was furious, quick, and decisive. Within moments, Moroni's men had the upper hand and Pachus' remaining men surrendered themselves and were marched back into the city.

THE COUNCIL CHAMBERS had been restored to a judgement hall rather than a throne room. Pahoran sat as chief judge over the trial of the king-men who had promoted the insurrection that brought Pachus into power. The air was charged from energetic accusations, denials, and cross-examination.

"Enough!" Pahoran declared with vigor. "All of the Nephites are blatantly aware of the trouble you king-men have caused this nation. You shall each be tried to assess your loyalty. Those who played the most active role in this treason will be tried and executed as traitors to liberty. The rest of you will have the option of swearing allegiance to the Title of Liberty and the cause of freedom, or suffering the same ignominious death as your foolish brethren."

MORONI SENT SOME six thousand men and provisions to aid Helaman. Both Corianton and Shiblon were among those who eagerly volunteered to aid their brave brethren in the south. Six thousand more were sent to Teancum and Lehi. They were heavy laden with provisions.

Chapter 29

Moroni's Return

━━━◗◆◖━━━

Moroni was encamped with his men far from Zarahemla on their journey northward back to help Lehi and Teancum fight for the cause of freedom. He sat at a makeshift table with other newly recruited military leaders. These were men from among those who had joined him during the march to Zarahemla.

"Again, I appreciate your willingness to do the right thing and push back our foe. Now that we've cleaned our own house, we can send reinforcements to Helaman and also Lehi and Teancum. We can focus on the Lamanites that Ammoron had stirred up. I believe we can actually gain some advantage from this little escapade," Moroni explained.

"How so, Captain, sir?" an officer asked.

"I have no doubt that my few men and I were seen by Lamanite spies as we journeyed south to Zarahemla. What did these spies report to Ammoron?" Moroni pondered. "Probably that a small band of men have wandered away from the main army of the Nephites. Even if they were able to recognize me, they wouldn't be able to do anything more than speculate.

"The last thing they should anticipate is that our return would include not a dozen or so soldiers bearing provisions, but a vast army numbering in the thousands of you who have flocked to the standard of liberty. I believe as Ammoron's armies contend against Lehi's and Teancum's in the north, we should be able to overpower and surprise the Lamanites from the south. My plan is to push and conquer until we have them with their backs to the sea at the City of Moroni. Here!"

Moroni pointed to a specific spot on the map. "I have no doubt that Ammoron will be among that last group of men," their commander continued. "Helaman may have pushed him out of that area of land, but I have confidence that he'll make his way back to the main action with Teancum and Lehi. I also believe, if we succeed at pushing the Lamanites that far, we'll break their spirits. Ammoron will have to win back their loyalty and refuel their interest in continuing a war which has gone on far too long. I believe if it weren't for Ammoron and Amalickiah's dogmatic leadership, this war would have ended long ago. It's time to end it. Now.

"Now! So, we have to take the upper hand and do our most critical fighting. We need to push hard, quickly, and with determination. I want word to get back to Ammoron that there's an unexplained, unanticipated whirlwind of swords coming from the south. If Ammoron hears it, his men will hear it. We can pit their fear against them."

Moroni's face was firm, but impassive. He had no lust for blood, but a strong determination to end the conflict and return peace to their society. He was willing to pay whatever price necessary to secure that peace. The campfire light flickered across his face, while the shapes in the background were shrouded in blackness. The determination to take an aggressive offense in this lingering war was clear in Moroni's expression. After the meeting, the men retired to their tents. The only lingering sounds were those of the campfire burning and the night sounds of the jungle animals.

THE CALM MORNING light grew within the peaceful jungle. The enslaved Nephites unenthusiastically milled about their occupied city doing such menial tasks as fetching water from the wells and serving their Lamanite captors. One Lamanite purposely knocked down a cup of water brought to him by a conquered Nephite. The Nephite stooped to retrieve it while the Lamanite and his two companions laughed loudly, mocking his servitude.

The Lamanites were clearly in control, but there was not a large number of Lamanites in the city. High on the city wall, two Lamanite guards paced next to each other, preparing for what they anticipated to be another dull day. They stood on the catwalk of the south wall, but were facing north, looking beyond the city and passed the northern jungle, where they longed to join the battle.

"Well, friend, it's another day," the one guard offered.

"Yes, another exciting day in the middle of nowhere," the other guard blurted.

"I long to be up north in the middle of the action," the first guard whined.

"How do we end up with the dull duties? These people hardly need guarding. Why can't we go up north with Ammoron and the main army?" his partner moaned.

"Maybe then we could see some action—"

The guard was interrupted by a crude grappling hook that had been flung over the wall and now clung to the banister directly in front of him. He turned to see where it had come from, only to be met by a spontaneous flow of Nephites hopping over the wall which they had just scaled. They continued to pour over the wall and fill the catwalk.

The outer side of the city wall was literally covered with Nephites climbing with ladders or climbing spades. The two Lamanite guards were easily subdued. The remaining Nephites on the catwalk leaped down to the city square and quickly overpowered all of the Lamanites within sight. A large Lamanite commander, still half-dressed from being awakened by the commotion, wandered out from his bunk-house.

He was suddenly surrounded and captured as he still pulled at his robes. His Nephite captors whisked him to the center of the city square, toward the city gate. He was indignant and struggled. As he was brought to the gate, Nephites opened both of the large doors. Moroni strode into the city, with dignity and haste. He was followed by a banner bearer, proudly bearing the Title of Liberty. The freed captives cheered.

Shemnon, the Lamanite leader, was dumbfounded and dropped the ends of the robes in his arms. His lips stammered then he muttered, "Mo–Moroni!"

He dropped to his knees, pleading for mercy.

Moroni approached him directly and commanded, "On your feet! Set an example for your men!"

"Please, Moroni, spare us!" Shemnon pled.

"Spare you! What, do you think we'll just line you up and cut you down?" Moroni asked with incredulity.

"Yes, of course, Ammoron, said so!" Shemnon replied.

"Ammoron said so? He did, did he?" Moroni was intrigued. He added, "Let me show you how a real Nephite treats his captives. If

354

you and your men will swear an oath of peace, we will escort you to the land of Ammon where you can live out your lives in peace with your other Lamanite brethren who have already sworn that oath."

"I don't believe it," Shemnon declared defiantly.

"Believe it," Moroni responded.

Moroni took off his helmet and knelt. He placed the tip of his sword into the ground symbolically indicating it was not readied for battle.

"As the Lord lives and as I live, if you swear to this oath, we will consider you as our own brethren and will die defending your lives," Moroni swore.

Moroni then stood up tall, leaning over Shemnon, with his helmet held against his side with one arm, and the end of his sword still tipped into the ground. Shemnon was astounded, but could not doubt the sincerity in Moroni's voice and eyes.

"We will swear the oath," he said at last.

Moroni sheathed his sword and cheerily stated, "Excellent! An excellent choice, especially since the alternative was imprisonment or death to all those who resist or attempt to flee. I offer peace and trust as freely as some would offer pain and death, but I'm not one to be trifled with. Had you not accepted my offer, you could have paid with your lives."

Shemnon swallowed hard at this, but was still grateful for Moroni's offer of genuine benevolence. While Moroni eyed Shemnon, the banner bearer had scaled the city wall. He walked along the catwalk above Moroni. With pride and enthusiasm he posted the city's copy of the Title of Liberty. The air seemed sweeter as the Title of Liberty blew freely in the breeze over the liberated city's gate.

SOME HOURS LATER, Moroni was again in the city square talking with the reinstated leader of the Nephite city. The Lamanite leader, Shemnon, stood nearby with two of Moroni's men. The Lamanites were gathered together by the city gate. Nephites stood about them.

"Jothon, we appreciate your assistance," Moroni said. "Be sure your men get these Lamanites to the land of Ammon quickly and try to avoid open areas. We want to keep this little victory quiet from the other Lamanites for at least a few days. I'd like word of a couple of such victories to reach Ammoron all at once. We hope to be sending more through here on their way to the land of Ammon in the next few days. Make them feel at peace, and protect them with your lives. Many of them will have sworn to the oath of peace. The rest will have sworn to at least return to their own lands without causing more harm to our people. You should be able to trust them implicitly."

"Understood. And, my people and I thank you again, Captain Moroni. May God watch over you and prosper you on your way!" Jothon replied and nodded with appreciation and respect.

"Thank you. Just keep the Title of Liberty flying freely above your city walls so that all may know that it is by the hand of God that this liberty has been granted to you," Moroni admonished.

Moroni turned to Shemnon, the vanquished Lamanite leader.

"As promised, my men will guide you to the land of Ammon. Remember that they will be with you to protect you. They are not your guards, nor are you their prisoners. Having sworn to the oath of peace, you will be utterly defenseless otherwise," Moroni stated.

"I understand completely," Shemnon replied. "Captain Moroni, I thank you again for your trustworthy and noble dealings. You are a far different man than Ammoron has taught us to believe."

"Should that really surprise you, when you step back and look at Ammoron's actions more closely?" Moroni asked.

"No, I suppose not," Shemnon acknowledged. "But, when your fathers have taught you for generations to hate a people, it's hard to not believe a man who reinforces those teachings with more lies."

"Let's hope we can rid our civilization of some of this never-ending hatred and distrust our peoples have held for each other," Moroni offered.

Moroni sent him off with a smile, but inwardly he sighed at the burden of the task that still lay before him. As Shemnon and his men disappeared through the gate, Moroni thought, "I've got other cities to free before I can rest."

THEY WERE IN a thick jungle. Moroni and his leaders laid in waiting, watching for their scout to return. The rest of Moroni's men were concealed behind them. Moroni's scout came running up, keeping low. He jumped over the fallen tree, which concealed Moroni and the others. The leaders all huddled around him and kept their voices low.

"The Lamanites have taken the city all right. They don't look any more prepared for us than the last bunch," the scout reported.

"How many are on the walls?" Moroni asked.

"Less than a handful of fingers," the scout replied.

"Good. I see no reason to do this any differently from last time," Moroni stated.

Moroni turned to his leaders. "You've done this before, so I don't expect any problems. Remember, keep the casualties low. I want no needless killing."

"Understood," his officers replied.

"Inform your men. When I see each of you return, I'll assume we're ready for the assault. Go!" Moroni ordered.

THE FIELD THAT separated the city from the jungle was a dozen leagues wide, flat and covered with a soft grass that stood half a meter tall, and increased in height slightly where it butted up against the jungle. Moroni's face became visible at the very edge of the jungle. To his right and left, about ten paces apart, the other leaders' faces became visible, one by one.

Once all leaders were revealed, Moroni leaped forward, out of the jungle, and began a quick dash across the field toward the city. The entire jungle border became saturated with Nephites silently leaping out onto the field and following Moroni's dash for the city. The flow seemed to be an endless stream of countless soldiers leaving the jungle and quickly making their way to the unsuspecting, captive city.

Soon, the Nephites approached the city wall. They deftly pushed the spears and staves aside, clearing the path through the trench. They began scaling the great wall. Again, they covered it like ants. The soldiers climbed quickly, digging handholds with their climbing spades, and turning these into footholds as they scaled at a surprisingly rapid pace. They bore knotted ropes that they planned to tie off at the top of the wall to aid other soldiers after them. Some soldiers had ladders or ropes with wooden grappling hooks attached.

As the first wave of soldiers leaped over the top of the wall, they immediately engaged the few guards on duty. That first wave included a vast majority of Nephite soldiers who had no guards to engage, so they immediately scaled down the catwalk to take charge of the action in the city square.

The second wave stopped at the top of the wall to attach ropes and tie off the tops of ladders for those behind them to increase their ascent.

A small group of soldiers from the first wave who had leaped down from the catwalk now dashed to the city gate. As they pulled it open, Moroni was the first to enter—boldly, alertly, and without danger of attack. He was flanked by a large group of his soldiers. The city was already under Nephite control before Moroni was able to take a dozen steps through the gate and into the courtyard.

Moroni strode to the center of the square to meet his soldiers who had gathered Lamanite captives. Moroni showed satisfaction at their success, but not the impertinent pride often displayed by power-hungry conquerors. He made his victory certain, but allowed his foes to retain their dignity.

"You Lamanite brethren have fought bravely over the years, but on this day your fighting is complete," he declared in a loud voice. "We offer you a choice. You have three alternatives. You may choose to swear the oath of peace. You may choose to swear to return to your own lands without causing any further contentions or harm to my people. Or, you may choose death. The choice is yours, but the decision will have very real and very swift consequences. I urge you to choose wisely."

Moments later, oaths had been sworn and Moroni looked over the faces of the freed Nephites. Their looks of gratitude and rejoicing made his heart burn with thankfulness within him. He noted the sense of satisfaction in his soldiers who had played a significant role in easing the burdens of their brethren.

He also noted the faces of the Lamanite prisoners who had sworn to live in peace—an oath they had never before anticipated making. The liberated Nephite city had an air of enthusiasm and potential prosperity to it. The Title of Liberty again flew freely, hoisted high above the city gate.

THE SKY WAS gray and foreboding. A massive flash of lightning revealed Moroni's men dashing toward another city. The Nephites advanced at a furious pace in spite of the pouring rain. The hand-to-hand combat was quick and decisive. The Nephites' pounding rained down on their Lamanite foes with all the pounding fury of the unpleasant elements. They conquered that city. Moroni stood in the city square ignoring the torrent and gave his captives the option of death or peace. He watched as two of his soldiers posted the Title of Liberty high above the city's main gate.

The succeeding days brought similar attacks on other occupied cities. Moroni's army continued to regain control of several Nephite cities. His powerful army's confidence increased with each victory. The bare-boned troops left by Ammoron to guard the occupied cities were no match for Moroni's forces. The assaults turned into a series of routs fulfilling Moroni's objective of carving a path and raising the Title of Liberty through the lands that the Lamanites had occupied, on his journey to the sea, and Ammoron.

A sword slashed through a rope holding fast a beam that locked a city gate. The door began to open, as it had so many other times in other retaken Nephite cities, for Moroni to enter.

A CITY GATE partially opened. A ragged, breathless Lamanite pushed through the narrow opening just as two Lamanite guards on either side of the double doors pushed them closed and another guard replaced the large beam that locked the gate. The Lamanite messenger collapsed onto the dirt, then got to his feet.

"Where is Ammoron? I must see Ammoron!" the messenger cried out in desperation.

One of the Lamanite guards helped him up and helped him on his way toward the inner city.

AMMORON SAT WITH several of his leaders, in a large room converted into a throne room. The Lamanite guard entered with the messenger. Ammoron looked up upon their entrance.

"So, you must be the messenger my men spotted," Ammoron said with arrogant contempt. "What news do you bring? It better be good. With Teancum and Lehi holding fast, I can use some good news."

"Sire, I dare not share my news, if it's good news you await," the messenger responded.

"Don't play with me boy! Tell me the news, good or ill!" Ammoron warned.

"Yes, sire," the messenger replied.

The messenger bowed respectfully, and had difficulty getting back up, due to his exhaustion.

"I have traveled long and fast to deliver my message, sire," the messenger explained, seeking at least tolerance for his faltering speech, and perceiving from his king's mood and demeanor that he would not receive any compassion, let alone respect.

Ammoron allowed for the sacrifices of his loyal subject by giving him the courtesy of a polite, but somewhat demanding restatement of his question.

"What message is that?" he repeated.

"Actually, it's more of a warning than a message," the messenger respectfully corrected Ammoron.

Ammoron grew visibly impatient. The failure to conquer in his battles with Lehi and Teancum weighed heavily on his increasingly ill mood.

"Warning?! All right, what is your warning, then?" the king bit out.

"There is a large Nephite army cutting their way in this direction," the messenger declared. "They move as if on wings. It is as if God himself were leading them. None can stop them. And, the men are growing fearful. The Nephites grow in numbers with each city they retake."

The messenger's words finally struck a chord with the arrogant and volatile self-declared monarch. "*Each* city—What do they do with so many prisoners?"

"I've been told they don't take prisoners," the messenger responded—somewhat pleased, in an odd sort of way. Although the news was unfortunate for the Lamanite army, it was ironically rewarding for the messenger to be able to deliver news that was carrying an impact on a ruler for whom his respect was dramatically diminishing, the longer he spent in his presence.

"No prisoners?! Do they wipe them out whole, cutting them down even after they surrender?!" Ammoron said in shock. He was momentarily unable to suppress his surprise. He caught himself and tried to turn this into a political move by adding, "It's as I told you. These Nephites cannot be trusted. They are without honor!"

The messenger, no longer impressed with the megalomaniac with whom he conversed, mildly chose to interrupt and directly contradict Ammoron. By so doing, he thwarted Ammoron's attempt to debase the morals of their mortal enemies.

"No, your majesty," he stated calmly. "As I understand it, Moroni himself is leading this army—"

"Moroni!" Ammoron shouted, interrupting the report. He now began to pace, and turned to one of his generals. "I thought your men had him holed up with Lehi and Teancum?" he chastised. He paused and mused the concept. In a moment, he added with bitter harshness, "This is the first statement that has made any sense. I told you I was growing skeptical of your reports!"

The general's face flushed with worry and concern. He was on the verge of giving excuses and defending his troops' reports, but Ammoron was disinterested and turned back to the messenger. During his pacing Ammoron had produced a dagger and was impatiently thumping one of the flat sides of its blade in his hand.

"So, tell me more about what Moroni is doing with these captives, if he truly isn't slaying them!" Ammoron demanded.

The messenger continued, "They convert them to their ways and have them swear an oath of peace."

Ammoron had grown increasingly agitated throughout this discussion. Still standing, he mocked this statement. "An 'oath of peace!' Now *that* sounds like Moroni!" Ammoron scoffed. The thumping of the knife in his hand grew harsher. "Well, we'll just have to round up some of these soldiers who have sworn this *oath of peace* and get them back into action," he vowed.

The messenger dared to stand erect and defend the oath the Lamanites had taken, for the sake of the oath and their individual honor.

"These men have sworn an oath," he declared. "None who have sworn this oath will be willing to touch a sword!"

Ammoron was in a fit of pique by now and sincerely frustrated. Tired of being daunted by the Nephites at every turn, and having grown especially tired of the recent bad news, he took out his wrath on the messenger who he perceived as virtually taunting him in his support of Moroni's actions and successes.

"Enough!" he ordered.

"I only speak the truth, my king," the messenger responded calmly and bowed slightly in mock deference to the brutal monarch.

"I said *enough!*" Ammoron shouted as he let loose his anger and flung his dagger at the messenger.

His aim was slightly off, and it missed its target: the messenger's heart. Instead, it sank deeply into his left shoulder. The soldier staggered backward, but did not fall. The others in the room were taken aback by Ammoron's treatment of this messenger who had risked his life to bring this news to their king. Some of them had to restrain themselves from going to his aid. None of them dared to speak out against Ammoron.

The messenger winced with pain, then straightened himself. With the knife still soundly sticking into his shoulder he proclaimed, "These men have sworn an oath. To them, their word is their lives. They would sooner die than go back on it. If you try to force them to break their oaths, you will fail. I have suffered much to bring you news of an enemy who wants to conquer you. Your response to my sacrifices has taught me much, your majesty."

The last two words were spoken with emphasis and more than just a hint of contempt. The messenger bowed and turned to leave, without being given permission to go. He paused and turned back to face the king once more.

"I will leave you with one last word," he stated with a matter-of-fact tone, "Moroni is coming. He's coming for you. He knows where you are. He's going to find you. I advise you to leave this place if you want to live to see another dawn."

The messenger turned to leave and headed directly to the door.

Ammoron's blood boiled over the taunt and the insolence. "I did NOT give you leave to go. Stop!"

The messenger continued to exit.

"I said 'Stop!' You will stop!" the king cried out.

The messenger was at the doorway.

"You men, stop him this instant!" he ordered.

No one in the room moved except for the messenger as he disappeared through the doorway, and Ammoron, as he stamped his foot and raised his clenched fists in a wild, angry, frustrated, and worried scream. The scream was a name.

"Moroni! *Moroni*!!"

It was abundantly evident that he was losing control of his men's loyalty. The scream continued to echo and fade off as the would-be throne room emptied.

Chapter 30

Night Charge

*T*he Nephite camp was enveloped by the night. Most men slept, recuperating from the day's warfare, and preparing for more come first light. The campfire sporadically lighted Lehi and Teancum's faces. A shape moved in the dark beyond the fringes of the firelight. They looked up, curious. When they recognized the approaching figure, they stood with excitement and happiness flashing across their faces.

"Moroni!" they shouted in unison.

Their gleeful use of Moroni's name was in stark contrast to Ammoron's desperate and angry shout. Moroni stepped into the light and the three warriors shook hands enthusiastically and embraced as warriors do.

"It's been a long time, Captain, sir. It's good to see you well and to know that God is still prospering your efforts!" Teancum said, beaming with gratitude at the sight of his leader, mentor, and friend.

"Yes, we've heard much of the ruckus you're causing the

Lamanites! It's been a tremendous encouragement to our men," Lehi added with equal enthusiasm.

"By the grace of God, we're finally beginning to prosper. Pahoran is back on the judgement seat. The king-men are disbanded. The Title of Liberty flies bravely over many freed Nephite cities. Our Nephite brethren are reawakening to the duties of liberty. The Lamanites are being pushed out of our lands. The only thing left—" Moroni was cut off.

". . .The only thing left is Ammoron. He's the only thing still keeping this war going," Teancum finished with a very bitter edge to his voice.

Moroni eyed Teancum carefully, but agreed. Teancum's face and posture had visibly shifted to one displaying both annoyance and a determined malevolence at the mention of Ammoron.

"Yes, that seems to be true. But, we'll be putting a stop to his murderous ways soon enough," Moroni responded.

Lehi added with unbridled enthusiasm, "Yes, we will!"

With a small amount of reluctance, Teancum changed the subject, "Uh, Moroni, I mean Captain, sir, did you happen to—"

This time it was Moroni who interrupted, ". . . Did I happen to visit your wife? Yes. Yes, I did. She sends her love and wants you to know that she's doing fine!"

Teancum's face beamed.

"And, so is your son," Moroni added.

Teancum was taken aback and said with surprise. "My son? My SON?" he said loudly. "I have a son! I have a son!"

He shook Lehi's hand. Lehi slapped him on the shoulder congratulating him.

"Yes, his name is Nephi. From the looks of it, he's just learning to walk and talk," Moroni added.

"Walk? Talk? My word!" Teancum said astonished at his offspring's skill level.

"Yes, you should have seen him when he walked into the room. His face just lit right up and he called me, 'Papa.' It's obvious that Sephara's teaching him all about you," Moroni added with a smile.

Teancum was a bit distressed by this.

"He called *you* 'Papa?'" he asked with a touch of concern.

"Well, it was more 'Pa-pa,' but it was pretty clear what he meant," Moroni smiled.

Lehi nudged Teancum as he added, "It sounds like you have a bright young lad, Teancum. You should be proud!"

"Yes, I should. I mean, I am. I mean—hey, I've got a boy!" Teancum said in a daze.

Teancum sat with his thoughts to himself. Lehi shifted the conversation back to the business at hand.

"Captain Moroni, we know that the Lamanites are encamped in the city of Nephihah. We believe that Ammoron himself is with them. What do you propose we do? A full scale assault?" he asked.

"My men have been extremely successful as we made our way here. But, I have to tell you, quite frankly, that our success has been in cities that Ammoron left behind. For the most part, these cities only had enough Lamanites in them to keep their captives under control. Not enough to stage a true defense," Moroni began. "If Ammoron is there, then the bulk of his army will be with him," Moroni continued. "I don't want to blindly rush into this. If they do have a large number, we're much better off getting them to come out and fight us here, on the plains. I have my doubts that Ammoron will willingly convenience us in this way though. So, if he won't come out, I'm going to at least take a look and see what he has behind those city walls."

"How so?" Lehi asked.

"My men and I have become quite adept at scaling these walls. Once more shouldn't be too difficult," Moroni explained. "I'll go have a little look."

"You?! Now?" Lehi said with surprise.

"Certainly, me—now. Who else?" Moroni said with a smile.

He rose with determination in his eyes. Lehi rose as well. Teancum continued to sit. He mumbled to himself, "He should be calling *me* 'papa,' not someone else—"

THE SCENE WAS darkness. A singular man scaled Nephihah's city wall. He worked the wall with skill and made good progress. He was as silent as the night, which surrounded him. This proved difficult at one spot when a large chunk of dirt gave way to his climbing spade. For a moment, he lost his footing and clung by one hand. His body twisted and his back hit the wall. He righted himself, paused and continued his ascent.

As he reached the top, he again paused, raising his head warily over the edge to watch for guards. He saw a tower guard fast asleep to his left. He made out another guard to his right, also asleep. He dared climb over the edge and stood on the catwalk. He peered over the edge and saw that even the inner city guards were asleep. He could not spy an alert soldier anywhere.

"Well, I'll be," Moroni whispered to himself. "Fortune smiles brightly tonight!"

He quickly climbed back over the edge of the wall and descended.

BACK AT THE campsite, Lehi paced restlessly.

"I don't like this! I don't like it at all," he repeated for the umpteenth time.

"He's our commander. I think he knows what he's doing," Teancum pointed out.

"He's being foolhardy I say!" Lehi bit back. "We could have sent one of our spies. Why did he have to go himself?"

"Because I wanted a firsthand view of what awaits us," Moroni explained.

He entered the area lit by the campfire.

"Moroni! You're back safely!" Lehi exclaimed.

"Of course I am. But, thank you for your concern, if not your vote of confidence," he responded.

"I only meant that—" Lehi began stumbling for the right word at this awkward moment.

"He only meant that we've missed your leadership terribly these past few weeks and we would hate for it to be a permanent loss," Teancum completed.

"I know, I know. No matter. Meanwhile, I have news," Moroni said.

"Yes, well, what *did* you manage to learn, other than how to give me stomach cramps?" Lehi asked.

"They're there all right, but sound asleep. I think if we do this right, we can catch them wholly off guard," Moroni announced.

"Now? Tonight?" Teancum questioned.

"Yes, now. Yes, tonight," Moroni answered.

"Excellent! The sooner we put an end to this, the sooner we can return to our families!" Teancum said with genuine excitement.

"It has been a long, lonely battle," Lehi agreed.

"Yes, well, perhaps we can end it now. Gather the men quickly and quietly. I fear daylight may come too soon this night and actually work against us for once. Have the men bring their ropes. We'll go up the wall and let ourselves down into the city square. They're all encamped on the east side of the city. We'll scale the west wall, so as to get as many men into the city as possible before being noticed," Moroni commanded.

"Marvelous!" Lehi said.

The leaders hustled off to prepare for a night assault.

THE CITY WALL remained bathed in blackness. Moroni sat at the top and was silently urging the men onward. The outer wall was swarming with soldiers furtively making the ascent. They began to gather on the catwalk as more joined them. Moroni had them begin to tie their cords off and shinny down to the city square. Several dozen were in the square, many more were on the catwalk, when, suddenly, a loud horn sounding the alarm blared from the watchtower above the catwalk.

For a brief moment, the Nephites froze in their tracks. Then, realizing they had been discovered, they moved into action. An archer saw one of the tower guards blowing the signal-horn and took aim. He was successful and the guard collapsed, falling out of the tower and onto the ground far below. The alarm had been silenced, but the damage was done. The Lamanites were roused and gathering. Ammoron himself leaped into action wholly shaken from his former slumber.

"Hurry men, out the east entrance!" he commanded.

Ammoron chose flight over sudden defense and led his men on

a hasty retreat, abandoning the city without hesitation.

Moroni hastened his men, but was concerned about charging with too few. If they attacked without a sufficient number, it would be a suicide attempt. He shouted over the wall.

"Quickly! We need at least enough men to stage a decent charge! Hurry!" he urged.

The men on the wall now scrambled quickly and poured over the edge, down the ropes, and gathered into the square.

"Open the city gate! Hurry!" Moroni shouted as he anxiously estimated the number of men in the square.

He was anxious to ensure that their number was sufficient. He finally felt comfortable with their tally when the front gate was forced open and his men came charging through. He led them on a charge through the city, hot on Ammoron's trail.

"Quickly!" he yelled, "Before they're gone! Run!"

Moroni and his men ran at full speed across the city through the main streets, around the houses, and entered the eastern side only in time to see the last of Ammoron's men closing the eastern gate behind them. On the other side of the gate, two of Ammoron's men hastily tied off the door.

Still inside, Moroni anxiously encouraged his men to pull the gate open. After some struggle, it was opened enough to poke their swords through the opening and hack away at the thick ropes on the outer side of the gate. They finally cut it free and threw the gate open. With the rising of the morning sun, Moroni could see that Ammoron's men were moving quickly and were already far away.

"After them!" he commanded. "Catch them before they can make it to safety! This must end!"

Moroni's men charged after the Lamanites. Far ahead, Ammoron led the retreat; Moroni led the charge. Men from both armies simply ran as fast as their muscular legs could carry them. Eventually, Moroni's men overtook the rear part of the Lamanite army and a battle commenced. Ammoron saw this happen, but continued urging his men on.

"Ignore them!" he bellowed, "You men, hurry! We can make the city of Moroni by the seashore if we hurry! We should be safe there."

Ammoron then muttered to himself, "Now, there's some irony for you—"

The conflict between Moroni and Ammoron's rearward, now-abandoned men, was in full flame. Both sides fought fiercely. Moroni's men quickly gained the upper hand, however, against the still-groggy Lamanites. Soon, the Lamanites were surrounded and had to concede the battle. Moroni pointed to a group of his soldiers.

"You men, take these prisoners back to Nephihah. The rest of you, continue on with me!" Moroni ordered.

As Moroni turned to continue on, Teancum was by his side.

"The rest have gained ground. Ammoron is way ahead of us now!" Teancum lamented.

"Yes, but if we keep up a good pace, we should be able to catch up with them when they camp for the night. I'm not letting him slip away again. Not when we're so close," Moroni replied.

"I know. I can almost hear my love's voice again!" Teancum stated.

Moroni and Teancum charged off at the head of their large and determined army.

THE HILLSIDE OVERLOOKING the valley was steep and covered with dense, green undergrowth. It was the evening. The heads of Moroni, Teancum, and Lehi slowly rose into view.

"We've at least caught up," Moroni detected.

"It looks like the whole Lamanite army is down there!" Teancum added.

"Well, you've certainly succeeded at rounding them up. This really could be the final battle," Lehi pointed out.

The Lamanite encampment was already within the walls of the city of Moroni, on the border of the east sea. Thick jungle was to the south. The steep hill Moroni and the others were spying from was to the west. To the north, beyond a field and a less dense jungle, the triumvirate could see their Nephite camp. The Lamanites had nowhere to run. The conflict was inevitable.

"Yes," Moroni acknowledged. "Let's hope tomorrow proves to be a good day. Tell the men to get well-rested tonight."

"Yes, Captain," Lehi responded.

Moroni and Lehi backed down from their perch on the hillside. Teancum lingered. His face bore an uncharacteristically serious and sullen expression.

"It's been too long," he muttered inaudibly. "Too many lives disrupted. Too many good men dead. Too many widows. Too many children growing up without their fathers. It's all too much. And for what? For Amalickiah and Ammoron's own vain glory. This has got to end!"

Moroni, who descended with Lehi, stopped and turned back to Teancum.

"Teancum, are you coming?" he called in a hushed tone.

Teancum was shaken out of his thoughts, and turned.

"Yes, captain, I'll be right there," he replied.

He glared at the Lamanite encampment once more before joining Lehi and Moroni.

THE TRIO RETURNED to their campsite. The sun was now setting. Brilliant red and orange colors shined on the trees, the tents, and the faces of the three as they headed to their central tents. They paused before parting.

"Sleep well, my brethren. If we fare well tomorrow, we should soon be sleeping in more comfortable surroundings," Moroni said.

"Yes, *if,*" Lehi added.

The two did not notice the uneasiness in Teancum's face at Lehi's statement. It had made him wince. When Teancum parted from the others, he headed to his own tent. As he opened the tent flap and sat on his bunk, he muttered to himself.

"Yes, '*if.*' And 'if *not*' then this will go on and on forever. It's been too long already. This has got to end. Ammoron is to blame. If we could just get rid of Ammoron, then we could end this. He and his brother have upset too many lives. He must be made to pay. No, he must be taken out. If we can take him out, this will end."

As Teancum sat mulling over the situation, his face changed to a look of determination.

"I took out Amalickiah. I can do the same to Ammoron. This ends tonight!" he declared to himself, slapping his hand to his fist. "As soon as the others are asleep—" he concluded.

Teancum looked around his tent and silently began gathering supplies such as rope and his dagger. He put on his darkest clothes.

THICK BLACKNESS PERVADED the area. Only the weak and dying

campfire made the outside of Teancum's tent flap visible. Teancum's face poked through the tent's door. He looked around, then crept out. He had a small amount of rope, and his dagger at his side. He sneaked through the Nephite camp, and then toward the jungle, being careful not to be seen by the guards.

He hustled silently through the small wooded area that separated their encampment from the occupied city of Moroni. Before he entered the clearing that led to the city, he paused a moment to size up his next task, and ensure there were no Lamanite guards looking his way. Feeling secure, he silently burst across the field and stopped at the base of the city wall.

He quickly scaled it and tied off his rope at the top. He planned to use it to get both in and out of the city. He let himself down into the inner area. The Lamanites slept soundly after the day's long march. No guards appeared conscious. Teancum crept into the Lamanite encampment that filled the city square. He saw more tents beyond the first row of buildings, as well as several Lamanites lying in the open.

He was bent on finding Ammoron's tent. He was certain it must be in the central area, beyond the city square. He assumed Ammoron would want to put as many guards and soldiers between himself and Moroni as possible. He made a direct line for the city center that lay beyond the first row of buildings. He was soon deep within his enemy's temporary and hastily prepared lair.

He carefully walked through the street that passed through the first row of builds. He kept to the corners and shadows, dashing quickly from one spot of refuge to the next. Coming into end of the buildings, he found himself on the outskirts of the central plaza. He looked into it and saw a large tent among several others. He supposed that this one was Ammoron's.

He quickly made his way to it and peered in. To his surprise, he did not see Ammoron, so he continued on to the next. The third tent he came upon had spears set up crossing over each other in the door-way, in a crude, booby-trap fashion.

"This *must* be it," Teancum whispered to himself.

He gingerly pulled a corner of the flap open, just enough to peer into the tent. He allowed his eyes to focus in the tent's blackness and eventually his persistence was rewarded. There, lying on his back, completely asleep, lay his deepest enemy, Ammoron. Teancum nodded to himself and smiled with the satisfaction of finding his prey.

He attempted to pull the flap open more, but the spears began to fall. He caught one, preventing it from falling to the ground and alerting others to his presence. Still holding the spear, he again tried to enter the tent. His movements made the other spears even more unstable. He saw he would not be able to enter.

He looked at the spear in his hand and determined to use it. He turned it, pulled it inside the tent flap, took careful aim, and in spite of his awkward position, hurled it at Ammoron. He struck Ammoron directly in the chest. But, he had missed Ammoron's heart, allowing Ammoron a brief moment to sit up and cry out as he grabbed the spear with both hands. The king's life quickly ebbed out as he slumped forward in bed, leaning on the spear.

In this instant, Teancum saw success and failure both. The enemy king was dead, but now the camp was stirring because of their mur-derous monarch's death-cry. Teancum abandoned all thoughts of a careful stealthy flight. Instead, he simply turned and rapidly fled at full speed.

He made it to the short street before Ammoron's servants were even able to determine what the noise from their king's tent had meant. While Teancum ran, Lamanites dashed into their king's tent. A servant came out of the king's tent and cried out. "He's killed the king! Stop him! He's killed the king!"

By now, Teancum was entering the city square, dashing toward the city wall and the rope that would lead to his escape. A horn was blaring from the plaza behind him. Lamanites were becoming alerted even as Teancum jumped over tent ropes and around tables and smoldering campfires that filled the city square.

Several Lamanite soldiers were hot on his tail. Some bore spears, others bows. They all planned to strike him, but were unable to take clear aim because of the maze of tents. He dashed with all his speed, zigzagging through the maze.

To his advantage, Teancum gained ground on those who attempted to stop and aim. He dashed across the city square and quickly grabbed his rope and climbed the city wall. There would not have been time for him to untie the massive knots the Lamanites had used on the city gate. He tossed the rope over the other side of the wall and let himself down, dropping the last dozen feet in a free-fall.

He ran with brilliant speed across the field with arrows raining after him and passing him on either side. The city wall in the background was now littered with Lamanite bowmen. Just as he entered the safety of the jungle, he had a sudden, sharp look on his face. He continued on, running at a good pace, but with an arrow sticking out of his left shoulder blade. When he detected no one in pursuit, he first slowed, then stopped. He leaned on a tree for a moment, tried vainly to pull the arrow out of his back, but was unable to get a hold of it. He quickly chose to simply struggle on again.

A NEPHITE GUARD looked toward the woods. He detected some form of movement. Animal? Monkey? Lamanite? It was definitely human.

"Who goes there?!" the guard demanded.

Teancum staggered out of the woods. The guard recognized him. His eyes grew wide with surprise and concern.

"Teancum!" the guard exclaimed. "Captain! Captain Moroni! It's Teancum!"

The guard raced to aid Teancum while Moroni and others came from their tents. As Moroni approached, Teancum stumbled and fell. The guard knelt down and turned Teancum onto his side, careful to avoid putting pressure on the arrow. He held Teancum's head on his lap.

"Teancum, what have you done?!" Moroni cried out.

Teancum dimly opened his eyes as he heard his commander's voice. He smiled bravely.

"I've killed Ammoron," he declared in a weak, but triumphant voice. "I've brought peace! Tell my wife—" He paused, gasping for breath, "Tell my wife that I've brought peace for our child!"

Teancum stiffened suddenly, groaned, and went limp.

"Oh, Teancum! Teancum!—" Moroni mourned with tears in his eyes.

A full moon pulled out from between thick clouds and lit the tragic scene.

DAWN WAS JUST beginning. The field before the city of Moroni was full of morning mist. The roar of the ocean waves was heard faintly in the distance. Moroni and his mighty army stood at the edge of the forest, covering the latter end of the field. The city of Moroni, housing the now leaderless Lamanites lay naked and vulnerable before them.

The Nephite army stood frozen in time, waiting for the command. Half a dozen Nephites stood with torches burning. A jungle bird squawked a horrid sound. All eyes were on Moroni. He raised his sword high and straight above his head. With deliberation he lowered it, keeping his arm extended, and pointed it at the city. As one, the Nephite army filled the air with a war cry that split the soul. The Nephites began their charge.

INSIDE THE CITY, the remaining Lamanite leaders argued as to how to lead their defense. They still stood huddled around Ammoron's uncared-for and lifeless body.

"I say we mount the wall and pick them off with our archers," the tallest officer, Zenephi, proclaimed.

"They're too numerous. We'd stop the first wave, but soon our archers would be outnumbered!" a shorter, more practical Limhah pointed out with bitter accuracy.

"What was Ammoron's plan?" a third officer, Jacom, asked desperately.

"You know as well as I do that he shared very little!" Limhah again pointed out. He paused momentarily, then added with bitterness, "He probably made it up as he went along!"

"I agree. I don't believe he had a plan either. He was on the run," Zenephi stated.

At this point, the sound of the Nephite war cry penetrated their ears.

"My word, what is *that*?!" Jacom blurted out, unable to conceal his shudder.

"It's coming from everywhere!" Limhah shouted.

A Lamanite guard charged up to them.

"It's the Nephites! They're charging the city! I can't even see the end of the horde! What do you want us to do?" the guard pled.

"Put up the best defense you have," Limhah commanded. "Post archers on the walls. Put armed men in the square. Hold them off as best as you can! Hurry!"

"Yes, sir!" the guard replied and rushed off to fulfill his duties.

"Hold them off as best as you can? What kind of an order is that?" Zenephi chided.

"The kind which should give us enough time to escape out the back gate with the rest of our army," Limhah replied without shame.

He paused and looked the other two in the eye.

"Do either of you have a better idea?" he asked.

Neither spoke.

"I didn't think so. Now, summon your men. If we don't make haste, we may never see another day!" he shouted.

THE NEPHITES HAD charged the outer wall. The Lamanite archers were taking aim and letting fly. Two rows of Nephite archers had paused in the field and were picking off the Lamanite archers, thus limiting their effectiveness. Nephite wall-scalers ignored the shower of arrows that flew in both directions over their backs as they vigorously scaled the wall. The torch-men had lighted the city gate and waited for it to weaken enough for them to push through. It was only a matter of time until it would burst open as they pounded it with logs.

The wall-scalers mounted their summit at the same time that the city gate gave way. Nephites flooded the city from two levels. The hand-to-hand combat was nothing short of intense, but the Lamanites who remained near the gate were pitifully outnumbered. Moroni entered as all resistance crumbled. He raised his sword to stop the slaughter. He looked around, surprised at the low number of Lamanites. A Nephite came running along the wall's catwalk and came into view of the city square.

"Captain!" he shouted. "The Lamanites are fleeing out the back gate! There are many more than what you see here! It must be the rest of their army! Do we follow?"

"No," Moroni called back calmly and confidently. "I believe we declare victory. Teancum's sacrifice has secured peace in our land. Post the Title of Liberty men. It's time to go home!"

The Nephite warriors cheered. Even the now-kneeling, well-guarded Lamanite captives looked relieved.

For Home

———◆———

*M*oroni had regained his horse and rode slowly and alone along a lonely alley. He approached the home of Sephara. He dismounted and approached the door. His steps were long and deliberate. He carried Teancum's cloak, belt, and dagger. He knocked on the door.

Sephara opened the door. Little Nephi was now about two years old. He stood by her side looking at Moroni with curiosity. He still wore the handkerchief Teancum had asked Moroni to give him. As Moroni handed her the items he bore, she broke down in tears. Moroni tried to comfort her.

He told her of her husband's sacrifice and last words. She was proud, sad, shocked, heart-broken, and thankful all at once. Her tears continued to flow as she wrapped her arms around Moroni, thanking him for his thoughtfulness and support, and wishing—just wishing—that Teancum had come home.

Little Nephi held the cloak and belt. His expression showed that he was filled with wonderment about these new things and where his father was. He wandered away, deeper into the house as Moroni said farewell. Sephara watched him go and then slowly closed the door.

MORONI AGAIN RODE his horse along a path. He rounded a bend and saw his home and farm come into view. His heart leaped with anticipation and satisfaction. He could see two of his sons tilling the ground. When he was within about fifty yards of the home, the sons saw him and shouted. Moroni's wife heard them and hurried out the door. She dropped the bundle she had been carrying when she saw who this "stranger" was and ran to him.

Moroni charged his horse up to the home, dismounted, and opened his arms to greet his family. They showered him with hugs and kisses. After a long embrace, Moroni looked his sweetheart in the eye.

"I'm home now," he said.

Moroni and his family stood reunited in a peaceful land. The lush fields and jungles of the area no longer harbored warriors and spies bent on death. The house was now a home, rather than a strategic location. The sky was peaceful and revealed a beautiful sunset. Life—true life—could begin again.

Chapter Notes

*A*general note about this book is that this is an adaptation of the *Book of Mormon*. As such, an attempt has been made to stay true to the original text where possible. There are many places where text has been taken verbatim from the original source, and others where it has been paraphrased. Verbatim text can most often be found in the content of the letters written between various characters. Some unnamed characters from the original source have been given names, while other characters have been created fresh. Some events have been consolidated, while others have been elaborated on or created from scratch. All of this has been done for the purpose of enabling the telling of the story in this format. This was not done in an attempt to improve on the original source.

The author highly recommends that readers of this book read the original text found in the *Book of Mormon* in order to gain the full impact of and appreciation for that account. The following notes summarize comments about the various chapters including commentary regarding which portions of the story came from the original text found in the *Book of Mormon* and which events have been fabricated.

They also give dates for when events occurred and references for where the original text for the storyline can be found.

Map Notes:

Over the years, many scholars have attempted to map out where Nephite cities were located, both in relation to each other, and where they were physically located in Central or South America. To aid the reader in identifying and distinguishing between the many cities named throughout this book, the author has devised and included a "Map of Nephite Cities." The author acknowledges that he and the scholars disagree in some instances. The map included in this book is not intended to be a scholarly work, but simply a resource for the reader.

The author acknowledges that when the Nephites established their cities, they would have placed them near the seashore, in valleys, near lakes, rivers or streams, or along significant thoroughfares. No attempt has been made to identify such features on this map. This map simply arranges the cities in such a way that they represent the author's interpretation of the arrangement implied in the original source material. While the author has put great effort into establishing the arrangement, the placement is still subjective.

Prologue & Chapter 1 Notes:

74 BC. This chapter based on: Alma 43:27–45:1.

The story picks up in the middle of an ongoing battle between a faction of the Lamanites, led by Zerahemnah, and the Nephites led by Moroni. In the original account, it was made clear that Moroni was not surprised by the Lamanite's attack because he had approached the Nephite prophet, Alma, to seek divine guidance on where he should plan to head off the Lamanite army. He had also sent out spies to find and watch the Lamanites' movements.

The Lamanites became surrounded when they haplessly marched in between Moroni's divided army on the hill Riplah. Moroni had intentionally divided his army because he knew the direction of their march and had hidden his forces to the north and the south. He assigned Lehi to command the forces on the south.

The rest of the details played out pretty much as described in Chapter 1. The dialogue between Moroni and Zerahemnah was essentially a paraphrasing of that recorded in the original text. The original text was more prophetic and contained more references to divine guidance.

The concept of swearing an oath of peace was taken from the original source. The concept of the importance both the Nephites and the Lamanites placed on the oath was taken from the current understanding of the emphasis such societies placed on oaths. Based on the usage in the original text, phrases such as, "as the Lord liveth and as I live" were common and significant points in the oaths they swore.

The contrast in the physical preparations in the two armies was taken from the original source. Although there isn't a literal description of either side, Zerahemnah did complain that ". . .It is your cunning that as preserved you . . . it is your breastplates and your shields" (Alma 44:9). While of the Lamanites, it pointed out that ". . .their naked skins and their bare heads were exposed to the sharp swords of the Nephites" (Alma 44:18).

The conversation and action between Alma and Moroni was contrived, but was based on the reference to Alma recording the event as the last entry in the records he kept (Alma 44:24). The names "Jeshua" and "Korimur" were fabricated. The other characters were taken from the original text.

Zerahemnah was most likely a Zoramite rather than a pure Lamanite (Alma 43:5). This is as per a somewhat complicated portion of the Nephites' history, which this book does not deal with. In short, the Zoramites were a group of Nephites who split off from the main group of their society and formed their own city. This group apostatized from the beliefs of the Nephites and became bitter towards those who continued to believe in the Nephites' teachings. They were especially bitter towards those from their own group that decided to return to the Nephites.

The original text states that the Zoramites went and joined the Lamanites and incited them to war against the Nephites. They then placed men from apostate Nephite groups as commanders over Lamanite armies because it was easier for them to stir up and maintain a hatred among these men than it was among the pure Lamanites (Alma 43:4–8).

Chapter 2 Notes:
73 BC. This chapter based on: Alma 45:2–19.

This chapter was intended to establish the fact that the Nephites kept a written record of their society, and the manner in which that record was kept. Beginning with this chapter, the remainder of the events described in this book were based on the record Helaman kept.

The dialogue between Alma and Helaman at the time Alma announced his intention to transfer ownership of the records to Helaman was a paraphrasing of the original text. Most of the other events depicted here were supposition and extrapolation of how they may have occurred, such as the blessing and the sermon before the congregation.

The reference to Alma possibly being translated like Moses was taken from the original text ". . . the scriptures saith the Lord took Moses unto himself; and we suppose that he has also received Alma in the spirit, unto himself" (Alma 45:19).

Chapter 3 Notes:
73 BC. This chapter based on: Alma 45:20–46:10.

The late night scene and dialogue in the tavern was fabricated, but the concept of the meeting was based on Alma 46:4 where it pointed out that Amalickiah wanted to be king and his greatest support came from "the lower judges of the land, and they were seeking for power."

The preaching of Helaman was not directly based on the original text, but was a summary of events described in other sections of the *Book of Mormon* and Bible. It offered some insight into the origins of the Nephite nation. This was included to give juxtaposition to the slanderous activities of Amalickiah, and to establish Helaman as a teacher as described in such areas as Alma 45:22 where it stated that "Helaman and his brethren went forth to establish the church again in all the land."

Amalickiah's speech and the events surrounding it were fabricated, but based on the concept of his attempted rise to power.

Chapter 4 Notes:
72 BC. This chapter based on: Alma 46:11–33.

While the original record did not specify that Moroni was tilling his farm at the time he got word of Amalickiah's deeds, it did say that after the battle with Zerahemnah "the armies . . . of Moroni, returned and came to their houses and their lands" (Alma 44:23). It is logical to presume that Moroni may have been a farmer too. It was clear that he was not present during Amalickiah's speeches as it said that, "When Moroni . . . heard of these dissensions, he was angry with Amalickiah" (Alma 46:11).

Moroni's creation of the Title of Liberty out of his own coat played a key role in the physical manifestation of covenant making in ancient days.

Much of his speech was fabricated, other portions however, were para-phrased from his speeches found in the original text.

The portion of the battle between Moroni and Amalickiah where Amalickiah's men second-guessed the justice of their cause and eventually fled rather than fight was based on the original text. The description of the chase through the jungle, Amalickiah's breaking away, and Moroni's reply was based on supposition, although the text did say that "Amalickiah fled with a small number of his men, and the remainder were delivered up into the hands of Moroni" (Alma 46:33).

Chapter 5 Notes:

72 BC. This chapter based on: Alma 46:34–47:1.

The scene of Amalickiah laying plans to infiltrate the Lamanites was not documented in the original source. The scene of Moroni dealing with the traitorous king-men, and declaring that the Title of Liberty be posted throughout the land of the Nephites was documented, but only briefly. It also stated that this was the beginning of establishing peace in the land that lasted uninterrupted for four years (Alma 46:38). This being the case, Amalickiah's infiltration into the Lamanite army likely did not occur as quickly as was implied in this book. The original text also pointed out that the Lamanites "feared to go to battle against the Nephites lest they should lose their lives" (Alma 47:2).

The words of Amalickiah to the guards and the king were not recorded, but the original text did point out that "he [was] a subtle man to do evil" (Alma 47:4). Hence, the enticing words described in this chapter to lure the king into his confidence were likely in line with his actual approach.

It was perhaps a confusing fact that the stronghold of the Lamanites was referred to as the "land of Nephi" (Alma 47:1). The first settlement of the Nephites, upon arriving in the land became the "land of Nephi." (It was on occasion also referred to as "Lehi-Nephi," being named after both Nephi and his father, Lehi.)

It became a strong and prosperous city. During their first few skirmishes with the Lamanites, they eventually lost the city. The Lamanites took it over and made it their own stronghold. Over the succeeding generations several battles were fought over the contested land. Each side claimed rightful ownership of the land, not unlike the ongoing disputes over modern-day Palestine/Israel.

The description of the large, solid stone door that safeguarded the entrance to the main records chamber was inspired by a similar stone door built by King Ludwig II of Bavaria, Germany in the late 1800's for his grotto near the Linderhof castle.

Chapters 6 & 7 Notes:
72 BC. These chapters based on: Alma 47:2–34.

The original text stated that Amalickiah had to send word to Lehonti four times before luring him down for a meeting, not three.

Regarding the poisoning of Lehonti, the original text merely stated that "Amalickiah caused that one of his servants should administer poison by degrees to Lehonti, that he died" (Alma 47:18).

The original text gave several details about the murder of the Lamanite king. An attempt has been made to faithfully recreate them in these chapters, including paraphrasing of the recorded dialog.

Regarding the report to the queen, the original text records, "when the queen had received this message [that the king had been slain] she sent unto Amalickiah, desiring him that he would spare the people of the city; and she also desired him that he should come in unto her; and she also desired him that he should bring witnesses with him to testify concerning the death of the king . . . Amalickiah took the same servant that slew the king, and all them who were with him, and went in unto the queen, unto the place where she sat" (Alma 47:33, 34).

Chapters 8 & 9 Notes:
72 BC. These chapters based on: Alma 47:35–36, 48:1–25, 49:1–30.

Regarding the wooing of the queen, the original text simply stated, "Amalickiah sought the favor of the queen, and took her unto him to wife; and thus by his fraud, and by the assistance of his cunning servants, he obtained the kingdom" (Alma 47:35).

The accounts of the attacks, or attempted attacks, on the cities of Ammonihah and Noah were intended to be true to the original text, with the exception of the specific dialog between Ammoron and Ishmael (who was never named in the original text). The original text also pointed out that "if Amalickiah had come down out of the land of Nephi, at the head of his army, perhaps he would have caused the Lamanites to have attacked the

Nephites at the city of Ammonihah; for behold, he did care not for the blood of his people," as was alluded to in this chapter (Alma 49:10).

The city of Ammonihah had a significant history prior to this story. When two missionaries, Alma and Amulek preached in the city, the people bragged of their strength and independence from God. The missionaries' converts were burned alive in a pit of fire and the two missionaries were imprisoned and threatened with death. They were saved by a miraculous earthquake.

The city was later laid waste in a single day by Lamanite soldiers who were angry with the Nephites who had converted several of their people and had them swear the oath of peace. (These people became known as the "people of Ammon" and ended up playing a key role later in this book.) Amalickiah chose to attack this city because he knew its recent history and destruction. He assumed it would be an easy target.

Chapters 10, 11, 12 Notes:
72–67 BC. These chapters based on: Alma 50:1–36.

The author of the original text was very impressed with Moroni's great character stating that he "was a strong and a mighty man; he was a man of a perfect understanding; yea, a man that did not delight in bloodshed; a man whose soul did joy in the liberty and the freedom of his country, and his brethren from bondage and slavery; yea, a man whose heart did swell with thanksgiving to his God, for the many privileges and blessings which he bestowed upon his people; a man who did labor exceedingly for the welfare and safety of his people. Yea, and he was a man who was firm in the faith of Christ . . . if all men had been, and were, and ever would be like unto Moroni, behold the very powers of hell would have been shaken forever" (Alma 48:11–13, 17).

Moroni spent a great deal of effort fortifying the Nephite cities, "Moroni did not stop making preparations for war, or to defend his people against the Lamanites; for he caused that his armies should commence . . . in digging up heaps of earth round about all the cities, throughout all the land which was possessed by the Nephites. And upon the top of these ridges of earth he caused that there should be timbers, yea, works of timbers built up to the height of a man, round about the cities. And he caused that upon those works of timbers there should be a frame of pickets built upon the timbers round about; and they were strong and high. And he caused towers to be erected that overlooked those works of pickets, and he caused places of security to be built upon those towers, that the stones and the arrows of the Lamanites could not hurt them. And they were prepared that they could cast stones from the top thereof, according to their pleasure and their strength, and slay him who should attempt to approach near the walls of the city" (Alma 50:1-5).

The record did not give an account of the tribulations, if any, that Morianton's army encountered on their trek, but it did relate the battle similarly to the account in Chapter 11, and pointed out that "the army which was sent by Moroni, which was led by a man whose name was Teancum, did meet the people of Morianton; and so stubborn were the people of Morianton . . . that a battle commenced between them, in the which Teancum did slay Morianton and defeat his army" (Alma 50:35). This was the first place where Teancum was named in the original text.

Sephara's name was not recorded in the original text. Her character is based on the account in which "Morianton being a man of much passion, therefore he was angry with one of his maid servants, and he fell upon her and beat her much . . . that she fled, and came over to the camp of Moroni, and told Moroni all things concerning the matter, and also concerning their intentions to flee into the land northward" (Alma 50:30–31).

There was no record of Teancum having any form of relationship with Sephara, but he was such a noble man, it's only fitting that he had some sort of home life outside of the many battles in which he fought. The marriage ceremony and resulting celebration as described in Chapter 12 had as much basis in pure imagination as it did in comparisons to ceremonies performed by various religions or groups. There was no such ceremony, ritual or practice described in any manner within the original text. What was described here was simply a liberal dose of poetic license.

Chapter 13 Notes:
67 BC. This chapter based on: Alma 50:37–40; 51:1–21.

Beginning with this chapter there was some divergence between this work and the original text with regards to where Moroni was located at various times of the story. The essential impact of the action was left in tact, but some of the events have been consolidated.

Although the name Elam has been artificially generated, it represented a group of characters in the original text who "had sent in their voices with their petition concerning the altering of the law . . . to establish a king over the land" (Alma 51:3, 5). The description of the vote and voting apparatus was not in the original record, but "their contention was settled by the voice of the people" (Alma 51:6), as illustrated in this chapter. The description in this chapter of their manner of voting and tallying of the votes was simply intended to be an imaginative proposed means of how it may have occurred, and not a statement of fact of how it did occur.

The original text related that the conflict between the king-men and freemen was significant and not focused solely within the city of Zarahemla. Moroni was actually out in the field during the conflict of words and opinions. Rather than turning to Pahoran while standing next to him, he "sent a petition, with the voice of the people, unto the governor of the land, desiring that he should read it, and give him [Moroni] power to compel those dissenters to defend their country or to put them to death" (Alma 51:15).

The resulting conflict was also much grander than this chapter described. "Moroni commanded that his army should go against those king-men, to pull down their pride and their nobility and level them with the earth, or they should take up arms and support the cause of liberty . . . there were four thousand of those dissenters who were hewn down by the sword; and those of their leaders who were not slain in battle were taken and cast into prison, for there was no time for their trials at this period" (Alma 51:17, 19).

Chapter 14, 15 Notes:
67 BC. These chapters based on: Alma 51:22–28.

Amalickiah's devastation of Nephite cities was much more intense than depicted in these chapters. These chapters related essentially one fateful day in which three cities were captured. According to the original account Amalickiah's attacks lasted over a great period of time and impacted multiple cities. For example, at one point it read, "And thus he [Amalickiah] went on, taking possession of many cities, the city of Nephihah, and the city of Lehi, and the city of Morianton, and the city of Omner, and the city of Gid, and the city of Mulek, all of which were on the east borders by the seashore. And thus had the Lamanites obtained, by the cunning of Amalickiah, so many cities, by their numberless hosts, all of which were strongly fortified after the manner of the fortifications of Moroni; all of which afforded strongholds for the Lamanites" (Alma 51:26, 27).

Chapter 16 Notes:
67 BC. This chapter based on: Alma 51:28–37.

The original text made the following comparison between the Lamanites and Teancum's men, Amalickiah "met with a disappointment by being repulsed by Teancum and his men, for they were great warriors; for every man of them did exceed the Lamanites in their strength and in their skill of war, insomuch that they did gain advantage over the Lamanites" (Alma 51:31).

The depiction of the death of Amalickiah was based on this description, "when night had come, Teancum and his servant stole forth and went out by night, and went into the camp of Amalickiah; and behold, sleep had overpowered them because of their much fatigue, which was caused by the labors and heat of the day. And it came to pass that Teancum stole privily into the tent of the king, and put a javelin to his heart; and he did cause the death of the king immediately that he did not awake his servants. And he returned again privily to his own camp, and behold, his men were asleep, and he awoke them and told them all the things that he had done. And he caused that his armies should stand in readiness, lest the Lamanites had awakened and should come upon them" (Alma 51:33–36).

The original text also pointed out that when the Lamanites "found Amalickiah was dead in his own tent; and they also saw that Teancum was ready to give them battle on that day . . . they were affrighted; and they abandoned their design in marching into the land northward, and retreated with all their army into the city of Mulek, and sought protection in their fortifications . . . the brother of Amalickiah was appointed king over the people; and his name was Ammoron" (Alma 52:1–3).

Chapter 17 Notes:
67 BC. This chapter based on: Alma 52:1–14.

The time that lapsed at this point in the original text was longer than was implied within this chapter. Something over two years passed while Teancum prepared to go to war against Ammoron, and Moroni dealt with Lamanites in his area of their world. There was a lot of "preparing for war" (Alma 52: 7) as well as harassing of the enemy in attempts to take back various cities that were not accounted for in great detail in the original text.

This chapter and the succeeding ones were written as somewhat of a summary of these events and highlight some of the better-described incidents. An example of these details includes the section where it stated that Moroni "sent orders unto him [Teancum] that he should retain all the prisoners who fell into his hands; for as the Lamanites had taken many prisoners, that he should retain all the prisoners of the Lamanites as a ransom for those whom the Lamanites had taken" (Alma 52:8). Moroni also said in his message, "I would come unto you, but behold, the Lamanites are upon us in the borders of the land by the west sea; and behold, I go against them, therefore I cannot come unto you" (Alma 52:11).

A point of interest is that a careful reading of the text could lead one to believe that much of this action took place near Panama or even Nicaragua. There were frequent references to protecting the land by the borders of the East Sea, as well as others that reference protecting cities by the borders of the West Sea. It would seem this would need to take place in an area where the distance between these two oceans would not be impractically expansive for an army to travel. There was also reference to Moroni instructing Teancum to "secure the narrow pass which led into the land northward, lest the Lamanites should obtain that point and should have power to harass them on every side" (Alma 52:9).

The "narrow" pass could be a reference to a narrow area of land that was surrounded by water on both sides, presumably lakes, seas, or a lake and a sea such as is the case in Nicaragua's geography. Or, it could be a reference to a pass through mountainous terrain that was difficult to traverse. Determining the exact location of their civilization by basing it on such references in the original text is made especially difficult however, because later portions of the text reported that a century after these events there was a massive earthquake during which mountains tumbled and covered some cities, while other cities sank and fell into the sea. In a word, their entire geography was highly altered.

Some of the many instances the record gave were as follows: "there arose a great storm, such an one as never had been known in all the land. And there was also a great and terrible tempest; and there was terrible thunder, insomuch that it did shake the whole earth as if it was about to divide asunder . . . and the city of Moroni did sink into the depths of the sea, and the inhabitants thereof were drowned. And the earth was carried up upon the city of Moronihah that in the place of the city there became a great mountain. And there was a great and terrible destruction in the land southward . . . the whole face of the land was changed . . . many great and notable cities were sunk, and many were burned, and many were shaken till the buildings thereof had fallen to the earth . . ." (3 Nephi 8:6–14). Given this, references to the geography of the area at the time of this story would not coincide with the lay of the land today.

Chapters 18, 19 Notes:
65–63 BC. These chapters based on: Alma 52:15–40, 53:1–9, 54:1–24, 55:1–35.

General Jacob and his men were lured away from their city, and the city was captured during the pursuit in a manner very similar to what was described in this chapter. It was interesting to note that Jacob was referred to with the rank of "General." Moroni was never referred to as anything higher than "Captain." Perhaps the Lamanites were more title-hungry than the Nephites. Or, it may simply have been that their specific ranks weren't tied in with those used today. These terms could have simply been words that best translated into English from the original text.

With the exception of Ammoron's first message to Moroni, the messages between Moroni and Ammoron as listed in this chapter were paraphrased directly from the original text. Much of the text was included verbatim, which was why it had a bit of a different (better) writing style than the rest of the chapter.

The discussion between Laman and the guards who asked for his wine was taken from the original dialog. The taking back of the city of Gid was depicted very closely to the description in the original text.

Chapters 20, 21 Notes:
64 BC. These chapters based on: Alma 53:10–23, 56:1–48.

The original text spoke extremely highly of the 2000 young men who volunteered to aid the Nephites in battle, when their fathers could not. It said that, "they were all young men, and they were exceedingly valiant for courage, and also for strength and activity; but behold, this was not all—they were men who were true at all times in whatsoever thing they were entrusted. Yea, they were men of truth and soberness, for they had been taught to keep the commandments of God and to walk uprightly before him. And now it came to pass that Helaman did march at the head of his two thousand stripling soldiers, to the support of the people in the borders of the land on the south by the West Sea" (Alma 53: 20–22).

The action and several pieces of dialog were based as closely on the original text as possible throughout these chapters, particularly the portion where Helaman asked his young soldiers if they were willing to go back and fight the Lamanites who had been pursuing them.

Chapter 22 Notes:

64–63 BC. This chapter based on: Alma 56:49–57, 57:1–5.

The original text described the battle between Helaman, Antipus and Giddoni (although Giddoni was not named by name) as follows:

"I did return with my two thousand against these Lamanites who had pursued us. And now behold, the armies of Antipus had overtaken them, and a terrible battle had commenced. The army of Antipus being weary, because of their long march in so short a space of time, were about to fall into the hands of the Lamanites; and had I not returned with my two thousand they would have obtained their purpose. For Antipus had fallen by the sword, and many of his leaders, because of their weariness, which was occasioned by the speed of their march—therefore the men of Antipus, being confused because of the fall of their leaders, began to give way before the Lamanites.

"And it came to pass that the Lamanites took courage, and began to pursue them; and thus were the Lamanites pursuing them with great vigor when Helaman came upon their rear with his two thousand, and began to slay them exceedingly, insomuch that the whole army of the Lamanites halted and turned upon Helaman. Now when the people of Antipus saw that the Lamanites had turned them about, they gathered together their men and came again upon the rear of the Lamanites. And now it came to pass that we, the people of Nephi, the people of Antipus, and I with my two thousand, did surround the Lamanites, and did slay them; yea, insomuch that they were compelled to deliver up their weapons of war and also themselves as prisoners of war" (Alma 56:49–54).

Helaman was concerned about his young army and "numbered those young men who had fought with me, fearing lest there were many of them slain. But behold, to my great joy, there had not one soul of them fallen to the earth; yea, and they had fought as if with the strength of God; yea, never were men known to have fought with such miraculous strength; and with such mighty power did they fall upon the Lamanites, that they did frighten them; and for this cause did the Lamanites deliver themselves up as prisoners of war" (Alma 56:55–56).

It also recorded the taking of Antiparah in the following manner: "I [Helaman] received an epistle from Ammoron, the king, stating that if I would deliver up those prisoners of war whom we had taken that he would deliver up the city of Antiparah unto us. But I sent an epistle unto the king, that we were sure our forces were sufficient to take the city of Antiparah by our force; and by delivering up the prisoners for that city we should suppose ourselves unwise, and that we would only deliver up our prisoners on exchange. And Ammoron refused mine epistle, for he would not exchange prisoners; therefore we began to make preparations to go against the city of Antiparah. But the people of Antiparah did leave the city, and fled to their other cities, which they had possession of, to fortify them; and thus the city of Antiparah fell into our hands" (Alma 57:1–4).

Chapters 23, 24 Notes:
63 BC. These chapters based on: Alma 57:6–27.

In the original text, Helaman wrote of capturing the city of Cumeni when they "did surround, by night, the city Cumeni, a little before they were to receive a supply of provisions . . . we did camp round about the city for many nights . . . we did sleep upon our swords, and keep guards, that the Lamanites could not come upon us by night and slay us, which they attempted many times . . . at length their provisions did arrive and they were about to enter the city by night. And we, instead of being Lamanites were Nephites; therefore, we did take them and their provisions . . . we should take those provisions and send them to Judea, and our prisoners to the land of Zarahemla . . . the Lamanites began to lose all hopes of succor; therefore they yielded up the city unto our hands" (Alma 57:8–12).

The account did not say whether the siege was led by the young warriors, or not. The implication of Helaman's use of "we" and the portion at which the convoy thought they were Lamanites lends some credence to the concept that the soldiers involved could have been the young warriors. The dialogue used in these chapters was not found within the original text, but the situations could possibly have played out roughly as described, with the exception of the depiction of the trenches and the dialogue between Jershon and the Lamanite leader.

The fiasco of trying to take the prisoners to Zarahemla, followed by the mighty battle outside of Judea played out very similarly to the account within the original text.

Chapters 25, 26 Notes:

63–62 BC. These chapters based on: Alma 57:28–36, 58:1–41.

The original text had no reference to how the Nephites regained control of the city of Zeezrom. It listed it as one of the four cities occupied by Lamanites in the early part of the account of Helaman's battles. It also later stated that the Nephites regained control of all Nephite cities, so it was liberated in some manner. It must be presumed that it was not a very eventful retaking, or it would likely have been recorded as such.

A strong effort has been taken to ensure that the events described in these chapters coincided with those described in the original text. Helaman's closing remarks in his letter to Moroni were nearly word for word from the original text.

The scene of Helaman speaking to Jershon on Judea's city wall was not recorded in the original text. The dialogue was not from the original text directly, but was influenced from passages or themes recorded in various places within the original text and other sources.

Chapter 27 Notes:

62 BC. This chapter based on: Alma 59:1–13, 60:1–36, 61:1–21.

The original text related that "when Moroni saw that the city of Nephihah was lost he was exceeding sorrowful, and began to doubt, because of the wickedness of the people, whether they should not fall into the hands of their brethren. Now this was the case with all his chief captains. They doubted and marveled also because of the wickedness of the people, and this excuse of the success of the Lamanites over them. And it came to pass that Moroni was angry with the government, because of their indifference concerning the freedom of their country" (Alma 59:11–13).

The letters between Moroni and Pahoran found in this chapter were paraphrased from the original text.

Chapter 28 Notes:

61 BC. This chapter based on: Alma 62:1–13.

There was no account that Teancum and Sephara were married, or that they had a child, or that Moroni looked in on Sephara. Had it been the case, that Teancum did have a wife and child near where Pahoran was located, it can be assumed that Moroni may have taken the time to look in on them and give them greetings from Teancum, had he been requested to.

There was no record of what transpired in Pachus' throne room. The battle between Pachus and Moroni was described in the following manner, "Moroni and Pahoran went down with their armies into the land of Zarahemla, and went forth against the city, and did meet the men of Pachus, insomuch that they did come to battle. And behold, Pachus was slain and his men were taken prisoners, and Pahoran was restored to his judgment-seat. And the men of Pachus received their trial, according to the law" (Alma 62:7–9).

Chapter 29 Notes:
61 BC. This chapter based on: Alma 62:14–17.
    There was little in this chapter that came from the original text, other than the point that Moroni made an aggressive return to the front. The original text did point out that "they took a large body of men of the Lamanites, and slew many of them, and took their provisions and their weapons of war. And . . . caused them to enter into a covenant that they would no more take up their weapons of war against the Nephites. And . . . sent them to dwell with the people of Ammon" (Alma 62:15–17).

Chapter 30 Notes:
60 BC. This chapter based on: Alma 62:18–38.
    This chapter contained several bits of dialogue that were not found within the original text, but the events themselves were based on that text. Of Teancum's last act, the text read, "they did not resolve upon any stratagem in the night-time, save it were Teancum; for he was exceedingly angry with Ammoron, insomuch that he considered that Ammoron, and Amalickiah his brother, had been the cause of this great and lasting war between them and the Lamanites, which had been the cause of so much war and bloodshed, yea, and so much famine. And it came to pass that Teancum in his anger did go forth into the camp of the Lamanites, and did let himself down over the walls of the city. And he went forth with a cord, from place to place, insomuch that he did find the king; and he did cast a javelin at him, which did pierce him near the heart. But behold, the king did awaken his servants before he died, insomuch that they did pursue Teancum, and slew him" (Alma 62:35–36).
    Of the final victory it read, "Now it came to pass that Moroni marched forth on the morrow, and came upon the Lamanites, insomuch that they did

slay them with a great slaughter; and they did drive them out of the land; and they did flee, even that they did not return at that time against the Nephites" (Alma 62:38).

Epilogue Notes:
60 BC. This section based on: Alma 62:43.

After the final battle in the city of Moroni, the original text recorded that, "after Moroni had fortified those parts of the land which were most exposed to the Lamanites, until they were sufficiently strong, he returned to the city of Zarahemla; and also Helaman returned to the place of his inheritance; and there was once more peace established among the people of Nephi. And Moroni yielded up the command of his armies into the hands of his son, whose name was Moronihah; and he retired to his own house that he might spend the remainder of his days in peace.

"And Pahoran did return to his judgment-seat; and Helaman did take upon him again to preach unto the people the word of God; for because of so many wars and contentions it had become expedient that a regulation should be made again in the church. Therefore, Helaman and his brethren went forth, and did declare the word of God with much power unto the convincing of many people of their wickedness, which did cause them to repent of their sins and to be baptized unto the Lord their God" (Alma 62:41–45).

Nothing more is written of Moroni in the original text, other than that he eventually died. It is assumed he lived a long and peaceful life. The text does have an extended account of how his son, Moronihah, later was called into service to save the Nephite nation from another onslaught brought on be deviant Nephites who join up with Lamanites to wreak havoc on their otherwise tranquil society. They even go so far as to capture the Nephite capital of Zarahemla, but that account is best saved for another time.